GIVEN
TO THE
SEA

MINDY MCGINNIS

↢ G. P. Putnam's Sons ↣

G. P. PUTNAM'S SONS

an imprint of Penguin Random House LLC

375 Hudson Street

New York, NY 10014

Library of Congress Cataloging-in-Publication Data is available upon request.

Printed in the United States of America.

ISBN 9780399544613

1 3 5 7 9 10 8 6 4 2

Design by Abby Dening.

Text set in Granjon LT Std.

For Jim & Joe—I'm not dead yet.

CHAPTER 1

I T IS IN MY BLOOD.

It is in my bone.

It is in my brain.

One day my body will betray me, dancing into the sea, my mind a passenger only. The water will close over my head and I will drown, my death bringing a reprieve for those who are not me. This is what I've been born and bred for. The food passing into my mouth, the clothes covering my body, every breath I draw—these are smaller offerings, each a promise that I will endure, bear my own cursed daughter, and then succumb.

How that will happen I do not know. My mother suffered the touch of another at least once, long enough to fulfill her duties and bring me about. I know it was badly done. I see it in the faces of my Keepers, these people who care for me without caring. I hear the small things in their voices. They worry I will not be pleasing to the sea, that my mother and her chosen mate created something less than perfect. I understand their concern, but cannot share it. Why should I care if the tides rise again, if I am only a corpse riding the waves?

To live aware of your own doom is no easy thing. I spend my days at lessons, my body fulfilling the expected duties, though my mind is elsewhere. The Keepers are worried that I have not prepared well, have not set my face in the appropriate response to their commands. "Happy," for instance, is an emotion I cannot be expected to parade, but they tell me it is necessary. "Melancholy" I excel at.

My mother and grandmother had other lessons, ones to please at table and dancing. Proper chewing, proper speaking, proper walking—only expected, of course, when we are in control of our limbs. My lessons have taken a different course, my other instructors quietly dismissed once I learned all that was expected.

All except how to contort my stone face appropriately.

The Keepers have tried, their emotions chasing through their faces so quickly I can't keep up, my own trying to mirror what I see. They say to me, "Pleased," but look nothing like it themselves, and I am easily confused on this point. So I often retreat, my mind escaping the room where I learn to mimic emotion, returning itself to some well-ordered facts absorbed from a musty book, its scent still lingering on my fingers, a source of comfort.

Their pages follow me through the day, their words imprinted on my mind. I know the history of my land better than the Scribes, better than the royals who rule it. I can recite the names of my predecessors, from the woman who gave birth to me all the way to Medalli, one of the Three Sisters whom the sea gave back after the wave that took nearly all. Seaweed was pulled from their hair, their locks drying as they worked alongside other survivors to rebuild what had washed away, not knowing they would be taken again, the first of the Given.

The sea waited until the sisters had married and had children of their own before it called for them, the price of its leniency the blood of their line. For the children went too, and their children after them, the first twitches of their childhood pulling them toward the water, the final coordinated movements driving them deep into the waves, the dance of death one their kingdom deemed the will of the sea. And so it continues. Their footprints in the sand not returning, my feet now itching to follow. Medalli's line—mine—remains strong, the other two Sisters falling short, the last names in their column females who did not produce heirs, the ink that wrote them now faded with time.

I rub my fingers together, drawing the scent of the book pages from them as my male Keeper says, "Sad." Sad I can perform, closing my eyes and picturing my name, *Khosa*, the ink slightly darker than my mother's name before me, *Sona*.

"Don't close your eyes," he says.

I open them again to see my Keepers, their faces so easily read. *Disappointment.*

CHAPTER 2

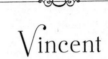

Vincent

I'M SORRY YOU HAVE TO WAIT, MY LORD."

"Not a concern," I answer the guard, but my eyes are on my hands, the clean nails freshly clipped, the smoothness of my palms interrupted by the lines that Madda insists hold my future.

In any kingdom other than Stille, the future of a prince wouldn't need to be read in his hands. It would be clear in his actions, the preparations taken to ensure he sits the throne well, does his duty, leads his country. Somewhere else I would be wed already, the announcement of my own child eagerly anticipated, the girl I keep on the side politely excused, with her pockets lined for her trouble. Instead I sit outside the throne room at the age of seventeen, awaiting my turn to speak to King Gammal—my grandfather—healthy, hearty, capable. At his side, my father Prince Varrick, already gray and lined, but still sitting in the lower throne.

I shift on the wooden bench, and the trapman next to me slides farther away, the smell of sea salt rising from his clothes. "I'm sorry, my lord. Do you need more room?"

"More than enough room," I insist, patting the space between us.

He's quiet for a moment, and the lady on the bench next to ours fills the hall with the clicking of her wooden knitting needles. One foot rests casually on the ball of coarse wool to keep it from rolling away as she works. She's assured, content. As a citizen of Stille, she is entitled to speak to the king, and her turn will come. Eventually.

I look back at my empty hands and the lines that Madda the Seer wrinkles her brow at. Her answers to my questions are always vague and muttered.

"Am I right to say *my lord*?" the trapman asks. "Is that what you're called?"

The words *it doesn't matter* are half formed in my throat, but I choke them back.

The woman's needles continue to click. Her hands are gnarled and work-worn, but her color is good, and the hat she is knitting small. For a grandchild. Or great-grandchild. They are lucky to have her. I tell myself these things every day: Stille is fortunate. Stille is healthy. Stille is strong. Years of peace and prosperity mean that the old linger and the middle-aged flourish, while the young inherit only boredom and aimlessness.

"Just Vincent," I say, finally answering the trapman's question. "No title necessary."

"You're of royal blood," the woman says, not glancing up from her work. "It should not be taken lightly."

"No . . ." My voice fades away. I have no words to explain succinctly, only memories from my childhood when I was called the baby prince, and then the young prince, and now there's a hesitation, a slight pause before acknowledging my rank. There is no name for the third in line, one whose hands will wither with age long before they hold the scepter.

I've come to hate the blank space before my given name, the deferential glance of the servants as they search for a title that represents nothing. So I make it easier for them, and for myself.

"Just Vincent," I reassert. The old woman makes a disapproving noise in her throat and keeps knitting. The trapman smiles at me, his teeth even, strong, and white in a face lined with wrinkles.

"I'm Agga." He holds out a bent hand, gnarled from years of pulling in the crab traps, the lengthy ropes rubbing it raw. Even the trapmen don't go into the water, letting the tides carry out the traps. His skin feels of age and the scars of work, years of absorbed salt water pressing back against the softness of my own hands.

"How is the sea, Agga?" I ask.

He shakes his head. "Eating the beach with hunger. We'll be needing her that's given to the sea, and soon."

"I will pass that along," I say. I don't add that my voice doesn't carry in the great hall, only echoes back into my ears.

"Here to do it myself," Agga says, and I wonder if he followed my thought.

"I saw when the last one was given," the woman says. "She danced beautifully."

"They all have," Agga says.

"But their faces, they do . . . twist," the woman adds, her own mimicking the memory, a brief mask of horror that slides off easily as she counts her stitches.

"Do they want to go?" I ask.

Agga shrugs. "It's their own feet taking them. No one in Stille makes them go. We're not the Pietra, feeding sea monsters with the flesh of their aged."

"No." The woman shudders, dropping the first stitch since I've sat here. "We're not the Pietra."

There's laughter in the throne room. It reverberates under the closed doors, my grandfather's hearty one underscored by my father's, which has never ceased to produce goose bumps on my skin, even in a lifetime of hearing it.

"I'm sorry you have to wait, my lord," the guard says again.

"Not a concern," I repeat, looking back at my hands, where lifelines extend forever, marching right off the palm.

Waiting is what I'm good at.

CHAPTER 3

Dara

THE TWINS MOVE THROUGH THE FOREST, THEIR FOOTFALLS lost in the leaves, their shadows blending with the trees. Their hunting cloaks waft around them, bulky hoods resting on their shoulders. Donil hesitates a moment, his eyes catching something in the dying light of the setting sun. He steps purposely on a stick, the sharp snap gaining his sister's attention. Dara comes to his side, her eyes not as trained at deciphering the forest floor.

"It passed through here, headed west," she says, her voice pitched low. She pushes leaves aside with the end of her bow. "Recently?"

Donil smiles. "You were right to make that a question."

"Not recently." Dara stabs her bow into the ground. "Then why stop?"

"Because of that." He indicates another sign, barely visible. Dara squats to the ground, eyes tight in concentration.

"This one is headed east . . ." Her fingertips trail in the impression. "Is it the same creature?"

"It is, judging by the size. I thought the farmer's daughter was going to faint when she saw the print."

Dara rises, leaning her cheek against her bow. "An animal with tracks we've never seen before raids a Stillean flock and flees into the woods. We follow it for days on Gammal's orders, and now it's changed direction. So I ask again—why did we stop?"

"Because of that," Donil says, pointing at a third sign.

Dara doesn't bother to look. "Save my breath and just tell me."

"And waste my own?" Donil teases, but the set of his sister's mouth tells him she's nearing the end of her patience. "The third track points east again, and is fresh. Whatever this creature is, it passes through here often."

"We'll wait, then," Dara says, pulling her hood forward and lying flat on the ground near the crisscrossing tracks. Donil does the same, his shoulder touching hers, their cloaks overlapping to share heat as the sun leaves the sky.

Dara exhales softly, a low hum, and the leaves that were softly drifting to the forest floor change direction. The twins hardly notice the first few settling on their backs, but as Dara continues her quiet call, the leaves layer on top of them, their slight weight a comfort that keeps them warm and hidden.

"You have your uses, even if you can't track," Donil says.

"You track it, I'll kill it," she shoots back.

"What then?" he asks. "That creature is huge; getting it back won't be easy. And we've got a full day of travel in hot sun between us and Stille. The meat will spoil before we return."

"No one is hungry in Stille," Dara says, her low voice twisting the words to make it sound like a bad thing.

"Maybe in the city proper, but perhaps the trapmen—"

"The traps are always full."

"How would you know that?"

"I listen when people talk."

"Then why kill something for the sake of a few sheep? You said yourself the bellies in Stille won't be empty without them."

"Because Gammal asked us," Dara says. "And because Vincent seemed concerned."

"Vincent . . ." Donil says their childhood friend's name quietly. "No matter how hard you try to please him, you'll always be Indiri, and not fit to wed."

"Asking me to kill something and asking me to marry him are two very different things."

"They are," Donil agrees. "I'm making sure *you* know that."

"Put your teeth together and keep them that way." She lashes out in irritation to punch his arm and dislodges half the leaves she'd called down to them. She swears in Indiri, a word that only they can understand. Dara hums again, but the sound is weaker now, and threaded with strain. The leaves that are falling drift toward them for a moment, then return to their natural course, the breeze stronger than the little magic Dara has left in her.

"More will fall while we sleep. It'll be enough to keep us from being seen," Donil says, all teasing gone.

They lie quietly as night settles in the forest, the leaves falling of their own accord and not Dara's will. Her breathing evens out as her temper settles, and Donil chooses his next words carefully.

"I had hoped you no longer thought of Vincent in that way."

"I hope for that too, brother. But the only thing that will avert my eyes is one marked such as us."

"So what will you do?"

"Jam your teeth down into your gullet if you don't stop your hole. The way your mouth runs, you'll have us both eaten by this thing we track, the last of the Indiri rotting in its dung heap."

"At least we'll be together."

Dara gives him a dark look, the one that has kept stable boys and Stillean nobles alike from troubling her. But Donil's smothered humor only vibrates through his body, spreading to her own until her smile is drawn out.

"I'll keep first watch," Dara says. "Get some sleep. Dream of women."

"You're confused, sister. They dream of me. And what is it you think of, if you ever rest easy?"

Dara's mouth tightens, all traces of humor gone.

"Revenge."

CHAPTER 4

Witt

WITT WAKES TO THE SOUND OF THE SEA IN HIS EARS and a filthy word in his mouth. The tide always brings out the worst in him, and the worst of the Lithos of Pietra can lead to very dark things. He covers his face with his hands, the thin bedsheet sticking to the film of sweat that gathered on his body as he dreamed. Tiny muscles in his face twitch under his palms as they fight to reassert the stony mask he must wear by necessity, as unrelenting as the shores of his people.

If his council knew that the sound of the tide resurrected faces in his sleep, he'd be usurped, and rightly so. No Lithos can lead with the weight of emotion upon his shoulders. To be the Lithos means making decisions that can lead to deaths, and having compassion can only complicate things. The teachings of his people echo in his head, trying to banish the faces of his loved ones for the last time, to force them to a place where the tides will not bring them back while he sleeps.

Years have passed since his arms, just burgeoning into manhood, pushed his mother off from the shore in a boat with no oars, her face shining with tears as she told him how proud she was. Next, his young brothers, each in their own boat, the smallest not even able to sit up yet. They all went to the sea and the Lusca, the weight of his love for them a burden lifted. After that final assertion of his abilities, Witt was recognized as the Lithos, with splinters still prickling his hands from the rough-hewn boats he'd made to carry his family away, one by one.

He watched, night after night, from his tower room to see if the sea could be forgiving, if it would return his loved ones and all the anguish that caring brought. In his waning boyhood, he imagined that he would save them, reeling them in under the light of the tide moon and hiding them secretly in a cave while he led their people to victory, bringing them before the council later to prove that one could love and lead at the same time.

But the sea did not relent, and Witt grew, the softer spots of his soul slowly shaved away as his gray-haired mentors deemed themselves no longer assets. The forest always rang with axes, as the old and infirm built their own boats from the Hadundun trees, and Witt performed his duty to shove them into the tide, and the waiting bellies of the Lusca. Now in his twentieth year, his palms are embedded with splinters, his heart a wearied thing that has retired under the reign of his mind.

A heavy knock at the door brings his hands away from his face, now rigid. "Come in," he says, all trace of tears shed in the night evaporated.

"My Lithos." Pravin ducks his head briefly as Witt sits up.

"My Mason." Witt nods at his lead advisor.

"Reports from the field bring no surprises. Our soldiers are positioned near Hyllen, ready to attack. The village has many men, but they hold pitchforks better than swords."

"A pitchfork can wound," Witt reminds Pravin as he dresses. "If our men believe this village will prove nothing but a lark, they might discover that such a wound can fester."

"Perhaps something to impress upon them before taking the field."

"Anything else?"

"More Feneen attacks in the night. They dragged off another sentry."

"That's the third in a moonchange," Witt says, as he laces up leather boots cracked with years of wear. "What are they doing with them, do you think?"

Pravin shrugs. "The Feneen are always swelling their numbers, collecting rejects from Pietra and Stille, even the nomads. How they feed so many mouths, I don't know."

"Perhaps that's why our sentries are disappearing," Witt says. "A starving man will eat anything."

He glances up from his boots to see Pravin running his thumb along the silver band on his middle finger, the metal there giving him the right to take a wife, his bloodline lending more strength to Pietra. He was lucky to have kept it after his first child was born with a grotesquely large head. It was left on the inlet where the Feneen came to examine those freely given, sometimes choosing to include the abandoned as their own.

Pravin's child was taken not by the Feneen, but by the Lusca.

"Although if they were hungry, they'd take everyone who is offered to them, if for nothing other than meat," Witt finishes.

"True, my Lithos."

"So why our guards?"

"Fresh blood, maybe? With no one but themselves to breed with, their babes can't be too healthy."

"Then why take a man and not a woman?"

"I . . ." Pravin shifts uncomfortably. "A man's body can be at odds with his mind when it comes to such matters. If they wanted to breed a man against his will, there are ways to make it so. But I shouldn't talk of such things with you. The Lithos is—"

"Not to be distracted. I know."

Pravin clears his throat. "As I said, a detachment is near Hyllen. Two days' journey will have you in camp, a night of rest, and we can attack."

"No, I don't need to sleep." Witt turns his back to the sea, his unflinching face hard as the stone floor beneath their feet. "Why wait?"

CHAPTER 5

Khosa

MY LESSONS ARE OVER FOR TODAY, THE KEEPERS' FACES exhausted after showing me an array of emotions to mimic. They don't know I take another kind of knowledge from them in the dark as they speak to each other in their bed, their words rising to my mattress in the loft. Because of their nighttime conversations, I know what worry sounds like, trapped inside a voice.

I go to my bookshelf for distraction, fingers rippling over the uneven spines. Stillean histories are laid bare to me in these pages, the long, fruitful past of the kingdom that I will die to preserve. A slim volume, warped with time and edges curled with rain, falls to my hand instead. It is a guilty pleasure, one that the male Keeper has chided me for spending long hours over. But the sketches of spotted Indiri skin hold a fascination for me that the long columns of Stillean nobles do not.

"They were savages," my male Keeper had said once, pulling the book from my hands as I leaned close to a candle's light. "Strange creatures that walked at birth and spoke as soon as they drew breath. Good that they live now only in the ink you see there."

"Not so," the female said, pulling tight the thread as she mended near the fireplace. "Two escaped the Pietra, or so our messenger from the castle told me."

"Two too many, then," the male said, sliding the book back into its place and handing me a larger one that smelled of mold and must and long years of being unread. "Learn of Stille," he told me. "Stille is what you were made for."

That memory is farther back in my mind than my first blood, but more bitter. What I've learned of the Indiri has come in small snatches, evenings when I snuck the small book up to my loft bedroom under my skirts. I pass over it today, not even the pages on the shelf calling to me as they usually do.

I leave our small house behind, the hills open to me if I trusted my feet to wander without pulling toward the east and the ocean I've never seen. But I know it lies waiting, so I don't go far, only to a rock on the hillside, more dear to me than any people I have known during my lifetime in Hyllen.

Tendrils of the Keepers' voices from the night before echo in my mind, captured to be examined later. The female is worried. Though my seventeenth Arrival Day has come and gone, I have shown no inclination to choose a mate, and the fine lines around my Keepers' faces have deepened as I grow older, well aware of what ails me.

Since childhood I have watched Hyllenian children nestled against their mothers' hips as they walked side by side, fingers entwined. What would bring a smile to another serves only to sadden me, a reminder that even my female Keeper tucking a strand of hair behind my ear produces a rising revulsion from my gut. I shy from their skin on mine as others would from a snake in the grass, though the poison comes not from them but my own mind.

My Keeper has tried to ease me into comfort by laying her hand on my shoulder while speaking, or wrapping her arms around me before I climb my ladder to bed at night. The only response my skin knows is a shudder, my bones and muscles rigid as death until she releases me.

Their positions as Keepers are enviable. A home in Hyllen. Food supplied by the villagers. They successfully raised my mother, the male Keeper taking her to Stille for the dance. The female Keeper was left behind with my infant self, a baby infuriated by her cuddling and affection. If I cannot bring my own girl child forth, they will have failed in their duties.

As will I.

It weighs heavily on her. Last night she suggested the male Keeper perform the role himself. Fear had me scrambling for my shoes before I heard his answer, but he was as revolted as I, maybe more. He said no man could be expected to perform under the scrutiny of my blank face, no matter how beautiful. It's a cold reprieve, and I sit on the rock, handling his words carefully so as not to shatter what little confidence I have.

The rock comforts me now as I spot Abna approaching, the solid feel of it beneath me something that will anchor me through a slippery conversation. Another Given in my place might have found him suitable, and he could've fathered the next cursed daughter.

"Khosa," he greets me, the morning breeze tossing his light hair. "How does the day find you?"

"Well," I lie, fitting my face to match the word. It must be convincing, for his natural smile answers my false one as he joins me on the rock. Either I've improved with my daily lessons or Abna is as apt at pretending as I am.

"I've not seen you since taking the sheep to the high meadow," he says, eyes skipping over me in a way part of me welcomes. My skin may not call for a man, but my blood does. And of late it has boiled.

More than ewes are bred in the high meadow, and well I know it. The young shepherds and shepherdesses who receive that duty come back with secretive smiles and healthy glows, not a few having their waists thicken in the following moonchanges.

"You've become prettier," Abna says.

"As have you," I say, which is certainly not a lie.

In the distance a rhythmic sound toys with my ears, and my fingers drum along, blunted nails striking the rock beneath my palm. They're stopped by Abna's own hand, strong on top of mine, which clenches.

"Khosa," he says again, his voice low, "my father returned from Stille yesterday. The trapmen become restless. They say it is time for you to be Given."

I nod. There are no words to agree with my own death.

His hand tightens on my own. I can feel bones beneath skin, his and my own, pressing nearer to each other. I focus my entire will on not pulling away, teeth grating behind lips still peeled in a practiced smile.

"You cannot go to the sea yet," he goes on. "All who live in Hyllen know this, but what of Stille?"

My eyes close, following the example of my throat. Yes, Stille knows that nothing grows inside me, that even the shortest wait for my dance is at least nine moonchanges long. Nine moons in which the sea can choose to become tumultuous, demanding me as my belly stretches, tiny feet inside performing a prelude of what is to come for both of us.

"I can help you," Abna says. "I know what must be done will not be easy for you, but . . ."

"But it must be done," I finally say, raising my eyes to meet his.

"Yes," he says, drawing courage from my words. "And I know that I can provide you with what you need, easily."

He plows on, his face growing red. "I was with Allas, just the once, and she quickened with child, though it was lost. And now Anja, after only once. If you can bring yourself to bear me for a short while, I can help you, and I wouldn't . . . mind the doing of it."

If he can promise me it will be just the once, maybe I could look at the grass or the clouds, distract myself sufficiently for as long as it will take. I force my palm to turn upward, meeting his.

"Abna," I say, but the agreement is lodged in my throat, unwilling to be voiced.

His attention is elsewhere, and I realize the noise I was drumming my fingers to earlier has grown louder while I deliberated, its pulsing rhythm now distinguishable as the slap of marching feet. Hundreds upon hundreds, they flow into our valley, the black armor of the men making them like ants marring the waving grass as it is shredded in their wake.

Abna and I stand, fingers still intertwined, as they overtake the first Hyllenian. He falls at the single swipe of a sword, his bewildered sheepdog hunching near his body as the horde swarms past. I feel my face changing, contorting into one of the only emotions I can feel honestly: fear.

Abna whirls me to face him, hands strong on either of my shoulders. Even among the rising screams of Hyllen, I flinch. "Khosa," he says, face close to mine, "listen to me. You must run. Far away, as fast as you can."

"Where?"

But he has already left me, running back to the village though he has no weapon and no knowledge of wielding one.

"Where?" I ask the question, though panic has already taken me, my feet slyly making the decision while my mind is lost. I ask the question, though I know there is only one direction for me.

I ask the question even as I head east, toward Stille.

And the sea.

CHAPTER 6

---∘⊙∘---

Vincent

THE REALITIES OF RUNNING A KINGDOM ARE MUCH LESS interesting than one would imagine.

My grandfather listens to trapmen claiming that the weavers are negligent in their work, the fibers that bind the traps together not as good as years past. The weavers claim the fault lies in the quality of the wool, the shepherds blame faulty grain for their stock, and the farmers lay blame on a wet season. Unable to bring the sun down from the sky to mount a defense, Gammal soothes tempers, sprinkles well-placed compliments, and sets everyone at ease until the entire assembly is smiling as they rise from their chairs.

I can't help but notice that even though they are my father's age, there are no cracking joints, or complaints from hours spent sitting in futile argument. Their skin may sag, but not the muscles beneath. My father is the only one whose attention wandered during the meeting, and it does so again as a shepherdess makes her exit, his gaze falling somewhat south of appropriate.

I know that boredom has taken a toll on him as he waits for the throne, but he has found his entertainments in pursuits that leach all happiness from my mother. Donil and Dara were a balm of sorts for a while, their childish mouths conversing with her like adults, their oddness requiring protection from those who feared them. But now their appearance matches their speech, and my father's reluctance to sire more royals for Stille leaves Mother a floating presence with less worth even than myself. It's her wan face I see when I clear my throat, drawing my father's attention away from the shepherdess.

"Prince Varrick." I keep my voice distant and formal, though the commoners are gone, Gammal and his guards exiting with them. "Yesterday the trapman waiting for his session shared his concerns about the sea with me. What are your thoughts?"

"I think that those who spend too much time by the sea are addled in their brains," my father says, turning his gaze to mine as the guards draw the doors shut.

"He claims the sea is tempestuous and calling for the Given," I say.

"Memories that stretch long cannot be trusted. Ask any Elder, and they will tell you the weather in their youth was more mild, the people kinder. That this trapman finds the sea more temperamental now than in the past is not surprising."

"So you don't think it's true?"

"What I think doesn't matter; I am not the king." He doesn't remind me with words that the same is true of me. It's in his dismissive glance and the way he rises from his chair—the conversation over in his mind if not in my own.

"What does Gammal say?"

"He says that the opinion of the trapman matters little. The girl has not borne a successor yet and cannot be given until then. We've sent men to Hyllen for another report, good men who can hold their tongues. If all of Stille knew that she has not bred yet—" Father breaks off. "She is of age, and her Keepers aware of their purpose."

"As am I," I say out of habit, though the words have grown stale in my mouth of late. The path to my kingship is long, but I am in no hurry to travel it. The cold seat has never called to me.

With the meeting over, the day stretches in front of me. Madda will be in her dark room. Whether she waits patiently for me to return or prays for me to stay away, I don't know. She has always claimed that the lines in our hands can change with time but laughs when I press for answers, saying that she can no more give me truth than predict where a gull will land. We frustrate each other, my pointed questions an amusement, her vague responses bringing less comfort than the cakes she would offer me as a child.

I look at my palms, the sun dancing back off their softness. Milda claims they are lover's hands, but I still feel a mild revulsion at the sight of them, so like my father's and grandfather's. I remember Agga's suddenly, cracked and wearied with work.

My feet had been taking me toward Madda, but now I jam my hands in my pockets and strike out away from the castle grounds to the sea. My Seer may not see hard labor in my palms, but I imagine nothing can change lines quicker than hauling in traps.

There's enough of a breeze to bring spray to my skin, though—like all Stilleans—I'm sure to keep a safe distance from the water's edge. It taunts and plays, whitecaps tossing. My people were once drawn to it, entranced by the play of light on water, white dancing on blue. But they learned the danger of toying with such strength, a forcible lesson taught by a predator that can appear meek and beautiful, but destroy in a breath. Like children we were taught roughly, and like children we took the fear to heart.

I shudder as my eyes follow the trapmen's lines, which extend deep into the sea, past even the Horns—a pair of rock pillars that jut from the water at low tide. I've caught the trapmen as they are returning to pull their catches in, fins and pincers erupting from the woven sides in a futile struggle.

Finding Agga is not easy. All who work close to the water are darkly tanned, their hair the same color as the salt on the waves. I ask and am directed farther down the line, near where the trees—less frightened than other living things—come perilously near the sea.

"Agga," I call as I approach, one hand raised in greeting.

He peers up at me, eyes squinted against the sun. "Ah, Prince Vincent . . . who prefers to be just Vincent. Strange to see you on the beaches. What brings you here?"

"I wondered if you'd let me pull a trap?"

Agga's lined face draws together in confusion, but the corners of his mouth are turned up. "Why would someone who doesn't *have* to pull a trap *want* to?"

"To see if I can."

He nods, as if this makes sense to him. "It's hell on the hands," he warns.

"Good."

He wasn't lying. I've lost layers and raised blisters before the first trap is in, while Agga wades into the surf to bring it the rest of the way. I can't hide my fear as the water breaks around his bare legs, leaving glistening skin in its wake.

"Bah," Agga says, noticing my face as he drops the trap at my feet. "Trapmen know a thing or two about the sea. She's a wily monster, yes, and one we'll never tame. But you can learn her ways if you've been around her long enough. And right now she's no more danger to you or me than a housecat that's filled her belly with cream."

I watch the surf come in again, pulling at the feet of the older trapmen who share Agga's confidence. The younger ones stay back, content to let the muscles in their arms do the work rather than give the sea a chance to take out their legs.

The scream takes us all by surprise, sending the gulls that had gathered to pilfer from the traps into the air, their own voices blending with the growing swell of agony. Agga and the others are as lost as I am; all of us search for the source, our bodies poised for some action not yet decided.

She breaks out of the trees like a wraith, her tattered dress barely keeping her decent as she spins, her body exultant in its throes as she clears the beach, her face a twisted display. I cannot tell if she is beautiful or horrific, and it does not matter for I know who she is in the second that all the trapmen instinctively take a knee to bear witness to the dance.

To see a Given dance is a blessing and a comfort, assurance that the sea has taken this generation's offering, her death solidifying our hold on life. Yet I cannot let it happen. Whether it is because she has not delivered a replacement yet, or because of the helpless terror I see, I do not know, but I run to intercept her. The beach fights me, sucking at my naked feet as I head for her, demanding the right to take what is being freely given.

"Vincent! No!" Agga yells behind me. His voice mingles with the dismay of other trapmen as I interfere, hitting her convulsing body with my own and pinning her to the ground.

She fights me—her limbs wanting the sea as badly as it wants to take her, and a well-aimed fist drives the breath from me as she craves to answer the call. Rough hands hold me back as she crawls for the surf, the water rising above her wrists before I draw air back into my belly and yell, "She has not bred yet!"

The hands leave me to find purchase elsewhere, tearing the girl away from the tide. It takes four of them to still her, one on each limb, and even after being pinned by callused hands she twitches, anxious to finish the journey.

But her face relaxes. The rictus of fear is suddenly gone, and her features return to their rightful place to paint a portrait of beauty. Her eyes meet mine briefly before rolling back, and the most meager of smiles plays on her lips for one moment, as if it's an action they don't know well enough to hold.

"My lord," Agga says, the title in place, "what shall we do?"

Any victory I felt at stopping her dash is instantly deadened as I look at the expectant faces of the trapmen, each still clinging to the Given's delicate arms and legs.

"Take her to someone with authority to decide," I say. "Take her to the king."

CHAPTER 7

Witt

FUNNELS OF GRAY SMOKE DRIFT INTO THE NIGHT SKY AS the ashes of Hyllen cool. Witt sits on an overturned trough, bloodied sword across his knees as those who did not fall are brought forward.

Witt warned the men not to take the villagers too lightly, that those who fight with their backs against their own homes fight hardest. As always, his words were given weight, the methodical press of his soldiers unbroken in their goal when they swarmed. As a result, there are not many left to question, and those who are brought to Witt come on shaky legs.

He waves a man to the right, an elderly shepherd who could give no account of those who may have escaped or where their feet could have taken them. To reach Stille on foot would take three days, the farther outposts even longer. A soldier takes the shepherd into one of the few remaining houses. The line of villagers has seen many go in and none come out. Yet they stand docile as children, waiting for a turn to face Witt and follow the same path.

He motions for the next in line, a handsome woman with a streak of gray in her hair, who bows as she comes forward. One of the guards behind him snickers when her chemise gapes, but the slightest tilt of Witt's head brings the noise to an abrupt halt.

"Did you see a girl, sir?" the woman asks, her eyes moving from Witt to the men who flank him. "Small and fair? Any of you? It's important, sir. She's the Given."

"Lots of fair girls been given tonight," one of the men says.

"Do not distract the Lithos with such talk," Pravin growls.

The woman goes down on her knees, hands raised in supplication. "Please, sir, Given to the Sea, is what I'm saying. It'll be the doom of us all if she goes to death before dancing."

"Filthy fathoms, this again?" a soldier mutters.

"What's the sea to one who faces a blade?" Witt asks

"It's for Stille's sake I ask, sir. I'd keep it from the waves if I can."

"What do you know of Stille, other than old wives' tales?"

"More than most." She draws herself up with a hint of pride. "My husband and I have raised three of the dancers and taken them to the sea when their time came."

Pravin motions for the woman to be taken to the left, the first to go to Witt's own tent instead of the unlit house. The next person is brought forward forcefully and driven to his knees in front of Witt by two men. Blond hair has been burned away on one side of his head, ashy, brittle tendrils still clinging in patches to his angrily shining scalp. A wound above his eye has crusted over, but seeps again after his struggle with the soldiers.

"You look as if you fought today," Witt says.

"As best I knew how," the boy answers through swollen lips. "We're farmers, not soldiers, but I'll stand against anything that brings harm to Hyllen."

"You're not standing now, are you?"

"Have your men take their hands off me and I'll rise."

"Abna!" a girl cries from the waiting line, her hands tight around her swollen belly. "Please!"

"Be still," he calls back to her. "It's all the same ending. I'll come to mine out in the firelight with the moon shining on me, not in a black room with smoke choking what little life's left."

Witt nods to the soldiers, and they step away from Abna, who comes to his feet as promised. Witt rises, circling his prisoner.

"Brave words. Do you have the actions to back them?"

Though Abna's eyes are bright and his bearing proud, his tone speaks of defeat. "I've never held a weapon in my life, and you are the Lithos of Pietra. Do what you do best and kill me now. Stop playing with me like a toy, for you never were a child."

Witt confronts him, dark eyes lost in the shadows of his face. "What do you know of being a Lithos?"

"Hyllenians may be quiet people, but that means we listen better than most. I know how Pietra live, their Lithos chosen young and molded fast. You were marked a killer before you could walk, and I've only to glance at you to know they chose well."

Witt's sword slashes quickly, the blade a mere flash in the night, back in the scabbard before Abna's head reaches the ground.

"Yes," he says. "They did."

The girl howls, falling to her knees while those around try to calm her.

"Take them away," Witt says, suddenly weary.

Pravin goes to work directing the prisoners into the animal pens and setting guards around them for the night. Witt shoves into his own tent. The guards stand at attention, one on either side of the woman he sent in earlier.

"Leave us," he says to them, handing her a flask to drink from as they go.

She takes a sip, her eyes never leaving his face. "What is it you want with me? I thought the Lithos took no woman."

Witt ignores her question, answering with his own. "You know Stille?"

"I do," she says cautiously. "But if you think I'll be useful, you're mistaken. I know the way in is a road, and the way out the same. I'm a Keeper, and the trips I've made in the past were spent tending to the Given, not minding much else."

"A Keeper." Witt takes the flask from her and drinks himself. "You raise these girl children from infants, watch them bear children, then take them to the sea when their time comes?"

"I do," the Keeper says. "And raise her babe the same, only to bring another into the world and make the trek to Stille again. One in the cart, one left behind."

"Then you know much of keeping the doors to your heart shuttered fast, and that's a lesson no Lithos can learn too well. Your life is safe, should you wish to impart some of this knowledge to me."

The Keeper tears the ragged edge of her sleeve away, wiping her face with the remnant. "Seems you have little need of such instruction, or Abna's head would still be on his shoulders."

"Like any blade, a craft can always be honed," Witt says. "If you have no interest in my offer, I can remove your own head as well. Do you wish to keep your life?"

"What's left of it," she says grudgingly. "With the Given lost, the sea will be lapping our heels."

Witt takes another drink, fighting the urge to roll his eyes as his soldiers had done. "Yes, the sea. What terror it does cause, that Stilleans cower at its very mention?"

"Even you Pietra fear it," she lashes back. "Your trees grow leaves that slice men to ribbons so that the roots can drink spilled blood, yet water keeps you at bay."

"Not the water, but what swims in it," Witt corrects her. "The Hadundun trees may thirst for blood, but they stay rooted. The Lusca are not so easily escaped should we venture to the sea."

"So you come here, take our lands and flocks instead. Do you think I did not see the hollows under your soldiers' armor? Metal may sit well on them, but it covers thin arms and near-empty bellies," the Keeper says with a bitter smile. "No worries, young Lithos, if the Given does not dance, your people will not suffer hunger pains long."

"Dear lady," Witt says, raising the flask in mock toast, "I too believe the sea will get us in the end. But not as Stille expects."

CHAPTER 8

Dara

DARA ALLOWS HER TWIN TO SLEEP THROUGH THE NIGHT, not waking him when she hears the first rustling of underbrush as the day breaks. She draws back her bow so that the tip touches both their ears as they nestle together under their shared cloaks. Donil doesn't stir until she releases the arrow. The slight *twang* brings him to his feet, daggers in hand, as the creature's body hits the ground, dead before Donil is even fully awake.

"Thanks for the warning," he says as he resheathes his daggers and pulls Dara to her feet.

She shrugs. "You track it, I kill it."

They pace around the body, stepping lightly over splayed limbs. The rising sun draws colors from its scales, creating a beautiful dance. But the stench gags Donil when he peers more closely.

"It stinks of the surf," Dara says. Even when she breathes through her mouth, the air feels wet, weighed down with salt and the unmistakable scent of the deep.

"And these feet are of the sea," Donil agrees, spreading the toes to show the webbing between. As he does, an otherwise buried claw pushes forward with a tuft of wool still hanging on the tip.

They gather at the head, and Dara pulls the wide lips open to find two rows of teeth, long and sharp as any tool in a weaver's kit. Tiny eyes betray its affinity for the dark, the pupils now wide and unseeing.

"A creature of the sea come on land," Donil muses, spreading the eyelid wide to get a better look. "You're far from home."

"Farther than you think," Dara says. "Not only of the sea, but not even from our waters."

"A Lusca, you think?" Donil stands back, arms crossed, while he looks at the creature. "Why would a Pietran monster come to our shores? They feed them willingly enough."

"If this is a Lusca, then that was a badly placed arrow," Dara says, leaning against her bow. "I'd rather have turned it back toward Pietra, sent it home for more flesh."

"Leaving fewer Pietran soldiers for you to kill?" Donil asks. "That's not the sister I know."

Dara loops her bow onto her back. "Tales of a Lusca on land won't be welcomed, and from the mouths of Indiri, no less. Gammal will believe us, but how to convince the Elders?"

"We'll take the head," Donil suggests. "The smell of the thing itself is testament enough of the sea."

"Two feet as well. The webbing says much."

"One stands in evidence alone. Why take two?"

"Because feet come in pairs."

They lose the morning to sawing and hacking with dagger blades that dull quickly from strange work. Scales stick to their skin as they brush against the massive rib cage, which rises high enough that they can barely see each other over it. They fashion a sledge out of branches and Dara's cloak, striking for home as the afternoon wanes into evening.

The smell precedes them, sending smaller creatures into hiding and attracting predators in their wake. A day of travel doesn't improve the stench, and as Donil struggles against a tree branch that pokes through the sledge, the rot-heavy air hangs in his lungs.

"Wait," he calls ahead to his sister, who has crested the hill and stands peering down the road to Stille.

"Not long, brother," she says as she returns to him. "I can just see the castle spire from here. We'll have warm food tonight, and our own beds."

"First a bath," he says, rocking back on his heels as she disentangles the sledge.

"A bath," she agrees. "Although I don't believe I smell it anymore."

"They do." He gestures toward the Tangata cats that have gathered behind them, thick whiskers betraying their presence behind trees. An older female, heavy and lazy, doesn't even bother to hide, and her coiled tail, wide as Dara's wrist, twitches in the fading sunlight.

"Begone," Dara shouts, tossing a rock. It bolts, ringed tail raised in alarm, but not before hissing at Dara to display teeth as long as her fingers. "They're only that bold when there's a clowder of them. We need to move."

Donil rises to his feet, but his sister takes the rope. "My turn."

Dara pulls it over her shoulder, easing down the hillside toward the road. Donil follows, eyes on the lashes they've secured the legs and head with. The eyes shriveled quickly in the rays of the sun, and the sockets have gathered flies.

Donil keeps pace as they come upon the first village, where the children run to the sight of strangers and possible news from elsewhere—then wildly change course when hit by the smell. Donil waves at a cluster of young boys as they pass, answering calls muted by shirts pressed around their noses. Some of the braver boys follow behind, shouting questions.

"Go home," Dara yells over her shoulder. "The Tangata are out, and they're curious tonight. Best not to satisfy them with your own skin. They'd have your hide off before your scream woke the oderbirds."

The smallest boy stalls at her words, little feet coming to a halt. His hesitancy catches quickly, and soon they are all left behind, the unbroken line from the sledge lengthening the distance between them and the Indiri.

"That was less than kind," Donil says, as they approach the castle walls.

"You're the pleasant one, and what good has it done you? Away a handful of days, for all anyone knew slain by a horrible beast in the black of night. And we come home to find the gates closed against us."

Donil comes to a halt, and Dara rests beside him, opening and stretching her hands, stiff from clenching the sledge rope.

"True," he says, eyes roaming over the double guards set at the lowered portcullis. "But the main hall is lit up as if it were the summer festival."

They stand in silence for a moment, letting the noisy rise and fall of a gathering drift to them from the castle.

"Sister," Donil says, "I believe there's a celebration we've not been invited to."

Dara glances over her shoulder at the rotting mound of flesh. "We're here now."

CHAPTER 9

I AM BEING HONORED.

There is little to be said about what I will do to earn this banquet, but a story of everything I did to get here is printed on my skin. My feet are torn from days of running, my shoes lost somewhere in the hills between Stille and Hyllen. The fine skin of my legs is lashed red with the marks of underbrush, and I am told that weavers were called to pull the embedded thorns. They say there were enough to make many carding combs.

The weavers were pleased when they left me, the physician exultant in the exhaustion from which he would deliver me. The trapmen who held me down have earned a place in the histories for stopping my mad dance that came too early. The blind terror that drove me for three days toward Stille has become legend in moments, anonymous souls now drawing glory from my pain.

There is pain, and there are bruises. When I first came to, my eyes skipped past bloody scratches from thorns and the swelling of my feet, landing instead on the purple marks on my wrists and ankles, shadowy spots in the shape of hands. People had touched me without my permission or knowledge.

Now I sit at the head of a table, a demurely cut dress in place to cover all the damage. The king's daughter did my hair, unperturbed by my flinching when her fingers brushed my scalp. Dissa says that I am beautiful, and the sea will be pleased. She says this as if I should be as well. In the mirror I see her plain face twitch slightly, perhaps wondering how she fares in comparison, and what her handsome husband with wandering eyes will make of me. Though the dress covers my wounds and ornately braided hair crowns my head, no one knows that it's only raiment for a deficient offering.

I am trying. The lessons of my Keepers run fast and true, the muscles in my face conforming to their instructions, though I doubt the mouths that voiced them will ever move again. Hyllen was burning when I ran from it, but I hear their words from years of practice, and now comes the test. The Keepers will never benefit from the lifetime of work instilled in me, the timing of a smile, the curiosity conveyed by a tilted head. I curtsy to the royals, lower my eyes when spoken to, and accept all compliments when hands are pressed against mine, though the rich drink in my belly threatens to overflow like a boiling pot.

They have no idea that I am measuring them, the width of a thumb, the distance between fingers. The exact imprints of my bruises have been carefully cataloged, and I will know the matching hands when I see them again. The playacting wearies me, and I settle into my seat after receiving the line of people who are so anxious to meet the girl who will die to save them.

"Hello," the boy to my right says quietly, as if a loud word may break me.

He is a royal, so I lower my eyes an extra finger span when responding. "Hello." I keep my volume the same as his, and our tones matching.

"Are you recovering?" he asks, and I feel a black wave in my stomach at such a question. What does it matter if I heal, when I only go to rot?

"I am well," I answer, all traces of the buried darkness removed.

"And yourself, Prince . . ." I stutter a moment, no amount of training able to cover the fact that I've forgotten his name.

"Vincent," he supplies quickly. "Just Vincent, please."

"Vincent," I repeat, raising my gaze to meet his, curious about the boy who forgoes his rightful title.

He is without the lines of work and outdoor living that the Hyllenian boys carried. Our eyes meet, and his sweep across my face in a practiced gaze, his own training in memorizing features, names, and titles at work. And work is what it is to both of us. His movements are too smooth to be natural, too kind to be authentic. Together we playact as the eating begins and the lives we have been trained for are set into whatever motion the occasion calls for.

I am served first, food from the sea piled upon my plate. I eat for so many reasons. To quell the hunger born from my mad run, to stop the necessity of conversation with the boy beside me, and because there is some satisfaction in knowing that I'll devour some sea creatures before they're able to devour me.

"It's good to see you up and about," Vincent continues, having to speak loudly as conversation grows around us. Many eyes cut to me while we talk, measuring my hunger and no doubt balancing it against the slimness of my waistline.

"It's good to be about," I lie, vastly preferring the isolation of my chamber and the guards at my door. "How do you fill your days here, Vincent?"

His eyes return to mine, and I see a flicker there, a real person underneath the façade he's accustomed to presenting. "There are things to do, but I admit you must search for them. Though a city, you may find Stille differs little from . . ." He stalls, tongue stiffening.

"Hyllen," I say quickly. I'm happy to pretend he has only forgotten the name of my village, not that he has just recalled rising smoke and screams that followed me as I fled. Most girls would be bothered by those memories, but to me it is like a painting I am observing from outside the frame. It may be a curse that my Keepers tried to leach from me with pointed lessons, but it proved useful when King Gammal asked me to share what I could about the destruction of my homeland, his military advisors leaning in to catch my words.

"We had our pursuits," I say, filling the gap that Vincent's stumble created. "Hayrides at harvest and new lambs in the spring. I imagine Stillean royals have grander ideas of fun."

"If we do, I'm not aware," Vincent says, a practiced joke that falls flat. I turn back to my plate, disappointed that what had come close to a real conversation has deviated back to mere puppetry. From the corner of my eye, I see him set his fork down, and take a deeper draw of wine than necessary before turning toward me.

"My best distraction is in visiting my Seer for palm readings." He pitches his voice low, only for me, as if aware that I tire of our being on display for the public, and holds his hand out to illustrate. "It's not always good news, but it passes some afternoons. You're welcome to come with me if—"

The illusion of a private conversation between us is cut dead at the idea of inviting one who has been Given to the Sea to have her future read. Yet it's not his suggestion that has stopped my throat, but the fact that his hands so perfectly fit the bruises at my waist, deep and dark. I choke on a crustacean.

"Khosa?" he asks, leaning forward. "Khosa, are you all right?"

His face is so concerned that I know it's not feigned. I almost want to tell him I am not all right and never can be, that this time the sea will not be pleased and every one of them will pay. But I don't get the chance. The doors of the banquet halls are slammed open, and the reek of salt and rot rolling in tells me the sea already knows, and it's coming.

CHAPTER 10

─────◦❦◦─────

Vincent

I AM A FOOL.

A fool who knows how to pace myself through these steps, the casual conversation that is actually calculated, mimic interest in this girl who will be dead before the ink in the histories has dried upon recording the name of her child. Yet her own practiced responses have awoken something in me, the tilt of her head at enough of an angle to acknowledge that she too, is pretending. And so in faking concern, I have wandered headlong into honesty, resulting in my asking Khosa if she'd like her future read, when this evening celebrates that she has none. She ran with death on her heels to another in front her, fire in her wake and the sea on the horizon. And now she must endure conversation with a boy who spouts nonsense punctuated by horror.

I was among the trapmen when we brought her to the castle, but she was quickly taken from us to be tended to, washed, and healed. I was not included in the whispered meetings held in the two days following, and though her arrival was all the talk of Stille, she had wandered from my mind as soon as she was out of sight. As a royal, I have been taught to think only of those who serve my immediate interests, and though I find those lessons abominable, I realize now that my interests had tended more to Milda's bed and welcoming skin than to a girl who is not meant for me.

But she has my attention now, the skilled set of her face in deep contrast to the tortured contractions on the beach, and I can't help but wonder why she smiled at me on the sand, as if I'd saved her, rather than interfered with her destiny. When I show her my hands, she blanches, what little color she has draining away, her mouth suddenly slack and eyes dull.

Panic edges out over manners at the thought that she might be choking. "Khosa?" I say, grabbing her shoulders to feel frail bones beneath. "Khosa, are you all right?"

Anyone can see she is not, and my first thought reveals how deeply royal I am when I think not of her well-being, but *what will become of Stille if she dies?*

The doors to the hall crash open, and my hand drops to the sword at my side, though it's only a ceremonial one. My other arm instinctively goes in front of Khosa, rigid as iron, but she curls away from my touch, her spine digging into the back of her chair.

My adopted sister bursts into the hall, her dark hair a wild halo, her face mottled with the shades of falling leaves and her own emotions. Dara is a maelstrom, and though the guards at the door fall back at the sight of her, I can't miss that they keep their weapons at the ready. Donil follows, his color high as he drags something into our midst.

The smell hits me, and I gag. To my right, my father does the same, though he hides it better. A few of the court ladies swoon; one of them vomits into her lap and then tidily closes her knees so that her skirts pocket the mess.

"Dara!" King Gammal is on his feet in a second, his guards rising with him. "What is the meaning of this?"

Dara strides up to the raised royal tables, confident as the dawn, her deferential bow to my grandfather more deeply imbued with her own pride than any respect for him. "We return triumphant, Father's-Father, though I doubt you'll find any comfort in our success."

Beside me, Prince Varrick stiffens at her familial address. Though Mother considers the twins part of our family and has given them permission to address us as such, I feel resentment rolling from him whenever the lilted speech of the Indiri lays claim to it.

"Show them, Donil," Dara says, her gaze sweeping the room.

Donil pulls the covering away, and the crowd gasps, the brave leaning closer while the leery shy away. Decay fills the air, and my mother raises a scented handkerchief to her nose, her eyes following Dara as she returns to her brother's side.

"What is it?" someone cries.

"It's water moving among us," Dara says, savoring the nervous looks traded among the nobles. "The tide with legs and claws."

"The surf no longer constrained by beach." Donil adds his voice to his sister's, but without her cutting edge. His eyes meet mine for a second, and the tiniest twitch there gives away his amusement. He opens his mouth to deliver the next line in whatever devilry the two of them have planned when he stops short, gaze no longer on me, but on Khosa.

She peers back at him like a bird tempted to peek at a cat, and her small voice pipes in my ear. "Is that truly an Indiri?"

I've heard the serving girls whisper among themselves about Donil's snapping Indiri eyes, the width of his arms and chest, deeply aware that I fail in comparison and have to look up when I speak to him. A familiar spear of jealousy tears through my middle as I tell her, "Yes. You'll notice there are two of them."

"And why have you brought this monstrosity to us *now*?" Gammal asks pointedly.

"You said to share what we learned with you upon our return. We have returned, and have much to share." Dara plunges a hand into the rotting mass and raises a scaled arm above her head to illustrate.

"Dara girl," Mother whimpers, her weak words barely penetrating the linen protecting her nose.

"What did you expect, Dissa?" Father replies in a low voice. "You bring a Tangata kitten home to nest and are surprised when it bites with grown teeth?"

My grandfather's guards are looking to him for direction, no doubt expecting to haul the Indiri from the room, a task none would envy, given Dara's renowned temper. A noble slumps forward, having held his breath too long. I see a muscle twitch in Gammal's cheek, which could signal anger, but I know him well. My grandfather is trying not to laugh.

"Your timing could be better," I say, saving the king a response. "We are in the middle of a banquet."

"Then the timing is perfect," Dara counters instantly, her tongue as quick as her sword. "We're starving."

She drops the arm unceremoniously, and a fresh wave of rot rolls from her clothes as she approaches the nearest table. Nobles push away from their plates as she reaches casually for a platter. One woman actually shrieks when Dara smiles at her.

Donil has lost all interest in his sister's provocation, his quick eyes moving over the room and assessing the size of the gathering, the amount of noble blood gathered in one place.

"What is this?" he asks. "What do you celebrate?"

Father pulls Khosa from behind me. A light groan escapes her as he clamps onto her wrist, and I stifle the desire to strike his hand away.

"The Given has come," Prince Varrick says, his tone drawing all eyes away from the monster the twins have brought us and reclaiming the evening.

All over the room, heads bow in silent recognition of the moment. Khosa's very presence is a sacrosanct thing that has been marred by the arrival of two Indiri and a pile of decaying flesh. Donil stays still, gaze riveted on her. Dara is the only one to move, teeth crunching down on a bone as she stalks toward us. Khosa draws deeply for air as Dara approaches her, and though she shrinks from Varrick's hand, it may be the only thing holding her up.

"You are the Given?" Dara asks, her tone suddenly cold.

Khosa nods, eyes on the ground.

"Then why are your feet on dry land?"

CHAPTER 11

Dara

"THE STENCH MAY STICK," DISSA SAYS AS SHE DRAWS A comb through Dara's hair, still wet from a thorough bathing.

"Better the stench than a claw," Dara says, watching the older woman carefully in the mirror of her dressing table. "You're unhappy with me."

Dissa sighs before speaking, her fingers catching in Dara's dark locks. "Unhappy, no. I'm bone weary and worn with the arrival of the Given. To have a rotting creature brought to me during a celebratory dinner requires a new word entirely to illustrate my feelings."

Dara's head sinks under the weight of her hair and Dissa's disappointment. The girl who would snarl at a reproach from any other is undone by the light reprimand from the only woman she can call mother. "We meant only to have some fun, and had no way of knowing the Given had come."

"I realize," Dissa says, releasing the comb and resting her hands on Dara's shoulders. Their eyes meet in the mirror. "But others may take offense."

"Gammal seemed more amused than anything," Dara argues. "He has great patience."

"Patience you try mercilessly," Dissa says, smacking the back of Dara's head with the hairbrush. "And he is not of whom I speak."

"Your husband," Dara says.

Dissa sits beside Dara on the cushioned bench, their knees touching. "Will you never give him the honor of his title in speech?"

"Varrick's title was earned only by marrying you, and none of his actions since have recommended him highly."

"Titles are often given where not earned," Dissa says, the argument between her and Dara a familiar one. "Even if bedding me is his only achievement, he remains the prince and will become king."

"If bedding is all it takes, then we could call him by many names—Lord of the Stable, Prowler of the Kennels, Frequenter of Brothels." Dara ticks off her fingers as she speaks. "He recently acquired the title Defiler of Shepherdesses, if I'm not mistaken."

"You're not," Dissa says calmly.

Dara picks up the dagger she keeps on the dresser and begins paring away at her fingernails. "Why do you persist in this?" she asks quietly, eyes on her work. "There is no dignity in the man or the marriage. You age in loneliness while he takes pleasure as he will."

Dissa's gaze lingers on the Indiri's skin, still lush with blood from her hot bath, dark lashes long around light eyes, full lips pressed tight against emotion.

"Does he pester you often?" she asks.

Dara glances up in surprise, her grip on the dagger tightening. "Not often, no. That he does at all makes me wish for the sight of his blood on the floor. My hand is stayed only because of the pain it would cause you."

Dissa folds her hands over Dara's, unpeeling the Indiri's fingers from her weapon. "I cannot expect one born into violence to understand the heart of one raised on promises of love. He may turn to me yet, and you would do well to remember that harming him would mean your death."

"Ah, Stille," Dara mocks. "How can it flourish when the best of its blood is relegated to the bedroom?"

"I have my ways," Dissa says, replacing the dagger on the dresser. "Not as impressive or memorable as your own, but I make my mark."

"The Indiri women lead as often as men. And they bed whom they please, when they please," Dara says.

"Oh, to be Indiri." Dissa's wry smile brings out Dara's laugh, but it is soon quieted.

"And what of when Varrick becomes king? Will your ways keep him in check even then?"

"I can only hope," Dissa says, her fingers prying into the tines of the comb to tear free Dara's hair. She holds the ball in her hand, untwisting it for the weavers to use in a tapestry.

"Stilleans would not like Indiri hair entwined in a tapestry meant only for that of the royal family," Dara says.

"Then Stilleans interpret the word *family* too strictly," Dissa says. "And with my hair growing silver, Varrick's thinning, and Vincent's pale as the moon, the weavers could use some color."

Dissa is quiet then, her fingers smoothing out the lump between her fingers. There was another color running through the tapestry once, the dark brown of her older son, gone to death too soon. Dara's hair is darker than Purcell's was, but close enough that the weavers accept the locks when Dissa brings them, claiming to have kept Purcell's trimmings.

"Would that I'd known him better," Dara says, her thoughts following Dissa's. "But I don't believe he felt the same. Babes speaking with the mouths of adults did not sit well with him, and once we were children, his sickroom was closed to us."

"That you should call it a sickroom," Dissa says, shaking her head. "I still think of it only as *his* room, though the door be barred and closed forever."

"It is for the best. I know you wish to look upon his things again, touch the bed he lay on. But the Stoning moves quickly, freezing limbs in the span of a day. Your father is right to leave Purcell's room untouched, for it may linger still in the air."

Dissa closes her eyes. "Can I trouble you?"

"Of course," Dara says, accustomed to Dissa's request. She closes her eyes and relaxes her hands at her sides, letting her mind wander back in time through her own memories and ones inherited from ancestors.

"He was tall and dark, would have made a handsome man, given a bit more time," Dara recounts, her memory sharp as her knives. "More lashes around the eyes than the average boy, with a tiny white scar across his top lip."

Dissa smiles, eyes still unopened. "That was from the kitchen cat."

"Never trust a cat," Dara says. "More?"

Dissa shakes her head. "No, I'll not be selfish tonight. I know how looking drains you."

"Only if I delve deeply. My own memories are near and close; those inherited from my mother and hers from her own are the ones that tire."

"He was a good boy," Dissa says. "His brother is as well. Would that there were more children to follow, but . . ."

"An emptiness your husband could easily fill," Dara reminds her.

"So I filled it myself, and brought the last of the Indiri into my family," Dissa counters.

"Yes," Dara allows. "You drew us in, while in turn drawing no love from your people for sheltering Indiri with your skirts."

"And here you are, my daughter in all but blood, grown to a woman and dragging dead animals to my feasts. Any suitors warmed to you by my well-chosen words may find their effect cooling."

"I'll not hear of suitors, and well you know it. The last of the Indiri must wed another Indiri, not dilute her blood with that of a Stillean."

"Even a noble Stillean?"

"Especially a noble Stillean," Dara huffs. "I could break any one of them over my knee like a twig. I do not find that a desirable quality in a mate."

"Not Vincent," Dissa counters, her voice making it a question, her eyes searching Dara's face.

"No," Dara says slowly, all boldness lost. "Though I don't believe he's an option."

"No," Dissa echoes. "He is not. My influence extends only so far. An Indiri on the Stillean throne would surely bring about an uproar. As it is, it pains me to hear a single voice raised against you."

"Which doesn't stop them from muttering behind your back."

"Perhaps if you gave them less cause?" Dissa raises an eyebrow, and Dara drops her gaze. "The Stillean people would not accept you as their queen, and neither would you care for it. Your blood is too wild, and it searches for a heat to match its own."

"Too true," Dara says. "I can fill your wish for a daughter only so far. My ways are not yours."

"No, but *you* are. Not by blood and never by marriage, but you are a daughter in my heart, and I love you as one."

Dissa clasps her hands with Dara's, speckled fingers entwining with unmarked ones as the tide comes in.

CHAPTER 12

———◦⟨○⟩◦———

Vincent

MILDA'S BED OFFERS SOLACE. THE KIND HER BODY OFFERS, of course, but others that she doesn't know I indulge in as she sleeps by my side, her mouth partway open. Her mattress is lumpy; the scuttle of mice comes from the corner, bold now that she and I are quiet. Here I can pretend for a time that I am a regular boy, waking up next to his girl, the smell of baking bread in the air. Her eyelids flutter, and she rolls against me, body seeking body beneath the ratty quilt.

Her father's bakery sits on the outskirts of the city, storefront hanging over the main road, one I rode past without noticing until the flash of her red hair caught my eye. Father saw, on one of the rare days we went together to meet with the weavers' guild, and made an arrangement that part of me finds reprehensible but not so much that I don't take advantage of it. I visit whenever I wish. The baker's door is always open to me, and he pays no tax to the city.

I curl a strand of Milda's red hair around my finger, and she reaches for me, wrist brushing against my hip.

"My prince is awake."

"Your prince wishes you would call him by his name," I remind her, but she only smiles at me. Neither of us harbors any daydreams about what we are to each other; she is my chance to pretend to not be royal, and I am her opportunity to bed one.

She smiles and her hands slide lower, more practiced than they were when we took up with each other. I wonder for a brief moment if she takes other lovers in my absence, and realize that I don't care if she does. I have no wish for my shadow to loom long in her life, making demands even when I'm not present. I know well enough what it is to lead a life not fully your own.

"Your mind is not in my bed," she chides, pushing playfully against my chest.

"Is it required?" I ask, and she giggles, burrowing into the covers and running her bare feet up my leg.

"No," she admits. "But I know when it's far from me. What's troubling you?"

"The Given has come," I tell her, rolling onto my back to stare at the ceiling.

"I heard as much," she says. "What is she like?"

So I tell her about Khosa, who seems to me a small, frightened thing, despite all her well-executed pleasantries. Milda asks what she wears, the color of her hair and eyes, and I tell her as best I can recall, although my strongest impression of the Given had nothing to do with her appearance, but with her overwhelming resignation to a fate decided at her conception. Still, I give Milda what she wants, well aware that these snippets of court gossip raise her in high esteem with the other merchants' daughters.

"She is not bred?" Milda asks.

"No. I think Donil caught her eye, though I don't know if she was fascinated or frightened by him."

"Donil catches all the girls' eyes," Milda says.

"Does he?" I ask, playfully pulling her back against me now that we're both fully awake.

"Not *all*," she says. "There's a certain baker's daughter who prefers her prince."

"Tell me more about her," I say, and she smiles as the sun rises and I decide that the castle can get on without me a little bit longer.

Madda is not happy with me, and makes no attempt to hide it.

"A Stillean prince who doesn't come to his Seer," she mumbles, a lifetime spent in the darkness of her own chambers reducing most of her conversation to fragments of speech directed mostly at herself. She putters through her small room, disturbing clouds of incense that waft around her gray hair.

I say nothing, familiar with her moods. Madda has held the hands of Stillean kings before me, the world passing by outside her windowless corner of the castle while her eyes followed only the creases in hands. She is an old woman who has never seen the sky, ensconced in the stone room she was born in, her mother's talent passed to her, both their lives choked by smoke and lit only by fire, for fear that the brightness of the sun might tear away the shadows that allow sight of the future. Madda's irritation is a constant stream of muttering that smells of the dried nilflower she burns, her lungs so lined with the smoke of years that her very breath carries the tint.

"Hands out, then, young prince," she says as she unceremoniously plops into the chair across from me.

I sigh, my usual amusement at her constant dissatisfaction eaten away by my thoughts. I try to focus on the task at hand, aware that my palms and the palms of my father are her only purpose in life, and that this duty was not her choosing but what she was born into.

Much like me.

"Oh, yes, a heavy sigh. What trying times when the young prince has to sit with an old woman who knows much and could share more. Just breathing in this room could teach you something, but I hear that you prefer the air in Milda's bedroom."

I glance up, all boredom evaporating. "What would you know of how I spend my time outside this room?"

"What would you know of how I spend my time when you're not in it?" she counters, and I sit back in my chair.

Madda knows well enough that she is a faded relic, her gift reduced to mere tradition. Generations of Stillean kings have asked their Seers for pointed answers, and grown bored with vague replies. Even Madda's childless womb drew little concern from the Elders or Gammal's advisors, for who needs to know the future written in their skin when the past has taught us that we will live long lives, uninterrupted by trial or terror as long as a Given dances when her time comes?

Madda's face is as familiar as my mother's, the lines there deeper than in my childhood, furrowing into skin sallow with lack of sunlight and gray with the film of burnt incense. Yet as I look at her now, familiarity falls away, her face not fitting the mold I've set for her in my mind, that of the cantankerous old woman who speaks whether anyone listens or not. Instead I see a craftiness I've not noticed before, a thread of amusement in her voice that could be easily dismissed as bitterness to those who do not know her well.

"An old woman who knows much and could share more." I repeat her words, drawing my hands away.

"Oh, you were listening," she says, an eyebrow cocked, its long gray tendrils almost snagging her unruly hairline.

"I still am," I say.

She leans back as well, each of us watching the other for a few moments. "The old women may know much, but it's the young girls who do most of the talking. Go back to your baker's girl. See what she's heard."

"It's the elderly who have my attention at the moment," I counter, which earns me a lascivious cackle.

"Mmmm . . ." She settles into her chair, her body seeming to sink deeper into the pile of rags she wears. "There's talk in the halls. The Given has come with the ash of a burnt village on her heels and nothing growing in her womb. She's not hard to look upon, I've heard, and would have had no trouble finding a willing Hyllenian boy to plant the seed."

"She is indeed fair," I agree, remembering the face that studied mine in the few moments when our public masks had slipped at the banquet.

"Yet there is no little Given swimming inside her, which must happen before the mother takes her own dip," Madda says.

"Madda, please," I say. "That's crass, even for you."

"And what do you care?" she snipes back. "The Given swims—or sinks, rather—with or without a few bawdy jibes before she goes. And you'd do best to remember that, young prince."

"Ah, I see. The talk in the halls doesn't concern only the Given, does it?" I lean forward, the legs of my chair thumping to the stone floor. "There were many eyes on us at the banquet."

"And little space between you," Madda says, wiggling her eyebrows.

"I thought she was choking," I defend myself. "I have no interest in the Given, pretty as she may be." Though my words are true, they don't ring that way, maybe because her beauty isn't what drew me to her but our shared moments over dinner. I smile at the thought that I feel bonded to someone because we wore false faces with each other.

"Nothing amusing in it, my prince," Madda chides me, misinterpreting the smile. "That's the other side of the talk. Someone must breed the Given, and this one seems . . . reluctant."

I remember Khosa frozen under my father's grip, how she burrowed against her chair when I leaned close to speak in confidence. "I don't think she cares to be touched."

"She'll have to bear it, and soon," Madda says. "Before the less scrupulous take matters into their own hands—"

"The Given cannot be forced," I remind her, my voice louder than necessary at the thought of violence brought upon the frail bones I'd felt folding under the very touch of my palms.

"Ooh, you're a bit piquey at that, aren't you, now?" Madda says, actually squirming in her chair with delight at my discomfort. "You'd best abandon those scruples, young prince. To be a good king you'll need to aid and abet in some unsightly things for the sake of Stille."

I nod, but my eyes are on the smoke swirling in the air, my thoughts no longer on Khosa. "A good person does not necessarily make a good king," I say.

"And that's as true backward as forward." Madda nods, all teasing gone. We're quiet for a moment together, the wax of the candle pooling on the table.

"I do not want the throne," I tell her, the words that have long been in my heart finally finding my tongue.

"Ah well." She reaches for my hand and unfolds my fingers, gaze sweeping over the lines of my palms. "Best get used to the idea."

CHAPTER 13

———⚬❦⚬———

Dara

DARA KNOWS HER BROTHER HAS TRACKED TRUE WHEN they find the Tangata cats. Their once-lithe bodies are twisted, dead paws set in a perpetual swipe that forces sheaths open. Claws rake the air in search of an enemy who has already won. Dara and Donil slip through the group cautiously, sidestepping the claws that could slice them open even in death.

"Tides," says Vincent, pulling his shirt over his nose even from his vantage point astride a horse. "They've been in the heat a bit, haven't they?"

Donil nods as he bends over the bodies, their muscles hard under softening skins. "Five days, at least. I've never seen so many taken down at once. Looks as if they thought they had safety in numbers, but the prey was new to them. This one's got a bite taken right out of his belly."

"They attacked the sea beast, you think?" Vincent asks.

"Surely," Dara says, plucking a scale from a cat's hide. She holds it to the light, but its iridescence was lost as it dried and curled. "Tell me again the worth of following an animal I've already killed?"

"To see if there are others," Vincent says, echoing his grandfather's words. "The sight of the sea on land threw fear into a great many people, something perhaps you intended by dragging half a rotting corpse into a banquet."

Dara flicks the scale into the breeze. "Your mother says Stillean banquets need flavor."

"The reek of death wasn't what she had in mind," Vincent says. "Gammal was sequestered with his advisors until the dawn trying to decide what to do about it. The Scribes tore through their shelves, searching for references of Lusca coming onto land in the past, and in Stillean territory, at that."

"Did they find any?"

"No, and that did little to alleviate their fears."

Donil rises from a Tangata body, his brow furrowed against the sun. "They'd be better served to fear the Pietra, after the attack on Hyllen."

"The Scribes say Pietra attacked Hyllen in retribution for Stille pushing them onto the cliffs years ago, time out of memory," Vincent says. "They found references in the histories."

"Nonsense," Donil argues. "Armies don't march for revenge only."

"Remind me of that if there's ever a Pietran neck under my blade," Dara says. "I'll gladly kill to settle a score."

"You with the memory of our mother's death fresh in mind, not buried in old books that no one reads anymore," her brother counters. "Pietra has the strength to attack Stille, certainly, but why would they?"

"The Pietra need no reason, brother," Dara reminds him. "Surely you of all people know that."

Vincent shifted in his saddle, sensing an argument brewing. "Nonetheless, Gammal is rousing the army," he says, voice muffled by the shirt still covering his nose.

"*Rousing* is the right word, indeed," Dara says, happy to shift her ire from her brother onto the Stillean soldiers. "Your army has been

napping since your father's-father's-father got a good look at his wife."
She reaches up, tugging the shirt from his nose. "Breathe deep, Vin.
This is what all of Stille will reek of soon enough, should the Pietra
march."

"Dara's right," Donil says. "Stille has had peace far too long. You're
the best fighter they've got, and that only because you grew up crossing
blades with us."

"Our army stands many men deep," Vincent argues. "Stillean soldiers teach their sons the art. It may not pass to them at birth like the
Indiri, but much is taught to them in their youth."

"Yes, training in backyards from soft fathers who never saw battle,
while their mothers look on and gasp at every nick of the blade," Donil
says. "Your army may stand deep, but they'll fall in a tangle at the first
swipe."

Dara swings into her saddle and flicks a scale from her boot. "I
could beat five men from the Stillean army. I might need a weapon,
but I doubt it."

"You wouldn't," Donil says, taking his horse by the reins and
leading him through the fallen Tangata. Dara's and Vincent's mounts
follow.

"We can test your confidence when we return. Father assured me
the army was a sight to see," Vincent says.

"It's not confidence," Dara answers, pulling her heavy hair away
from her neck in the heat. "It's the way of it. Donil and I have lost
one home, and our entire race. I see a threat to my new one, and my
adopted people ill-fit to defend themselves. 'A sight to see' may well be
true, but saying kind words about the shininess of their armor doesn't
change the fact that it shines from lack of use."

"And a man who doesn't use his sword soon loses his nerve.
Though from what Milda tells Daisy, there's no end to Vincent's
nerve. Or his sword, at that," Donil says, bending to pick up a stone

and toss it toward the prince's head. But it's easily plucked from the air by Dara.

"A man who dips his sword in every well soon finds it spotted with rust," Dara says to her brother.

"Among other things," Vincent adds, catching the stone when Dara tosses it to him, then winging it at the back of Donil's freckled head. The Indiri leads his horse on, his low chuckle the only evidence that he felt it at all.

Vincent reaches up to pluck a leaf from a red tree and hands it to Dara. She takes it, only too glad to play a childhood game. Vincent watches as the speckles on her hand and arm change colors, matching the leaf in her hand and flowing up to her face in a ripple.

"You'd do better to be more mindful of your own blood, brother," Dara chides, letting the breeze pluck the leaf from her hand as her skin settles back into its normal tones. "The last thing Stille wants is half-Indiri children."

"I'm careful," Donil says. "Daisy takes the nilflower brew that Madda makes for Vincent's girl as well."

"You're foolish," Dara snaps, her voice unusually harsh at the mention of Milda. "You'll get some girl with child, nilflower brew or not, and dilute all that's left of our blood."

"And you're angry that the only man who will have anything to do with you is Unter Hoff, and him only to put a fresh bud to your skin to make you turn green."

Vincent smothers a laugh, and Dara lashes at him, her anger only half pretended. "That's not true."

"You *did* turn green. I saw it."

"And that's not the only thing our Dara turns green over," Donil says, and the kick aimed at her twin is not in jest.

"And Unter Hoff is not the only one who will have anything to do with me," she says, face suddenly hard as she spurs her horse past

Vincent's, roughly brushing her twin out of the way. "At least I can turn," she shoots at him as she passes. "Magic runs through my whole body, not just between my legs like yours."

Donil sighs heavily as Vincent's horse pulls alongside him.

"Were all Indiri women so prideful?" Vincent asks.

"For the sake of my male ancestors, I hope not."

CHAPTER 14

※

Vincent

DARA REFUSES TO GO INTO THE CAVE, EVEN THOUGH THE tide is low. The teasing on the trail sent her into a black mood she won't be removed from.

"You go on and invite the sea to come for you, if you want," she says to us, her feet firmly planted at the edge of the beach where the last of the trees end their march. "I'll not offer myself up so easily."

"The tide doesn't come in that quickly," I assure her. "We won't be in danger."

"Yes, Vin has spent *an entire day* hauling traps. He knows these things," Donil says. I give him a shove, but Dara's scowl remains.

"I'm sure Khosa's ancestors thought they knew the sea," she says. "Then the great wave took the Three Sisters, and she's fated to be Given."

"And if it comes, standing back here will do you little good," Donil tells her. "May as well die with us, sister."

"I'll die as I please and with whom I choose."

"Enough," Donil says, rolling his eyes. "The beast had a path through the underbrush. Any sign on the beach is erased, but that cave is the only good shelter we've come across. If there are any more of its kind, we'll find them there."

"Should we come back with more men?" I ask, remembering the litter of dead Tangata behind us. But Donil shakes his head.

"You know our opinion of your men. Even with Dara standing at a distance, she's more use than ten of them flailing in a small space, like to cut off each other's arms." He claps a hand on my shoulder. "I've not seen fresh leavings. I'd bet my left hand there's nothing in the cave, and it's the one I prefer."

"In that case, I'll kindly ask you to release me," I say, shrugging out from under Donil's grip. We head for the cave in the dying light, leaving Dara as she sinks into the sand, a mistrustful eye on the restless sea.

"Does the Given find the castle to her liking?" Donil asks.

"I believe so." My simple answer evades the truth—that Khosa has retreated to the library in the seven days since her arrival. She seeks no company, and the one time I attempted to speak to her, she murmured half answers, eyes locked on a page and not my face. Though Madda's words had worried me for Khosa's safety, the guards my father had set at the library doors seemed sturdy.

"Where are your thoughts, brother?" Donil asks me. "Nowhere good, I think."

The familiarity of calling me "brother" goes far past the spoken word. Donil knows me down through my skin. "I met with Madda yesterday," I tell him, and my Indiri friend snorts.

"You know what I think of your Stillean Seer."

"Yes, and brothers we may be in heart, but our ways are still not the same," I tell him. "Plenty of Stilleans share your opinion—my own father among them. But she's said things to me that have come to pass, so I won't dismiss her as easily as others do."

"Fair enough. What did the old lady say that has you looking like a crushed sea-spine?"

I take a deep breath, remembering how my body relented to the weighty air of nilflower in Madda's chamber, my mind following as thoughts unspooled into nothingness. Father's wandering eye, Mother's unhappiness, Purcell's shadow falling darkly even now, a long wait for a throne that was never meant to be mine, the speckles that mark my best friends as something to be feared by others, the bright red hair of the girl I bed to pass the time . . . all those had floated with the smoke in the air. I had been left with Khosa, and the one smile that flickered briefly in the spray of the surf.

"I asked her if I will marry," I admit to Donil.

"Course you will," Donil scoffs. "I don't need the Sight to see that. What was her answer?"

"She said I'll have two great loves in my life."

"Doesn't mean you're married to either of them."

"I'll not be a false husband," I snap, thinking of my father and the lines around Mother's eyes, deepening with every lover he takes.

"Easy, brother," Donil says, halting at the cave mouth. "I didn't say you would. You're a good man, Vincent, and take too seriously the words of a mad old woman in a tower. You've told me yourself the lines in your hands can change, and that the fate she sees in them today can be altered by your actions tomorrow. No one thing is set in stone."

I think of Khosa's body pinned by the trapmen, the sea lapping for the Given even as she lay still.

"One thing is," I say. "We best see what the cave holds before the tide comes. Dara will have our hides if we have to camp on the beach tonight."

"Hides and heads." Donil draws his sword as I do the same, and we enter the cave together. The floor is littered with scales, shining colors catching the last of the fading light. We tread carefully, feet sliding in spots.

"Bit of a reek to it," I say, stymieing the urge to cover my face again.

"Our beast's place, for sure." Donil sheathes his sword as he nears the back of the cave. "And no one home."

"My grandfather will be glad to hear it. He feared we'd find a nest, send half the people panicking and the other half on a trek to the beach to see."

Donil doesn't answer, his attention captured by the wall.

"What is it?" I ask.

"Not sure. We're losing the light but I think . . ." Donil backs away from the wall, eyes squinting in the dark. "I think someone has painted here."

"Nonsense." I join him. "No Stillean would chance being drowned." But my words lose their conviction when I spot a figure on the wall.

It could be explained away as a pattern in the rock when I focus, but when my eyes wander, it springs out again, arms and legs and head too pronounced to be anything but human.

"I see another." Donil's fingers trace a pattern higher on the wall. "And you're right, no Stillean would risk it."

"Who then? The Indiri?"

Donil shakes his head. "I have no memory of this. And I can tell you the color of my seven-times-great-grandmother's eyes."

"And what good is that, when the ones in your own skulls are useless?"

I spin to the front of the cave to find a man leaning in the mouth, picking his teeth with a dagger. "I've heard that there were only two Indiri left in our world. I slip past one and find the other boxed in. It seems as if we Feneen were right to leave the speckled babes."

"No Indiri babe would be left out for your filthy Feneen hands," Donil says, words coming as swiftly as his sword is drawn. Mine follows, half a shade behind.

"You'll want to improve your draw, young prince," the Feneen says to me. "Your tame Indiri may not always be at your side."

"How do you know who he is?" Donil demands.

The Feneen pockets his dagger and smiles. "Many questions, and the tide rises too fast for a long talk."

"Then I'll slit your throat quickly, and you can suck wind through your second mouth as we leave." Dara's hand flicks from behind him, smooth as silk in the wind. "You didn't slip past me."

The Feneen stiffens in surprise, and Dara's blade presses all the more closely. "Hear me out, and I think you'll find it worthwhile to stay your hand."

Dara and Donil share a look I'm not included in as she adjusts her grip on the dagger, the pressure lifted from the Feneen's neck.

"I wasn't looking forward to a night ride home, anyway," Donil says, relaxing his sword arm. "The cats are restless with the smell of this creature in the air. We relieve you of your weapons, and you share our fire—fair?"

"Fair," the Feneen agrees.

CHAPTER 15

Vincent

MY ARM IS TENSE AT MY SIDE, UNABLE TO RELAX, EVEN though Donil and Dara move easily before the enemy. Dara's hands slip through the Feneen's clothing and relieve him of a dagger before we exit the cave. I will the blood to drain from my cheeks as we leave the shadows. I do not want the twins to know how I flushed when called out on a slow sword draw. It did not go unnoticed either, how Donil had stepped slightly in front of me, angled to protect me from an attack.

"You travel light," I say as we emerge from the cave into the twilight, looking at the single dagger that Dara now carries.

"My true weapon lies here," he says, tapping a pouch that hangs around his neck, but the easy smile that follows takes all threat from his words. My steps falter as I look at him.

All of my life I've used the fine lines around eyes and mouths to decipher whether I'm speaking to a mother, grandfather, or great. In some of the noble families, the resemblances are so close I have to count crow's-feet before I pronounce a name, like counting tines of my fork to know which to use with what course. But this Feneen has told me much in a glance, all of it at odds.

The smile remains as he watches my confusion, dimples sunk deep in cheeks still plump with youth. His lips are full but pull back over yellowed teeth, a few missing already. The fingers at his necklace are rough with years of work, the nails as thick as my grandfather's. My eyes travel back to a face as smooth as mine, and eyes that are laughing at me.

"As I said, I think you'll find it worthwhile to hear me out, young prince."

"You know me," I say, not phrasing it as a question as we pick our way across the beach, Dara gingerly flicking the surf from her boots as if she were a forest cat herself.

"I'm Stillean—or would have been if my mother hadn't left me on the rocks," he amends as we pass into the coolness of the woods, the long shadows of the trees closing around us. "I've kept an interest in my people, whether they had one in me or not."

"What is your name?"

"The Feneen call me Ank, and I don't know that I ever had another," he says, sinking down to the ground as Donil and Dara set to making a fire. Their capable hands have a flame within minutes, and Donil pulls food from his sack while she tends the horses, their noses brushing against her for treats.

"Oh, beasties," she says quietly, pulling an apple from her pocket and slicing it. "Can't keep a secret from you, can I?"

"Bread, cheese, and would've been some fruit if my sister hadn't fed it to the horses," Donil says, carving up chunks of both among us.

"They need their strength, same as us," Ank says. "You were right earlier; the cats are restless. You'll want the legs under your mounts if you need to outrun them."

"They don't attack people," Dara says. "Only if they're desperate."

"Or the people particularly foolish," Donil adds.

"Perhaps," Ank says. "None of you strike me as foolish, but the cats are desperate, though not for food."

"What do you mean?" I ask him, my eyes still crawling over his young face in the firelight, his aged hands a stark disagreement.

Instead of answering me, he looks to Dara. "What do you know?"

Her eyes go to her brother, and he nods. "The cats have gone to the trees," she says, and my heart sinks.

My childhood was littered with tutors to teach me stars, letters, sums, manners, and the history of my people. Books rested on my bedside, heavy with necessary reading, but the one that captured my attention held it because of the fear it evoked. Tales of the great wave that took nearly everything, illuminated with Tangata cats climbing trees in the margins, water lapping at the lower branches.

"What do you make of it?" Donil asks Ank.

"The cats aren't the only ones behaving oddly. Something of the land is taking to the trees, something of the sea taking to the land. I've seen worms burrowing their way to the sun like there's going to be a hard rain, but none falls. And the birds aren't making nests."

"Why not?" I ask.

"Because there aren't any young," Ank says.

"Sister?" Donil's question hangs in the air.

"He's right," Dara says quietly. "I've not seen Tangata kittens or wolf pups, no oderbirds' eggs from toppled nests in the woods."

A silence settles over us, and the fire pops, brilliantly lighting Ank's young face. "What are you?" I ask.

"I'm a Feneen, made so by the caul I was born with."

I'd heard of those born with cauls, a membrane covering their faces as they exited their mothers' wombs. It was rare, but like a lamb with a fifth dangling leg or a pup with two heads, it was not looked on as a good thing. A merciful midwife would cut it away before presenting the babe, the parents never the wiser. Whoever attended Ank's mother on the birthing stool was not one of those.

"You were abandoned?" I ask.

He nods. "Left on the rocks for the Feneen, the cats, or the gulls— whoever got to me first."

I shudder, but he raises a hand. "There's a reason why those born behind the veil aren't welcome, and I can't say I disagree with it. Seems that having a mask given to me as a babe means I can see past whatever the living wear now."

Dara clears her throat and hugs her cloak tighter around her chest.

"Nay, girl," Ank says, but not without a smile. "I mean I can see to the insides of you, know who you are in truth, not the face you present to the world."

I think of Khosa and me at dinner, careful to make conversation, share food and drink, and never once say anything of importance to each other, the polite manners and court politics keeping us from sharing one true thing.

"A rare gift," I say to him. "To know someone fully."

"And one that might make keeping friends a bit difficult," Donil adds.

"Harder still to find people I'd want to call that."

Dara smiles, but her eyes are serious. "So you know our thoughts?"

"No, I can't see what's in your mind for the good or the bad. But when I put my hands on you, I can be sure which you *are*, no matter how hard you try to be the other."

"A useful trick," I say. "Though I can't see how much it's worth when you're in the woods alone."

"But I'm not alone, am I?" Ank says.

"You were following us," Donil says.

"I've got business in Stille. What better path there than following a Stillean royal?" His hand goes back to the pouch at his neck, the smile gone.

"You said that was your weapon?" I prompt, hoping he'll elaborate.

"My caul, withered and old, though it kept my face young a good long while." He answers me, eyes on the fire. "I was left out still wearing my veil, for what use is it to uncover a face that will not look long on the world? The Feneen have had a few caul-bearers amongst them. They believe the longer we wear our mask, the greater our power grows, so they did not cut it away. I wore my veil until my thirtieth Arrival Day, and it protected me from sun, wind, and rain. So here I am with the task of a man and the face of a boy, hoping he who sits the throne will hear me out."

"What task?"

His eyes, carrying all the weight of his years, despite the lack of wrinkles around them, land heavily on me. "Our world is dying. You know, Indiri," he says to Dara. "Your magic fades as the earth around us gasps for last breaths. And the animals know. They won't bring their own young to bear because it's futile."

"You were coming to warn Stille?" I ask.

"Nay, for there's no forewarning can save anyone. The cats have shown me there's no escape. They go into the trees and come back down, prowling the earth only to attack what they can find of the sea. It's futile, but they've always been the violent type. Like you," he adds, eyes cutting back to Dara.

"Don't forget it," she says darkly, but he only chuckles.

"Not much of a bedtime story, I'm afraid," he says, rolling onto his side and pulling his cloak tight about him. "But it's rest I need, and the castle tomorrow, perhaps a glimpse of she who is given to the sea, though I don't know that Stillean superstition can save us."

I tense, and I can see the lines of laughter in his shoulders as his words land right where he wanted them to.

"What do you know of Khosa?" My voice is harsh, more defensive than I meant it to be.

"Khosa?" he asks. "Of her, nothing. But I knew much of her Feneen father."

CHAPTER 16

Khosa

THE WRONGNESS FLOWS STRONG THROUGH MY VEINS today, weighing down my blood and dragging my mind into dark corners. I can hear the tide through the castle walls, but my feet are not itching to feel the sand beneath them again. So it is not my mother's curse I feel in this moment, but my father's. And though Sona's will be the one to kill me, it is his that makes my life a misery.

The servants tend to me, something I cannot adjust to with ease. They are on my steps, following my shadow, whispering in my wake. I dismiss them, not anxious to have anyone at my elbow as I make my way to the library. The discovery of its book-lined walls has been my saving grace; it is the only place I can go where others do not follow out of curiosity. My not-quite-right smile and the slightly wrong angle of my head as I try to appear curious when spoken to have not gone unnoticed. I am no longer paraded about for the public to rejoice in, their savior come, though a bit off in her timing.

The king has given me permission to wander the castle as I please, hoping, no doubt, for me to have a chance encounter with a male I find pleasing. But it is here as it was in Hyllen; I take comfort only in the ink-stained pages in front of me. The castle library is well-lit so that I can read as early as the sun rises, but the sound of the surf finds its way to me through the high windows, and my guards cannot rest easy.

The sea always calls me, a dull throb like a headache biding its time, though I never know when it will spike into the blindness of the dance, and have found no precursor that brings it on. My dance is not like the tide, with predictable ebbs and flows. It is a fever in my veins, abaiting at will and surging forth when it wants, bringing twin spots of desire to my cheeks as I spin to my death.

King Gammal has a guard set at all times, ready to stop any mad dashes like the one Vincent saved me from. I do not share with the king that a few hours of rustling paper tends to send them into deep sleeps from which they wake, opening their eyes to find me where I was before.

They always look guilty. My bloated corpse will be on their hands if I lose control on their watch. The younger ones smile at me sheepishly, and I feel a rush of forgiveness inside, a warm wave that rises from my gut but fails to illuminate my body. I want to reassure them, but I know my face looks as blankly at them as at the paper under my fingers.

The king has been patient in his questions, Prince Varrick less so. They know I carry nothing within me; my mate is not yet chosen, and no seed has been planted. The Scribes have reasserted that the Given is a willing sacrifice, the sea placated by my subservience. To drag a thrashing, wailing girl to her death could agitate it. I assure them the same holds true in other aspects, keeping my eyes on theirs without flinching, daring any one of them to cross my bedroom threshold without my consent. Only Varrick holds my gaze.

I always return to the books, because they do not mind my imperviousness.

Today it is the annals of the castle that leap to my hands. I found it quite by accident, a heavy book toward the bottom of the pile, one I had to wrestle free in order to inspect. The cover was wordless, the date entry on the first page the only indication that I had discovered an intimate history of my new home. With nothing to do and the light snoring of my guards filling the air, I searched for mention of Sona, my mother.

Her name was not recorded. She was called only the Given, as I must be in a book with newer ink and fresher pages that someone here in the castle is likely writing this very moment. Yesterday I read of my birth, and the celebration that followed, culminating with the waves closing over my mother's head. Mention was made of my Keepers carrying me from Stille, and now my fingers run over those words, recalling faces that did not light with affection exactly, but at least with recognition.

The next page tells of Vincent's birth, the story taking up fewer lines than my own. My arrival saved the kingdom, while his only reiterated that his blood would fill the throne one day. I feel a kinship with him as I see our stories set side by side in this book, lives recorded in facing pages.

Two good years followed Vincent's Arrival Day, with healthy herds, full grain bins, traps brimming with food from the sea. Even on my stone stool, I feel the comfort rolling from these pages, the contentment of an age past. I turn the page to find the same hand at work, but the letters are ragged, now, written in haste or anger. The word *Indiri* catches my eye, and I am instantly lost.

The Indiri have come, tiny feet leaving bloodied footsteps behind them. Their infant mouths speak words as they lie in the arms of Princess Dissa, and she tends to these as if she shares their abominable speckled skin. They tell their stories, small bodies sitting upright on the table to address the king, quick eyes darting not in the surprise of babes but with the cold calculation of warriors.

The Pietra came for them, why they do not know. The Indiri have shared a border with the people of the Stone Shore since deep into their memories, and while they would not be called friendly, a tenuous peace held. And so the Indiri, though stronger and more able, were caught by surprise when battle came to them.

The female child tells a hideous tale of their mother, heavily pregnant with the two of them, running into the fray, sword in hand. She spoke of her arms entwined with her brother's, safe inside the womb, even when their mother's head was struck from her shoulders. Dissa cried openly, her own arms shielding them when the boy spoke of their mother's body being dragged into a pit, where they lay surrounded by the dead, waiting for the invaders to leave and for their mother's body to cool before they birthed themselves and clawed their way through filth and blood.

Even this unnaturalness will not draw the princess's affection from them, though the king and Prince Varrick wear heavy faces, brows drawn together as they find themselves interrogating infants. These babes now share a cradle with Stillean blood, their ableness in stark contrast to the infant Vincent, who gurgles and taps at their faces while they carry on discussions, one on either side of him, their foreign words filling the air while their spots rub against his unblemished skin.

I shiver, pulling the worn cloak I keep here in the library tighter around me.

"Would you like me to set a fire, my lady?" one of the guards asks.

"No," I say quickly, as always. The thought of crackling flames in this room of brittle paper makes me more uneasy than the tides coming in at night. "I thank you, though," I add, willing my eyes to soften, my lips to form the small twist that my female Keeper wore when placating me.

It does not work. I see it in his face as he resumes his position at the door. In time, my guards may become as practiced at keeping their thoughts from showing as I am. But for now I spot every subtlety, the tiniest flicker of muscles around the mouth, the precise sheen of moisture in the eyes, all declaring that I am as much of an outsider as the Indiri twins.

Unlike the Scribe who penned these pages, their Indiri skin is not what sends the blood pounding in my veins, though I can't help but notice it. Their gazes have burned through me whenever we meet, and so I have taken steps to ensure our paths do not cross. The girl especially overwhelms me if I stare too long into her light eyes, where emotions flicker like flame. Each one wars with the next, and I've found myself dizzy in her presence, a leaf caught up in a storm that it did not foresee.

The boy, Donil, is more cautious, but burns just as brightly, if not more so. In Hyllen the act between men and women was never hindered or wrapped in embarrassment. I know what desire looks like, and saw it in his bright eyes when they met mine at the banquet. Keeping my path from his has not been easy, as my limbs ache to run not toward the sea but to find *him*.

It is not fear of his desire that sends me away from Donil, but fear that I might acquiesce to my own. It's not his broad shoulders or easy smile, or even curiosity about his skin that casts my handmaids into simpering smiles whenever he is in their sight. There is a tenderness in him that carries with it an echo of Abna's hand pressed into mine, a touch that I *could* bear, one that might have led to more if not interrupted by the march of an approaching army. Abna's hand, undoubtedly cold now, perhaps in a pit not unlike the one Donil's Indiri mother was thrown into.

I shiver once more, and the same guard opens his mouth, undoubtedly about to suggest a fire again. He catches himself in time, and our eyes meet, an unhampered smile spreading across my face as I guess his intent at the same moment that he stilled it. His own smile answers mine, reaching to his earlobes so that he looks less like a soldier and more like the child he once was, caught in some shared joke.

"No fire, I assume?" he says.

I look to the walls, the ancient maps that have stared down at me while I stared back, memorizing the lines of coast, wondering which might represent the place where my feet will cross from land into sea.

"I would never risk it," I answer, gesturing toward their crumbled edges, yellowed with age.

"Very good, my lady," he says, eyes holding mine for a moment longer than necessary.

I look to his partner, slumped in a deep sleep on the other side of the door. "Speak freely, if you wish."

He clears his throat, awkward in the moment where I change from being more than a duty. "I was wanting to say that you should smile more, is all. It might . . . help."

There is much truth in what he says. My happiness, when it does come, is pure and unpracticed. If I knew how to conjure its ghost, the fake twist of lips I see worn on the court faces, it would help. Help to find a mate, help to build friendships, help ease the guilt of the young prince whose hands I still have bruises from, now faded to yellow.

Vincent wears his court-appointed mask well, but I have spent years mimicking emotions and read them as easily as the books that line these walls. His gaze may have registered the cut of my dress or the shape of my face, but it was the idea of both rotting in the sea that filled his mind, not lifting the hem or touching my lips. He looks at me and thinks of my death, guilt fast on the heels of that because for his throne not to float in water, my body must.

Why should I work to assuage that guilt? What use in making friendly with him or any other when it would be a short-lived friendship indeed? Nine moonchanges at the most, should I find my mate—whom I hardly need to care for in order for the deed to be done.

A wave crashes in the distance, the impact carrying into the library, the sea invading even this place as its scent billows through the window, wiping away the last traces of mirth from my lips.

"What would be the use?" I say to my guard.

CHAPTER 17

Khosa

THE WALK BACK TO MY CHAMBERS IS NOT LONG, AND I manage to convince my guards that I will be safe in the company of the sconcelighter who precedes me, her flame lighting the way. The younger guard bows his head as if I'd given an order, but I hear his footsteps turn the corner as mine do and know that he shadows me. The sconcelighter walks alongside me without speaking, pausing to light the wicks as she goes. We are a silent and odd group, our footfalls stopping together and picking up again.

Raucous laughter echoes from around the corner, and the sconcelighter yelps as two men collide with her, one of them rescuing her torch and flame before it falls to the ground. Too late I see the fingers that have caught it are speckled. The fire reflected in Donil's eyes is brighter than his companion's.

"Careful, Reah," one of them says, taking the torch from Donil and offering it to the sconcelighter. "You'll light your skirts on fire, and the castle too."

She snatches it back with an annoyed huff, but can't hide a smile. "And what are my skirts to you, Rook? I hear you like the way the kennel master's daughter's breeches look."

"I like the look of them on my floor, anyway. And would offer the same spot to your skirts should you be so inclined," Rook answers her, and in Reah's torchlight, I can see two bright spots of drunkenness in his cheeks. A sideways glance at Donil shows the same; the sound of steps drawing near tells me my guard has noticed as well.

"I'll not drop my skirts for you when your bed's still warm from her," Reah chides Rook, but by her voice, I think she would be happy to once it cools.

"Would you consider lifting them, though?"

"Excuse me," I say, trying to slip past.

"Hello, there," Rook says, tipping an invisible hat to me. "Who is your fine-looking friend, Reah?"

"She is the Given," Donil says. I feel his gaze on me, a weight heavier than the sea. My chest tightens, what little breath left smoldering within.

"Given to the Sea?" Rook steps back to look at me better. "That's a waste, then."

"Rook," comes a warning voice, my guard closing the distance between us, "we know you well, and that you jest. The Given may not be inclined to laugh along with you."

"Merryl." Rook nods at my guard as he comes in the light. "Good to know you're here, keeping the young lady safe from a good, thorough . . . laugh."

At his words, I feel exactly that—a bubble of humor coming from inside of me, a place I thought could be filled only with sadness after I arrived in Stille. My laugh takes everyone by surprise, weak as it is, a light thing in this dark corner lit only by Reah's flame.

"See, Merryl, she's the Given, but a girl no less," Rook says, lacing an arm around the sconcelighter's waist. "We're headed to the tower. I've got a bit of water to add to the sea if you take my meaning."

"I hear you're not likely to reach it," Reah teases, and they head back the way we came, ducking into a stairwell.

"Would you like to go to your quarters, my lady?" Merryl, my guard, offers.

I would not like to, but I don't know how to say as much without sounding brash, sending him away to be alone with Donil. I can see the tips of the Indiri's boots as I stare at the floor, too embarrassed to raise my gaze.

"Come with us, Merryl." Donil neatly saves me, his hand cupping my elbow. My body tenses, but the shudder I'm expecting does not come.

"It's a clear night, and the moon is on the rise," Donil continues. "Fresh air is best for what ails you."

"All that ails me is duty, and mine is to see the Given to her bed," my guard says.

It's a poor choice of words, and one that Donil leaps on.

"Oh, is it?" he exclaims with mock incredulity, dropping his hand from where it had rested at my elbow. I miss the pressure immediately. "By all means, don't let me stop you," Donil says, motioning us forward with a sweeping bow and a wink for me.

"That's not—" Merryl chokes on outraged words, his face flushing bright red. "My lady, I meant nothing—"

"I know it," I say, raising my hands to tide his embarrassment. "And some air would be welcome."

I head for the stairwell to follow Rook and Reah, only to have Donil's hand fall on my arm once again, our skin separated only by the light fabric of my dress. "You might give it a moment, first," he says.

"Oh . . ." I glance down at his hand, unfamiliar with the feel of warmth that spreads from him to me, no revulsion alongside it. "Do they need privacy?"

"Well." Donil smiles. "Reah might wish for it after she sees Rook pissing over the parapets."

"I grew up in Hyllen," I call over my shoulder as I ascend the twisting stairs, Donil and Merryl in my wake. "I've seen plenty of men relieving themselves. Girls too," I add, for good measure.

I climb quickly, the muscles in my legs enjoying the stretch after being deprived of the hills of Hyllen. I've missed night air, too, I realize when I burst onto the parapet, filling my lungs with it. Reah rests against the wall, snuffing her flame with a pinch of wetted fingers as Rook finishes his business over the ledge.

"You missed it," he chides me when he turns.

"Not much to see," Reah says, and I laugh again, enjoying the sound on the coolness of the air, how it reaches out to the sea, floating above where its wet fingers cannot reach.

Merryl stands by the door, his duty still heavy on his mind and eyes always on me. Donil comes into the moonlight and, captivated, I can look nowhere else. We ease away from the others by silent agreement, coming to the ledge, where I glance at the surf below.

"Your guard watches as if I'd fling you to the water," Donil says, and I feel his gaze pouring over me as the sea wishes to.

"I don't believe you would," I say, turning to look at the sea.

"No, I'd rather have you in front of me," he says, and extends a hand. "I don't know that we've formally met. I'm Donil."

"I'm Khosa," I say. I place my hand in his, palm to palm, flesh to flesh, and the only shiver I feel is one of anticipation.

"Khosa," he repeats, and I realize that he was never told my name, only that I am the Given.

"Khosa," I say again.

And for the first time, I wish to be only that.

CHAPTER 18

Witt

WITT'S EYES WANDER OVER THE FLOCK, HUNDREDS strong, their nubbed tails twitching in the morning light. His men lean against a pen, watching the animals chew their cud peacefully, oblivious to their new company.

"What's a soldier to do with a bunch of sheep?" one of his men asks.

"Eat 'em," another answers.

"If we slaughtered all of them, we couldn't eat a third of the meat before it spoiled, and I'd rather go into battle with empty hands than an overfull belly," Witt counters.

"I could take on three Stilleans with no weapon and a whole goat in my gut," comes the response.

"Perhaps." Witt nods. "But I'd rather see mutton walking around than lying on the ground after you've been gutted by a chance blade."

Beside him, Pravin smiles. "The Lithos speaks true. We didn't take Hyllen only to spill blood. There's land here, and food. These people are shepherds and farmers, and none of you could tend an animal or harvest a crop if your life depended on it."

"And it does," adds Witt.

"We are soldiers, sir," one of the men responds, the inherent pride in the fact making his tone border on insubordination.

"Soldiers must eat to fight," Witt says. "Our Lures haven't caught enough fish from the cliffs to feed Pietra in some time. Armor that fit fathers sits loosely on their sons, while the Lures spot schools in the distance, where lines cannot reach. Would you rather learn to tend a flock, or take to the sea?"

The soldier's face hardens to equal that of his ruler. "Boats are for the dead."

"They are," Witt agrees, though he walks away from his men before any trace of his nightmares can betray him, the memory of tears falling from decidedly living eyes as he shoved them away from shore.

Pravin stays in step with him. "I didn't expect this much resistance."

"They've been raised to live by the sword," Witt answers. "Their hands won't fit to the staff or plow overnight. We'll finish speaking with the Hyllenians, sort the meek from the brave, and spare an equal number of capable shepherds and farmers."

Pravin nods. "The sorting shouldn't take long, at least."

Witt's palm brushes the tops of the grain as he walks. "They are as peaceful as we are fierce, but we need them. The Lures will not take to the sea to catch fish for fear of the Lusca, and neither would I ask them to. We must learn to grow our food, or make the Hyllenians do it for us."

"I know which I prefer," the Mason says.

"And I know which we excel at, but if we refuse to set our hand to the plow, we must allow them to multiply, always passing their trade to the next generation. Those who would submit to a harness themselves will not wish it on their children. And so grows unrest and rebellion."

"Yes, my Lithos," Pravin consents, but Witt notices he keeps his own hand on his sword pommel, not touching the grain around them.

"You disapprove?"

Pravin stops, his fighter's eyes roving the hills even as he speaks. "I know what I am, and what our people are. It is not in our nature."

"No. But the world is changing, and we must change with it."

A muscle in the Mason's jaw flickers. "I know. And I'm not ashamed of the fear in me at the thought. I'm glad I'll be gone to the dark long before I see the days that are coming."

"Maybe not as long as you think. The Lures claim—"

"I know what they say."

"Then you understand that keeping the Hyllenians for labor so that our pride might be spared is a luxury we cannot afford. People require space, and it's my duty to ensure that every handful of earth is minded by the Pietra."

Pravin exhales slowly, a heavy breath that brings the tiniest wheeze, which Witt closes his ears to. He is not ready to set Pravin's boat to sea.

"These are odd days indeed," Pravin says with a humorless smile, "when the Pietra worry about what happens inland, and the Lithos makes slaves instead of bodies."

Witt shrugs as they approach the next holding pen, still stocked with Hyllenians, their eyes heavy with fear. "They are no threat," he says. "They are not the Indiri, passing strength and fury in their blood."

"No," Pravin spits on the ground. "They are not the Indiri."

"And there is no clemency in letting some live," Witt adds, resting his elbows on the fence as the Hyllenians scatter away from him, their clothes whispering together, recalling the sounds of the sea. "As there will be none for us."

CHAPTER 19

Vincent

I'VE BEEN ALLOWED A SPOT BESIDE VARRICK IN THE COUNCIL chambers only because it was I who delivered Ank to the castle and announced him as something more than an ordinary citizen. To have a Feneen alongside me carried enough confusion through the ranks that I assumed a chair before anyone could object.

Ank should look out of place here, his travel-worn clothes in stark contrast to the vibrant tapestries around him, his bare feet inelegant against the smooth floors. But he seems more amused by his surroundings than awed, and I see my father trying to sort him out from across the table.

"My grandson says you are Feneen?" King Gammal begins.

"Stillean to begin with," Ank corrects. "Feneen in the end."

"And for what reason did your mother reject you?" my father asks. "You seem well made, and quick-witted enough."

"Perhaps it's best to not focus on the wrongs done to me by your people, when I've come to offer aid," Ank says, smoothly avoiding the question.

"Aid?" My father laughs. "Does the builder look for stones in the rubble he tossed aside?"

Ank's face hardens, settling into an anger I never glimpsed last night in the woods. "Only once the house is fallen."

Varrick's laughter chokes out, and Gammal shifts subtly, his hand resting on my father's arm to quiet him.

"Ank," the king says, "by what title should I address you?"

"There are no titles among the Feneen. People are only people to us, and those we take in are happy to be recognized as such. I am a messenger, bearing the will of my kind to yours."

"And what is the message?"

"You lost the village of Hyllen to the Pietra. Do you know why they attacked?"

Around me the less-trained advisors share glances, eager to know the answer to a question much debated. For my part, I remain still, eyes trained on Ank.

"The Scribes advised me of a moment in our shared histories when our people pushed theirs to the stony shores, depriving them of grass beneath their feet and leaving them only fish to feed on. They are a bloodthirsty and violent people," my father continues, "and I find it believable that they would nurse such a grudge long after we had forgotten why it would be held."

"Believable, maybe," Ank says. "But is it likely?"

"For a messenger, you bear little information," my grandfather says. "And ask many questions."

"And for a king, you do not ask enough."

I've fought to keep my face dispassionate, my eyes locked on Ank, but at his disrespectful words, my gaze shoots to Gammal. The king is smiling, though, the laugh lines around his lips deepening as he regards the Feneen.

"Ruling Stille does not require many questions beyond inquiring how full the larders are this year, how fat the sheep."

"How rough the sea," Ank adds, and all around the table, bodies stiffen.

"Yes, always the sea." King Gammal nods in agreement. He and

Ank watch each other in silence. The waves outside crash twice before it is broken.

"What aid have you come to offer a kingdom without hardship?" Gammal asks, all amusement gone.

"Hyllen was not an exercise in revenge, and will not be the last you see of Pietran soldiers on Stillean soil," Ank says. "They wiped out the Indiri and paid for it. Their pit may have been filled with Indiri bodies, but the ash from burned Pietre rested fingers thick on the ground. The Pietra lost as many lives as they stole, if not more, and it took a generation to fill their ranks again."

"Then their soldiers are young." My father shrugs.

"And yours inexperienced," Ank says. "The Pietra will come, and old throats open easily under young blades."

"And the aid?" Gammal prompts again.

"The Feneen will fight with you. Grant us homes, land, a place to live after the blood has been spilled. End our days of debasement and let us call ourselves Stillean, and we'll fight at your side for that right."

Ank's words are for my grandfather, but his eyes trail over my father, and then to me.

"To be clear," my father says, "you ask us for land and the intermingling of our people, in exchange for which you'll provide the odd and the unable, the weak-minded and the rejected, as soldiers in our army—an army facing a battle that at present exists only in your mind."

"At present," Ank says. "But tomorrow comes quickly."

One of the advisors leans near my grandfather, whispering into the king's ear. The others are a constant ripple of movement around me. They fidget with their sleeves, drum fingers on the table, eyes swiveling in their sockets as they look to one another in what they assume are furtive glances. My father and I sit still, ourselves and Ank the anchors in the room that swirls around us. My grandfather waves his advisor away, turning his attention back to Ank.

"You would give us some time to confer, I hope?"

"Two days," Ank says. "And then I make the same offer to the Pietra."

Even I can't sit still. "You'd fight alongside people who put the ill and the elderly to sea with no oars?" The words are out of my mouth before I can remember that I've retained my place in this meeting so far by making my forebears forget I'm here.

Ank shrugs. "I have morals. First I offer my sword to those who drown young girls in the sea."

"Two days." Gammal nods, ignoring the jibe. "How shall we send word of our decision?"

For the first time, there's a tremor in Ank's boyish face, the tiniest slip of muscles that betrays his disappointment. Emissaries are usually invited to stay within the castle walls, where they dine with the servants—if not the nobles. But Ank is Feneen, and now this slight has been piled on top of a lifetime of rejection. He covers it well; the blank look of bored insolence slips back into place before any but myself can decipher it.

"I'll bring word," I say, and all heads turn toward me.

"Vincent—" my father begins, but I cut him off.

"In two days' time, I'll bring you the king's decision at the cave where we first met."

"Agreed," Ank says.

The king rises, my father with him, and the advisors scurry to follow suit. Ank gets to his feet slowly, his body betraying its age even if his face doesn't. He leans across the table, hand extended, and my grandfather and father return the gesture.

My breath catches in my throat, an audible click, remembering too late the pouch at Ank's throat, the gift his caul brought him alongside the curse of being not wanted. Ank's eyes meet mine as he shakes hands with Gammal and Varrick, eyebrows raised to ask why I should fear him knowing what truly lies in their hearts. And as I watch their palms meet, I wonder the same.

CHAPTER 20

———⚬⊂◯⊃⚬———

Dara

DARA PICKS THROUGH A PILE OF GOOSE FEATHERS SHE'S assembled in the haymow, a half-fletched arrow in her hand, dagger within reach. She heard the barn door slide open, knows too well the footfalls of the man who entered, body tensing as he climbs the ladder to the loft where she works.

"You're a hard girl to find," Varrick says, lightly stepping off the ladder and into the hay.

"That is by design," she says, without raising her eyes. "Would that you realized as much."

"Perhaps I wished to find you alone," he says.

"I can't understand why," she says, sliding a feather into place. "Last time that happened, you left with a slash across your belly."

"That I did," Varrick agrees, lifting his shirt to show her the healed scar, his muscles still tight underneath. "Yet I think I left a mark upon you as well."

"Not a lasting one," she counters, sliding the last arrow into her quiver and rising to her feet. "And only one among the hundreds of bruises I've had. Easily healed and equally forgettable."

He grips her wrist as she tries to slide past him. "Dara." He says her name somewhere between a threat and supplication. "That you deny me only makes you more desirable."

"And here I thought it was only my skin that caught your eye, a conquest where you've not planted your flag before. The stables, the meadows, the seaside, the kitchens, the kennels—all their women know you. But Indiri women remain untouched, and I'll see it remains that way."

She twists her wrist from his grasp, but Varrick blocks the path to the ladder, his eyes making himself as familiar with her body as he can be from a distance.

"That's certainly a part of it," he says, leaning against a pillar. "But I've always loved the hunt, and you're the first woman who hasn't responded to the crook of my finger."

"I'll have your fingers off if you lay them on me again."

"I don't doubt you'd like to," he says. "But you can't harm me."

"Royal blood means little to me, weighed against my own," Dara snaps.

Varrick watches her carefully, a slow smile spreading on his handsome face. "I don't think that's quite true."

"The Indiri before all—"

"Yes, yes, I know your mantra," Varrick interrupts her. "But I've seen the way you look at my son. And while there is the light of affection in your eyes, I'm too familiar with cold calculation to not recognize it in another."

"What are you saying?"

"Only what you yourself have thought, and I have followed your line of thinking." Varrick takes a slight step forward, as if approaching the most feral of Tangata with a collar in his hand.

"Long years have passed, Dara," he says, voice dropping low. "No men of your kind have been found, and you've grown into a woman. Deep passion resides in you, I see it. Just as no average soldier should cross swords with you, not just any man should take you into his bed.

You are Indiri. You deserve more. You've set your sights on my son, overlooking the father."

Dara watches him coldly, hand resting on her knife but not unsheathing it. "I overlook the father because he's repulsive."

"I am many things, but not that," he says. And though she would argue, Dara knows her words would ring false. Varrick's looks have not faded with time, but have achieved a luster of experience, eyes of both women and girls following him when he enters a room.

"Perhaps not outwardly," she says. "Though an unknowing glance would wonder why Dissa is your wife, those who know both of you realize that she is the true treasure."

"Is that why you reject me? Out of respect for my wife?"

"I reject you out of respect for myself," Dara yells, voice spiking with anger. "Now stand aside or I'll see you at the foot of the ladder by the quickest route."

Varrick steps away from her smoothly, and she keeps her gaze on him as she goes to the ladder, never turning her back. She is halfway down, each rung trembling beneath her fingers when his voice reaches her, casual and assured.

"Think on it, Dara. I will be king sooner rather than later, and if I say speckled children can sit the throne, who will argue?"

She leaves the barn at a run, too aware that his words have gained traction in her heart.

CHAPTER 21

———— ❦ ————

Khosa

"K HOSA . . ."

My name, whispered furtively, as delicate as the strands of a dream that fade away as a hand touches my shoulder. I sit up quickly, shrugging it off as I come awake.

"Don't touch," I say, the bite in my words one of the more honest intonations I can make.

"I'm sorry." Vincent stands before me, hands up in the air as if to show he means no harm. My skin crawls where we made contact, a reaction that has nothing to do with him but gives offense nonetheless. I can see it in the flicker of hurt across his handsome face; I doubt many Stillean girls would react as I did to having his hands upon them.

"I apologize," I say, and though I mean the words, they come out as hollow as any others.

I tuck a strand of hair behind my ear, and he looks away as I compose myself. The dust motes that had alighted upon me while I slept in the library now floating freely again, the dying light of the sun barely reaching us from the high windows. My guards slumber too, and Vincent frowns at the sight of them.

"I'm hardly about to drown myself while sleeping," I tell him, drawing his attention back to me. "Please don't punish them."

"If that is your wish," he says, but his words are as stiff as my own, his manners and my inability keeping us from saying anything important to each other. His eyes linger on me for a second, and his mouth quirks into a smile.

"You've got some ink just here." He reaches for my face, then thinks better of it and points to his own forehead.

"Oh, tides," I sigh, licking my fingers and running them across my skin to see them come away black. The manuscript I'd fallen asleep on is smudged, and there's a plunge in my stomach at the sight of it.

"I've ruined it," I say.

"Nonsense." Vincent comes around behind me, careful to keep a distance. "It's still legible." He clears his throat, reading aloud. *"The Indiri continue to dominate the practice field, even the female easily overpowering young Vincent in swordplay, memory of violence feeding her combative hands, while he can only defend himself with the first strokes the swordmaster teaches the noble children."*

Vincent fades off, his finger no longer trailing the words of the bitter Scribe.

"Lovely," he says. "You couldn't have found it in yourself to drool a little, ruin this page entirely?"

I laugh impulsively, and his own smile stretches, breaking the mask of manners he wears, perhaps making room for more than apologies between us.

"How do you find the castle?" he asks.

"Confining," I answer, before I have time to wonder at the indelicacy of slighting the very walls that protect me from the sea.

"You must be safe at all times," Vincent says, back once again straight and face formal. "I'm sure it brings some discomfort to you. For that I apologize."

"Then Stille may never rest easy, for the sea calls." I tell him. "What a task—to ensure the well-being of one who must die for the kingdom's own survival."

Vincent stiffens further, and my hand goes to my mouth.

"I'm sorry," I say. "I do not mean to sound ungrateful—"

He stops me with a dark glance, leaning into my space and dropping his voice though my guards still sleep. "Does it frighten you terribly?"

"Frighten . . . I . . ." There is no way to explain that my drowning is not a terror to me. I cannot find words for my resignation, and have never been asked my thoughts on the matter until now, until a boy who is destined for a throne broke through his noble demeanor to ask me something real.

Perhaps I don't need to find the right words. Perhaps he already knows them.

"It does not frighten me," I tell him, holding his gaze. "It shall come to pass, and any dread on my part is ill used in the interim. The sea waits for me . . . much as the throne waits for you."

The court trappings fall away from him, each muscle relaxing and visible relief showing in his eyes as he reaches for the stool opposite me.

"Is it so obvious?"

"Not to those who see only what they expect to see," I reassure him. "My Keepers taught me much of false emotion, and so I can spot it easily in another. Your desire is not for the throne."

He nods. "It should have been my brother's."

"Purcell?" I ask, my mind skipping through the pages of the castle history that I've absorbed in my long afternoons.

"Yes," Vincent says. "The Stoning felled him almost overnight, though he drew breath for a day or so after."

I shiver at the thought. "What a world we live in, where your brother finds death in lying still, and I find mine in a dance."

"We're a sad lot, aren't we?" Vincent says, laughing ruefully. "Why can we not behave as others our age, running wildly on the beach?"

"Or eagerly awaiting a trip to the high meadow?" I add, though he will not know my meaning.

"I suppose we weren't meant for it, after all," he sighs. "Though I do sometimes wish . . ."

"Wishing is for the spring lambs, and them our supper in the fall," I say, repeating a Hyllenian saying.

Vincent pulls a face. "That is truly horrible."

I shrug. "Which doesn't make it any less true."

He sits forward suddenly, "Khosa, would you like to leave the castle for a bit?"

My interest perks, but I can't force the lightness into my tone the way he does. "What do you propose?"

"I volunteered to deliver a message, something any Stillean could do, but I must find some worth in my days. You too should have something other than pages beneath your fingers to fill your time."

"The pages bring me all I need," I tell him, though the very mention of fresh air makes my lungs feel as if they will burst.

"You would be in no danger," Vincent goes on. "We would have guards alongside us—ones that are awake. Donil and Dara, as well."

"Is that necessary?" I ask, too quickly.

"Are you frightened? I assure you, the Indiri are not monsters."

"I . . ." I think of Donil and his watchful eyes, my skin warming to his and rising to meet it.

"I forget, they can be difficult to adjust to," he says. "But if you agree to come with me, they'd best be along."

"Come where?"

Vincent glances at my sleeping guards, dropping his voice still further. "What do you know of the Feneen?"

My eyes go to the blot on the page, unable to meet his. "They would come into Hyllen from time to time, for trade. My Keepers didn't allow me out at those times, but I saw them through the window once."

"Just the once?"

I nod. Once was all it took.

"Why do you ask?"

"We met a man in the woods, a Feneen," he says. "He claims that Hyllen's destruction is the beginning of a larger offensive, and that his people would stand with ours in exchange for a place among us afterward. I'm awaiting my grandfather's decision, and will deliver it."

I trail my finger along the edge of the book, the brittle flakes of paper feathering beneath my touch. "And you would take me with you," I say, filling the blank space he left after his words. Though I have felt some connection not born of touch with this prince of Stille, I understand nobles better than he can imagine, having spent my entire life studying them. "Why are you doing this, truly?"

Vincent watches me carefully. "I would gain you some small semblance of freedom."

"And?" I prompt him.

"The Feneen—Ank—says he knew your father."

I stop moving, a sliver of paper wedged under my fingernail. The pain is bright and sharp, shooting past my finger into my arm, but my mouth is stopped.

A Feneen. My mind cannot even create words, but pictures flow with ease, framed by the window of our cottage in Hyllen, memories of a humped back, an extra limb dragging in the ground, guttural noises escaping from a malformed mouth wrongly placed in an awkward face. Then my Keeper's arms around my waist and a much-deserved tongue-lashing that stung far less than the things I could not unsee.

My father one of them, whether ill in body or mind.

"It would explain much," I finally say.

"Ank wishes to meet you," Vincent says. "I thought to bring him to you in the castle, but the king was anxious to send him away. There was no chance—"

"I will come with you," I say, pinching the sliver of paper between my fingers and pulling it away, leaving a white scratch beneath the nail that quickly fills in red.

"Will you be safe enough with guards?" Vincent asks. "If you should . . ." He trails off, my spinning, crazed dance undoubtedly on his mind.

"It is always with me," I tell him. "It could leap at anytime, and I'd be none the wiser until the moment was upon me and the sea at my neck."

"Perhaps it is best you remain," Vincent sighs. "If the Given is lost before . . ." He stops again. It seems we are unable to speak to each other without bordering on unmentionable things.

"Before I am bred," I say for him.

"You say it easily enough," he laughs, his color rising.

"Saying and doing are two different things," I confess. "I cannot . . ." My words halt, a lifetime of the Keepers' teachings to hide my inadequacies still in place, though the teachers are now gone.

"I understand," Vincent says. "Many noble families are uncomfortable with showing affection."

"No." I shake my head, unable to find words to describe the feeling of my skin coiling into itself, rolling back like the shedding of a snake in an attempt to avoid others. "It goes beyond not caring for it. I cannot bear a touch."

"Oh . . ." His face collapses at my frank admittance, my oddness widening the space between us. "I guess that would complicate things," he says, producing a shy smile along with his weak joke. "Although . . . it is good to know it is not . . ." He clears his throat. "Perhaps then it is not *me* you flinch at?"

"No, people are equally unbearable," I say.

But he surprises me with a true and honest laugh, and a smile equally so. I feel an answering smile, one that may become more common to me, should I spend more time with Vincent.

"I will go with you," I tell him. "The prey being stalked by the predator cannot spend its whole life skulking in fear. When the sea leaps is not my decision, but what I do in the interim is."

"Very well," he says. "For my part, I'll be glad to have you along."

"When do we leave?" I ask, and close the book before me.

CHAPTER 22

Dara

"WHERE ARE YOUR THOUGHTS?"

Dara speaks Indiri, her words meant only for her brother, and not the guards who trot behind them.

Donil pulls his gaze from Khosa and her mount, riding alongside Vincent as the horses pick their way over the sandy beach. The moon is bright, and the sea so still that its light casts a broad path across the water, almost daring the more adventurous to try to walk upon it—exactly what they are there to prevent.

"Why bring her at all?" Donil answers his sister, jerking his head toward Khosa. "Having Khosa so close to the sea is ill-advised."

"The Given," Dara corrects him. "And cursed or not, she'd never reach the surf before I cut her down."

"Which would hardly help, since they need her to bear a child."

"I can stop her without killing her."

"You won't need to. Khosa tied a scarf around her waist; the other end is around Vincent's saddle pommel."

"So if she makes a leap for it, she won't drown, but be trampled under his horse instead. Lovely plan."

"Speak a language the rest of us understand," says one of the guards, urging his horse between theirs. "I'm not keen on taking the

Given and the third of the blood out with so few swords at their backs. Hearing your tongues make words I don't know doesn't settle my nerves any."

"We are saying words you know, but we're saying them in Indiri," Donil says easily, flashing his smile.

"Them pearly teeth won't look so nice in a rotting corpse," the guard growls.

"We don't rot," Dara says.

"What's that?" The second guard brings his horse forward slightly.

"The Indiri don't rot," Dara repeats, but doesn't explain, her attention focused on Khosa and Vincent, whose heads are close together in conversation.

"Of earth we are made, and to earth we return," Donil says. "When the Pietra slaughtered us at Dunkai, they burned their own dead, since they were too far inland to put them in boats for the Lusca. They returned to the pit where they threw the Indiri, and found it filled in—not with bodies, but with freshly turned earth."

"And how would you know that?"

"We were watching," Dara says, her eyes leaving Khosa to find her brother and the echoed memory of their frail newborn skin, pricked with thorns as they hid in the brush.

"I've heard about that," the first guard says grudgingly. "Shared a drink with a man once, said there's a stretch of land there on the Dunkai plains where nothing grows. Someone told him it's on account of the Indiri underneath, their blood poisoning the dirt."

"They *are* the dirt," Dara corrects. "And if nothing grows, it is not the blood that is to blame. You can't kill the people of the earth and expect their dirt to yield for your benefit."

"Light ahead," says Donil. "Seems Ank made a fire in the cave."

The first guard moves into the lead, telling Vincent he should check to be sure the Feneen is alone before they go farther. The second guard keeps his horse beside Dara's, too young to be able to hide his fascination with her skin.

"I rather like the idea of you making not a corpse," he says. "Seems a waste."

"Oh, I can make a corpse," she says. "I've made many." With that she spurs her horse forward, and her brother smiles again.

"Better luck next time," he says to the guard.

CHAPTER 23

Khosa

T HE CAVE IS DIM, THOUGH THE FIRE THAT THE FENEEN
has started burns brightly. I turn my back to the cold light of
the moon and follow Vincent into the cave, his hand tight on
the end of the scarf that cinches my waist.

"Is that the Feneen?" I nod toward the back of the cave, where a
man stands by a small fire, the flames sending orange ripples of light
along the damp walls.

Vincent nods. "Let me speak with him first." He hands the scarf
over to someone behind me. I keep my eyes on the Feneen as he greets
the prince with a familiarity that most Stillean royals would bristle at,
but Vincent accepts in stride.

"Careful on these rocks. They're slippery," a voice at my elbow
warns, and I feel a slight pressure on my arm. I recoil without thinking,
recognizing Donil's voice a moment too late.

"I'm sorry," he says, pulling away as well. "I didn't mean to give
offense."

"No, it . . ." I bluster as every bit of my skin sings to pull away from
my own body to be closer to his. "It wasn't entirely unpleasant," I finish.

Donil laughs, the sound filling the cave. I cannot tear my eyes
from the pulse of the sound in his throat, his Indiri skin rippling. "It's

not the warmest invitation I've ever had," he says. "But I'll accept the encouragement."

Dara shoves her way in between us, spotting the end of my scarf now twisted around her brother's knuckles. "I see you've got yet another girl on a leash."

"Speaking of being entirely unpleasant," Donil says.

"Come into the light," Ank calls to us. "The tide will return soon, and I'd rather make words over a dry fire."

Vincent's guards search the Feneen, but find no weapon. Vincent waves them away and they move to flank the entrance of the cave. Dara stays by the prince's side, the crossed swords on her back casting an eerie shadow on the cave wall.

Vincent clears his throat. "I must inform you that my grandfather, King Gammal, declines the Feneen offer of aid in a war against the Pietra that has yet to exist."

"I'm not surprised," Ank says smoothly. "He'll rue that decision when the war does come, and us siding with them."

"Stille will chance it."

"No," Ank corrects. "Gammal will chance it. Your father will chance it. Stille and its people had no say."

Dara shifts slightly, hand resting on a dagger at her side. Ank watches her move with amused eyes.

"I'd like to put my hands on you," he says.

Vincent's knife flashes from his side, more quickly than I would have expected. "Watch how you speak to her."

Ank laughs, brushing aside Vincent's blade. "For the purpose of my gift, to see how deep that ferocity really runs."

"Pretty deep," Dara says.

"Mmmm." Ank's eyes shift back to me. "We've not been introduced."

I step forward. "I am Khosa. The next to be Given, daughter of Sona."

"Was that her name?"

"Yes." My voice is nearly lost in a crashing wave, and I wonder if Donil can feel the scarf shake in his hands as my body trembles. "Vincent said you knew my father?"

"The Given pick their mates, is this true?" Ank asks, ignoring my question.

"Yes. We're given that freedom in exchange for our sacrifice."

"Your mother chose well."

I take another step toward the fire and the Feneen, the length of scarf between Donil and me growing taut. In it I can feel the tensed strength of his entire body, prepared to pull me back from danger if necessary, and the tremor that thought sends through my body has nothing to do with fear.

"What was his name?" I ask.

"If he had one, he never shared it. Your father came to us half mad, a child from the woods. A Tangata had been at him, bit clear through his leg. But when our healers tried to tend to him, he lunged at them like a wild animal himself, wouldn't be touched. He couldn't understand them when they said the wound was festering."

"He didn't speak your language?" Dara asks.

"No, fierce one. The Feneen have cast-offs from all the peoples, and all the languages as well. Whoever birthed that poor boy kept him alive long enough for him to learn to fend for himself, but whatever tongue he learned in the cradle had long since gone from his head.

"I know that people say we're monsters, and worse. And yes, some of us aren't easy to look upon, and there's more than one whose wrongness is of the head and not the body, but pity runs deep in our kind. Pity for those whom the rest of the world chooses to cast away.

"We fed him as best we could, but he came only close enough to take the food we laid out, then retreated into the woods to eat it. Eventually, his wound was so rotten a fever laid him low, and a healer found him one morning, out of his head. She brought him in, cleaned him up. Even as he grew into a man, he wouldn't let anyone touch him."

Ank looks at me as my skin tightens against my own bones, shrinking into myself as I learn why I am the way I am. Though the Feneen's words are heard by everyone, we both know they are meant only for me.

"Your mother came to us looking for a mate, and knew her business well. She was a bold one, lined up all the men and inspected them, asking what their defect was if it was not obvious. Your father was skulking in the shadows, curious about what was happening, but unable to understand any of it. She spotted him and he ran off, like a deer with its tail in the wind."

Ank smiles to himself, lost in the memory. "She insisted on him."

"Seems a poor choice," Dara says. "I've hunted many deer. They're leery of a leaf falling, and impossible to get next to."

"For Khosa's mother, that was the whole point."

"Why a Feneen at all?" I ask. "If my mother was so bold why not take her choice of any man?"

"She was more than bold, child," Ank goes on. "She was bitter about the fate that sent her to the waves and demanded her child do the same. There was no escape for her. Yes, she could slip her Keepers and visit the Feneen, but her will wasn't strong enough to control her own feet, and they would lead to the sea, eventually."

"Yes," I agree. "Eventually."

"She did her part," he goes on. "It took many moonchanges to draw your father to her, and in the end, a bottle of wine overcame his dread of touch. You've got him in you, and you won't be bred, which was as your Mother wished."

I feel a sinking in my belly, as if a cold stone from the sea has found a place there before I danced into the waves.

"Your mother knew any baby born of her with an extra limb or a missing eye would come right back to the Feneen and land her in someone's bed to get a healthy baby before she went to the waves. So she picked something that would bide its time, hide in the small things. And here we are—she's gone to the sea, and you the only one left, a taint in your blood that means you've no inclination to make another."

My strength goes out from my knees, and I sink to the cave floor slowly.

"Oh, Mother," I say to no one at all, my voice echoing hollowly. "Mother, you've ended the world."

CHAPTER 24

Khosa

THE WETNESS OF THE STONE FLOOR SEEPS THROUGH MY skirts, but I hardly feel it. My mind can see only a madman, shying away from people, and a girl with a glint in her eye and a determined heart.

I had hoped it would be better, a story of caring and trust, an echo of the bearable pressure of Abna's hand on mine, affection that grew from conversations like the one I'd shared with Vincent, or even a flash of desire as I have felt for Donil. Instead my mother picked my father with cunning, and won him over with a wine bottle.

I am meant to fail at the only thing I was born for.

A numbness sinks in, not of the chill in my skirt or the heavy air around me. I know this feeling, following in the wake of strong emotion. I slip away from my surroundings, my body left behind as my mind recoils from whatever I have felt, slipping deeper into myself so that I can be affected no more.

I hear Vincent and Donil saying my name, but my ears are hollow recipients of the words being spoken, caught and stored for later when I can process them. My hands rest in my lap, thumb and forefinger rubbing a fold of my skirt for comfort. My tongue is slack, and my teeth have caught the inside of my cheek. They clamp down, pressure holding my mouth shut against the scream that wants to erupt.

My eyes have found their own solace, a pattern in the rock above Ank's shoulder. They run over it, my mind jumping at this new distraction, this logic amid the rushing inside of me. I follow the rise and fall, a picture forming that I'd not expected. A hand was pressed there once, faded ink left behind that barely holds the outline now. But it's there. And another—my eyes skip to the next, deftly comparing the two to see if it's the same person, or many. A game played by a wandering child or something meant to be seen by more than a proud mother.

Conversation continues; the fire pops and sends a spark that alights on my hand. It sputters into nothing. The pain is not worth my attention as I go to the wall, fingers tracing the drops and curves of what could be dismissed as shadows forming patterns I know, pictures I have looked on for quite some time.

I grab a stick from the fire, holding the flaming end aloft as I follow the walls of the cave, out past the glow of Ank's fire. There is a tug at my waist as the scarf meant to protect me from the sea pulls tight, but I push on, and the resistance falls away. I know Donil has followed me, but I don't look back.

"What is it?" Donil says, as I press my hand against the rock.

"We have to go," I say. "I need to get back."

He doesn't question me, only nods. "Vincent," he calls toward the fire.

I'm already leaving, with or without them, my feet slipping over rocks and my ankles bruising against their sides. Donil is beside me, his hand still wrapped in the scarf that loops my waist.

"Is it the sea?" he asks.

But I have no speech, no room for pain, no ears for hearing. There is only an image in my mind, and the deep conviction that though the sea may get me eventually, I won't be alone.

CHAPTER 25

—◦~◯~◦—

Vincent

W E RIDE ALL NIGHT, LEAVING ANK AND THE GLOW OF the fire behind as the tide finds its way to the horses' hooves. The moon sinks, the sea enveloping even that as my mount tires. Dara is beside me, her face grim and determined as she watches the end of Khosa's scarf flutter behind her, long pulled from Donil's hand in this mad dash for home, this run driven by something none of us understands, but we had no chance to question.

Donil keeps his horse between Khosa and the sea. I hear him call to her once or twice, but she shares nothing, only spurring her mount to go faster when it flags for even a moment.

We break into the city, the clatter of hooves against stone bringing people to their windows before sunup, curses littering our path. Khosa is the first into the courtyard, jumping off her mount and falling into a pile beside it while the horse heaves for breath. I rush to help, but she's already gained her feet and goes ever forward, her dress dripping sea spray, her soaked scarf dragging behind her.

"What the depths is wrong with her?" Dara hisses at my side, keeping pace with us as we follow Khosa through halls still sleeping, the first of the servants making their bleary-eyed way toward fireplaces that hold only cold ash.

"I don't know," I tell her. "Maybe something Ank said? Donil, do you know?"

He shakes his head as we follow Khosa deeper into the castle, following the wet trail she leaves behind. "She saw the hands on the cave wall, and it sent her into this . . ."

"Madness?" Dara supplies.

"She's not a lunatic," I spit back as Khosa wrenches open the double doors to the library. We follow to find her spinning in circles, eyes to the ceiling, muttering to herself.

"For certain?" Dara asks.

"There!" Khosa halts, pointing at a map that hangs from the vaulted ceiling. "Do you see it?"

"What?"

"On the cave wall, there were paintings," Khosa says, shoving her hair out of her eyes.

"Vincent and I saw hands, last time we were there," Donil says, watching her carefully.

"There's more, if you know how to look," Khosa says, turning to a wide, low shelf and pulling aside scrolls. She unrolls five before she finds the one she wants, flinging it wide and heaving it onto the stone table in the center of the room. "There," she says triumphantly, and looks at us as if a point has been made.

It's a map of the shore, faded with age. Even I can see that the city is much larger now, sprawling farther down the coast. The edges of the paper are dark with smudges from fingers long dead, the ink faded with time. No one has looked at this for centuries as it rotted here, obsolete. Now the four of us gather around it, wet and shivering, its musty smell filling our noses.

"What are we looking for?" Donil asks gently, and I can hear that he hopes as much as I that there is some logic at work here.

"Here." Khosa's finger stabs at the map. "The Horns."

Two fingers of rock, colored black and looming high, jut from the sea, a trail of smaller rocks leading inward to meet the shore like the curve of a sickle moon.

"That's not the Horns," Dara argues. "They're not half so tall, and too close to the shore, anyway."

Khosa nods as if she's happy with what Dara says. "And look there." She points to the ceiling again, where the hanging map has begun to undulate with the first of a morning breeze off the sea, the black ripples drawn long ago being given real life. "See the Horns?"

I squint as the gray light of dawn breaks in through the window, illuminating two spires, shorter than in the earlier map. I glance between the different drawings.

"I don't understand . . . ," I say, and then my eyes fall on the curve of smaller rocks. The map above shows fewer, the shorter ones no longer existing.

"Khosa," I say, my breath coming in shallow gasps. "What did you see in the caves?"

"It's barely there," she says. "When they first painted them, they never guessed the tides would touch the ink, but it has. Slowly."

"What does the cave have to do with the maps?" Dara asks, no patience left.

"I saw the Horns," Khosa says. "Painted there, strong and tall. I've spent days in here, brooding over books and maps, memorizing shorelines, and all the while, that map stared down at me. I saw the Horns tonight, in the cave, unmistakably. There were people on them."

"Nonsense," Dara snorts. "No one would go that far out to sea."

"You're not understanding," Khosa says. "The Horns were close by, and easy to reach by climbing from these rocks to the next." Khosa trips her fingers along the paper beneath her fingers, alighting from the shore, jumping from rock to rock to land on the Horns.

"If those are the Horns, then where have all those other rocks gone?" Dara argues.

"They're underwater," Khosa says, still smiling as exhaustion finally overcomes her and pulls her down in a tangle of wet skirts. "Underwater and far out to sea, with the Horns barely peeking out at low tide."

She laughs, the sound jarring as the gray light of morning fills the library. "The waters are rising. My blood may mark me as the Given, but eventually all of Stille will drown."

CHAPTER 26

Witt

"How is the sea today?" Witt's unpracticed eyes scan the horizon from the cliff outcropping, glad to be back among the stones of Pietra.

"Sparing," the Lure answers him as he reels in an empty line.

Behind them the wind whistles in the cave where the Lure lives, his life dictated by the rise and fall of the seas, the duty of feeding his people a daily weight. Many such caves dot the cliff side, the sound of lines singing in Witt's ears as hooks sail out to sea, most of them coming back empty.

"Fish don't want to be caught," Witt says.

"It's more than that, begging your pardon, my Lithos," the Lure says, rebaiting his line from the tackle box that rests by his side. "I've tried all the tricks, everything my father taught me, and his before him. Fish never *want* to be caught."

"What is it, then?"

"They're moving away. I watch the sea. I know how it flows when it's moving over a school of fish. I can see the flash of a scale halfway to the horizon, but no one can see what isn't there."

"I was told they had simply moved farther out?"

"At first, yes." The Lure nods. "Some of my fellows thought

perhaps the Lusca had taken to eating them, but it's human flesh they want, and we feed the beasts well enough as it is. Now the schools are out of sight entirely, gone from these shores."

"For what? There is nothing else."

The Lure shrugs. "They're fish. They don't need land."

"Fair point."

Silence passes between them as the Lure casts again, the feathered bait he chose this time flashing red in the morning sun as it arcs out to sea. He has a practiced hand and a knowledgeable wrist, the slightest of movements sending the line far from the cliff side, never tangling with the gossamer strands of other Lures' lines, which hang from the cliff like spider webs.

Webs that catch little.

The Lure watches Witt for a moment, measuring the irritation in the Lithos's eyes before speaking. "I've got an idea about what the fish might be thinking, if I can speak freely."

"Please."

The Lure takes a deep breath. "I remember my old cave. Down lower. It was flooded out years ago, and I moved up here, more and more Lures joining me as time passed. Used to be the sea was far below; now I can count the chops even on a misty day."

"It's no secret," Witt says. "The Pietra have long known the sea is rising. We send out bodies in boats, so as not to use the soil for the dead. The Lithos before me had the foresight to clear out the Indiri before they guessed at the sea's intention. Their land is ours, useless as it is to us now that we know nothing can grow where Indiri blood was spilled. What's this have do with fish?"

"They're leaving the shores, my Lithos. Won't come near us for even the tastiest bait. Sea's been rising since before my time, but I've never reeled in so many empty hooks. This is something different, something more. Like the land itself is telling them to keep a distance for their own good."

"So you think the land is talking to the fish?" Witt raises his eyebrows.

"Stranger things have happened."

"Not that I'm aware of."

"You've never met an Indiri, then," the Lure grunts.

"Very briefly. I was there when they were cleared from the land."

"Then you should know better than most that just because you don't understand something doesn't mean it's not the truth. The Indiri carry the memories of their forebears at birth, right down to holding a sword and shearing a head from its shoulders."

"I remember," Witt says. Children had fought alongside their parents that day, blades flashing just as quickly, tiny hands taking out unsuspecting horses at the knees as they rode past. Some of the Indiri had been as small as he was at the time, a line of Pietra boys sitting on ponies to watch the massacre, an advisor standing nearby to see who wept at the sight.

Witt hadn't even flinched.

"I remember things too," the Lure continues. "I've had a lifetime to watch the sea, and I've never seen anything like this. The fish are leaving, and the Lusca come in more numbers. What we live on is going, and what kills us draws nearer, like they know more bodies are coming to the water soon. There's something wrong in our world, my Lithos. And though I can't tell you what, it stands true."

"Very well," Witt says. "We've brought back sheep and seed from Hyllen. People may not like it, but they'll learn to farm before they starve. We won't need the fish anymore."

"And what of the Lures?"

Witt smiles. "I guess we won't need you either."

CHAPTER 27

Vincent

TELLING MY GRANDFATHER THAT EVENTUALLY OUR ENTIRE
kingdom will be underwater falls to me. Our hasty arrival,
Khosa's wild cries from the library, and our wet footprints
through the castle created a rush of whispers among the servants that
I had no chance to stem before being called for. As I enter the meeting room and Gammal's heavy gaze falls upon me, I'm reminded that
though he is my grandfather, he is also the king. And though I had
felt the beginning of something between myself and Khosa, gossamer
threads of a web just being spun, I'm forcefully reminded that she is
still the Given.

"Vincent," he says, "I woke to a bit of a clamor, and you at the
center of it."

"I am sorry, Grandfather," I say.

"Sorry?" he repeats. "You took the Given out of the castle. And to
the sea of all places. Tides, boy!"

"It's a blessing that I did," I tell him. "She learned things in the
cave where we met the Feneen, saw patterns where the rest of us saw
only ink."

He pauses for a moment, my voice holding enough edge to

penetrate his own irritation. "And what did she learn? Nothing good, by the look on your face."

There is a soft knock on the door, and my mother enters, needlework in hand. "Father," she says, looking to Gammal. "You called for me?"

"Sit down, Dissa," the king says. "Young Vincent has acted rashly, but he assures me there was reason at work."

I tell them of meeting Ank, of Khosa's reaction to the ancient pictures on the cave wall, ending with the Given's prediction that we are all going to the sea, though she will undoubtedly be first.

The king sits quietly, face as unreadable as Khosa's often is. Mother's needle dangles from the thread, long dropped from her fingers.

"What are your thoughts?" Gammal turns to my mother, who shakes her head as if to clear it.

"Call the Scribes," she says. "If the sea rises, we must know how quickly. The histories go deep, and may hold some clues."

"Khosa should be included as well," I tell them. "She is as well versed as our own Scribes as to what our library holds, and without her keen eyes, we'd be none the wiser."

Gammal nods, his fingers going to his beard to twist the white hairs there, as he does when in thought. "The Indiri could be of use as well," he says. "If their ancestors noted such a thing, the twins will remember it. As for the cave, I'll see these paintings myself."

He rises to his feet, joints popping.

"Is that wise, Father?" Mother asks, rising also, her needlework falling from her lap.

He waves his hand. "Wise. Unwise. What does it matter? Will I have it said that the Given walks in the surf while the king sits idly by?"

Gammal is already calling for his horse to be saddled as the doors to the meeting room close behind him, leaving us alone. Mother bends to retrieve her needlework, and I recognize her bridal pillow, corners darkened from years of resting on her forearm while she worked.

"Still?" I ask, nodding toward it.

"Still," she agrees, smoothing out the embroidered top, decorated with symbols only she can decipher, one chosen carefully for each year of her marriage.

What each picture represents only she knows, but some are easier to decipher than others; the blossoming salium at the time of Purcell's birth, and the same, cast in dying shades twelve years later. I count backward now, finding the two deep red fiverberries that surely stand for the twins, near what I believe is my own symbol—a pale green bud, newly opened. Mother's pillow begins well enough, with oderbirds and their young, the royals from a set of ridking, side by side. But later there are Tangata with teeth out, the scratching leaf of a barbar weed, and the prickly back of a sea-spine.

"Vincent," Mother says, drawing her pillow back into her lap and reeling in the needle at the end of the swaying string. "Your grandfather may have been stirred to action by your story, but I still wonder why you would risk exposing the Given in a night ride by the sea."

I cannot tell her that I wanted to give her the freedom of fresh air, this girl who spends her life waiting for an end she doesn't want, as do I. My eyes go to what Mother works on now, the symbol for this year. A rankflower, opening to spread its stench.

"The Feneen that Grandfather met with said he knew Khosa's father," I tell her. "Once I shared this with her, she insisted upon seeing him."

It's a version of the truth, one I can tell with a straight face.

Mother rolls the needle between her fingers, the deep purple thread she's using for the rankflower twisting as she does. "It would explain much, if she were part Feneen," she muses. "I cannot pretend that she isn't . . ."

The needle stops as she searches for a word, one that can encapsulate the oddities of this girl whom I have lately found much in my thoughts.

"There is nothing wrong with Khosa," I say too quickly, and Mother's eyes go to me, suddenly bright.

"You would do well, Vincent, to call her the Given," she says quietly. "So that you remember what she is. Not a girl, but a sacrifice."

She unthreads the needle, ripping out the rankflower with a few practiced tugs.

"What are you doing?" I ask. "You were nearly finished."

"I think I'll call for the weavers to dye some blue thread," she says. "This year is surely one for the sea."

CHAPTER 28

Dara

DARA FINDS VINCENT ON A CASTLE PARAPET, HIS SLUMPED shoulders in contrast to the Horns, visible in the low tide of evening. She joins him to lean against the rock, their arms close together but not touching.

"You truly think Khosa is mad?" he asks.

"I think a life spent knowing it is meant to be ended soon would make a meal of anyone's mind."

"A lovely way to avoid the question."

Dara sighs, her own eyes drawn to the Horns. "My answer is two-fold, and I don't like saying either half of it."

Vincent turns to her, taking in the irregularities of her skin in the glare of sunset. On another face, he might have found it garish, but he'd grown up drinking in the sight of the Indiri. Others might shy from them, but for Vincent, the twins were both beauties, their skin bringing back memories from a simple time when swords were used only for practice and the revolutions of the tide meant the next day was nearer, but no one was counting.

"Dara of the Indiri, not speaking her mind?" Vincent teases. "Toss the maps. This is all I need to know that truly the world is coming to an end."

His words draw forth her smile. "I'll toss you, and right over the edge. Royal blood be damned," she says, a gust of wind turning her hair into a storm around her face. She wrestles with it for a second, the dark strands finally acquiescing to be tied at the nape of her neck.

"Go on, then. Tell me the things I don't want to hear and you don't want to say," Vincent says.

Dara's eyes are back on the Horns, the dull tops as wide as their hands, even from this distance. "I think she's right."

"The king's advisors say the same," Vincent admits. "After I reported Khosa's discovery to them this morning, they went to the caves themselves. The maps are not dated, but the existence of certain outposts, the size of the city, all of these things can give us a rough idea of when they were made. Everyone agrees. As the maps march forward, the Horns diminish, so the sea rises."

"How long do we have?"

"The Scribes will try to discover exactly that. It would be a great help if you could search your memories, anything your ancestors may have known about the sea."

"We have nothing to do with it," Dara says dismissively. "Indiri take to the sea as well as a Tangata cat."

"But a Tangata can't remember its seven-times-grandmother's face, or what her home looked like. I remember the game you and Donil played as children, each of you reaching as far as possible, daring the other to go farther and see something new. Why not do it now, when it could save people?"

"It's not that easy!" Dara shouts, her words cutting across the air, sending panicked birds from the treetops. "It's not easy, and it is not a game. In order to go back, we have to *see*, Vincent. We watch lives unspool in reverse, gray hair to tufted baby crowns, starting with our predecessor's dying moment. And the last thing our mother saw before her head was parted from her shoulders was a line of Pietra children brought to watch a hated race dispatched.

"My mother could fell any man with her sword, and she'd brought many low that day until she saw those children . . . and one of them—" Dara's breath catches, her eyes closed against the memory and her mother's feelings as they sweep over her. "One of them sat unmoved, not blinking against the sight of children as young and younger than him, skulls crushed open under Pietra hooves."

"Dara," Vincent says softly, hands reaching for her as guilt blooms in his stomach.

"Khosa isn't the only one who dances, you know," Dara goes on. "The Indiri know the dance of death, and perform it well. My mother's sword sang songs that day, but that boy . . . his stone face broke her rhythm, and she faltered for one moment, one misstep that should have been a parry. And her life was gone."

Dara's eyes open, the memory seeping from her. "I have to see that first, Vincent, every time."

"I was wrong to ask it of you." His hands are still caught midair, as if he'd rethought touching her. As if she were Khosa, not this girl he'd known his whole life, whose dark head had rested next to his fair one in sleep time and time again.

"You were wrong, yes." Dara swipes at a tear. "But I'll do it."

The air between them is tense as a bowstring, the last errant tear slipping down her face unnoticed. Again, Vincent moves to touch her, and again finds himself stopping. Their ever-fought argument over Dara's Indiri pride has led to something he'd never known his childhood friend harbored inside of her: her mother's death and the destruction of her people as the terrible precursor to any further mining of memory. They look away from each other, back to the Horns and the ever-biding sea, the rocks beneath their hands cooling as the day's heat is released.

"You said your answer was twofold," Vincent breaks the silence. "As to whether or not Khosa is mad—you must not think she is, because you agree with her about the rising tides. So what's the second part?"

Dara's hands flatten against the stones. "That being right doesn't mean she *isn't* mad, a taint of her father's blood running free in her veins. And even if she is, it won't matter to you or Donil. You're both taken with her—don't bother denying it."

"I don't know that I am taken with her," Vincent argues, but his words carry more of a question than Dara wishes to hear.

"She's beautiful, I know," Dara goes on. "Beautiful and damned and tragic, born to breed and die. An enticement, I'm sure."

Vincent closes his eyes against the cut of her tone.

"You're beautiful too, you know," he says.

But she is already gone.

CHAPTER 29

Khosa

I STEP INTO THE LIBRARY TO FIND MY FORMERLY QUIET REFUGE a hive of activity, robed Scribes pilfering stacks that I had organized according to my liking. I feel a wave of irritation, then remind myself that the books are no more mine than the dress I wear on my back. Everything belongs to Stille, including me. My guard Merryl senses my discomfort and pulls a stool into a corner.

"Have a seat, my lady. I'll discover what the fuss is about."

"Thank you," I say, climbing onto the stool.

I hear my name spoken in a voice that has become familiar, as Vincent comes into the room. The Scribes pause in their work to nod to him, as do the guards, but he waves to them to continue with their work.

"I'd hoped to arrive before you, to apologize in advance for this disruption," the prince says, as he pulls a stool next to my own.

"You and I have made a habit of apologizing to each other," I say, meaning only to state fact, but a smile has bloomed on my face at Vincent's appearance, and the words come out with a lilt that is almost teasing.

It draws an answering smile from him, and a light in his eyes that I'd not spotted there before. I drop my own gaze quickly, aware that nothing between us could end well. My lips may have turned upward at the sight of him, but my arms have wrapped tightly around myself to escape accidentally brushing against his.

"The Scribes are gathering a few volumes, but I've instructed them to work elsewhere. I know that you find some solace here from . . ." His words fall away, not able to find the appropriate description from that which I wish to escape.

"Everyone?" I supply, damning my face for still smiling even as the word escapes with an intonation that invites more.

"Hopefully not *every*one," Vincent says.

"No," I have to admit. "Not quite."

"Good," he says, but leaves it at that, not taking the opening as an excuse to put his hand on my own, as another boy might have.

"What is their work?" I ask, moving the conversation from us to the Scribes who bustle around the library.

"The sea," Vincent says. "Our history is long, but the written record deep. This library holds writings from many generations of Stilleans, and they hope to find references to the tide among them. Where it reached. The depth of it in spots."

I grasp their goal, appreciating the endless days of work ahead of them. "And when," I add. "If you could find references to those three things, you could create a timeline, and some idea of how quickly the sea rises."

"Precisely," Vincent says. "Your mind is quick. Which is why—"

"You would ask my assistance," I finish for him.

He nods. "I told the king you know these shelves as well as the Scribes, maybe better. I'd wager you've read lines that haven't been seen since they were penned."

And while this is true, I can't help but feel the bitter taste of irony behind it all. "So I'm asked to save Stille from a wave *and* the tide? My body for one, my brain for the other?"

Vincent's smile falls, the light in his eyes gone as quickly as if the very water we speak of had extinguished it. I slide from being a pretty girl back to being the Given in that moment, and regret my words.

"I'm sorry," I say, and he raises a finger to my lips as if to touch them, but leaves a breath of space.

"No more apologies, remember?" he says, and though his tone is light, it is also full of sadness. "There are many minds at work on this, and it need not tax yours. My grandfather suggested the Indiri memories may be an aid, and so they will be working with the Scribes."

"Will they?"

Though I've tried to tell myself my fingers have sought books at random here in the castle library, it cannot be denied that often they've alighted on those that mention the Indiri. Since his skin brushed against mine, Donil has been present in my thoughts, the only person whose touch I wish to revisit. And I have, often, my imagination lengthening and embroidering upon that innocent moment until it becomes something less than decent that brings a blush to my face even as I think of it now.

I could bear Donil's touch, even welcome it. Now that it has happened I understand the young Hyllenians who wait for the long winter to be over, bringing spring and trips to the high meadow with whomever they choose. And for the first time, having to make my own choice feels not like a burden to bear, but something to celebrate before I go.

"I will help," I tell Vincent. "Send the Indiri to me."

CHAPTER 30

Vincent

THERE IS MUCH WORK TO BE DONE. THOUGH THE KING and my father chose to toss aside Feneen aid, that doesn't mean they don't believe the Pietra pose a threat. Meeting after meeting I've sat through, looking over notched pieces of wood meant to be our soldiers as they are knocked over with little effort.

Gammal believes that even if a battle were not imminent, the city walls need fortification, and our men could use some real training—something Dara has been saying loudly and often since she was to their knees. As I walk the martial field with Donil, I know she'd rather be here with us than inside the castle, where I sent her to work with Khosa in the library. I ignore the rising emotion that has begun in my head whenever Khosa is mentioned, and tell myself that I sent Dara to her instead of Donil only because he can do more good at my side, rather than by hers.

Two different types of battles are being fought; the bodies here on the field strive for physical dominance against enemies who can bleed, while in the castle ink is spilled and calculations made to judge how fast the sea devours the land. Gammal sat with Mother and me late into the night, suddenly aware that our army must ready itself not only against an attack, but prepare for an invasion as well. Our seaside perch is picturesque and easy to defend—but now we know there is an enemy behind us too. We can only hope there is time to build an army that can stand against the Pietra, and claim good land so Stilleans can move inward.

Men mill around Donil and me on the field, gathering in groups, their excited conversation rising above the grounds.

"The smith hasn't made a real blade since a faded memory," Donil scoffs. "Everything that's come from that forge since your grandfather's time was meant to be worn in a parade, not used in battle."

"He'll learn," I say.

"Quickly, I hope. Till then we have only these poor excuses to train with," he says, spinning a blade in his hand. "Doubt this could cut air."

He makes a sudden lunge toward an invisible enemy, sword halted midswing. "Nope." He shakes his head. "Stuck."

Finally, he gets the laugh he's been angling for. "Point taken," I say. "I'll have a talk with the smith myself if you think it might put a keener edge on a blade or two."

"As long as a good sword lands in your hands. One less back for me to watch so closely," Donil says, as we pass a team of men headed to the forest, saws in hand. "But I can tell you there's an easier way to take a tree down, and being of the earth makes all the difference. You'll need my sister, though—she's the one with the magic."

"Oh, I wouldn't be so sure about that," calls a kitchen girl, cheeks rosy and smiling for Donil even as she hauls a massive stew pot, empty at the moment. "You've got a bit of magic in you, to hear Daisy's stories."

Donil's smile changes in a second, from the easy one that rides the air between us to one that quirks too far in the corners, bringing a glint to his eye I've never been able to compete with, royal blood or not.

"And what does Daisy say?" Donil asks, changing direction as easily as a leaf in the wind, his sword now sheathed and his hand on the stew pot.

"A few things to make a roomful of girls blush, and if you don't know what *those* are, then her stories aren't true," the girl says, and their conversation fades as he walks with her over the hill to where the cook has fires banking.

"Hopefully he's not so easily distracted in battle." Dara is beside me, her eyes following her brother.

"I doubt there will be any pretty kitchen maids on the field," I tell her. "Though it seems girls do wander onto it even when a Stillean prince requested their presence elsewhere."

Dara's eyes narrow, and her mouth makes a flat line that usually is a precursor to someone getting punched in the nose. "A Stillean prince would be wise to not relegate an Indiri to a dank library when the sun shines on a field of battle."

"Donil says you know of a better way to get a tree down than an ax," I say, changing the subject.

"That I do," she says. "My own voice."

The men blanch when I give the order. They're well into their work, halfway through the trunk of the tree and sweat running down their faces. They resent me taking advantage of royal blood to tell them to stand aside for her, yet I am obeyed. But I cannot banish the disgust on their faces when she sails past them, cape swirling.

Even though I've known them a lifetime, the Indiri never fail to amaze. Dara lays a hand on the tree, says a few words in her own language. "This one wasn't ready," she chides the workers. "It gave you trouble."

"Changed the blade twice," acknowledges an older man. "But it doesn't seem overly bothered by the bite of metal."

"Too late, even so," Dara says, eyes on the green gaping wound at its base. "Finish the job after I'm done. That's not work I'll take part in."

A few of the men nod, but many of them glare at her. She ignores them, moving on to a tree as thick as her waist, roots wound deeply into the ground. "This one, maybe," she says to herself, again resting her palm against the tree. She closes her eyes and her brows twitch, a string of words no one but Donil can understand flowing from her lips. Dara relaxes slightly, now pressing her whole body up against the trunk.

It starts beneath my feet, a slither I mistake for a snake. My hand goes to the sword that Donil had informed me moments before was little better than useless. It's not a snake slipping between my ankles, but the rough root of a tree unwinding itself from the soil.

"Filthy fathoms!" The first man in the group of woodcutters notices, leaping and knocking into his brethren, who look down to see an army of roots—large and small—unspooling around them as the ground shifts.

Jaws agape, we all look to Dara. Her eyes are still closed, mouth purring in Indiri as the tree wilts beneath her touch, the limbs drooping low, green leaves being sapped of vitality as they curl into themselves. The trunk tilts slightly, like a drunk wandering home, using its own limbs to lie down quietly and die softly, her body easing to the ground with it.

There is silence in the woods when she's finished, and her body lies prone on top of the dead trunk. When the men take down a tree, there is a crash that shakes the earth, the violent descent tearing branches from neighbors as it falls, crushing saplings beneath its weight. The silence that fills the forest after a tree is cut down is a watchful one, a quiet that means every living thing knows a predator has won a struggle.

This is different. This tree fell where it would, not harming as it went. The silence here is awestruck and reverent, like a deathbed passing of one whose time had come. And while it's a death that occurred, the air is thick with life, and the thought of a bed not far from my mind as I look at Dara sprawled, cheeks warm with blood. The tree's smallest branches curled around her as it fell in a way that brings a pang to my chest similar to the one I felt when thinking of Donil sifting his Indiri memories alongside Khosa in the library, little space between them.

It's jealousy, something not even a royal is immune from. But how it found its way into my heart at the sight of a tree wrapping limbs around Dara, I don't know.

"Depths, woman." One of the men comes forward. "I've cut down many trees. What in the name of my ancestors did you do to that one?"

Dara opens her eyes, brushes aside the limbs that hold her to the trunk, and rises. "I asked it to fall," she says. "For me."

"Seems a rather large favor," says another, sidling up to the tree and toeing it cautiously, as if to check if it's actually dead.

Dara shrugs, bright eyes meeting mine. "You just have to know when they're ready."

CHAPTER 31

Khosa

I AM NOT GOOD AT MAKING FRIENDS.

It can't help that Dara doesn't wish to be here any more than I wish to see her. When she sailed through the library door instead of Donil, I'm sure that even my stone face registered disappointment. We sit among piles of books and charts, her dark head and my light one bowed, mine over my notes, hers with the weight of memories far back in time.

"Tides," Dara shouts, pushing away from the table between us. "Ask me something different."

I sigh, and cap the inkwell. The Indiri memories are deep, but the very width and breadth of them make them hard to navigate. Dara can flip through them quickly when looking for something specific, but I have only vague outlines to give her, guesses stitched together from moldy maps that I'd prepared in hopes of seeing Donil.

The last prompt was an attempt to judge the rise of the sea near Sawhen, a small outpost near the base of the mountains. I thought it might be easier to look for mountains, large and looming in anyone's memory, then tease out details. Instead, I got this outburst—another in a growing line—and no notes to add to the fairly short list of information I've gleaned from her so far.

"Let's take a breath," I suggest, and Dara waves her hand at me as if it is nothing to her, but I know different. Diving into the memories wears her down, even if she won't admit it. I fill a glass with water from a pitcher and offer it to her, which she takes without a word of thanks, her other hand massaging her temple.

"Does it pain you?"

"No," she growls back, though she pinches the bridge of her nose. "Why do you persist in this?"

Surprised, I glance up from the notes I had been making. "To calculate the—"

"No," Dara says again. "Why are you, of all people, doing this work? Stilleans would feed you to the water, yet you strive to save them from it when a cadre of Scribes can do the same?"

I finish what I'm writing, the beginning of my sentence drying while the end remains wet, the words on the page easier to manage than those in my head.

"I go to the sea regardless," I say, blowing on the ink to dry it. "From birth I have been called the Given, a girl born only to be taken away. Yet here in Stille, I have become other things as well, a friend, a girl named Khosa—"

I cut myself off, unwilling to go farther and reveal that I would become a lover too, taking her brother to bed.

"I am Given still," I go on. "But I would not see this place ruined, my friends sharing my fate."

Dara sighs and takes a drink. "Pretty words."

"That fall on deaf ears, I presume?"

She considers that a moment. "I hear you, but do not understand. If an entire city wanted me dead, I'd raze it to the ground and piss in the ashes."

"Not if Vincent was in it," I counter. "Not if Donil was."

She only shrugs, and peers at me over her cup. "Maybe."

When her glass is empty, we face each other again, my quill at the ready. I look to the map, searching for a location that might prove more fruitful.

"How about the Forest of Drennen?" I suggest. Dara seems less prickly at the idea of delving into memories that relate to the woods. This morning I'd tried asking her to comb through memories about the sea, which earned me a snarl and a reminder that the Indiri have nothing to do with it. And while that has proven mostly true, the few memories of it she has pulled from the past have been shockingly clear, the novelty of the sight seared onto the mind of the beholder.

"Fine," she says, tilting her head back and closing her eyes. "Say more."

I flip open a book to where a marker with my handwriting indicates there is some snippet of information here, a recollection of Drennen from a time past that might help guide our delving.

It's only a few sentences, a brief description of the forest as the bored Scribe cataloged a list of goods Stille had retrieved as tithe from the farthest reach of the kingdom, the village of Hygoden.

"Look for . . . *shaggy undergrowth, enough to lend shelter to a colony of rabbits.*"

Dara makes no indication of hearing me, but her face spasms as it always does when she first tries to remember. I read on.

"*The timber here is plenty, rough-barked trees vying for the light of the sun against the smooth ones.*" I pause, giving Dara some time. She spins one finger in the air after a moment, and I continue.

"*There are clear markings where the cats have sharpened their claws, some trees nearly skinned. Early this morning, we ousted a family of them, the youngest of the kittens too slow to disappear into the violet-flowered brush, so it climbed instead, spitting at us as we passed underneath his perch, fur puffing him to twice his normal size.*"

Dara says nothing, her brow furrowed in concentration as she flicks through memories that she claims she's never found the beginning of.

The small candle I keep nearby burns down two finger-widths before she motions for me to continue. I clear my throat.

"The canopy is thick, the sun barely breaking through—"

"Oh, piss in the salty sea, you're describing every wood on the damn island," Dara yells, leaving her chair and kicking a nearby stool for no reason. I lean back from the table, not knowing what to say.

"Ooohh, there's trees in this woods—that's helpful," she goes on. "And the sun shines on them, and it has animals in it."

"Dara," I say carefully, but there's no point.

"Don't tell me," she mocks. "Next it says there's a breeze."

I glance at the pages. "Actually, yes. And it smells of fiverberries."

She was prepared to sneer at my next words, her face already twisting into one when she stops. "Fiverberries?"

I check again, to be sure. *"The breeze is soft and from the west, carrying with it the pleasant smell of fiverberries."*

Dara comes back to her chair and closes her eyes. "Fiverberries," she says to herself. "Something . . . once . . ."

And she's gone, lost somewhere that stretches far beyond anything I can imagine. I give her as much time as she needs, not even bothering to gauge the passage of it as the candle beside me shortens. The few instances when I've been able to find historical mentions of landmarks with a corresponding Indiri memory have been precious victories for both of us. Even though we may not like each other, I am learning my way around her, and Dara is on a scent now, keen to run it down like the hunter she is.

She is expressive with others' memories as she is in her own present, and I watch, fascinated as she relives moments from her ancestors' lives; grief, joy, pain, happiness, and finally a flaring ecstasy that is hers alone as skin that I relish on another lights with discovery.

"Fiverberries," she says, tapping her hand twice on the table, eyes still closed as if she's afraid the memory will escape her if she opens them. "And something about the brush . . ."

I glance back over the entry. *"The youngest of the kittens too slow to disappear into the violet-flowered brush—"*

"I'm there." Her jaw goes slack in concentration.

I abandon the history, switching over to the many maps that scatter my work area. An outsider would walk in and think me messy—or yes, I know it, *mad*—but there is a system here of my own devising, and I lay my hand to a pile that references Drennen with no hesitation.

"What do you see?" I ask.

This is the point where no amount of research on my part or concentration on Dara's will make any difference. She can see only what her ancestor saw, and if this Indiri moved inland instead of toward the sea, it is useless to us.

Dara's hands dig into her temples as she silently examines what she sees through the eyes of a many-times ancestor, and I hold my breath. While the Indiri have a unique gift of passing on their knowledge, memories are a tricky thing, colored by emotion. Dara warned me when we began that what resides in her head is not like the pages of the book under my fingers, a catalog of the day's events. She can no more tell me what her ancestor had for dinner that night than I can say what I ate a week ago.

"Because it's not important," she told me. "Unless it was poisoned," she had added. "They'd remember that."

And I can't help wonder as I watch Dara's lips move in the fading light of evening what could be so momentous about fiverberries and violet-flowered hedges in the life of an Indiri. So many of her recollections have been tinged with violence, bright, pulse-pounding battles that any warrior would carry with pride, handing it down to the next generation. But Dara's face flickers with happiness, the tug of a smile on her lips giving her a moment of beauty that disappears when she opens her eyes. The brightness of her gaze rips through me like sun through a morning mist, the vicious cast of victory claiming her face again.

"The Forest of Drennen, my third-great-grandmother, violet-flowered bushes—those are called waterleaf rue, by the way—and fiverberries."

I dip the tip of my quill in ink, ready to capture the fleeting moment as she reels it off.

"It's the same spot as your Scribe, as best I can tell. The tree he mentioned the cats sharpening on? Once they've picked a spot, the whole clowder uses it. An older tree can bear scars from cats long gone, the tree growing and widening the claw marks. If you can find one old enough, it'll look like a Tangata the size of a house has been at it."

"You're sure it's the same spot?"

She nods her head. "Waterleaf rue grows only in Drennen, and then only on the western edge where there's enough light for it to flower. Fiverberries come into season in waves, and there's only a very small area where you'd have the rue flowering and ripe fivers at the same time. Toss in the clawed tree, and yes, it's the same spot."

"And the sea?"

"She heard it, breaking on the land. I couldn't see it, but I could hear the tides even though it wasn't waves. Only the tide, in and out. Like now," she adds, cocking her head toward the window.

"So it couldn't have been far."

"No, I imagine if she'd gone even ten paces to the west, she'd have broken out of the forest and onto the beach."

I return to the Scribe's pages, searching for references to the sea. My eyes dash over the lines, his neat handwriting illuminating in rigid columns what a pound of clean wool was worth, but not giving me what I want.

"Wait," I say, my breath rushing out as one word stops me.

"My apprentice has developed a taste for the clams of this area, which have a sweeter edge than those from Stillean trapmen. But the sea is a half day's journey, so he'll have to be satisfied with—"

I stop reading, not caring if the Scribe's apprentice was satisfied or not. "Which ancestor again?"

"Third-great-grandmother."

I consult my list of her ancestors, their names and the ages they lived to listed neatly, back farther than my own bloodline.

I've made notations on the maps, some of which bore cartographers' names——whose births and deaths helped me narrow down when they'd been made. I do sums, checking the date on the Scribe's journal entry and jotting down Stillean calendar dates next to the Indiri names. Their lifespans are so chillingly spare when represented by my black slashes, yet so colorfully rendered inside Dara's head.

"Well?" she asks.

I glance up, surprised that the only light left to us now comes from the candle, even its flickering flame almost drowned in a puddle of wax. I was lost in my facts, and she let me be, as I have left her for long periods in her world of memory and dream.

"I can't say exactly," I tell her. "I have to guess how far a half day's journey would've been for them, which means first ascertaining how big their party was, although I'm guessing not large by the fairly paltry amount of tithes they gathered. You also have to take into account that while the sea is definitely rising, it may not be doing so at an even rate. It could gain three hand spans in a moonchange, for example—"

"Khosa." She stops me.

I look again at the date on the ledger, and at her third-great-grandmother's lifespan. Barely three generations separate them, but she could hear the surf, while my Scribe couldn't spare the time to reach it.

"Fast," I say. "It's rising fast."

I expect her to curse, maybe kick some furniture again, but instead her head sinks and she sighs. "I don't know how to fight an enemy that will only rust my sword," she says. The flame is down to a blue flicker, the shadows under her eyes dark as those that lurk in the corners.

"I'm done in." She rises from her chair and is to the door before I stop her, not finding the courage to ask the question to her face.

"Your memories," I call, "they're mostly battle and blood. What did your third-great-grandmother find in waterleaf rue and fiverberries, that you should know it now?"

Dara turns, the tiniest of smiles on her lips. "She was falling in love. Those moments burn deep and hot, down into the bone if you let them."

"Oh," I say, surprised that Dara who seems made of only sharp edges would know this. "I see."

"I'm not sure you do," she says, eyes dragging over my expressionless face.

She leaves me as the flame drowns itself, and I find myself alone in the dark with the lingering smell of smoke and thoughts of her brother.

CHAPTER 32

Vincent

I LOOK AT THE NOTE IN MY HAND, THE HANDWRITING UNFAMILIAR but the hand that wrote it intimate with me as no other.

> *My Deer Prince—*
> *You have not visitted me in some time, and so I rite instead of*
> *saying thees words to you. The word of the riseing sea has father*
> *thinking of the blod of his line. He wishes me to mary and get*
> *with childe, and I hav a man in mind. I wood ask you to release*
> *me of my servises to you, that I may mary him, though I ad that*
> *I will mis you.*
> *Milda*

I quickly pen a letter of my own, granting Milda her release to marry and telling her truthfully that I will miss her as well. My failure to visit was out of respect for her and not disinterest. With both Khosa and Dara swirling in my mind, I felt it would be unfair to bed Milda and think of another.

"My lord?" A servant knocks politely on my open door, a Stillean dress uniform in hand. "The queen sent this for you, and asks that you be in the great hall after breakfast."

"Tides, I'd forgotten." I say under my breath, as she lays the court uniform across my bed, curtsies, and leaves.

In my years, little has been demanded of me as a Stillean royal, but what tradition asks for I must see done. And today is a farce indeed, a passing of hours that will require nobility on full display, the truth of my thoughts buried deeply. I dress and make my way to the great hall, hoping to intercept Khosa so that I may explain before another does so, with less delicacy.

But I am too late. I find her already there, face inscrutable but tension visible in her spine, stiff as a sword in a white dress. She watches the servants placing chairs around the throne, softening them with pillows and following the instructions of the painter, whose canvas for now remains blessedly blank.

"Khosa," I say as I go her side, reminding myself not to touch her bare shoulders, though I want to.

"Vincent." She smiles, her face transformed as she turns to me. "What is all of this?"

"I should have mentioned it, but I forgot. I apolo—"

"Ah." She raises a finger.

"In that case I retract all of my regrets," I say, earning a smile. "Except one," I go on, and she stills at my tone.

"It's a rather morbid tradition," I tell her, leading her away from the others and into a corner where we may talk in private. "The Given is as honored as the royal line, and it is customary to accord her the honor of wearing the crown alongside the blood of the line in portraiture."

Though her face does not change, I have grown to know Khosa well enough to see the light in her eyes go out at my words, yet another insult disguised as a compliment delivered to her, and this one from my own mouth.

"So I'm to wear the crown of the kingdom that I drown for?"

"All rulers die for their kingdoms," I say, the throne's shadow reaching for me even now. "Though it kills some of us more slowly than others."

"There you are, my dear. You're looking quite lovely, but the finishing touch awaits." My mother's lady's maid crosses to us, the queen's crown resting on a pillow in her arms. Khosa's eyes remain on mine as the maid places the crown on her head, keeping up a constant stream of chatter.

Yet I hear nothing; I'm transfixed by the girl in front of me. The crown of Stille rests on her head as if it belongs there; the white dress outlines her body in ways that send my thoughts to places best kept private. This moment could be my wedding, this girl my wife.

Stilted words over our first meeting have become real conversations, her place in my life sliding from a sacrifice for our kingdom to an attractive, intelligent girl whose death would be a pity. And now my mother's crown on her head has transformed her once again, and I am at a loss.

This must be how love feels, I think as I take my place at her side, the artist arranging my mother and father as they arrive in the great hall. It is not the stab of desire that I felt when I realized that Dara had gone from child to woman, or the warm affection I hold for Milda. Those are already outstripped by the sudden conflagration in my heart at the sight of Khosa wearing Stille's crown.

This is all-consuming, penetrating so deeply I feel it throughout, both my body and mind suffused by a need for her so great I wish to tear out my father's eyes as he runs them casually over Khosa. And it is useless, even more so than passing thoughts of Dara, another girl who is not meant for me.

For Khosa is married to one thing only, and that is the sea.

I stand as I am told, take direction, and fulfill my duty as the painter's brush moves over the canvas, each brush stroke filling one more moment of the very few left in the life of the girl I have fallen in love with.

CHAPTER 33

Witt

"I HAVE MADE A BOAT, MY LITHOS."

The people wind down from the cliffs in a silent line, the only sound in the early morning air of Culling Day the heavy *clunk* of their boats as they drag them to the rocky beach where Witt waits, Pravin by his side. The girl who faces him now is younger even than he, and she cradles a babe still bow-legged from the womb in her arms.

"Why have you made a boat?" Witt asks, words that he will repeat many times, to the sick and the old. But this girl is neither. Wan and thin, yes, but with many years still ahead of her. If she wants them.

"My baby won't suck, my Lithos," she says, her voice dull. "She's nine days out of me and has had nothing except what I squeeze from a cloth into her mouth."

Witt glances at the baby. It is curled against its mother, jaw open and mouth slack. He knows nothing of infants, but enough about the pallor of death to be aware that her boat has been built only just in time. And yet, the sight of the tiny hand splayed against its mother's chest, each finger as thin as seaweed, sends him reeling from the thought.

"Have you not considered the Feneen?" he asks, and Pravin stiffens beside him. The Lithos is only to ask why the boat was made, accept the reason, and then push the dead out to sea and the waiting Lusca.

The girl wavers as well, confused by the departure from what she expects. "No, my Lithos. I could not bear the thought of leaving her alone on the rocks if she wasn't accepted."

Witt keeps his face in the straight, practiced calm that the muscles know so well, but his eyes sweep out to sea and the mist that rolls back from the shores. It climbs to meet the gray sky, forming a wall of sheer white. But Witt knows the boats will sail through it, and the claws of hungry creatures will break them to splinters.

"I used the last of my strength to build my boat," the girl stammers, and Pravin puts a comforting hand on her shoulder.

"As you should. That is what the Pietra do," he says.

Witt's tongue curls in his mouth, a muscle in his cheek flickering as he fights the urge to rail at the girl that she should have used that strength to find the Feneen and give the babe a chance. They could refuse it, certainly, but beyond the mist, there is only the water and the monsters—and they welcome all.

"Please, my Lithos." The girl reaches for Witt, her hand so small it can barely curl around his wrist. "I am so tired."

He can see as much. It is etched into the shadows under her eyes, evident in the frail grip she holds him in.

"I have nothing left to offer my people," she says quietly. "Let me go."

Witt pulls the boat from her side, a small thing meant for only the two of them, and pushes it into the surf. It was cut from a Hadundun tree, the barest indentation of a seat hollowed out.

"You have built a boat." He returns to the words he is supposed to say. "You may go."

Relief floods the girl's face as she climbs in, her hand tight on his shoulder to keep her balance as she takes her seat. The baby stirs briefly, hand reclaiming a strand of its mother's hair as it settles against her.

"Thank you," the girl whispers in his ear as he shoves the boat off, water lapping the toes of his boots. She fades from sight in moments, the mist closing around her.

There is a solid *clunk* as another boat falls at Witt's feet.

"I have made a boat, my Lithos," says an old man, a wheeze escaping him as he speaks.

"Why have you made a boat?" Witt asks, closing his eyes against the weak mewl of a baby's cry that penetrates the mist.

"Will there be anything else?"

Witt glances up from the fire to see the Keeper from Hyllen standing by his chair, a tray with his supper resting on the table beside him.

"I didn't hear you come in."

"Your thoughts seem far away." Her eyes go to his boots, still wet from the day's work, resting next to the fireplace. He doesn't answer her, and she moves to leave.

"Wait," he calls. "Stay. I doubt I will eat much. You'll be taking this back soon."

She takes the chair across from his, hands folded in her lap. "Your man Pravin doesn't like for me to be alone with you. Though I'm not much of a threat. I think you could break my neck quick as a chicken's."

Witt shakes his head. "It's not that."

"Ahhh . . ." She laughs to herself, throat long in the firelight as her head tilts back, more life in her than there had been the night he spared it. "Am I so tempting?"

He can't help but smile back. "A Lithos—"

"Cannot be distracted," she finishes for him. "Yes, I've heard that many a time. One of the scullery girls has a running bet with a Lure for his pole. She thinks she can distract you."

"And how fares she fishing?"

"Hard to catch anything when you don't have a pole."

They laugh together this time, and Witt snaps the legs off a crab, handing her one. She waves it away.

"That's the best of the lot, for the Lithos."

"I'm giving you some," he insists, and she takes it.

They crack shells in silence, the low fire drying Witt's boots and leaving a film of salt around the bottoms. "Are there many such wagers concerning me?" he asks.

The Keeper pulls some white meat from the shell with a quiet smile. "More than you'd care for, I'm sure. Quite the variety, as well. Some think you take your pleasure with other boys, but I've seen your eye caught by a well-turned curve of a girl's hip once or twice, though it's only your eye that goes to it and nothing more."

"The Lithos's only pleasure is in seeing Pietra safe," Witt says, in recitation.

"And you do revel in it."

"What else is there?" he asks, voice gone hollow.

"Many things, my Lithos. But none of them for you."

They are quiet again, the sound of the fire and the crack of shells the only noise as they eat.

"I know you only as the Keeper. What is your name?" Witt finally asks.

She pauses a second, a sliver of crabmeat pinched between her fingers. "Odd thing, a name. The little Givens I've raised called me only Keeper, and the man I raised them with . . . Well, when you've spent your whole life with someone, you call each other all kinds of things, but rarely your names."

"And what kinds of things do a man and a woman call each other, when they live together?"

"Nice things, if you're lucky. Though no matter how good you have it, we will use ugly words to each other sometimes."

"And you?"

"I was lucky," she says, the ghost of a smile on her lips. "He called me *Lamb*."

"And what became of him?"

"You killed him," she says simply. "So I think I'll keep my name to myself."

Witt nods in understanding. "Did you watch the Culling today?"

"I saw the boats go, yes."

"And what did you think?"

"I think pushing so many off into the sea must be a great weight."

"As is raising little girls who don't even get a boat."

"True enough," the Keeper acknowledges. "But in my lifetime, I have sent three to the water, and today I watched you send ten times that many. And I imagine the line from the cliffs at the next Culling will be as long or longer, with the next moon coming on again."

"Too soon," Witt says, before he can catch his tongue.

"You didn't kill me at Hyllen," the Keeper goes on. "Others were spared, and now they tend sheep and sow grain—things a Pietra won't. And yet I'm bringing food to the Lithos, a task any hands can do. I had thought in time you might make . . . other requests of me."

"It's the weight we both bear that caused me to spare you." Witt says, though he does allow his eyes to slide over her in the firelight, a harmless indulgence. "As I told you that night in my tent; you raise the Givens from small things only to know they go to die."

"And you look your people in the face every day, knowing they will all build a boat in time."

"Tell me how to bear it," he says, voice tight.

"There's no bearing it, young Lithos. All things die. We only hold their hands as they go."

Silence falls again, thick and heavy. She reaches across the space between them, her fingers entwining with his. "The best you can hope for is to find someone among the living to hold you up."

"I'm the Lithos. I'm not allowed someone."

"I'm here, aren't I?"

He squeezes her hand back, and they sit by the fire as the flames settle into embers.

CHAPTER 34

Khosa

I T'S DARA I EXPECT TO SEE WHEN I HEAR FOOTSTEPS OUTSIDE the library, but the polite knock on the already open door makes me raise my head—the Indiri girl would no more do that than embroider a marriage pillow. Instead her brother stands there smiling, the raised hand wrapped in a bandage that seeps enough to blood to send alarm through my own veins.

Merryl's eyes shoot to me in question, but I wave him away, "It's all right. It's only Donil."

My guard gives Donil a hard look, one that Dara would set him on his armored ass for. But he stands aside when Donil takes a seat across from me at my stone table, cluttered with dulled quills, ink splats, and piles of paper.

"You've hurt yourself?" I ask, nodding toward his bloodied bandage.

"Not so badly that it should trouble you," Donil peels back the end of his shirtsleeves from the wound, revealing the bright slash across his palm. "I thought I might see if my sister wouldn't mind patching a fellow, but she's not here."

"No, she's not. I don't think she much enjoys spending time with me," I say, rapidly searching for something to add so that he won't leave.

"Then she's a fool," Donil says. And I feel a rush of warmth as he winks. Behind Merryl clears his throat.

"You should let a healer look at this," I say, unwinding the makeshift bandage, the tips of my fingers as black with ink as his are red with blood. "It may need to be closed."

"I've had worse." Donil waves off my concern.

"Not that I knew of," I counter. "Would you worry me unnecessarily?" It's a tease, one I've heard Hyllenian girls toss to boys they fancy to gauge their reaction.

"Never." Donil smiles, and I see that he knows the game I'm playing, though he's doubtless more experienced at it than I am.

"What were you doing to be cut?" I ask, highly aware that my hand is resting only inches from his, our fingertips straining toward one another.

"What any man does when he's alone and bored—playing with my dagger," he says, and I laugh loudly, waking the other guard, who had slumped back against the wall.

"And how do you fill your time?" Donil asks.

My eyes fall to the book in front of me, a flush creeping up my face when I realize that it's a study of the Indiri, opened to a particularly detailed drawing of an Indiri male. I pull a loose paper over it quickly, but not before Donil sees.

"Khosa," he says, clicking his tongue at me. "Naughty, naughty."

I sputter, caught halfway between shame and amusement, the prim line of my mouth trying to squelch a giggle that pushes its way out anyway, the blood in my cheeks rising along with it. Donil spares me further embarrassment by pulling a different scroll toward him, one carrying the long list of Indiri ancestors that Dara had recited for me.

"My sister has been of some use other than killing, then," he says, glancing at it. "I could tell you all kinds of Indiri stories, if you have interest. Would you like to know how we got our spots?"

"Certainly," I say, happy to keep him near me under any pretext.

Donil leans back in the chair, kicking his feet onto the table and ignoring a protracted groan from Merryl.

"The Indiri are earth people, I'm sure you've read," Donil continues.

"Yes. Dara claims she can bring down trees at her whim, pulling their life out with her voice."

"That she can," Donil says. "Because of where our ancestors come from. Long ago, before there was a Stille or the Pietra had built a single boat, there was a heavy rain that brought life to the Indiri. The moon passed three times before it stopped, and the water soaked deep into the ground where we had been sleeping for time out of mind."

Donil's voice is low and lulling, and I find myself searching his face as he talks, not knowing where my fascination with the story ends and one with the boy telling it begins.

"We woke to find roots poking our eyes and soil in our mouths, so we dug for the surface, rising as the last of the rain cleared. It fell on our dirt-covered skin, clearing some spots away and leaving others still stained with the truth of our beginnings."

"Can you go back to it?" I ask. "Through your memories?"

"No. Many have tried, though not in my line. There was a man who went so far back in thought that he was fed by his relatives for many moons as he sat unconscious, trying to reach the story."

"With no luck?"

"No luck, and no love lost between him and his kin. We hold our gift of being born knowing sacred, but wiping another's ass while he searches has a way of detracting from that."

I smile again, relieved that he has no compunction around me, and our conversation is not peppered with apologies like with Vincent and me. "And how far have you delved into the memories you were born knowing?" I ask.

"Not nearly so deep." Donil's face is suddenly serious. "I've got one memory of climbing out of a pit right at hand. I'm in no hurry to find another."

"I'm sorry," I say, my hand closing over his before I realize it, the heat of his skin sinking into mine. "I read of your birth in the histories. I should have known better than to ask."

His smile returns, and I feel a bright spike of pleasure at the thought that perhaps it is brought on by my touch as well as my words. "Indiri know much, and very little of it pleasant," he says, his uninjured hand closing over mine tentatively. His fingertips barely touch mine as if in question, a sharp stab of anticipation following each brush of skin against skin.

"Tell me more of the histories, and the work that stains these fingers black," he says.

So I speak, my words coming easily as the candle burns low, Donil holding my hand. And I let him.

CHAPTER 35

Dara

"How many of these trees did you talk down, and how many were cut?"

Dara eyes the freshly hewn logs piled nearby, knobs still bleeding sap from where branches were cut away.

"I'd say half are my doing," she tells Donil. "And even with my help, that's not nearly what they'll need to reinforce the city walls. It's been rotting since the last time someone attacked it, and that's time out of mind."

The two are sitting under a shade tree in the middle of what the Stilleans call their *encampment*, something the twins find amusing. The tree was ancient, the early Stilleans neglecting it when they cleared the field. Dara imagined one Stillean saying to another as time passed that someone should see to it, each expecting the other to handle it, until it had grown large enough to present a daunting task. Its leaves spread wide, as if reaching for its counterparts that ringed the field, a distance it could never cross.

The field is used for marching drills and to host a few swordfights, none drawing blood but leaving a few purses lighter for want of smart bets, and there is a tent that serves as a mess hall, constantly doling out food to men who aren't even hungry.

"That fellow's on his third bowl." Donil nods toward a portly Stillean leaving the tent, out of earshot. "He delivers the fresh blades from the smith, puts them in a pile, rewards himself with stew, then drives back into town."

"He should feed it to the cart donkey; it's the one doing the work," Dara says.

"Quite," Donil agrees, halving an apple with his knife and handing part to Dara. "You look like you could use some feeding yourself."

She accepts the apple but says nothing.

"Does it drain you much to talk down the trees?"

"It tires me. But much less than it would a whole team of them to do the same task."

"Yes," her brother says. "It's important they reserve their strength for things like swapping stories of their heroic feats, as of yet unperformed."

Dara crunches into her apple. "And attending speeches."

"That's today?"

"This very moment, I believe," Dara says, gesturing toward the city with her bitten apple. "Why do you think I'm here?"

"What? You don't want to hear the king tell Stilleans it is time to make good on their proud history of . . . knitting sweaters?"

"I'd take the old ladies and their needles over the would-be soldiers I've seen."

"The old ladies are faster."

"I'm not entirely sure I jest," Dara says, picking a seed from her apple. "They put more work into reinforcing the walls than training the army. If they think the Pietra will see a wall of wood and go home, they're wrong. The Pietra will tear it down with their teeth and spit the splinters at us before shearing our heads off."

"They're Stilleans," Donil says with a shrug. "The last time any of them shed blood was when they lost their baby teeth."

A wave of sound rolls toward them from the city, voices raised in unison, and the twins exchange a look.

"Gammal must've said something decent, anyway," Donil says.

"Vin wrote the speech."

Donil doesn't respond, but watches his sister while she crunches through the last of the apple.

"What?" she asks.

He plucks some blades of grass from between his feet and begins to braid them together. "It seems like the two of you have been talking quite a bit lately, is all."

"He makes good conversation."

"Mmmm."

"What?" Dara asks again, this time accompanying her question with a slug to her brother's arm.

Donil ties off the braid and tosses it into the breeze, watching it waft away to float over the heads of the would-be Stillean soldiers, now pouring from the city like ants.

"I see our adopted people getting ready to fight battles they're not prepared for," he says. "I'd hate to see my sister about to do the same."

"No worries," Dara says as the men began to fill the encampment, and Donil relaxes slightly. "There's never been a battle I wasn't prepared for."

"Dara . . . ," he begins, but her hand clamps onto his shoulder, strong and sure.

"Brother, as long as there's a breath of hope that I can find a male Indiri, Stille is safe from speckled royal children."

"I'm glad to hear it," he says, watching as the king himself mans the pile of swords, handing one to each man who volunteers for the Stillean army. Vincent stands by his grandfather's side, stiff and formal, but squints against the sun and nods when he spots them beneath the tree.

Dara waves back. "And once I've determined there are no more Indiri, what better place for our blood than a throne? Besides, brother, you have no foot to stand on, speaking to me of such things. I hear you passed some time with the Given yesterday."

"What of it?" Donil shoots back, tone sharp enough to confirm Dara's suspicions.

"I'll tell you what of it. If blood of mine is in Khosa's child, I'll take it to the treetops with the Tangata, and all of Stille can go to the depths in a wave."

"Even Vincent?"

"Even him," Dara says, and her voice does not shake. "The Indiri above all things, brother. You need to remember that."

The first scream from the woods goes unheeded by all except the twins, the killing call of a Tangata being a familiar sound. But Dara's hand tightens on Donil's shoulder, a lifetime spent in the woods bringing her to her feet in alarm.

"Something is wrong," she says, seconds before a wave of Feneen burst from the trees.

"To arms!" Donil yells, his own sword unsheathed as he charges forward, ready to meet the entire line on his own.

The men waiting their turn for a sword panic, half of them running back toward the city empty-handed, while those who remain dive for a weapon, fighting each other instead of the enemy bearing down on them.

Donil cuts into the first Feneen he meets at a run, easily parting the soft pit of his belly open. The next feints, and Donil's sword takes his knees out from under him, a back slash ending the rest. Donil slips easily underneath the broad swing of his next attacker, a huge Feneen with an extra head resting on his shoulder, mute and blind. Donil takes off both with a single swing.

He turns, expecting to find Dara beside him. But she barely cleared the shade of the tree, the paleness of her skin even more evident in the stark light of the sun. Talking down the trees cost her more than she'd admitted, and he is about to return to her side when he sees her lips moving fervently, and the grass browning at her feet.

Dara's voice gains volume as the grass around her dies, its life flowing into her as she calls it, refilling the energy she's lost and then some. The brown swathe widens, creeping toward the tree as Dara's Indiri speech flows, the words dark and heavy, nothing like the ones she used in the forest. This call isn't asking, but demanding, and it echoes over the field with a clarity that slices through the cries of battle as the first of the untried Stilleans fall under Feneen might.

When the tree begins to crumble, it shakes the earth, and soldiers from both sides turn to watch as grass turns to dust and the tree itself sinks into the ground, enveloped by the pull of Dara's call. As many eyes are on her as the collapsing tree, her skin now flush and bright with life, her hair crackling with energy and eyes bright as stars. In the space of breaths, a circle of fallow ground surrounds her, and a tree that stood for ages is gone, all of its power inside the Indiri girl, who draws her sword, and charges.

The first Feneen who dares to meet her is cut in half.

The twins fight toward the king and Vincent, whose own swords are already bloodied.

"You've got to get back to the city," Donil says to both of them, yelling over the cries of men dying around them, the crash of steel against steel as untrained Stilleans try to hold their ground.

King Gammal shakes his head. "I gave these men a speech about courage. I can hardly be seen fleeing."

"And I wrote the speech," Vincent says.

"Backs together, then." Dara doesn't bother to argue. "Vincent, on my right. Father's-Father, we'll circle you."

"I would not see youth cut down in my stead. I'm an old man, Dara girl," Gammal says.

"And the king," she reminds him. "So shut up and do as I say."

Gammal's laughter rings out odd and lost on the battlefield, as alien as Dara's now vibrant skin and glowing eyes. They circle their king, Indiri on one side of him and Vincent on the other, a pattern they'd often practiced, always in play and never with blood underfoot.

"Vincent," Donil calls as he spots Ank among the melee, shouting orders, "our friend has declared himself anything but."

"Well, pull me under," Dara says breathlessly as she parries against a Feneen, driving him through the chest. "They're riding Tangata."

A cat breaks through a group of Stilleans, swiping open a man's face down to the bone before leaping onto another. Its Feneen rider swings his sword wildly, and Donil takes off his arm with a stroke as the cat passes near, ready to pounce on its next prey. Another cat bounds through the melee, a dead rider dragging behind but not slowing it down as it pulls a Stillean back by his heel, snapping his neck with a toss of its jaws.

Dara takes down another Feneen as they press toward the king. The body of dead around their protective circle grows, but her eyes are on the cats.

"My left arm for a bow," she seethes.

"That's your sword arm," Donil reminds her, but his glance follows hers and he sees the trail of mutilated bodies left in the wake of the cats.

"Go," he says.

Dara doesn't argue, crossing the field in a moment with her stolen energy, taking out a cat's back legs before it knows she's behind it. It turns to fight, the bloody stumps of its legs dragging through filth and spraying blood. The first swipe snags the tip of her cape, pulling her off balance and bringing her to a knee. The cat drags itself to her, its haunches curling for a pounce even as it dies. She finishes it with a slice across the throat and rises, blood-spattered, to face a Feneen who saw a chance to take her unawares.

He was mistaken.

Donil's sword makes wider arcs as he grows tired, Vincent barely keeping his breath by his side. Still, the Feneen come on, drawn by the sight of the king.

Gammal has pulled his sword, though it is a decorative one only. He grips the blade in gloved hands, swinging the heavy pommel through the air and dropping more than one Feneen at his feet.

"I see him," Vincent says to Donil. It's the first chance he's had to acknowledge Ank's presence.

The Feneen is the only one on a horse, and he turns its head toward them almost as if he heard. He carries a bow, and an arrow sails straight for Gammal the moment he spots him, Donil knocking it aside with a swing of his sword.

Ank rides for them as the sounds of the battle falter, the dead bleeding out, the wounded crying for help. As he comes closer, Donil can see that the horse wears a Pietran bridle.

"You were not long in making new friends," Donil says to Ank, arms shaking with the effort of holding his sword.

"The Feneen do what they must," Ank says calmly, eyes on Vincent.

"Like attack those they offer assistance to?" Vincent asks, chest heaving.

Ank shrugs. "The assistance was refused." His eyes shift back to Donil. "Stand aside, Indiri. This is not your king."

"Not my king, but an old man armed with a useless sword," Donil says. "I'll remain, like any decent person would, Indiri or otherwise."

"Let me see him." A female voice speaks. Ank turns his head to answer her, his horse angling so that Donil and Vincent can see a strikingly beautiful woman with no arms or legs riding in a basket on Ank's back.

"King Gammal," Ank says. "Meet Nilana of the Feneen, brightest and best among us."

"Milady," says Gammal, unruffled.

She inclines her head. "Ank tells me you are a good man."

"I'm pleased to hear he thinks so. Although his actions speak otherwise."

"During war, our actions sometimes go against our hearts," Nilana says.

"We weren't at war until today."

"Until today," she agrees. And then she spits.

Donil and Vincent are watching Ank, not prepared for a threat from Nilana. The dart she'd hidden in her cheek sails between them, burying itself in Gammal's throat. He drops instantly, the poison spreading through his body with one beat of his heart.

"A good man," Ank says as Vincent kneels next to his grandfather, fingers outstretched to cover the wound. "And a good grandson."

"Don't touch it," Nilana warns. "I've been building up an immunity to igthorn my whole life. One brush against your hand and you're dead."

"Why?" Vincent asks, arms around his dying grandfather.

"Because he *is* a good man, young prince," says Nilana. "And not many years left."

"I've seen inside your father, Vincent," Ank adds, pulling the horse's head back toward the woods. "I want to go to war against a man I can hate. Not one I respect."

Dara's shriek splits the air even from far across the battlefield, where the last cat and rider have fallen under her sword.

"Go," Nilana says to Ank. "Now."

Ank spurs his mount for the trees, bloodied mud flying up from its hooves. Dara gives chase, even with no hope of catching them. She screams an Indiri obscenity in their wake, launching her sword into the air. It hits the ground a hand span shy of the horse's rear legs and Nilana's laughter can be heard ringing back at them. Dara leaves the sword, running back to where Gammal lies, his life already gone, Vincent numb by his side.

"Father's-Father?" she asks, even though she is all too familiar with the pallor of death that rests on Gammal's face.

Donil shakes his head, and Vincent glances up to see Dara quaking, eyes bright as twin suns, hair billowing in a breeze as the borrowed life inside of her seeks a way out. Their eyes meet, and she fills his mind, so that he forgets even Gammal, though he is touching the cooling body.

"Sister," Donil says sternly. "Release."

Dara closes her eyes and sinks to the ground, head resting on her knee. A gasp rips from her throat and her cape flutters as hundreds of speckled butterflies rise from beneath it, diving to play in the breeze that blows above the dead and the dying.

CHAPTER 36

Vincent

FOR A MOMENT, DARA IS ALL I SEE, AND THE THIN THREAD of desire that has been weaving through my body suddenly becomes a tapestry that might smother me. Her eyes, skin, hair—everything that has always been Dara—comes together in a burning moment in which I want her so badly I would take her there on the blood-slicked grass, among the dead, with her brother watching.

Then she releases the butterflies, the life she took from the tree leaving her with each pulse of their wings, and the pull is gone. I see her as she is, the girl of my childhood, covered with gore. Blood spatters her skin, drying so that it is impossible to discern it from her speckles. Tufts of Tangata fur stick to her, and I spot a tooth in her hair, snared in a tangle. I realize it is human, and I retch.

I'm on my knees, losing breakfast next to my grandfather's corpse, when the trembling begins. At first I think it is only the weakness that comes after I train with the twins, a bone-deep exhaustion that promises to cripple me in the morning. But this is different. This travels from my knees into my gut, my whole spine trembling inside me as I roll to sit in the mud, one hand buried in the open gut of a Feneen soldier to keep my balance.

"Donil," Dara calls, and comes to my side. "Vincent has the shakes."

Her words reach my ears but not my mind. The trembling is so violent that I jab my own eye when I try to swipe the sweat from my brow.

"It's all right," Dara says. "It'll pass."

Donil sits on my other side, a hand on my leg. "You've not killed before, Vin. Not seen battle. This is what happens next. There's no shame in it."

He's right. All around me, the Stilleans that breathe are lost nonetheless, some managing to gain their feet, but most are like me, bewildered in the wake of battle. The twins sit with me as the tremors pass, easing off as the sun breaks through a cloud and warms my skin.

I rise when I'm able, moving through the wounded to do what I can. The dead are many, more Stillean than Feneen. The twins begin piling the enemy corpses, while I grab a Stillean who has his wits about him and we form lines of our own. People have begun to slink from the city, wary as mice. Cries rise up as they discover their own among the line of the dead—growing longer—and among the wounded, yet living. It's hard to tell joy from the pain, and I stop looking up when I hear them.

"I'll be drowned," Donil says. "Vin, Dara, come here."

We go to him, where he stands over a downed Tangata.

"The Feneen weren't riding them. They're sewn to them."

"Fathoms," breathes Dara as she bends in closer to see. "Makes sense. No cat worth its claws would ever be ridden."

"But why?" I ask, staring in horror at the dark seam running between human flesh and cat, each stitch held tight even in death.

"Terror," Dara says. "Our army split like ants in rain when they saw these. And look . . ." She prods the withered leg of the Feneen with her sword. "This soldier would be useless without a mount."

"So he chose to be sewn to a cat," Donil finishes. "How'd they manage it, though?"

Dara pulls back the Tangata's thick lips, curved teeth shining brightly white, and takes a sniff. "Darrow root."

I'd seen the kitchen maids taunt the housecat with darrow, sending it into a frenzy, followed by the deepest of tail-twitching sleeps.

"And they woke with Feneen on their backs," I say.

"They woke with riders they couldn't pitch. Pissed off, in pain, and with Stilleans in front of them," Dara says. "We had no chance."

"The prince!" A shout rises from the edge of the field as my father steps out of the city, clothes unspeakably clean amidst the carnage. He had left the speech to go with the advisors, the group of them checking grain storage against the number of army volunteers.

And now that number is much fewer, and my father is king.

"The king!" comes the corrected call, from a man who had been in battle, seen Gammal fall.

A hush rolls over the field at the full impact of those two words, and all around me, men bend a knee. I go down as well, not surprised when Donil and Dara keep their feet. A quiet sob breaks through the silence and I spot a woman kneeling over a fallen man, her grief too sharp for the change of sovereigns to penetrate.

My father walks though the field, nodding for everyone to rise. He places his boots carefully to avoid treading on the dead—whether out of respect for them or for his boots, I don't know. When he spots me, something like relief washes over his face, and I'm alarmed to realize that it surprises me.

"Son," he says, clapping heavy hands on each of my shoulders, "you're unharmed."

It's not a question, but if it were, I wouldn't know how to answer. The spasms that racked me have passed, but left an emptiness in their wake. I'm surrounded by the dead and dying, my king and grandfather among them, the blood of mutilated strangers on my blade, the friends of my childhood on either side of me.

Yet I feel utterly alone. I find myself wondering if Khosa is safe in the library, and if she is concerned for me.

"Father," I say, the word somehow alien and unfeeling, even if accurate. "Gammal . . . My . . . The king is dead."

He nods once slowly and squeezes my shoulders. "I know. It'll be all right, Vincent. I am king now. Not that it seems to matter to some," he adds, eyeing Donil and Dara.

"It'll take more than a crown to get me on my knees in front of you," Dara says.

"Dara!" Donil growls, and even I gape for a moment. She ignores both of us, the coldness of her voice mirrored in her eyes as she stares down my father.

"How did it happen? Take me through it." My father takes my arm, and Donil follows.

"They broke through the forest," Donil tells him. "We heard a scream. Could've been a cat, but I think we'll find what's left of a timber crew out among the trees later."

"The men didn't even have swords," I say, steering us toward what remains of the pile we'd been distributing. "They were lined up to receive them, and I was helping Grandfather—"

My throat closes against me as I remember the glint in Gammal's eyes to match the shine of the new swords, the pride he took in each Stillean he armed, sparing a word for everyone. The sun hasn't moved three finger spans in the sky since then.

"The men weren't prepared, which was part of their attack, I'm sure," Donil continues. "To be fair, even a trained and armed man would've been taken aback by soldiers such as these."

"Were they well practiced? Better armed?" Father asks.

"Some had clubs, others fought with bare hands," Donil says. "There were those with swords, but—"

"They had sewed themselves to Tangata," I say, spitting out the words.

"It's more than that," Donil corrects me. "Many of these people were thrown away because their mothers couldn't bear the sight of them. Raise a child on a lifetime of anger, feed him on the memory of rejection, then give him a weapon. It makes for a fierce soldier."

"And a frightening one," my father says, toeing over a Feneen corpse with three arms, all his fists still locked around daggers.

"There was one that had eyes all 'round his head." A Stillean speaks up, an open gash in his cheek showing that he faced a cat today. "Wasn't any way to come at him—he could see in every direction."

"And a woman," adds another, the battle stories coming thick now. "Did you see the one who ran on all fours, fast as I do on two at a sprint? She took Unga's leg out at the calf, ripped the muscle right through with her teeth and spat it out to go after another."

"A fierce battle," my father says, raising his voice so everyone could hear. "Many are fallen—Stillean *and* Feneen. We'll bury our dead tonight, and mourn them. Pile the Feneen and burn them. Tomorrow we'll have our revenge."

A cheer goes up from the group that has gathered around us, and I try to find the strength to answer with a halfhearted smile. Father grabs my hand and lifts it upward in his own.

"Revenge will have to wait until long past tomorrow, if he really wants all the dead buried," Donil whispers in my ear.

"What do you suggest?" I ask. "We can't burn our own alongside the enemy."

"It's quicker." He shrugs. "And this is war."

I'm pulled away from him as Father raises our arms together again. "For Stille!" he shouts, and an answering cry rises from those around us, echoing out in the field and drawing the attention of others.

"For Stille!" he shouts again. Again, my arm is jerked upward, and we're walking, bringing the crowd with us as we step over my grandfather's body and the first of the flames rises from the pile of Feneen.

CHAPTER 37

Khosa

SOMETHING TERRIBLE HAS HAPPENED.

I've spent my life studying faces, and there are volumes in the tight lips of the kitchen girl who brings a lunch tray to the library, stories buried in the red-rimmed eyes of the maid I pass in the hall, and untold tales in the taut muscles of the sconcelighters who keep eternal fires burning in windowless corridors.

Vincent does not come to see me, something I tuck into a dark corner of my heart, a place I've learned to hide worry. He's made it a habit to speak with me every day, asking about the progress of my sessions with Dara, and the lines of cramped writing that fill lengths of paper as I dash out my thoughts. His visits always start that way, then we veer off into other conversations, often losing much time telling each other things of little consequence that somehow bring me great happiness.

His absence today is conspicuous. Taken in hand with the tense shoulders of the servants and tear-streaked faces of the maids, I know there is news, and likely not the kind people want to hear. More than once my tongue has quaked in my mouth, wanting to ask after Vincent, to be assured of his well-being.

But I caught one of my guards tipping a wink at the other the last time Vincent came in, sliding one of his fingers in and out of a hole he made with his fist. I blushed scarlet, and Vincent had to pry every word out of me on that visit. He left with a furrowed brow and hunched shoulders, dejection seeping from him.

Merryl isn't on duty at the moment, and I won't ask the ones here about what happened, or about Vincent. Not when they think he comes to see me for one thing only. Blood seeps into my cheeks even thinking about it, a mixture of anger and humiliation that makes my fingers shake.

But even as I rage inwardly at their assumptions, I ask my own questions. Would it be such a surprise if that *was* why Vincent came to me? Should I be grateful that at least he puts on a pretense of courting me, instead of stating his duty to his people and pulling my skirts up?

The tip of the quill I'm using punches through the paper, and I swear under my breath just as I hear the soft scraping of feet across the floor and the rustle of weapons as my guards come to attention.

"I'm sorry, I didn't know anyone was here," an unfamiliar voice says, and I look up to see a Scribe in the doorway, a heavy book in his arms. Since Vincent asked them to work in their own wards so I could continue using of the library, I have not seen any of the robed men.

"Hello," I say awkwardly, the word tumbling out because it's supposed to, but with no welcome in it. "I am Khosa."

"Yes, I know," the Scribe says, his brown robes rippling as he comes toward me. "I am Cathon."

"Hello," I say again, and he glances over my table.

"I've come to return one of the histories," he says. "But I wouldn't want to disturb your workspace. Is there somewhere you'd like me to put it?"

"This room belongs to you more than me," I say, the coldness of my words not reflecting the warmth I feel inside that he is respecting my ink splotches and tottering piles. "Put it where you feel is best."

"I think . . . here." He casually knocks a pile of books off another table, a plume of dust rising as they fall. I'm so surprised I laugh, and he smiles in return.

"What are you working on, Khosa?"

"The rise of the sea, the same as you," I say, and find myself unfurling scroll after scroll, explaining my methods, sharing my calculations, pointing to maps and diary entries that have no bearing on the sea. Cathon nods as I speak, his hands occasionally pulling on his beard in thought.

"I admit, you've made more progress than the roomful of Scribes I come from," he says, when I am finished. "You have the mind of a scholar."

"And the body of the Given," I remind him. "The mind will go to the sea with it, when the time comes."

"Seems a pity," Cathon says, his eyes locking on mine.

A shiver passes through me, echoing one that gripped me earlier when I thought of Vincent breeding me out of duty. But this one is for my mind, and the idea I see in Cathon's gaze at the thought that it might not need to be flooded with salt water.

"More of a pity to end Stille for the sake of one," I say, looking away from him. "Mind. Body. They're both set for the sea."

"Because of Stille."

"Because of who *I am*," I argue, the heat of my thoughts firing in my belly but not seeping into my words. "Stille does not send me to the sea. My feet go on their own."

Even as I say it, I feel the tremble, so different from anything else a body can feel. It starts in my center, as if a string connected to the shore is tied there, pulling taut in this moment. My toes twitch, my fingers spasm, I feel my tongue curl in my mouth and my lips stretch across my face in an obscene smile.

I want the sea, more than I want Donil. It has been patient, and I have waited too long. And though there is a stone wall between me and the sea, it is nothing.

The windows are set high. I break for a bookcase even as Cathon yells for the guards, but my need outstrips their duty. My wrist slides through the Scribe's grip like seaweed, and I'm climbing the bookcase. The first shelf holds me, but the second groans as I ascend, the third warning me with a subtle shift that it's been holding its weight too long. The fourth splits beneath my foot, raining down books and scrolls onto Cathon and the guards.

I slide as it goes, my ankle within the Scribe's reach. He grabs it and pulls me back, my hands gripping the sides of the bookcase, screaming in misery. When I'm close enough to land a kick, I do, and the slight bridge of his nose caves beneath my heel. Cathon's blood drips on the fallen books, marring pages, something I would've mourned only moments ago.

But not now. There is only one thing for me, and my insides are screaming for it, wailing for want of the one thing they've been denied. I'm scrambling through broken boards, the strength of panic propelling me upward to shelves untouched for many lifetimes. I send them falling on the faces of my guards, and then the window is at my fingertips.

The stone window ledge is warm from the sun, almost pleasant, as my fingernails peel backward when I pull myself up. I hear the men screaming below me, but the sound is a dull cousin to the roar of the waves, the spray of the sea. I take a deep breath, the salt of the air touching me more deeply than any person ever will. The pull forward is so strong, I can't fathom the feeling when I start to fall back, until I glance down and see an arrow tip protruding from my shoulder.

There is a tug, almost polite in its tentativeness, and I'm headed toward the floor, the window growing smaller in my vision. Dust follows me down, arms try to break my fall, but my head meets stone. The last thing I see is the ripple of the ink sea in the map above me, the closest I could come to the place I'm supposed to be.

੭⊙੧

Vincent's voice is the first to break through, and I reach for him instinctively, the only familiar person in the room. His fingers close around mine before my eyes are open, and I bear it for a few moments before pulling away and wiping my fingers on the soft blanket of my bed.

"Khosa? Can you hear me?"

I nod, but my eyes feel like heavy stones, my skull a watery jam hardly capable of supporting them. My hands go to my temples, and I make a sound like a kitten without a mother.

"You're either the best shot in the kingdom, or the most ruthless man in it," Vincent says, and I peer through my fingers to see my guards, no longer smug and smirking, but pale and shaking under Vincent's glare.

"If I may, young prince." Cathon's voice is thick, blood still coating his chin. "The guard was the quickest thinker among us. If he hadn't shot her, Khosa would've cleared the window. And while an arrow ran the risk of killing her, the fall on the other side left nothing to chance."

"It's true, sir," one guard says. "She wasn't stopping for anything. I've sat in that room with her day in and out, not seen a single bit of violence. Then she breaks a Scribe's nose and climbs a bookcase like a cat up a tree. There was a spool of the stuff they use to bind the books, so I tied an end to an arrow and—"

"And you shot her." Vincent says, his tone making it clear what he thinks of that.

The guard's chin goes up. "I can place an arrow."

"That he can," I say, finding my voice. "My head hurts worse than the wound."

"It didn't nick a bone, slipped right through flesh," a new voice says, and I turn my head to see a woman rolling a clean bandage by my bedside. "You don't hurt much now because I put a bit of rankflower salve on it. Will take the kick out of any pain that ails you, though not much I can do for your head, dearie, I'm sorry. That hurt's on the inside, nowhere I can get to without cracking your skull apart, which I don't think Stille would thank me for."

I angle my head but can't quite see the arrow wound just below my clavicle, but the poultice carries a distinctive aroma.

"*I* thank you," I say to the healer. "And you," I add, nodding to the guard, despite the pain it causes me. "He saved my life," I tell Vincent, and the scowl that has been etched on his face since I opened my eyes lightens slightly.

"And I'm sorry about your nose," I add to Cathon, who waves away the apology.

"How many Scribes can say they've had their nose broken by a Given?" he says. "I may find my name written in a book one day."

"If anyone lives long enough to write it," I hear a guard mutter as Vincent waves everyone out of my room.

"What did he mean by that?" I ask Vincent when the door closes behind them. "Yes, the seas are rising, but even my most dire calculations give us at least a generation—"

But Vincent only shakes his head, and I know it is not the sea that brought on those words.

"What is it?" I ask. "What happened?"

"The Feneen attacked. Many were lost on both sides—the king among them," he says, his voice as empty and dull as mine.

I know that I should comfort him, that the hours we've spent together in the library have added up to something like a friendship, and that in this moment I should put my hand in his, say words of consolation. But my hand is in a fist, and my throat is closed against kindness. The madness that swirled in my center has quieted for the moment, but I know it will return, calling me to die for the land that my mother tried to end in the very act of birthing me, the kingdom that my father's people now wage war against.

I close my eyes against Vincent's pain, choosing instead to drown in my own.

CHAPTER 38

~⊙~

Vincent

MY MOTHER SITS, SILENT, AT THE FOOT OF THE BED WHERE
Gammal lies, one hand resting on his shin, as if touching
only this impersonal part of his body will make it less real. I
say her name, but she doesn't hear; her eyes are large and unfocused.

"Dissa," I say, her given name bringing her gaze to me.

"I never thought it would happen," she says. "Seems an odd thing,
to not expect that death will come eventually."

"Not in Stille." I sit on the other side of my grandfather's bed and
reach for her hand, our fingers warm over his cold skin. "We are a land
of length and plenty."

She grimaces at my words, and the ghost of my older brother,
Purcell, seems to fill the room in contradiction.

"The old linger here," I go on. "It is not surprising for you to think
he would live until your own hair was thoroughly gray."

"Instead of only a few hairs," she says, fingering the tip of the
braid that rests on her shoulder. "And those that I have I blame your
father for."

Her hand is still with mine, but her mind is far away, the ghost of
a smile that had traced her lips turning bitter.

"Did you think you could change him?" I ask. We have never

shared words about my father, only glances that spoke of mutual opinion.

"It was foolish," she says. "But I was young, and never very pretty. And he the handsomest man in the kingdom, with enough noble blood to raise his chin in pride even higher."

"You are beautiful," I argue.

"You look at me with eyes of love, and that can change many things." She shakes her head. "If I ever carried the gaze of a room, it was because of the crown on my head."

Which she wears less now than I remember as a child. It cannot be because her pride in it has soured, because it imbues her very spine. I look at her now with the eyes of a man and see a broad nose, hair a little too coarse to invite touching, lips a shade too thin. If she wore the crown more often when I was younger, I realize now it was an attempt to recapture whatever lure it had held for my father. But that prize was claimed the day of their wedding and cannot be rescinded.

"Is there no way—"

"I have turned it over and over, like a stone in my mind," Mother says, guessing at the question before I ask it. "Maybe if I had been born in a different age, Stille would have accepted the king's daughter as their ruler and not her husband. But we are in dangerous times—a barren Given, and the blood of Stilleans soaking our doorstep."

I listen in silence, knowing she's right but feeling that her very argument presents reason for her to ascend rather than my father.

"In such times, would not the strongest ruler be the best choice?" I ask.

Mother shakes her head. "I lost the love of many when I brought Dara and Donil into our family. I know what they are called in the streets, and that sometimes my name is mentioned with theirs. No, Stille would not have me. Not after that."

"Varrick will not rule well," I warn.

"No," she agrees. "But you will follow, and because of that, I cannot regret my marriage. You will bring honor to my blood, though it is tainted with his."

I look again at our hands, the lines of blue veins pulsing beneath our skin.

She sighs, her eyes on Gammal once more. "I am glad he went now, before he could see the depths we will surely sink to."

"Madda?"

I call up the winding stairs to the Seer's room, but hear only a rustling in response. I clear the last few steps, calling ahead to announce my presence.

"What's this?" Madda's voice comes from the corner where she emerges from the gloom. "A fine young nobleman come to see me, and to find me in rags . . . how embarrassing."

"I wouldn't recognize you in anything else," I tell her, and she wags a finger at me.

"You don't know how true that is," she says with a wink. "Why, only yesterday I put on a pretty dress and pretended to be a sconcelighter. I think you may have flirted with me by accident."

"Quite by accident," I tell her, ignoring the tug of a smile on the corner of my lips. "You spend too much time alone."

"And what else am I to do? The king is for the ground, and no one asks the Seer what she thinks."

"I'm here," I argue, but she waves a hand at me.

"After the fact, long enough for him to grow cold, and your father's head already bowed under the crown. No, used to be the days when the Seer was sought before the Scribes and the noble council."

I take a seat at her table, shooing a mangy cat out of the way, its tail nearly catching in a lit candle as it growls displeasure at me. "Perhaps people cared more for magic in those days."

"Cared for it," Madda agrees, and takes the chair opposite me. "That, and there was more of it in the world."

"What do you mean?"

She watches me for a moment, and the cat jumps into her lap, its purr the only sound in the room. "I heard your Indiri girl took down the big tree in the encampment, pulled all its life for herself."

I nod, remembering too easily the flash of Dara's magically lit eyes, her hair streaming as if the ripples of life flowing from her own body made it move. Then she'd released it, the butterflies she created with that power flying away, taking with them all the attraction I'd felt. Or . . . almost all.

I clear my throat. "Yes, she did."

But my pause didn't go unnoticed, and Madda leans forward. "You liked it, didn't you?"

"Madda," I warn with a growl to match the cat's.

She leans back in her chair, still smiling. "What would Stille think of such a match, I wonder? Better yet, what would your Mother think? And"—she fakes a gasp as if something has just occurred to her— "where does that leave the lovely Given?"

"Mother's made herself clear enough on that point," I tell her, before I can think better of it.

"Ah, well," Madda shrugs. "Someone else can always breed her."

"Of course," I say, desperately trying to sound uncaring, but the words can barely get past my clenched teeth.

Madda bursts out laughing. "Ah, my poor young prince, you need to release some tension. Too bad the baker's girl is no longer in your service. You should find a playacting girl and ask her to teach you a thing or two. You could use some lessons on keeping a straight face."

"I'm sure if I took up with a stager, it would send tongues wagging," I say.

"And the Indiri running about town with her blades bloody, all the shows canceled until new girls are trained," she adds, and cackles again at my dark look.

"You were saying about magic?" I remind her.

She waves a hand in the air, as if it no longer matters. "I hear that your Indiri girl pulled a tree into herself, and the whole battle stalled to see it."

"It was a sight."

Madda *garrumphs* deep in her throat. "Only because it goes unseen now, a display like that. When the Pietra slaughtered the Indiri, their bodies went back to the dirt, but I still think something was taken from the earth, nonetheless. Our land falls away, and there is only one female of a hated race left who can use magic, and it weak as an oderbird with a broken wing."

"Our land falls away," I repeat her words. "You think the rising tides sap Dara's magic?"

"I think the girl can do very little on her own. She has to drain strength from another, and that is a deed best left undone."

"Why?"

"Because it's a death, sure as slitting a throat," Madda says, finally reaching across the table for my hands. She pats the soft inside of my wrist reassuringly, her face suddenly serious as she pulls a candle closer to us. Her touch is warm and sure, resurrecting memories from when my hands were smaller, her chambers a mysterious place where I might ask if there was a new horse in my future, or if my father and mother were going to fight again.

"A death," I say. "Certainly not the first at Dara's hands."

"No," Madda agrees, "but she is of the earth and took one of her kind—only a tree, sure, but it's a living thing. She pulled its life to fill a hole inside her, one that I fear grows even as she does. She's more alone than even I am, up here in my tower. And a creature alone will fold into itself, feed its own fears."

"Dara fears nothing."

"Dara fears being alone," Madda shoots back. "And she's right to do so, if her eyes fall on you, and yours on the Given."

"Is there nothing about me people don't know?" I ask.

"They don't know what's in your palms," she assures me, my hands tight in her bony grip. "What's in the skin is between you and me."

We lean forward together, old head bent to young, my hands spread before us like Khosa's maps.

If only they were inked so clearly, and my choices easily made.

CHAPTER 39

─◦○◦─

Dara

"How goes it?"

Dara's voice no longer carries across leagues, but the sound of it makes Vincent jump, regardless.

"I didn't know you were there," he says as she emerges from the shadows to take a seat across from him, the low fire providing the only light in the great hall.

"I'm always somewhere." Dara slips off her muddy boots and curls her feet under her in the chair. "So—how goes it?"

"It was a clean shot. Khosa's healer says it'll close in a few days. She hit her head pretty hard—"

"I'm asking about you," Dara interrupts. "I assume Khosa is fine because the whole castle isn't wailing fit to end the world."

"No, their mourning is more the quiet kind."

"As is yours," Dara says gently. "Battle tactics aside, Ank was right about one thing. Your grandfather was a good man."

"I know," Vincent says, eyes on the fire. "And I can't help but wonder . . ." He trails off, loyalty to his bloodline closing his mouth.

"Say what you will, Vin. I've seen you naked. Might as well know what's on the inside, too."

Despite his mood, a smile cracks Vincent's mouth. "You haven't seen me naked since we were children."

"You can't have changed too much."

He tosses a throw pillow at her, which she catches easily. "I have, thank you," he says.

She laughs, tucking the pillow behind her head and giving him a minute of silence before pressing on. "Come on, then. Out with it."

Vincent glances around to be sure they are alone before continuing. "The quiet in the castle makes me feel as if the people mourn not only the passing of Gammal, but also the end of his reign."

"Ah," Dara says, understanding. "And the beginning of your father's."

"Yes," Vincent nods. "Ank said he wouldn't fight a man he could respect, but he'd go to war against one he could hate. Truly, Dara, what do you think of my father?"

Dara looks away from him, back to the fire. "I think he is a man."

"Lovely help you are."

"No, Vin." Dara pins him with her eyes, remnants of stolen life still flickering in their depths. "I think he is a *man* before anything else, king or otherwise."

"Dara, if he—"

"I can take care of myself, Vincent," she says, the fire in her eyes a thousand times brighter than the one that burns in front of them. He stares unabashedly, nearly as lost as he was on the battlefield.

"After you brought down the tree, why did Donil tell you to . . ."

"Release it? Because when I steal life like that, it fills me, gives me strength. But I took too much, and it overflowed onto everything around me. Life . . ." Her words flutter, her cheeks reddening in a way that has nothing to do with heat from the fire. She clears her throat, trying again.

"Life wants to celebrate being alive," she says.

"Ah . . . ," Vincent says, color rising in his own face as he remembers how Dara had affected him, the uncontrollable need for her that had risen. "But you didn't let it all go, did you?"

"There is a splinter of it lurking inside me still," she admits. "It will burn off in a few days."

"I can see it," he says, his voice hitching slightly.

"Yes, and you feel it," she adds, eyes avoiding his.

"Yes." He rises from his chair, cutting the distance between them, his fingers finding her speckled ones. "Dara—"

"I should go." She rises abruptly, pulling her hand from his.

Vincent reaches for her again, confused. "But I thought you—"

"I do." She cuts him off, almost violently. "I do," she says again, quietly. "But not because you can't help it. Not how Donil does it."

"What do you mean?"

"Tides," Dara mutters under her breath. "It's not the way it sounds."

"Dara." Vincent's voice is suddenly cold. "What do you mean *how Donil does it*? Is that why girls always—" He breaks off, anger closing his throat until he manages a laugh, the sound coming out choked. "And I thought he was just handsome."

"He *is* handsome," Dara bites back in her brother's defense. "Now, hear me out, or I'll tear your ears off."

Vincent goes back to his seat, but Dara remains standing, arms crossed.

"The Indiri are ancient," she begins. "Even with fighting buried in our bones and memories carried in our heads, Donil and I could spend our whole lifetimes and never learn everything there is to know of our people. It's all *here*." She points to her forehead. "But we have to look for it."

"I know all this." Vincent's voice is laden with impatience.

"Yes, you know us best, and yet you know the Indiri not at all. You can't possibly, when we ourselves learn something new every day. Our hands will turn to a task we think unfamiliar only to find our fingers know what to do because our grandmothers' did. When I pulled life from the earth, it was a reflex, my battle instincts telling me I needed strength and my body simply taking it, and it was done badly. I regret taking down that tree more than any Feneen."

Dara picks up a length of her hair and begins to braid it, her fingers moving as quickly as her words.

"The Indiri are earth. And if you know anything of nature, you know that it excels at two things—life and death. The trees are heavy with the nests of oderbirds in the spring, but how many fall to the ground before they can fly, their helplessness easy fodder for Tangata kittens just learning to kill?"

"Many," Vincent says, remembering a vision from his childhood, a Tangata sitting lazily beneath a nest as the baby oderbirds tried to fly. Tried and failed, not knowing they only had the one chance. He picked up a stick, and was about to run at the cat in all his foolishness when Dara had stopped him, a chain of salium in her hair.

It is the way of it, she said then.

"It is the way of it," he repeats now.

"It is. Death follows life, and life returns again, only to find the same shadow behind."

"What does this have to do with the Indiri, and Donil?" Vincent asks.

"We are the earth," Dara says, tying off her braid, fingers finding a new lock of hair to toy with. "Each Indiri has an inclination toward life or death. Which is why my blade flashes a bit faster than Donil's, why my voice can convince a tree to lay down its life at my request. Donil can't help what he is. When we were children, the animals of the forest would come to him."

Vincent nods, remembering snakes curling around Donil as he stood like a stone, his entire body a writhing mass of poison that he didn't fear. "Yes. Donil could call anything to him."

"And now . . . ," Dara prompts.

"And now we are older, and it is women who answer," Vincent finishes.

"It cannot be helped any more than you can help that you are of royal blood and bound to the throne by it. I give him some salt about it, but truth be told, I think he turns away many. He knows the difference between winning a woman who wants him for him and having one who is responding only to his body's call."

"And that's what you think you're doing to me?" Vincent dares to stand, approaching her next to the fire. "Using the life you took and making me want you?"

Dara studies the flames, tying off her last braid with an efficient twist. "I would have you on my own terms, and you never looked at me before."

"You don't know that," Vincent says, and she turns her head in surprise. "You were spilling death from your lips when you talked down that tree in the woods, and I suddenly saw a woman where the girl from my childhood had been."

His words hang in the air, which stretches tight between them.

"Our childhood," Dara echoes. "Do you remember the vow we made?"

"We said if neither of us found a suitable spouse before a gray hair, we'd marry," Vincent says, the words so close to his tongue she knew they had been in his mind more than once in the passing years.

"A vow made by those who were little, and knew the same, Vin. Childish minds that took no account of my skin, the throne, the will of the people, or your own mother."

"There can be no marriage between us, but . . ." Vincent agrees, and though she had said as much in her own words, his cut her to the bone because of the opening he left after.

"I am no baker's daughter," she snaps.

"No, you and Donil ensnare with more than a well-cut hip or head of hair," Vincent shoots back, angered by the rejection. "You draw others to yourselves like a Pietran Lure, but at least Donil makes use of his catch. You throw yours back to the sea, damage already done."

Most women slap, but Dara's hand knows the shape of a fist better than an open palm. When she punches Vincent in the face, he's knocked to the floor.

"I'll damage you all right, Vin, and worse than that if you dare to propose to have me as a kept woman again. Do you understand?"

"Yes, I understand," he says from the floor, touching the trickle of blood that seeps from his nose. "I understand that I never had a chance."

And Dara knows that it's not her he speaks of but Khosa. The anger she has left slips away, and she sinks to the floor beside him, the broken parts of each of their hearts unable to make a whole.

"Me neither, Vin," she says.

CHAPTER 40

Khosa

WHEN MY GUARDS COME TO A QUICK ATTENTION, THEIR mail rattles, pulling me out of the history I study and jerking my hand, which sends hot tea splashing onto my wrist. I hiss but otherwise ignore the pain, instead coming to my feet as the guards had.

For the queen has come to visit.

"Your Highness," I say, instinctively dropping into the deep curtsy that was taught to me as soon as I could stand on two legs, though it would come into use only when those same legs took me to Stille.

"Please, as you were," Dissa says, motioning to both myself and the guards, though I doubt they take her quite so literally, as one of them had been nearly asleep.

I go back to my bench, and the queen follows me there, her full skirts moving through the rushes and bringing an unfamiliar perfume into my library. The room is more hers than mine, and though I know it well, I can't help but feel an ownership for a place that she's yet to grace with her presence in my time here.

"Are you healing well?" the queen asks.

I lightly touch my shoulder where a bandage rests beneath my clothes. "Yes," I tell her. "The salve from your healer has done its work, and there is hardly any pain."

"And how goes your work?" Dissa asks.

This is a subject I can take to easily, the one thing I can speak of that won't involve practice and concentration, each gesture and word carefully thought out in the ever-fought battle for normalcy. I prattle on about tides and dates, fiverberries and Dara's third-great-grandmother, before I realize that the queen is watching me more carefully than she is listening.

"I forget myself in talk of the past," I tell her, pushing aside a sheet of my calculations. "I should have offered my condolences before anything else. I was sorry to hear of your father's death."

The queen accepts with a nod of her head, but I'm well trained in smiles, and hers does not meet her eyes. "I imagine it is hard to stay in touch with what goes on outside of the walls, when one is as isolated as you are."

"It is," I say slowly, searching for the buried meaning that is surely in her words. "I have left the castle only once, when Vincent—"

"Yes, when my son risked much to give you a moment of freedom," she interrupts. "Of late I have wondered what more he would wager on your behalf."

Tones and small gestures I cannot interpret, but words I can decipher, and she does not cloak these. My eyes drop to my wrist, and the angry burn left in the wake of spilled tea.

"The prince does not care for me beyond what is seemly," I say.

"I wish I were so sure," Dissa says. "A mother knows much, and what I've learned from watching him since your arrival could fill one of your books, if there were a language to write it in."

I meet her eyes, daring her to call me liar again.

"All things can be written," I say. "And between us there is nothing that could not be read by his own mother, or that would make a Scribe blush to copy."

Dissa is quiet, studying me. "I believe it is so, on your own part. But what of his?"

"I cannot speak for the prince more than I could a sea-spine," I tell her.

"And that is as it should be," she says, placing her hand on mine and holding it tight when I try to pull away. "It is the sea-spine you are meant for, and not my son."

I fake no courtesies as she rises to leave, the guards' faces as unreadable as my own as she sweeps past them. Outwardly, I return to my work, and I have no doubt that my guards find me a cold fish indeed, to be so unruffled by a royal threat. But inside I am reeling, for I have myself wondered if Vincent's feelings for me have intensified, and if so, what to do about it.

I lose myself in pages and ink, until there is a tapping at the door and my heart leaps at the familiarity of the pattern. Donil's knock is always hesitant, asking my permission before entering the library—a place that I've just been forcefully reminded I won't occupy for long. He enters at my nod with the same easy confidence as always, and I feel my face twist as the emotions I've tamped down force their way out.

"Khosa?" His own smile falls away at the sight of my distress, and I wave to the guards.

"Leave us," I say, my voice tight as I struggle to cap the rage I feel at the knowing glance they share, even if I am grateful when they judiciously shut the doors behind them.

"What is it?" Donil asks, and I go to him without preamble, falling into his arms as all the strength I've held on to by my very fingernails since escaping Hyllen leaves me in a rush. His arms circle me, and I sag against him, a deep sob rising in my chest.

He lowers us both to the floor and lets me cry, not asking for explanation. I revel in the safety of his touch, the brush of our skin, the only touch I've ever borne without revulsion. Since I was small I'd seen children run to their mothers, wives to their husbands, friends to one another, and never known the draw that made them do so. Until now. There is comfort within Donil's arms, and safety. And undeniably, buried deep but churning through us both, a throb of desire.

"What is it?" he asks softly, his breath stirring the fine hairs around my ear. "What has you so troubled?"

A gasp of fresh air does nothing but give strength to a new bout of tears, and he draws me even closer, our bodies pressed together, both of us surrounded by the pile of my skirts on the floor around us.

"The queen was here to visit me," I finally tell him, as he dries my tears with the hem of his shirt.

"She's not so frightening," he chides.

"She's a mother, and there is nothing so ferocious in nature as that," I correct him. "I was warned away from her son."

"Ah," Donil says, glancing away from me. "I didn't realize your heart went in that direction."

His jaw is tense, the pulse of anger at my words betrayed by the smallest flicker of muscles jumping beneath speckled skin. I reach for him, drawing his gaze back to mine and letting my fingers trail across his lips.

"It doesn't," I say.

He closes the distance between us, and my world is no longer made of water, but fire. In Hyllen I had often lain in my loft bed, wondering how any act of intimacy was performed, how nakedness could be seen and not bring shame, how embarrassment could be overrun by need. In only the space of a few moments, I know, as my body screams for his so loudly its voice alone would shed my dress if my hands weren't already at work. I don't know whether to tear at my own clothes or his, but then my fingers are buried in his hair and our mouths are saying things to each other with no words, things that have grown between us in more innocent hours.

"Khosa," he says, voice heavy as if drunk. "Khosa, wait."

I'm on my back in the rushes, hair spilling down my shoulders. "Wait?" I ask, partly brazen, partly confused.

"I can't do this," he says, rising off of me.

"You don't want me?"

"Tides, woman," he says, shaking his head. "I only wish I didn't." He pulls me onto my knees beside him, and I arrange my dress back into decency.

"Khosa," he says gently, hand finding mine, though we both still tremble with need. "What if I should get you with child?"

"It is my purpose," I remind him. "And you are my choice."

"And fulfilling the role would give me great joy. Until it was truly done, and then my love the reason your body floated in the sea."

"That *will* be," I remind him pressing my palm against his. "Whether by you or another man, I go to the water."

"And your child after you," he says. "Dara would drag me to the depths if one of the last Indiri was meant for the waves."

I untangle my fingers from his and rise, presenting him with my back. "Are your sister's wishes so great that they outweigh both yours and mine?"

Behind me, Donil sighs as he gets to his feet. "I have a role to fill, same as you, Khosa, same as Vincent. Though it seems we're all damned whichever way we turn."

The door slams as he leaves, sending the rushes at my feet trembling as much as my hands, hands that have just now learned the thrill of a touch, only to have it taken away.

CHAPTER 41

———— ∘⟨◯⟩∘ ————

Witt

WITT RUBS HIS FINGERS AGAINST THE ROUGH UNDER-
side of the table, picking at the sharp edges of splinters that
catch his skin. It serves to keep him focused as the long
parade of Pietran problems and requests comes to face him.

"You need to collect what, again?" He asks the Hyllenian shepherd
to repeat himself.

"Coilweed, my lord," the man says.

"My Lithos," Pravin, seated next to Witt, corrects him. "In Pietra
you face your leader on equal footing. The Lithos sits on the throne
only to deliver judgment. Today he sits in a chair like any other."

Witt is acutely aware of the fact that his chair is like any other,
on this day of all days. The Hyllenians were surprised that they
would have a chance, along with any Pietra, to speak to the Lithos.
The Pietra had not been pleased when some Hyllenians were spared
death, and more than a few fights among the two peoples had broken out.

As a result, the line of supplicants is much longer than usual. He's
been receiving all day. Witt's backside hurts, his head is pounding, and
his lungs feel as if they might collapse under the pressure of inhaling

the indoor air, stale with so many complaints. A sliver of wood slides underneath his thumbnail, painfully bringing him to the present.

"And what do you need coilweed for, shepherd?"

"It's time to take the tails off the young lambs, my lo—my Lithos. The coilweed, it reaches for other plants, squeezes the life out of those around it so that it can have all the sun, all the rain, for itself."

"I know what coilweed *is*." Witt pulls the splinter out from his nail with his teeth and spits it onto the table between them. "Why should I let you go looking for it?"

"Because the lambs . . . they're born with long tails, see? They can get stepped on, scraped open, fester. We take a bit of the coilweed, and it snaps around the tail at the base, pinches it off in a few days."

Pravin leans back from the table. "And you think *we're* depraved?"

"It only hurts for a moment, sir. Once it coils tight, they can't feel it. Like tying a string real tight about your finger. It's how we do the castrations, too."

Pravin covers his face with his hands. "That's knowledge I didn't need."

The shepherd looks between the Lithos and the Mason, his hands rubbing together nervously. "I thought maybe you would. For . . . for the next Lithos."

It is Witt's turn to cover his face, hiding the smile that blooms there for a moment.

"The Lithos is . . ." Pravin searches for a word, his color deepening. "Intact. He takes no one to his bed by choice. It is a sacrifice he makes for his people, as the Lithos cannot be distracted."

"Begging your pardon, but it can still be distracting, someone in your bed or no."

"Coilweed," Witt says loudly. "How much do you need?"

"I'd say a basketful, pulled properly along with the roots so we can plant them within distance of our flock to harvest at need," the shepherd says. "It grows easy as rankflower. I doubt I'd have to go far to find some."

"I'll send two of my men with you. And you'll be back by sundown, or we'll practice your methods on your own skin."

"Yes, my lo—my Lithos." The shepherd backs out of the room, nodding to Witt and Pravin as he does.

"A moment before the next one, please," Pravin calls to the guard at the door.

"And would you mind bringing something from the kitchen?" Witt asks the Keeper, who stands in the shadows of the hall. She nods and turns away, Pravin's frown following her exit.

"You've taken to keeping her close."

"I have. But not for any reason you need fear, intact or not." Witt stands, stretching his limbs and judging the passing of the day by the slanted light coming in through the window. "We've been at it all morning and a good part of the high hours."

"Bringing sheep and farmers into a world of stone and water was bound to set some tongues wagging. Let them have their words. They say them to the Lithos and leave without the weight of them. Besides, some of the Hyllenian women are not difficult to look at. A few high tides, and the Pietra will grow accustomed to them. The next Lithos will be sitting at this table across from their children, no doubt."

"With the water pooling at their heels," Witt says darkly.

"We can only do as we always have," Pravin says. "Send the dead to the sea to spare the land, and claim every last inch of earth for our people."

The door at the end of the hall is thrown open suddenly, banging against the stone wall and bringing Pravin to his feet, Witt's hand to his sword. A Pietran soldier runs toward them, face drenched in sweat.

"I'm sorry, my Lithos," the guard calls, hurrying to catch up. "He would not wait."

"It *cannot* wait," the soldier spits back, turning to Witt. "My Lithos, the guards who were taken by the Feneen have returned, bringing one with them."

"Bring their prisoner to me," Witt says.

"I think you'll find, sir, that it's the other way around."

Witt has no need of slivers under his fingernails, or the rough texture of wood grain against his hands to keep his attention focused. The man sitting across from him has spurred him into battle-readiness, though it is not the kind of engagement that would require any weapons other than words. Witt takes the measure of the Feneen quietly, well aware of the same being done to him.

"You took some of my men," he says.

"Rather easily," the Feneen answers. "And one horse. But I've brought them all back to you, having seen sights they'll not soon forget."

Witt's eyes flick to the Pietra who were returned. They stand, stripped of their armor and flanking the Feneen called Ank, almost as if they are his guards instead of soldiers in Witt's army.

"And what sights would those be?" Pravin asks them.

"I saw men melded with cats, sir," one of them answers, staring straight ahead. "Feneen who could not walk, submitting to be sewn onto Tangata in order to fight for their people."

"A show of loyalty, to be sure," Witt agrees. "But no more stunning than our own people who line the cliffs when the time has come to build their boats."

"Pardon me, my Lithos, but no," the other soldier says. "The Pietra who can no longer be of use to their people willingly go to the Lusca, a solitary death on an endless sea. The Feneen who believed themselves useless chose pain in order to become an asset. They rode wild animals into an enemy camp, knowing that even should they survive the battle, they would never dismount."

A prickle of irritation rises along Witt's spine. "You sound like you admire them."

"Is it so unbelievable?" Ank asks.

"What enemy were these Feneen set against?" Pravin asks, and Witt silently curses himself for not asking the more important question first.

"The same one you would conquer," Ank says. "Stille."

"What argument do the Feneen have with Stille and King Gammal?" Witt wills the growing uneasiness in his belly to not reflect in his words.

"The same argument any child would have against a parent who set them aside," Ank says easily. "More than half our numbers are Stillean born, and the walls of the city closed to them though they drew their first breaths inside of it. As for Gammal, one cannot argue with a dead man."

Pravin sits up straighter in his chair, and Witt leans forward. "You killed the king?"

"Not myself." Ank holds the younger man's gaze. "But I saw him fall."

Witt looks to the Pietra standing on either side of Ank. "It's true, my Lithos," one of them says.

"It seems you have done us a great favor," Witt concedes.

"I believe we can do more," Ank says. "We have an army of fighters, recently blooded."

"Pietra does not need favors, or soldiers sewn onto animals," Witt says brusquely, rising to end the meeting.

"And how does Pietra feel about the loss of its own in exchange for its leader keeping his pride?"

Witt's upper lip curls. "What loss would be that be, when you openly return what you take from me?"

"I speak of the Pietran dead when you take the field against Stille. As an army, they're laughable, but a lifetime of weeding your weak has left you outnumbered, and while your fish may feed bellies, I do not believe they are quite full."

"One Pietra is worth five Stilleans in the field," Pravin says.

"And if they outnumber you seven to one?"

"Then it's their blood flowing ankle deep," Witt growls.

"But they're the only ones left standing," Ank answers. "Even the strength of your cliffs is eroded by the sea, and the Stilleans are as many as the sea is endless."

Pravin and Witt exchange a glance, a lifetime spent together making their communication as easy as speech.

"What are you offering?" Witt finally asks.

"Feneen to fight for you. First on the field and last off of it. Send us headlong into terror, put us against the best of the Stilleans. Three Feneen to fall for every Pietra who even crosses blades with the enemy."

"In exchange for?"

"When the dust is settled and the blood dry, the Feneen who are left accepted as Pietra, equal in measure."

It was cleverly done, and Witt knew it. If he were to send Ank away, the Pietran soldiers who were returned would let their people know the Lithos rejected a Feneen offer of lives willingly given in battle, lives spent before Pietran soldiers were even endangered. With many already grumbling against him for the wandering sheep and buds of green grain, Witt could hardly afford more voices lending to their volume.

The offer was generous, but the price higher than the Feneen knew. The barb from before had hit harder than intended; Pietran pride ran deep, and not only in Witt. His people disliked the inclusion of the Hyllenians—and as Pravin had pointed out, they were pleasing enough to look at, and provided them with food and livestock, as well. Their customs were different, but the Pietra knew work when they saw it, and the Hyllenians labored as hard as any.

But what Ank asked was something more. If Witt put the unable and truly monstrous alongside those who got into boats once they could no longer contribute, he'd have more than a few turn against him. But as Ank had said, that would come when the battle was over, when there might not be many Feneen left to accept.

"What makes you think my men would even fight with yours?"

"They'll adjust to the men. It's the women who will take getting used to," Ank says.

"Your women . . . fight?" Witt is not able to keep the incredulity from his voice.

"Fierce as the men and some even more so. Why not let them have a weapon if they're willing to wield it?"

"Because it's unseemly," Pravin says.

Ank's affable nature slides away like rain from a downturned Hadundun leaf. "Don't speak to me of unseemly, when you put the old in boats, sending lifetimes of knowledge to the bottom of the sea."

Pravin leans toward the Feneen across the table, his color high. "And don't you lecture me about respect for elders, with that smooth face of yours. You're not much older than the Lithos, and I a lifetime of suffering behind."

"I've seen more than you know, and have more years than you can guess," Ank says easily. "I was there when you brought us your son."

Pravin freezes, and Witt's hand goes to his advisor's elbow, aware that with this man, the calm usually comes before the storm.

"Impossible," Witt says, to which the Feneen only raises an eyebrow and pushes his sleeves up, resting his hands on the table between them. They are old and twisted, marked with the spots of time and the swelling of joints.

"I am Feneen," Ank says evenly. "Anything is possible."

Words desert Witt, and he feels Pravin's arm go loose in surprise under his hand.

"What is this deception?" the Mason asks.

"No deception." Ank slides his hands back under his sleeves. "Only myself, as I was born. Some years before you imagine."

"We'll need some time to consider, of course." Witt finds his voice, though his tongue is dry in his mouth, the image of Ank's hands still before his eyes, though they are no longer in sight.

Ank nods in agreement, but his words hold a warning. "Do not wait overly long to make your decision. That was your mistake years ago," he adds to Pravin. "If you'd brought the babe a day earlier, we could have saved it."

Witt expects a lunge, and his hands tighten, but Pravin remains still.

"I've driven much harder bargains," Witt says, striving to keep his tone light. "Dead Feneen in exchange for living Pietra? I won't take overly long to decide."

"There is one more condition," Ank says. "You must take a Feneen wife."

It is so unexpected that Witt bursts out laughing, the sound startling Pravin back to life.

"The Lithos has sworn off women," he objects.

"That's his mistake," Ank says. "One to be rectified. I've lived a long life with no expectation to see the waters rise much farther. You striking a bargain with me is all well and good, but who is to say that you will honor it once I am gone? A Feneen wife for the Lithos would show your people that we can be accepted."

"And ensure my death by her hand or one of my own guards for abandoning our traditions," Witt says. "A Lithos taking a wife is as ludicrous as . . . as . . ."

"As a soldier who is one with a Tangata? As a man with the face of a child and the hands of experience?" Ank asks, one eyebrow raised. "We are the Feneen. We change as necessary to survive. The Pietra could take a lesson from us."

Witt rises to signal the meeting is over, choking back angry words that will only degenerate the debate to an exchange of insults. Ank makes him uneasy, his responses coming so quick on the heels of anything they say, as if he anticipates their every word and has answers for them all.

"We'll speak in three days' time." Witt offers his hand across the table as bond.

Ank's withered hand emerges, pressing against Witt's. The Feneen's skin feels like paper too often handled, thin and on the verge of tearing. Witt grinds his teeth to keep from gagging, and inexplicably, a true smile breaks across Ank's face, the youth there shining, despite the broken teeth that his lips reveal.

Taken aback, Witt's words slip out before he can weigh whether they should be spoken. "Why do you smile, when you offer your people to die for my own?"

The old hand squeezes his, a pulse of unmistakable affection buried there. "Because this world is endlessly amusing when the Lithos of Pietra is a better man than the king of Stille."

CHAPTER 42

———⚬◯⚬———

Vincent

"M Y LORD." THE SCONCELIGHTER SLIDES TO A HALT IN front of me, cap askew, her torch long extinguished in her rush to find me. Smoke floats in her wake, and I choke on it before questioning her.

"What is it? Is Khosa—"

She shakes her head, draws a shaky breath. "No, my lord, all is well with the Given. It's the Seer who sent me for you."

"Madda?" I turn, headed back the way the girl came. "Is she unwell?"

"I . . ." A polite hesitancy edges her voice, and I call back over my shoulder.

"More unwell than usual?"

"That's what sent me at such a pace, my lord," she says, pulling her skirts up past her ankles to keep up with me. "She's on a bit of a tear . . ."

Madda on a tear is not a sight I've ever seen, and is certainly not one for a servant. "You're excused," I say tersely, leaving her no choice but to return to her work, cut off from choice gossip.

I charge up the circular staircase to find Madda pacing in her tower room, sending tendrils of incense smoke swirling behind her.

She's muttering under her breath, hands wringing each other in search of comfort.

"Madda?" I say softly, pulling a torch from the wall to light what the sconcelighter had left untouched. "What troubles you?"

She turns at my voice, errant steps finally halted. "Much, young prince," she says. "Much and more. Sit."

Gone is the teasing Seer I know, who laughs at my romantic predicaments and finds the future of only mild interest. I take my familiar stool and offer her my hand. Her mouth quirks as she sees something there, and she falls into a routine, massaging the tiny bones in my hands, touching the slight webbing between my fingers.

She hums to herself softly, a Stillean lullaby that Mother still falls into out of habit when she works on her bridal pillow. It permeates the room, easing some of the tension from the air, and setting even my heart into a more normal rhythm, my mind onto paths it has traveled much of late.

Dara has not spoken to me in days, a flush rising in her skin and her eyes avoiding mine when we meet in the halls, reluctant to be near me after her confession of desire, met by my own and no release for either of us. I know that I appear much the same to Donil. My words to him are stilted and carefully selected, with an undertone of anger he identifies without knowing what he's done to deserve it.

I've taken lives, seen the friends of my youth covered in blood and reveling in it. The very pulses of our bodies are at odds with each other these days, disturbing childhood ties. Donil's blood calls to every woman who walks by, Dara's yearns for me, and mine is confused even as it flows from heart to mind—Khosa fills one and Dara the other. At times, the two change places and send me into a spiral that I can only call despair.

Madda's lullaby arcs, breaking into my reverie and drawing my thoughts to her, and her soft touch upon me.

"What has put you in such a state?" I ask.

She finishes the song before answering, the last bars threading off into nothing.

"I know when time is spent," she says, finally. "It's not only the royals who come to me, you know. I may have books with the inkprints of your line's palms back to the time of the wave, but in the past few years, the hands of the shepherds and curriers have said more than your ancestors, for all their importance."

"How so?"

"Their lines unwind, like spools of thread cut too soon. Many and more as time goes. The lines in the hands of Stilleans grow short. This morning a mother brought her baby to me. One whose palms were as smooth as his cheeks."

"How is that possible?" I ask, a spike of fear rising in my belly.

"Ask the Given," Madda spouts. "Ask the last of the Indiri, with no mates to be found. Ask them about a life with no future."

Madda releases my hands, and I put them in my lap, curled into each other like frightened Tangata kits. "And what of mine?"

It's her turn to sigh, the exhalation of nilflower filling my nose. "Young prince," she says, "I cannot speak for the Given, for I have never seen her hands. But I can say that you are surely headed for the sea."

CHAPTER 43

◦─◦◯◦─◦

Vincent

I T'S ALL ROT. DON'T LET IT FESTER YOUR MIND," DONIL TELLS me as he slings his sword across his shoulders, a runnel of sweat streaking down his nose.

We've spent an entire day at training with no time for words. Our sword arms as we demonstrated simple attacks and parries for the men provided a familiarity we fell into from habit, though I admit that my sword may have fallen more heavily than necessary. The thought of his Indiri blood calling more loudly to Khosa than mine lent some violence to my actions. But it is spent now and words came easily afterward, as I confess that Madda's words scared me badly.

I sheathe my own sword. "It's not all rot, though. Madda's told me things before that—"

"Like what?" Donil interrupts, returning the waves of a few men as they leave the field, his place among them more assured since he has bested them all at swordplay. The Indiri sits on an upturned log used for archery practice, kicking another onto its side for me. I sit, about to answer his question.

"Wait—let me guess." Donil grabs my hand and turns it over, brow furrowed in mock concentration. "You're . . . destined for great things. You may even be king."

"Go jump in the sea," I say, jerking my hand away.

"I didn't get to the good part yet. You're going to marry a girl and have children. You may own horses. You'll never go swimming."

Donil's laugh is infectious, even more so when I kick his seat out from under him, sending him rolling onto the ground, his shirt pushed up to show his speckled torso.

"Hey Donil, how far down do your spots go?" a kitchen girl calls as she passes by, a plucked chicken in each hand.

"Ask Daisy, if you want to know," he yells back, still laughing.

My own laughter dies as the girl smiles at Donil, eyes bright with invitation. When they slip to me she dips a quick curtsy, but that is all. By the time Donil rights his seat and is on it again, I am troubled once more.

"Madda," I reiterate. "She's told me things—admittedly vague, but accurate enough that her saying I'm headed for the sea made me dream of waves, and I woke with the taste of salt water in my throat."

Donil lays his sword across his knees, finally serious. "Your ways aren't mine, brother. The Indiri know the past because it is a thing already done. To lay claim to what lies ahead implies it is already decided, the actions only waiting to be fulfilled and you powerless to do nothing but."

"Am I not?" I ask. "I don't need my palms to see a line pointing to the throne, and me on it."

"So leave. If you don't want to be king, don't become one."

"And what shall I do? Leave my people on the brink of war for what purpose?"

"Come with Dara and me. We always find adventure wherever the king sends us, no matter how idle the task. Whether collecting tariffs or hunting bandits, a ride is a cure for restlessness. And, between you and me and where we sit, Dara's more restless than is safe lately."

My gaze goes to the wall that has been raised around the field after the Feneen attack, Dara bringing down trees day after day to make a safe place for the Stilleans to drill. I can see her moving among the men in the distance, hauling the last of the logs into place alongside them, her strength welcome even if they still shy away from her skin.

"What do you mean, restless?" I ask.

Donil scrapes some mud away from his ankle. "I mean that we need to find her an Indiri male, and then everyone can sleep more easily. Her included. Or, perhaps not." He rolls the mud into a ball and flicks it at my nose.

I bat it out of the air more violently than necessary. "There aren't any Indiri males left besides yourself. And I don't think you do much sleeping in your own nights, *brother*."

Our banter is the same as ever, but Donil catches my tone.

"Is that it, then? Daisy said that you'd excused Milda. Do you want me to say something to Anna or one of the kitchen girls? I'm sure any of them would be happy to—"

"No," I say, loudly enough to turn heads at the archery range.

"Depths, brother. Lower your voice unless you want the whole of the kingdom to know their prince needs a tumble."

"If that is in fact what I need, I think I can manage it on my own," I spit. "I may not be able to quicken a girl's liking by my very nature, but I do have a thing or two to offer, one of them being the throne."

"Which you were lamenting a moment ago," Donil reminds me.

"Not that it's ever helped," I tear on. "I could be wearing the crown, but with you beside me, their eyes will always land there, drawn by . . . by . . ."

"Ah . . ." Donil drops his eyes. "Dara must have told you."

"Dara says many things to me," I say.

"What does that mean?" Donil's head jerks up. "She's meant for an Indiri, Vincent, and if you *ever*—"

"There are no more Indiri!"

Donil comes to his feet, and I rise with him. "Even if that were true, Dara will settle for nothing less than a throne for her children."

"I can't marry Dara," I yell, ignoring the glances we're attracting. "Stille wouldn't have it."

"Then you can't have *her*," Donil seethes, closing the distance between us.

We grew up as brothers, and fights that began with small fists flying ended with arms slung about shoulders, black eyes forgiven as scrapes healed. But now we know how to throw punches that draw blood, and the words that pass between us aren't easily forgotten during a game of ridking.

"I believe I'll decide who can or cannot have me, brother." Dara's voice breaks over us, and we turn to find her watching, arms crossed.

"And as for there being no more Indiri," she says to me, "I'll not rest until I know. And after that . . ." Her lips twist into a hard smile I've only seen on the battlefield when she's about to deal a killing blow.

"I can have the Stillean throne without you in my bed."

CHAPTER 44

Khosa

I REACH FOR THE INKWELL TOO QUICKLY AS A LINE FROM the histories catches my eye, and a little gasp escapes as pain shoots across my chest. Merryl is at my elbow in a moment.

"Are you well?" he asks.

"Fine, Merryl, thank you," I say, the pain giving my words more inflection than usual. "I forget sometimes that I'm still wounded." I don't add that I had healed almost entirely before rolling around on this very floor with Donil loosened my stitches.

"Mmm . . ." is all he says, his eyes going to the bandage on my chest, where a fresh spot of red blooms.

"Your fellow guard did only what he thought was best," I remind him.

"Perhaps," Merryl's eyes lingering on my wound, lit only with concern and no hint of lechery. "Yet I worry that a man who would shoot a girl would not hesitate to . . ."

My eyebrows raise. "To?"

"To harm her otherwise," he finishes.

"I appreciate your concern, Merryl. But the Given has always chosen her mate, and if the next child for the sea is born from force, who knows what the waves would make of it?"

It's the threat I've leaned on myself time and again, in the darkness of my own chamber whenever I hear footsteps outside my door, my guards straightening at their approach.

"Perhaps," Merryl says again, and glances over his shoulder at his fellow guard, slumped against the stone in the heat of the day, a thin line of drool leaking from his mouth.

I put down my quill. "Speak freely."

Merryl takes off his helm, and for the first time I see his face clearly. It is not much older than my own, but already heavy with care. He sits next to me, resting an arm on the table, but careful not to disturb my papers.

"It's true that no Given has had violence done to her in the past," he says. "But . . . that was the past. And a different king on the throne."

"You do not have faith in King Varrick?"

"I do not have faith in every man," Merryl says, evading treason neatly. "And in the barracks there are talks of . . ." He pauses again, choosing words carefully. "Talks of a reward being offered for—"

"For impregnating me," I finish, for once grateful for the cold, clipped tones I produce.

"Yes." Merryl raises his eyes to mine. "By any means."

"I see."

"Some of the men vie for the duty of guarding you. If fate handed you two guards of a similar mind, I fear the result."

I nod; even the pinched tones I do manage have clogged in my throat.

"You can request your own guards. Myself, of course, and I can provide you with the names of others who are trustworthy."

"I would appreciate that."

"But . . . my lady—"

"Khosa."

"Khosa," he amends. "We can keep you safe only for so long."

"I am aware of my duties, and will fulfill them." It's a phrase I repeated often to my Keepers, a phrase that once meant something, some pride at being the Given leaking into me, even though I knew how the blessing would end. And yet, in Stille—the place where the Given should be most sacrosanct—I have become merely Khosa, a girl who found friends and would take Donil as a lover for the pleasure of it, not as a means to an end.

"Why is it that you dislike the Indiri?" I ask Merryl.

He sighs, avoiding my gaze. "I see how you light at the sight of him, and know that perhaps your duty may be more easily fulfilled at his hands. But if the sea should rage at her creature being forced by a mate not her choosing, then how would it accept a body polluted by Indiri seed? And what would the histories have to say of a Stillean guard who allowed such a thing to happen?"

"I cannot change your opinion of the Indiri," I say to him. "But you would do well to remember that I choose my mate, not you."

"And I took a vow when I became a guard to protect the sacred from the profane. To my mind, you are the former, and the Indiri, the latter. I cannot forsake that vow, and would not even were you to ask it of me."

"Very well." I push aside the inkpot, my irritation rising. "I appreciate loyalty to your vow, but you cannot be with me every moment. Decency stops my guards from entering my bedchamber, and it *does* have a window."

Merryl's face stiffens. "This is no game, my lady."

"If it is, then I am playing it very badly." I smack the table, tears rising to my ears. "What is this life, where I wield power over the entire kingdom, yet cannot bed whom I please?"

My head goes to the table to hide my tears, but my back rises with sobs I try to still. A light snore rises from the guard in the corner, and I hear Merryl shift in his seat. Moments later, there's a light pressure on my back, his hand resting there giving some comfort, his glove preventing a shudder.

"I know decent men," Merryl continues, voice low. "I myself am married and have an infant daughter of my own. I hold her after dinner sometimes, watch her sleep. The small twitches in her face make me laugh, and I told my wife I don't know how your Keepers could raise you up from that and send you to your fate."

"Well, my face doesn't twitch all that much." I raise my head, pointing to the blankness there.

Surprised at my joke, Merryl laughs, then covers his mouth as the sleeping guard changes position, head rolling to the other shoulder at the disturbance.

"As I said, I know good men . . ." he says, letting me draw the conclusion on my own.

"Men who would get me with child if I so desired?"

"Yes, with kindness."

I shake my head, and he holds up a hand. "Just remember that I said so, should the time come."

"I will remember, and thank you," I say. I return my eyes to the flowing lines of a Scribe long dead, and Merryl puts his helm back on, reclaiming his post. The tension flows from my shoulders as I work, the pain in my chest ebbing, for I know I am safe with him at the door.

But as he said . . . for how long, I do not know.

CHAPTER 45

WITT STANDS BENEATH THE LEAVES OF THE HADUNDUN trees as they rustle together; many of the group gathered with him edge toward the clearing at the sound. The rust-colored leaves could take off a finger if they fell at the right angle, slicing through skin and bone. More than a few Pietra have gone to boats after losing a hand to a combination of bad luck and a stiff breeze. But it isn't fate or weather that will bring the serrated edge of a Hadundun leaf to a throat today. It is treason.

"Willa of Pietra," Witt calls, and the woman steps away from the few family and friends who came along with her. "Share your crime."

Willa's chin goes up. "I have none."

Witt glances at Pravin, but his eyes are combing the woods, alighting on Hadundun trunks in a manner that puts an edge in Witt's voice when he speaks again.

"You sheltered one who was no longer useful. Food meant for bodies that can fight and work went into one that can do neither."

"Food that came from my hand went to my father," Willa says. "As he did for me when I was small, so I do for him when he cannot. I find no fault in that."

"And when you were a child, did you not work?" Witt counters.

"Did you not gather bait for the Lures and find edgestones for the smith?"

Witt doesn't wait to be answered, but instead motions to one of his men, who pulls her father from the crowd. He falls to the ground the moment the support of the soldier's arm is gone, hand impulsively going to cup a growth that springs from above his ear, creeping its way toward his eye.

"What is your father's name?" Witt asks Willa.

"Broca," she answers, and her father's head jerks up at the sound.

Witt nudges the man with his foot. "Pietra, what is your name?"

"Tan," he says, hand still covering half of his face as if the assembly would forget his growth if they could no longer see it. Willa's mouth goes into a thin line, but her chin remains high.

"And your daughter's name?"

"Tan."

"And what is your duty to Pietra?"

"Tan."

Witt steps back and addresses the small gathering. "This man is no longer capable of serving, something his daughter hid so that a boat would not be made for him. This deception weakens Pietra, at a time when strength is more important than ever before."

"I would not build a boat for the one who raised me," Willa says, speaking without permission. "My mother's last breath came when I drew my first. He's all I know."

"In a way, you have succeeded," Witt says. "There is no boat in your father's future. Or yours."

For the first time, she wavers, her eyes slipping up the black trunks of the Hadundun trees to the leaves. "I know what awaits me."

"Then let it be over with," Witt answers, and she goes to her knees beside her father. Pravin reaches up and carefully breaks a leaf away, handing it by the stem to Witt.

"Willa of Pietra." Witt raises his voice so that it can be heard by all.

"Your blood will feed the trees. May this drink speed their growth, so that all may have boats."

The slice is quick and clean, her throat not the first that Witt has opened. He steps to the side as the spray of red coats the nearest tree and is neatly sucked into the bark before it can even drip. Blood spills from under Willa's fallen body, and tendrils of black roots erupt, dark fingers crawling toward her. Witt moves to her father as the tree behind him groans, stretching higher as it drinks.

"Broca of Pietra," he says, and the man again reacts to his name, looking up at Witt. "What grows from your skull condemns you, yet a boat was not built. Do you have anything to say for yourself?"

Broca looks at his daughter's body as the shade from the Hadundun spreads, branches growing longer as life leaves her. His face contorts, pain and wrath chasing each other through the muscles that still work, and when he meets Witt's eyes all the grief pooled there is poured into his only word.

"Tan," he says, dropping his arms and baring his throat. "Tan."

Witt slices. And the tree grows.

"Have you given more thought to the Feneen offer?" Pravin asks, taking a seat beside Witt on the edge of the cliff.

Witt plucks a stone and tosses it before answering, and they both watch as it sails far out to sea.

"I have," Witt says. "There is no easy choice. Let Pietra die when Feneen could do so instead, but betray our customs by taking a wife. Or give up a battle advantage and make a new enemy when they could easily be an ally instead, which goes against all I know."

Pravin nods. "The Feneen is cunning. He gave you options that will betray your people either way. But if you deny him, his attack will be twofold. The guards he returned to us know the offer has been made, and our men will know that you willingly endanger them when not necessary."

"Dissent is sown from within, and we invite an attack from without," Witt says, thinking aloud. "There was a buried threat in his saying that many of their fighters are Stillean, ready to kill those who abandoned them."

Pravin pitches his own rock into the sea. "Meaning that many others are Pietra-born, and equally inclined."

"Indeed."

They watch the high arc of Pravin's rock, and the soundless white splash that follows.

"The girl this morning . . ." Witt finally says.

"It was treason," Pravin says. "And her father not pretty to look upon."

"Yes, treason, and how many more will I punish in the same way? The Pietra have always kept to their ways admirably, allowing their weaknesses to be fed to the Lusca, making us stronger in their absence. I saw many things when I was being tried for Lithos, but never did I witness a death under the trees."

"It does not happen often," Pravin admits.

"How rare?" Witt pushes. "I had to send the Keeper for a history to learn the words before I slit her throat, as you did not know them yourself."

"I have never seen one fed to the trees," Pravin says, eyes on the ground. "Nor did the Mason before me."

"But it is in my time as Lithos that a woman takes it into her head to shelter and save her father," Witt says bitterly. "She saw me show mercy to the Hyllenians, and expected the same for one of our own. How can I follow Pietran ways, sending one such as Broca to his death, then ask my men to fight side by side with a man who may have two heads, and welcome him as brother after?"

Silence falls between them and two Lusca tails break the surface of the water, scales flashing brightly in the light.

"The Feneen has trapped you neatly," Pravin finally says. "But there is a way for the Lithos to stay true to Pietra custom, without giving offense to Ank."

"I do not see it."

"Take the Feneen offer, use his soldiers, choose a wife but do not take her. Your word to Ank is good, and your bond as Lithos unsullied."

Witt considers it, tossing a rock from hand to hand. "But would the people believe I have not been a true husband to my wife? I cannot in good conscience cut oathbreakers' throats beneath Hadundun trees if Pietrans think me guilty of violating my own."

"Separate rooms, guards who are known to have wagging tongues . . . it could be accomplished. Ank will get what he wants if the Feneen live side by side with Pietra, but that doesn't mean the Lithos has to share his bed with one."

"It belies his goal, though," Witt argues. "He hopes to mingle our blood, truly make them no longer separate, much as you say will happen with the Hyllenians."

"I think with the Hyllenians, it's more easily accomplished," the Mason says. "Although the guards who spent time among them said there are many children born to Feneen who are as like any Pietra as you or I. For the most part, the Feneen are easily spotted and won't be sought after as bedmates. If a few of the less repulsive ones find their way into our bloodline, so be it. In a few generations, the Pietra will have absorbed what's left of both the Hyllenians and the Feneen, and if they stay to our customs, there is little harm done."

"And have the histories say that I suffered the Feneen to live among us?"

Pravin shrugs. "Pen the histories yourself, have them say what you would. You may be the only Lithos ever to take a wife, but she is only relevant in the moment to gain Ank's goodwill. The histories need not mention her. The matter is a minor annoyance, and at least you get to choose her."

"If I'm not bedding her, what does it matter?"

"You still have to sit across from her at mealtimes," Pravin counters. "Having only one mouth in her face would be to your benefit."

Witt laughs, the sound bouncing across the cliffs. The Mason smiles, but his eyes grow troubled as they go to the sea, and the wet cough that follows doubles him over.

"My Lithos—" he begins.

"Don't." Witt stops him. "I saw you choosing your tree today. It is not your time to build a boat. I won't allow it."

"And how can I stand beside you while you open throats with leaves, feeling a weight in my lungs and a hitch in my breath?"

"Your duty is to me. We strike Stille again soon, maybe beside an ally I don't fully trust. The next Lithos has not been chosen or groomed. I either face dissent in my ranks or inform Pietra that their leader abandons tradition and takes a wife. I need you by my side."

Pravin wordlessly holds out his palm, wet with saliva mixed with blood.

"Not yet," Witt says, shaking his head. "Not yet."

CHAPTER 46

Vincent

LTHOUGH IT IS MY FATHER IN FRONT OF ME, IT IS Madda's face I see, and her words that echo in my ears. Even my fight with Donil could not drive her declaration from my mind, and the thought that I am destined for the sea has played out in dark variations during the night hours: me clasping hands with Khosa when she dances and never letting go, Donil standing over me in the surf, one foot planted on my chest as the tide comes in. I even thought of Dara, sword in hand, her face stonily set as she drives me back from the shore as I try to come inland, my laughter at the idea of marrying an Indiri to be paid for with a wet corpse.

"Do you hear me?"

My father's voice cuts through the reverie, and I jump in my seat, the Elders avoiding my eyes as I rejoin the conversation.

"I'm sorry," I say. "I was . . ." There are no words for what I was doing, and I don't make the effort of concocting a lie.

"Leave us," my father says, waving one hand, and the others filter out of the hall, the last closing the doors behind.

"I asked you how it goes with the Given twice, Vincent. For the prince of Stille to pay no heed at an Elder meeting on a matter of high importance is an embarrassment to both of us."

"I apologize," I say, clearing my throat. "I have not been myself lately."

"No, Vincent," my father says, black eyes even darker than usual. "You've been exactly as you always have, and it needs to change. With your grandfather gone, and me sitting a throne at war, you need to be prepared to take responsibilities."

"I am. I was distracted."

Father snorts. "Shall we be as the Pietra, then? What is their saying? *The Lithos cannot be distracted?*"

I ignore the jab and attempt to answer the question originally asked. "The Given is recovering from her wound nicely—"

"To the depths with the wound," Father yells, slamming his hand against the table. "And with her too, if someone would get a child on her. Why you didn't take the opportunity when she was senseless from the fall, I don't know."

"That seems a bit unprincely," I say.

"Then allow someone else. It's clear the girl has no intention of choosing a mate of her own accord, and those around her lack the taste to—"

"To *rape* her?" I shout, rising to my feet. "To perform an act we publicly lash others for? Truly, Father—you call this a *taste?*"

I've always known my father as a man of appetites, seen his gaze travel down women he had no right to look at in the manner of a lover.

"She must be bred," he says. "It will happen, Vincent. If you prefer it be your doing, then so be it. Royal children are easily come by, and a daughter less of a loss than a son. This is not a question of what the Given does or does not want, but of what will happen should she not have a child."

"And what will happen? A wave of old? One to pull Stille up by the roots and leave only sand behind? If this is what we've come to, then so be it. I'll not take part."

I think of the Stillean babe with unlined palms, and my own, telling a story that ends with smeared ink and wet pages. If the sea will claim us all, I go knowing I've hurt none.

"You will take part," Father says, pressing down on the table so hard that his knuckles go white. "Choose the mate for her, or do it yourself. Take your pleasure, do your first real duty to your kingdom, and maybe you'll discover at the same time that some tastes *are* acquired."

"I will do no such thing."

"Your choice," Father says. "But be aware if the girl is not bred soon, I will make it so. I will fulfill my duty to my country through whatever means necessary. That is what great men do, Vincent."

I turn my back to him, denying my hands their urge to close around his throat. Behind me, I hear him walk to a window. His next words bounce back from the glass, echoing through the room.

"Did you know that they say the sons of great men are always a disappointment?"

"Then I have nothing to fear," I say as I walk to the door.

The slamming of the hall doors behind me sends servants scurrying out of my way, but the fear on their faces is nothing compared to what has taken root in my mind. I have always known that I cannot save Khosa, that her life was made to be short.

But no one said it had to be miserable.

CHAPTER 47

Khosa

THE LINES OF THIS BOOK HAVE SNAKED INTO MY BRAIN, the sweeping quillstrokes of the anonymous Scribe flowing so beautifully that I am pulled along, oblivious to my surroundings. I've picked a book from the Stillean histories today, searching not for entries that speak of the sea, but for a distraction so that I may not think of that very thing.

An eerie report today from a hunting party. They saw Tangata sunning themselves on the rocks, newly born kits tumbling beside them on the ground. The young were purely white, an anomaly spoken of by those before me, a cycle that their coats follow, a white generation born every hundredth harvest. Word of the white cats spread and people of Hyllen and Hygoden had come, bringing their children so that they would not miss their chance to see a white Tangata—something all of us can remember, no matter when it occurs in our lives. A white Tangata is a marker, splitting our time like a line in a palm. There is what came before, and what came after, the cat a common reference point for all.

But this generation's cats will be overshadowed by something more stunning, and they will speak of it before the cats, the white fur an anomaly—but one that will recur, eventually.

While the party stood at a safe distance, watching the cats and tumbling kittens, an alarming cry broke out, and a naked Indiri child scrambled onto the rocks with the cats. Mothers covered the eyes of their children, and those unable to look away watched, breathless, expecting one swipe of a claw to mark the day with blood and tragedy.

Instead the child curled into the warm body of a Tangata, and the mother cat licked it clean, while the Indiri made the deep purring noises of a cat, kneading the Tangata's skin, human hands following all the motions of a kitten content with its kin.

"Khosa?"

I'm startled out of the story, the image of sun-dappled cats replaced by the dust motes of the library, and Cathon's apologetic smile.

"I'm sorry to interrupt," he says.

I wave away the apology, biting down on my own as I notice the permanent bump in the bridge of his nose, the skin around it still swollen and yellow with bruising.

"Do you know this story?" I ask, tilting the book toward him. His trained eyes skim the lines quickly, and he nods.

"The wild Tangata child," he says, taking a seat next to me. "She was in the time of Konnal, who would've been Gammal's grandfather."

"What happened to her?"

"When the Indiri learned that one of their own was living feral, they tried to reclaim her, but the child was more cat than human. She sharpened bones and tied them to her fingers, swiping her claws at those who tried to come near, and eventually the Indiri had to admit defeat."

"I doubt that came easily," I say under my breath.

"It didn't," Cathon smiled. "They caught her finally, but their party was attacked by Pietra and the girl was lost."

"Dead?" I ask.

Cathon shakes his head. "No one knows. The Pietra and Indiri had no love for each other, so it wasn't unusual for a chance meeting of the groups to end in violence. Whether she died with them there or was allowed to remain with her cats is a matter of conjecture. There were tales for years afterward, though. Men claimed that they would feel a presence in the woods and look into the trees to see a grown woman staring down from above, only to disappear in the blink of an eye."

My fingers curl a page of the history, finding comfort in the touch of the paper much as the feral girl did in her mother's fur. "I prefer to think of her that way," I say. "Alive and wild in the woods, not dead by a Pietran hand with no knowledge of why it should be so."

"It makes for a better story, anyway," Cathon says, leaning toward me. "In some versions, the girl even has a tail."

He winks at me to show that he's teasing and I shut the book, uncomfortable with how close he is. I rise from my seat and cross to another table, one where I have laid out my scrolls with Dara's ancestry on it, paralleled with Vincent's so that an Indiri and Stillean time line can be created. I trace my fingers across Dara's line, the simple beauty of Indiri names out of place with the sharp edges of my handwriting.

"How did the feral child come to be as such?" I ask. "The Indiri do not give their children to the Feneen, and they put such an effort into reclaiming her."

Cathon crosses to me, closing the distance between us again. "Stilleans have made their own stories to answer that question. Some say the mother was taken by surprise by Tangata in the woods, and the babe's helplessness was somehow endearing to the cats. Another story goes that the child had always harbored fascination for the wild, and went to the cats on her own. But no one knows." His eyes land on Dara's bloodline. "Perhaps you should ask your Indiri."

"She's hardly mine."

"Just as you are no one's." Cathon's voice drops, but there's an intensity in his words I can't ignore, and I back away from him.

"Don't be afraid, Khosa. I mean you no harm." He glances at the guards, who are awake but lost in their own conversation by the entryway, while Cathon and I have wandered toward the window, our words drowned by the sounds of the sea.

"You belong to no one," he repeats. "Not a man. Not Stille. Not the sea. You are given to nothing, do you understand me?"

"So you say, while standing in a room full of histories that claim otherwise," I tell him, gesturing to the stacks of books around us, all of them holding at least one story of a dance that ended in death.

"There are those of us who believe you need not go. Some who penned the very books you mention have studied them long years, our lives dedicated to the history of Stille. We know what has passed and believe what is to come need not follow the same pattern."

A spark of hope in my chest is more painful than the arrow that pierced it, and I tamp it down. "You tried to say as much to me earlier, and my own feet denied what you say before you could even finish. They will go to the sea on their own."

"We can take you inland," Cathon insists, voice a mere whisper. "Farther even than Hyllen. You were safe there."

"Only for so long," I shudder, remembering the clamor as the Pietra descended upon everything I knew. "And still I danced," I remind him.

"Then we'll put more distance between you and the sea," he argues. "No Given has ever lived past her youth, or sprouted a gray hair. Who can say? Your fits may cease and a wave may not come."

My hand reaches again for paper and ink, for the solidity of truth beneath my fingers. "The histories all say—"

"The histories all say that nothing happens when we allow a young woman to drown. It is not the occurrence of *nothing* that provides proof but the occurrence of *something*."

My breath catches, his logic tearing down the very walls of the room we stand in. "A heavy wager. You would let the Given not dance, only to satisfy the curiosity of a handful of Scribes. If I do not go, and a wave rises, then you are wrong and your kingdom lost."

Cathon's eyes return to my time line, the heavy scratches of my ink and quill. "My kingdom is lost, regardless. Shall it go quietly, as your work shows, with lives shortened by rising inches? Or all at once, in a majesty of might?"

"The histories . . . ," I say again, their facts so ingrained in my mind that I return to them again and again to dispute him.

"The histories are books, written by men," Cathon says. "You live your life and would sacrifice it because of what is in these pages, but what of ones you haven't read, reduced now to ashes?"

"What are you saying?" I ask. "There are histories that have burned?"

"In some cases whole books, but in others, pages only," Cathon says, sifting through the pile on my stone worktable. "Here, for instance."

He fans the pages of a book I've scoured time and time again, but stops to show me something I'd missed, a small shred of paper still bound into the spine, the page itself missing. I touch it gently, and what remains crumbles at my touch.

"I didn't see this," I tell the Scribe.

"You cannot see what has been taken away," Cathon says.

"What did it say?" I wonder aloud, still touching the frayed edges of binding twine where the page had been ripped out.

"We will never know," Cathon says. "But an Elder Scribe who has since passed once told me stories that I've not found in books. Stories of how two of the lines of the Three Sisters died out, leaving only one."

"They were barren," I tell him, reciting what I've been told. "The strength of their line was spent, and the sea no longer interested in them."

"Or they birthed male babies," he says.

"The Given is always a female," I tell him. "And creates another in her own image."

"According to who?"

I spin in the shadowed library and wave my hands at the dusty shelves that surround us. "Everyone. Everything. Every book ever written."

"Again I say, written by people. And people . . . they often have agendas."

"The Given goes to the sea because she must," I say, but my words lack conviction, and deep inside me, I feel something foreign. Something like hope.

Cathon does not answer, but his eyes pin me, bright as an Indiri's. And a flicker within me answers.

"What would you have me do?" I ask.

CHAPTER 48

Vincent

THERE HAVE BEEN CHANGES IN THE WAY I'M TREATED since my grandfather's death. The throne is one step closer to being mine, which makes everyone around me take one step back. Servants whom I know by name and call to every morning now drop a deeper curtsy or incline their head farther, any joke or familiarity I aim for now bungled on their end as they try to mix their response with deference instead of the friendliness we've grown accustomed to.

The newly acquired power has paved a way for me, so it comes as a surprise when the guard at Khosa's door puts his hand to his blade at my approach, an inch of steel flashing above the sheath.

"I would speak to the Given," I say.

"She is sleeping," he responds, tacking on a "my lord," after a pause.

I hear rustling behind the door, combined with the light humming of an unfamiliar tune, and I raise my eyebrows.

"She is about to sleep," he amends, unflustered.

I meet his eyes, the same color as his blade, and see that arguing would be pointless. After the conversation I had with my father yesterday, I should be thrilled to know that Khosa is so well protected, but I'm not the one she needs to be guarded against.

"Khosa," I call, raising my voice, "it's Vincent. May I speak with you?"

There is a scraping sound as the bolt is shot back, and I can't help but give the guard an imperious look as I slide past him. Khosa's fine bones are nearly lost under the layers of her dressing gown, but she clutches it tightly closed against her throat nonetheless.

"Vincent," she says, her voice as flat as when we first began speaking to each other, "how can I help?"

I've never been in her chambers before, and make a concentrated effort to keep my eyes on her face, not letting it wander to her body or—fathoms—the bed. Once I lock gazes with her, though, I cannot look away. The fear evident there is at odds with the stillness of her face.

"Depths, Khosa," I say. "Don't you know by now I would never harm you?"

She closes her eyes for a moment, a deep exhale escaping from her parted lips. "I believe so, but a Given in my position . . ."

"Must be cautious," I finish for her. "Which is why I came to speak with you." I look to the door, still standing open, her guard making no attempt to hide the hostility in his gaze. "Privately."

Khosa nods to the guard. "It's all right, Merryl. We can trust Vincent."

He flinches at the use of my proper name, as I do at her use of *we*, but the door closes all the same, with Merryl on the other side. I gesture for her to sit at one of the chairs facing the fireplace and take the other, conscious of the fact that she wraps an extra blanket over her dressing gown despite the heat.

"You're very much in the right to be cautious," I begin. "And it's good to know that you have a dependable guard."

"Merryl is trustworthy. But he cannot be with me at all times. Even he must sleep."

"As must you. Though the circles under your eyes tell me that hasn't been easy of late."

Khosa readjusts her blanket, but says nothing.

"Khosa, I . . ." There is no pretty way to phrase what comes next, so I aim for truthfulness. "Until you are bred, you are not safe here."

"I know it," she says, eyes still on the fire. "Merryl tells me that the soldiers in the bunkhouse drew lots to guard me until I requested him personally."

"Lots may be the least of it," I tell her. "My father has quietly offered a reward to whoever . . . accomplishes it."

"Yes," Khosa says simply. "I am aware."

"I can help you," I say, and her eyes shoot from the fire to me, alarmed. "Not in that way, at least, not in truth. Please—hear me out."

Khosa nods, and I continue.

"You said yourself Merryl cannot be by your side always, and with your mate not chosen you are a target for gossip and worse. Allow me to sleep here, at your feet. If my father believes you have made your choice, it will buy you some time, and a measure of safety."

Her face is blank, her eyes staring me down with an intensity I can bear only because of a lifetime spent with Dara.

"You can have a standing order for Merryl to come in and clean my head from my shoulders at your first cry of alarm," I say, garnering a smile.

"Stille would love me all the more for that," she says. "No child in my belly and the prince dead at my feet."

"You are safe with me," I tell her.

"It is not your actions I fear, but your mother's anger," Khosa says. "She warned me away from you. Nicely, and with pretty words, but her meaning was clear."

"Am I a child, still to be ruled by my mother?" I ask, feeling the heat flush my cheeks.

"Vincent . . . ." Khosa drops her eyes, fine hands toying with the front of her dressing gown. "She is only protecting her son. Any feeling you harbor for me would end badly."

"But there would be a beginning," I say, voice suddenly hoarse. I reach to cross the distance between us and our hands touch. "And a middle," I add. A flicker of discomfort lights her face, and she pulls back in a moment.

"It could only hurt you," she says, but I reach for her hand again, ignoring the tug as she tries to pull it away.

"I know what you are. I go into any agreement between us aware that you are the Given, and accepting that our time together would end in death for you and misery for me. Yet I accept that, for what would come before."

But she is shaking her head, tears now running freely on her cheeks lit by the fire. "That is not the only way I can hurt you," she says, and my heart dips in my chest.

"Donil. You are drawn to him," I say quietly, and she nods. I clear my throat, eyes on the fire. "You are aware that he has certain abilities?"

"I know of Dara's," she says.

"Donil's are different," I say, ignoring the flare of conscience in my belly. "He's able to charm . . . women."

"Oh," Khosa says again, her voice calm and flat, in stark contrast to the tempest in her eyes. "I did not know."

I let my words continue to hang in the air, aware that saying more would only illuminate my jealousy.

"Would you be amenable to my sharing your room?" I ask. "For your protection only?"

The smile that cracks her face is not one I've seen before, almost mocking. "I need no protection from Donil. He would not harm me."

"You would not perceive it as harm, at the time," I say. "Ask any of the kitchen girls who are made of laughter on the days they have his attentions but cannot be drawn from their depths when he is finished with them."

The smile is lost quickly, the heat of conscience in my belly soon overridden by victory at her next words.

"Yes, Vincent," Khosa says, face once again blank as she stares lifelessly into the fire. "You may share my room."

CHAPTER 49

Witt

HYLLEN FELL EASILY, BUT STILLE IS NO SHEEP TOWN. It's a city, with deep roots and many to protect it," Witt says, glancing around the room at his commanders, who nod. "We drew back to return what we had captured to our people, much needed meat brought to our shores, and Hyllenian shepherds to tend the sheep that provide it. It will be with fuller bellies that we approach their city, but they outnumber us greatly."

"Yet those numbers are untrained, uncounseled in war," says a commander.

"True. Still, many are more than few. To that end, we've enlisted aid to ensure our victory."

There is nervous shifting in the room, muttering that Witt can attribute to no one man. He knew that rumors of their alliance with the Feneen would spread before he had the chance to confirm or refute them, but to see Pietran commanders uneasy in their own war chambers drops a weight on his heart.

"Speak so your Lithos can hear you," he says. "Or do not."

"The aid, my Lithos," Hadduk, a commander who rode against the Indiri, says. "There are whispers that the Feneen will ride with us."

"And not with horses for mounts," adds another.

"It is true we will have Feneen at our side." Witt raises his hands to quell the rising voices. "Whether they ride horses or their own mothers is their business."

He is rewarded with a deep rumble of laughter, but Witt can still feel an argument brewing.

"Why bring inferior fighters to a battle we can easily win?" Hadduk goes on. "The Pietra have never needed their help before."

"No, but we've never attacked Stille, have we?"

"The Indiri were three times their worth in fighters, and we bested them," Hadduk says, puffing out his chest.

"And their numbers four times less than Stille's, if not fewer," Witt says. "Why waste your men's lives—or your own—when others are willingly given? You think less of the Feneen? Fine, let them die for you, so that you and your children may inherit every speck of dirt until the sea takes all."

Hadduk glances at the men around him, gauging their reaction to Witt's words before trying once more. "We heard a bargain was struck that allowed surviving Feneen to become Pietra in name, and I think very little of that."

"What you heard is true," Witt answers, drawing more muttering. But it slowly dies out as he smiles, something they've learned to dread. "And tell me, how many Feneen do you think would survive a battle where they face Stille, with Pietra behind?"

Witt wipes the sweat from his brow before it can flow into his eyes. One misstep on the steep cliffs of Pietra could put a new Lithos on the throne long before he is ready. More than one Lithos has been replaced in that way, falling victim to the very path that led to where those vying for his role train.

Pravin clears his throat for the third time during the climb, and Witt turns to him. "Out with it, before I push you to the Lusca to clear the air."

"Today, at the council . . . ," Pravin begins, taking a deep breath before continuing to climb. "I don't see you as the type to betray an ally, even the Feneen."

Witt scans the rocks above for a handhold before replying. "I promised a place for the Feneen who survived the battle, not to make sure that they did."

"Which isn't quite the same thing as telling the men a Stillean sword in a Feneen chest is all the same to you as a Pietran arrow in the back."

Witt hauls himself over the top of the cliff, then lies in the cool grass to wait for Pravin. The older man clears the top and rests as well, the cool breeze tossing his hair to reveal the multitude of gray underneath.

"What would you have me do?" Witt asks. "I can't fight a war on Stillean soil, only to face another at home after."

"I don't have an answer, my Lithos. But I do know this is below you."

Witt doesn't respond, the sound of small voices making it unnecessary.

"The Lithos, the Lithos," they cry, the youngest of the children breaking out of the pack, their little legs bringing them to Witt ahead of the older ones too proud to run.

They crowd around him as he sits up, eyes still bright with the enthusiasm of youth, and Witt has to bite the inside of his cheek to keep from telling them to go back home to their mothers.

"Have you come to see the rock?" one of the smaller ones asks, little fingers winding through Witt's as he makes a show of helping the Lithos to his feet.

"Not entirely," Witt says. "But I'll have a look."

The rock from Witt's generation had been dark and smooth, easy to mark with a slash for each boy who would be Lithos, and just as easy to strike through when one failed.

The boy releases Witt's hand and points to the white rock they'd chosen, the black slashes from burnt sticks scraped there like dark sentinels.

"Jannan has gone," the boy says, pointing to a fresh mark that bisected the original slash, pale from years of rain. "He was caught with a girl who had been making the climb to see him."

"Why would he do such a thing?" Witt asks playfully, and the boy pulled a face.

"Who knows?"

"Who is this?" Witt asks, pointing to another slash.

"Paduit," the boy says quickly. "He refused to kill his oderbird."

The oderbird trial wasn't easy. Each boy was given a fledgling to raise when his family sent him to try for Lithos. They would wake one morning to find that someone had gone through the cages in the night, neatly snapping one wing on each bird. The question was simple— waste time and resources to heal the bird, or finish what had begun?

"You killed yours, I take it?" Witt asked.

"Yes, my Lithos," the boy says immediately. "His name was Baden, and I broke his neck like that." He snaps his fingers to illustrate, and Witt suppresses a shudder.

"I'll make Lithos one day," the boy goes on. "I heard you sat like a stone when the Indiri were slaughtered. That you took the head off a Hyllenian because he sassed you, and that you made boats for your whole family in one night, not a tear shed. I want to be just like you."

Witt goes down on his haunches and looks the boy in the face. "You would make a fine Lithos," he says, and the boy beams at him before running off.

"But no one should wish to be as I am," he adds to himself.

CHAPTER 50

Khosa

MY OWN IDIOCY ASTOUNDS ME.

The memory of Donil's hands on my body draws a blush even in the chill dark of the library. That I could touch and feel nothing was an anomaly, that I could touch and feel pleasure, remarkable. To learn that it was all smoke and mirrors, the natural product of his Indiri gift misleading me, has painted my mood black, and I know that my irritation with Dara is born from that.

"Look for . . ." My eyes roam the history in front of me. "Anything to do with the village of Dosdos. I've found a mention here of the high tide that could be useful to compare."

Dara waves me off. "It's a Stillean village by the sea. No reason for an Indiri to venture there."

"Would you mind looking, though?" My words are polite enough, and delivered in my usual monotone, but my eyes remain on hers when she challenges me with a glare.

She sighs, hands going to her temples as they always do, an involuntary twitch that accompanies the beginning of her journey into memory. I study the dark circles under her eyes, which aren't new, but the swelling underneath is, as if the Indiri girl hasn't slept. She squeezes her head tighter, and I see that her nails are ragged and bitten, not the usual clean edges pared down with her dagger.

"Never mind," I say. "It's not worth chasing."

Dara opens her eyes, hands dropping. "Why?"

"Because I doubt we'll learn more than we already have." I tip my hand over the table I've claimed as my own, charts, diagrams, time lines piled on top of one another. All of them telling the same story.

"And what have we learned?" Dara asks.

I hedge on answering with numbers, their impersonal nature not able to convey all I've ruminated on in the waning hours while sitting in this chair. "One of the Hyllenian shepherdesses was delivered of child before I came here," I say instead. "He may reach her shoulder before the water closes over all our heads."

"So soon?"

"If my calculations are right and Indiri memory can be trusted—"

"Indiri memory is faultless," Dara says, cutting me off.

It's my turn to rest my head in my hands, an argument I hadn't wanted burgeoning in front of me. "I'm not so sure."

"What are you saying?" Dara asks, learning toward me across the table.

"When was the feral Indiri child raised alongside white Tangata, according to the Indiri?" I ask, rising from my table and going to another, where her bloodline lies next to Vincent's.

"My great-grandmother has that memory," Dara answers easily, the monumental moment right at hand. "Agarra."

I hold up the scroll with her ancestry. "Yet Agarra lived during the reign of Philo, Gammal's father. I can show you here on the time line."

Dara shrugs. "Agarra remembered the feral child."

"She didn't," I insist, my voice breaking. "The Stilleans keep detailed records, and the Scribes write down daily events as they happen, Dara. You're reaching through years' worth of memory, distanced by time and warped to match the mind of whatever Indiri passed it on."

Dara comes to her feet too. "Warped?"

I hold up my hand to still Merryl, who is watching Dara carefully. "Yes, warped," I insist. "Who holds dear the memories of failure? Agarra may have passed on to you that she saw the feral child because she loved the story so much, she wished that she had."

Dara says something under her breath in Indiri, and I don't need to know the language to be aware I've been deeply insulted.

"Truly, Dara," I barrel on, "would you hold tightly to a memory of when you were wrong or acted poorly, knowing it would be passed on to your children?"

"I have none," she seethes. "And if ever do, I'll be sure to pass along all that happened here in this room, so that they may know it is a grave error indeed to throw an Indiri mind open to one who would pick it clean only to mock it."

"I'm not mocking. Only correcting."

"Oh, correcting," she says. "Adjusting what my ancestors claim so that it will fit the Stillean version? There may only be two Indiri left, Given," she sneers, "but we'll hold the truths buried in our minds more sacred than lines of ink written by strangers long dead."

"And thereby disputing facts," I plunge in, ignoring the shake of Merryl's head pleading me to stop, as well as the fire in Dara's eyes.

"Facts," Dara laughs. "Yes, and what of those? Tell me, these long days spent over your books and histories, draining one inkpot after another—what have they told you?"

My hands unclench at her words, my stomach dropping. For all of the anger clouding her mind, she's right. If the Indiri memories are inaccurate, all my work is undone.

"If this is true, then we know nothing more than at the outset," I admit. "The cave paintings and the evidence of our own eyes when looking at the Horns tell us that the sea is rising, but we don't know how quickly."

Dara shakes her head. "You mistake my meaning. I'm asking instead, what could the Given learn of the rising sea, when she is destined for it, at any depth?"

I have no answer, and the slamming of the library door sends a shiver down my spine, whether at her words, or because it reminds me of her brother's exit, I do not know.

CHAPTER 51

Dara

"THE SOONER SHE SINKS, THE BETTER." DARA FINISHES OFF her flagon of wine and slams it to the table, leaving a bloodred ring.

"A bit harsh, don't you think, sister?" he asks, polishing off his own wine to keep pace and refilling both their drinks.

"She's headed there anyway. And I'll not be sad to see her go, no matter when it happens."

Donil says nothing, only turning his drink on the table and eyeing the basket of bread laid out for the early-rising servants.

"Oh, and you will be?" Dara asks, drawing meaning from his silence.

"I doubt Khosa meant to offend—"

"By implying that the Indiri history is a long string of bragging, and those half lies at best?"

"Are those your words, or hers?"

"Mine," Dara admits, downing a gulp of wine before continuing. "But her meaning is intact."

Donil smiles. "My sister, always ready to find a fight."

"My brother." Dara smiles back coolly. "Quite the opposite."

Her words still him, and they watch each other carefully over the table. "Are you calling me coward?" he asks, the calm in his voice deceptive.

"You know I'm not. I'm saying you'll take any other path before crossing blades, even if the blades are only tongues."

Donil raises an eyebrow, and Dara tosses a roll at him. "That was a bad example. You'll cross those readily enough."

Donil sighs. "You'd rather settle an argument with fists than words. As for the tongues, I know your opinion there."

"I only think yours is loose, in more ways than one. I know you've passed more time with the Given than is seemly."

Donil takes a deep drink, eyes in his cup when he answers. "And your tongue? How can it not curl upon itself, twofold?"

Dara's eyes narrow. "Why should it?"

"You told Vincent about my Indiri gift, which has caused no little harm, sister. He and I nearly came to blows over it."

Dara's mouth twists, and she drains her cup for the second time. Donil refills it and adds to his own.

"No little harm?" she repeats his words back to him, somewhat subdued.

"Vin may have taken your meaning a bit . . . rashly, in connection to the Given. He has eyes for her, and maybe more than that."

"She's new and different," Dara says, too hastily. "A rare creature inspires awe, which fades. As for your gift, I told him only that you have life, and it rises within others to answer you."

"Whatever your wording, it raised his temper. That's why we were fighting the other day when you came upon us."

"Over a girl? What are you, stags in the woods?"

"May as well be, for how it ended. We've shied away from each other since."

"I'd talk to him myself, let him know you're not magicking girls into dark corners," Dara says. "But we're not speaking, either."

She doesn't say why, but the jagged echo of Vincent's laughter on the training field at the thought of marrying Dara still grates on both their ears.

"Life was easier when we hit each other with sticks to settle our problems," Donil says.

"We're still doing it, brother. But now the sticks are swords."

"And how go your men with those?" Donil asks his sister, ready to change the subject. More than a few Stilleans who saw Dara against the Feneen asked to train under her, speckled skin and femaleness notwithstanding.

"Surprisingly well," she admits. "I told them if they couldn't look past my breasts, I'd cut them off right in front of them. Someone shouted that would be a shame, and we had a good laugh. Then I beat a few of them to a pulp with the broadside of my blade and showed the rest how. They're mediocre soldiers, but you don't need a lifetime of warfare behind you to fight well when you're defending your home."

"I feel the same," Donil says. "When the Pietra come, some will run, but most will stand."

"And many will die," Dara adds. "But not me, and not you."

"Or Vincent." Donil tips his cup to get the last of the wine. "Shall we go to him together and clear the air?"

Dara's cheeks are warm with wine, and her kinder nature near the surface. "I suppose. Be a shame to have the Pietra take anyone's head off when we have something of meaning left to say to those we care for."

"Up, then," Donil says, striking the table as he rises. Dara follows, and they walk shoulder to shoulder through the halls to Vincent's chamber, only to clear the corner and see his head ducking into another's door.

"Where's he going?" Dara presses forward to follow, until her brother's hand clamps onto her wrist, as unrelenting as stone.

"Donil?" she asks, eyes searching his face as a muscle in his jaw jumps.

Dara looks down the hall to the door where Vincent disappeared and recognizes Khosa's guard, eyes flickering to the shadows that hide them before sliding away. She grips her brother back, fingers tightening into a bone-grinding pinch.

"He's with the Given, in her chambers." She can barely whisper the words, her throat is so tight.

Donil spins away, and Dara's hand falls limp at her side as he goes, his anger fueling him forward, while her own abyss of sadness brings her to the floor.

CHAPTER 52

———— ❧❦❧ ————

Vincent

I CLOSE KHOSA'S DOOR BEHIND ME AND COME FACE-TO-FACE with a Scribe.

"My lord." He inclines his head, and I take the moment to meet Khosa's eyes, my confusion evident. She holds up a placating hand, and I hope I've recaptured some royal imperviousness when the Scribe looks back up.

"Cathon, correct?" I ask, offering a hand.

"Always nice to be remembered by a royal," he says, returning the shake.

"You took my Arrival Day measurements," I say, taking a seat by the fire. "How can I forget columns of numbers tracing my path to manhood?"

Those pages are seared onto my memory, it is true, but not for any good reason. On the anniversary of my birth, my hands are splayed, fingers painstakingly traced, feet measured, inked palms recorded, the top of my head to the flats of my feet written down and compared to the royals that came before. I always hovered over the pages as a child, eager to see how I'd grown, only to find that the answer was usually *not much*, and my measurements tallied well below my ancestors.

But I keep my voice light when I answer Cathon, not wanting him to know that the sound of his quill scratching, though quiet, always seemed to leave my head aching in its wake.

"Ah, yes, the measurements," Cathon says, taking his own chair as Khosa seats herself in the remaining one. "A task for the lowest of Scribes, if you don't mind my saying."

"Quite all right," I reassure him. "And how do fill your time outside of my Arrival Day measurements? I recall your penmanship was remarkable. Are you inking the lines of the histories?"

Cathon colors and looks away, although I don't know what I've said to offend. "The Elder Scribes hold tight to their quills," he says. "My tasks are relegated to bringing new histories to the library, and delivering older ones to those who require them for study, and recently of aiding with the calculation of the rising tides. I have my own projects, of course, but advancement is slow in coming."

I nod, too familiar with the feeling. Cathon bides his time waiting for blood to stop flowing in withered fingers that are ink-stained to the first knuckle, his place in life advancing only with the death of another.

"Vincent," Khosa says, "I would speak with you . . ." Her words die off, and her eyes go to Cathon, wary and unsure.

My heart stutters as much as her tongue, to see her so undone. The Khosa I know stares down maps that spell the doom of all without flinching, forgives the man who fired an arrow through her chest without a quaver in her voice.

"Khosa, what has happened that can put a tremor in you?"

"It's not what has happened, Vincent. But what I would have happen."

Cathon clears his throat. "My lord—"

"Please," I say, raising my palm. "Call me Vincent. I have no use for titles in this room. As Khosa is Khosa only, and not the Given here."

"There are some who would like that to be so regardless of where she stands," Cathon says.

He watches me as the words sink in, each one ripe with treason and punishable by death. I could call the guard in and have his head off here, and well within my rights to do so. But his words raise no anger, or even fear inside me. All I feel is hope, and know the same thing is what pulses through Khosa, bringing a lilt to her voice and a flicker in her face unknown until now.

"Count me among them," I say without hesitation. "If there is a way to deprive the sea of Khosa, I will see it done."

Cathon lets out a deep breath, and Khosa's smile illuminates the room.

"I said as much to Cathon," she tells me. "I told him that you would stand with me, but it is no small thing, Vincent. If you see this through, you will be reviled by your people, stripped of your future throne, and remembered in the histories as the Stillean royal who betrayed his country."

"What is that to me when the throne is underwater, and the histories floating in it?"

Khosa exchanges another glance with Cathon, who nods at her to continue. "It may not be so, and I would not mislead you to save my own skin."

"What is this?" I ask, looking from one to the other. "With the Horns underwater, we cannot deny the rising of the sea."

"It rises, assuredly," Cathon tells me. "But the offering of a Given prevents a great wave and sudden destruction, not the slow degradation of water enveloping land."

I think of the pictures from my childhood book, Tangata desperately clutching tree branches as fingers of water try to tear them loose. "A terrible wave," I say. "And an equally terrible choice, to send someone I care for to her death in order to stop it."

"What if I told you that I and others among the learned do not see it as so?" says Cathon. "The wave has come before, but the idea that the Given is what stops it from returning is shoddy thought, at best."

"In Hyllen we had a shepherd who had a favored crook," Khosa says. "It was his constant companion, with him night and day. He said it brought luck, ensuring easy lambing for his ewes, and that none wandered from his flock while it was in his hand. In his old age he even slipped it under his cot, believing that it kept his dreams tranquil. One morning he stepped from bed and snapped it beneath his heel. He crawled back to bed, proclaiming doom upon his herd and uneasy days for the rest of his life."

"And?" I ask.

"Many of his ewes delivered healthy twins and triplets that year. As for uneasy days, it could be argued that was so, as he had to build additional paddocks," she says.

"So the lucky crook was in fact only a crook like any other, and the good fortune he had attributed to it nothing more than coincidence," Cathon said.

I take a moment, tossing the logic in my head. "Likewise in Stille the absence of a wave is not due to the sacrifice of a Given but because . . ."

"I'm saying the absence of a wave signifies only the absence of a wave," Cathon shrugs. "The Given doesn't come into it."

"You take a great chance," I say. "Your theory can only be proven wrong with the death of a kingdom."

"I know it," Cathon responds. "And it took some effort to convince Khosa her own life is worth keeping, even if I believe the risk to Stille is small."

"And what of the risk to yourself?" I ask. "If you are caught out before proven correct, Khosa goes to the sea, and your neck to the chopping block."

"It's exactly because I value my neck highly that I run the risk," Cathon says. "Most Scribes are content to write others' names, use their own breath to dry the tales of deeds they took no part in. I'd see my name in ink, not be the one writing it."

"There is an immortality in words, Vincent," Khosa says. "We are not the Indiri, cannot recall our predecessors by closing our eyes. Stilleans know the names of the Three Sisters only because a Scribe penned them."

"And I, too, would be worthy of such a mention if I subvert beliefs we've long clung to, knowing no better," says Cathon. "It's a risk worth taking."

"On your own, yes," I tell him. "But you bring this to me, of all people? The prince of the kingdom you destroy if you're wrong?"

"In all truth, I was against it," he says. "Khosa assured me. She has great faith in you."

"And I in her," I say, looking at her as the fire plays across her delicate features, every line of her face emblazoned on my heart. I cross the distance between us and place my hand over hers. For once she does not pull away.

"Whatever you need," I tell her. "Stille holds nothing for me without you in it."

A light not born of the flames dances in her eyes, and I press upon her hand, only to have it slide out from under mine.

"It's a lovely sentiment," Cathon says, reminding me he is in the room. "However, moving Khosa away from Stille is our intention."

I reclaim my chair, spine humming with anticipation. "There is a safe place in the Forest of Drennen, known only to the royals and personal guards. It's well stocked with dried food and could shelter us for a day or two. Once my own disappearance is noticed, it would not be wise to tarry there."

"Perhaps that means you should not accompany us," Cathon replies, and I shoot him a look learned from Dara across boards of ridking.

"I go with Khosa," I say. "You are right to trust me. But I come along, or no one goes."

It's a harsh threat, and not one I would make good on, but neither will I set Khosa into the hidden halls beneath the castle with a man I do not know.

"I would have him with me," Khosa says, placing her hand on my arm. It remains there, and I shiver despite the fire at my back.

Cathon frowns, but nods. "Be that as it may. There are a few Scribes who will assist us, though they prefer to remain anonymous."

"And your guard?" I ask Khosa.

"Merryl is with us," she says, "and would be to whatever end, except I forbid it. He has a wife and child whom I will not see dragged from their home for a life of wandering. He will take a sleeping draught, and appear victim to those who smuggle me away."

"A life of wandering?" I ask. "What plans have you after Drennen?"

Khosa's hand tightens on my arm, her frantic pulse beating within. "I do not know, for my plan had always been simply to die."

CHAPTER 53

Dara

THE FOREST HAS ALWAYS CALMED DARA, THE DRIP OF rain from the leaves, the touch of wind on her face. Even when storms approach, sharp cracks of dead trees falling and dragging down the living ones nearby, she loves it. The wildness of the woods, with the heady scent of life bursting forth, undershot with the constant rot of death from an unlucky animal or the carpet of leaves beneath her . . . this is her home.

She has come to it for comfort more than once, but as she's grown older, the calm emanating from dirt and mud can't compete with her desires, her need for Vincent to see past the flecks on her face and into her heart. He was close, that night at the fire, but Dara will accept nothing short of an absolute acceptance of his untarnished love for her, buried—she is convinced—somewhere deep inside.

A branch snaps beneath her hands as she bends it for firewood, her anger vented on what she cares for, as usual. Brush rustles nearby, a deep-throated growl warning her that Tangata roam. She tosses half the branch in their direction, followed by an Indiri curse, and the cats fall quiet. Tonight Dara fears nothing, except the spinning of her own heart, freed now from the tethers that held it for so long.

Seeing Vincent go to the Given's chambers unmoored it, and she felt it slip around in her chest like a pebble in a bottle, glancing off her insides while each sob tore everything loose along with it. She'd never been one to cry and nearly choked on her own misery while she made her way outside, not wanting any in the castle to see the Indiri girl was weeping.

Now in the dark she can see the castle, a wave of light passing from one end to the other as the sconcelighters make their rounds. She knows all the windows, Vincent's most of all, and the dark spot where a light should be gnaws through what is left of her resolve as the dam breaks and tears flow again. Even now, after she dragged herself from the hall, wandered into the woods, and set a fire, he is not where he belongs.

He is with the Given.

That he should go to her was not in itself a shock. Dara was not immune to the tug of the flesh, and had seen the fire in men's eyes spark at the sight of women. Though she has allowed herself the daydream of Vincent taking her to wife, she has always known that he would wed a girl with unmarked skin, a Stillean of good blood.

That he would find another she knew. That he might actually love the girl, she has not prepared for. The fire climbs, and Dara watches it, letting the heat obliterate the shed tears on her cheeks. Quietly, the forest falls silent around her, and she with it, her heart slipping back where it belongs, bringing with it a darkness that had not been there before.

CHAPTER 54

———⊶◯⊷———

Witt

THEY WON'T BE LURED OUT, NO MATTER THE BAIT," Pravin predicts, brow furrowed as he bends over a map of Stille and the surrounding area. "With Hyllen burned, there's no good place to launch an attack from, and only a fool would march unblooded soldiers for days and then ask them to fight."

Witt nods his agreement. "A long march takes the fight out of many a man, no matter how great the speech at the beginning of the trail. It would be unwise, but what do we know of this new king in Stille?"

"He is rash and driven by greed," Ank speaks up. "But not a fool. He's correct in that he's not going to leave a stronghold with an army he can keep happy, fed, and warm in their beds until the battle comes to them."

Witt and Pravin both turn in surprise at the smooth-skinned Feneen's contribution, and he smiles, exposing his stained and broken teeth.

"I've met the man, after all," Ank says. "Can you claim the same? Or did you invite me to a war counsel only to look upon my pretty face?"

"If it's a pretty face we want, we'll ask you to turn your back,"

Hadduk says, and a hearty laugh erupts from behind Ank, where Nilana sits in her harness.

Witt avoids the Feneen woman's eyes. As the Lithos, he is not to be distracted, but her alarming beauty combined with lack of limbs would bring stares from anyone, man or woman. Her eyes dance over the map, and she mutters something to Ank, who tilts his head so that the others cannot hear.

"I offered my people to you as lambs to the slaughter," Ank says, once they are finished conferring. "But we may surprise you by being useful as more than flesh shields for Pietran soldiers."

"How is this?" Witt asks.

"We can take you across the river," Nilana says, pinning him with her eyes as if daring him to contradict her.

"There is no bridge," Hadduk counters. "The ones built in the past have been washed away, with no solid soil to rest on. And as for boats—"

"Boats are for the dead. Yes, I know," Nilana interrupts in a tone that makes it clear what she thinks of the Pietran belief, making Hadduk's black eyebrows come closer together.

"No Pietran soldier would set foot in a boat before fighting a battle." Witt smoothly steps in between them. "Even if their Lithos told them to, it would unsettle them badly. No man fights well with a shaking sword arm."

"We don't swim either," Hadduk goes on, arms crossed defiantly. "And we're in no hurry to learn."

"No one is asking you to," Nilana says. "Come to the banks with your men, and we'll get you across the river."

"Maybe earning your respect at the same time," Ank adds. "The Stilleans will expect a frontal attack, our first wave announced by the sound of the timber fence they've built crashing to the ground. What an advantage we will have if instead we approach from the beach, feet silent on sand."

Witt studies the map, mouth set in a thin line. He doesn't like Ank making suggestions that uproot his entire battle plan, but at the same time, he can't argue the logic of it.

"Assuming you can get us across here," Witt says, touching the map where the river cuts through the Hadundun forest, "we can then follow the river on the opposite side, making our way toward Stille where none would look for us to travel."

Nilana nods, seeing Witt waver. "The Pietra and Stilleans both dread water. Overcome your fear, and give them a new nightmare."

Witt doesn't glance up, eyes still on the map, finger trailing the five-day march to Stille, where the river empties into the sea. "We recross here?"

"By what unknown Feneen magic?" Hadduk demands, but stills when Witt raises a finger.

"No matter their method, once on sand, our footsteps will fall quietly, the tide hiding the rustle of sword and spear, and the unguarded belly of Stille before us, defenseless as a pried-open clam."

"You may have won my respect already," Witt says, meeting Nilana's eyes and stifling the shiver that threatens to tear through him when she winks.

"Wait until I fight at your side," she says. "Imagine what that will win me."

"Tides, woman," Hadduk says. "How do you intend to fight with no arms and no legs?"

She cocks her head, and a slight bulge appears on the side of her cheek right before she curls her tongue and spits at him. A thorn flies through the air, embedding itself in the leather of Hadduk's belt, right above the groin.

"You'll want to put on a glove before you remove that," she says. "The poison will drop you dead in a moment."

Witt prepares to stop a lunge from Hadduk, but instead his commander's lips spread into a misshapen smile. "I always said women were snakes, but I never met one who could kill the same way. Tell me," Hadduk goes on, smile slipping into a leer. "When you're on your back do you writhe like one, too?"

"I imagine if you were to learn the answer to that, *I'd* drop dead from the amount of wine it would take for it to come to pass," Nilana answers coolly, and Witt covers a smile.

"Enough," he says. "If you say you can get us across the river, I'll take you at your word, but I won't wager all my men on it. Hadduk, you'll take a battalion to the banks in the morning. Ank, you'll perform whatever miracle you have at your employ to get Pietra to the other side, and I'll trust you with more."

"They won't even wet their feet," Ank assures him, and Witt leaves the room, nodding to Nilana as he goes. Hadduk and Pravin follow, their boot heels echoing down the halls along with his.

"Hadduk, you'll keep a civil tongue in your head to Nilana," Witt reproaches him, and his commander heaves a sigh.

"You may not be distracted, my Lithos," Hadduk says, "but it's easy enough to get my attention, even if she is only a torso with a pretty head attached."

"Hadduk," Pravin growls, and the commander waves him off.

"Fair enough, my Lithos. But if it comes to making half-Pietran babies with a Feneen to honor a bargain after the battle is done, I'm willing to make the sacrifice of taking a tumble with her."

"Your selflessness will be remembered," Witt says evenly, earning a slap on the back as Hadduk slips down a side hall that leads to the barracks.

Pravin waits until his footfalls have died away before speaking. "You realize that Ank brought her to the proceedings to illustrate that your choice of Feneen wife may not be such a hardship after all, yes?"

"It had occurred to me," Witt admits. "But my own thoughts on the matter change nothing if the people will not have a Lithos with a woman by his side."

"First things first," the Mason says. "Win the war, then worry about the woman."

"First things first," Witt echoes. "Move an army across a river with no boats and no bridge."

"And I say if the Feneen can do that, then perhaps they deserve more than Pietran arrows in their backs," Pravin says.

"Perhaps they do." Witt wills his answer not to be influenced by the invitation in Nilana's eyes when she looks at him. "Perhaps not."

CHAPTER 55

Khosa

MY NERVES HUM, FOR ONCE WITH SOMETHING OTHER than the assurance of my death. This is the last time I will sit in this library; my fingers will never hold this quill again. The words I write are still wet, and I'll not linger over them, once dry. The dust sifting onto my shoulders from the maps above as they sway will land on the floor tomorrow.

For I will not be here.

I work, even so. Vincent thought it best for me to keep to my habits in the days leading to my escape, and I am not one to fill my scrolls with drivel. My hand shakes a bit as I remind myself that all of it is exactly that, if Dara's memories are as compromised as I think. I steady the tip of the quill on the edge of the inkpot, only to hear a rhythmic tapping as it strikes against the glass. Tiny convulsions are running through my hands, nerves come to life in a body that now has the hope to live. Tension ripples down my spine, into the meaty muscles of my legs and down into my feet.

My feet.

"Not now," I say and bite down on my lip to feel pain instead, anything other than the beginning of the dance, though it may only be an echo of the tremor in my hand.

"And usually the girls are happy to see me," a voice says, and I turn to find Donil leaning in the archway, his smile so comical next to Merryl's obvious disapproval that I feel an answering one bloom on my lips.

"It wasn't meant for you," I tell him, and he takes this as an invitation, striding to my side. The leap of my heart at his voice drives my senses away, any shame I feel from our last meeting driven out by the pulse of my heart. Too late, I remember the lure that Vincent told me resides with Donil, an Indiri magic that no doubt is the reason within I ended up on my back the last time we spoke.

"Nonetheless, I am busy," I find myself saying, my stony voice sliding back to what it knows best.

"I know, and it's a fine bit of work you've set upon yourself here," he says, completely unfazed by my tone. "Khosa is going to save the world," Donil yells over his shoulder at Merryl, who only grunts.

"You are," Donil says, reaching out to pat my hand as he says it.

I let him, savoring the rush of warmth that slides up past my wrist, tingling all the way to my shoulder and burrowing toward my heart. Even if it is planted falsely, I can't dislike it. Vincent has been the promised gentleman every night in my bedroom, never suggesting he even lie beside me to pool warmth. I've lain in my feather bed night after night, listening to him turn on the stone floor at my feet, knowing he will not suggest another arrangement. And neither do I want him to, for even though he will give up a throne to save my life, his touch still brings a shudder to my skin that I cannot ignore. Yet with Donil I seem able to outrun my father's dark heritage, if only for a few stolen moments.

I slide my hand out from under his to clear my head. "I don't know if I will save the world, after all."

Donil grows suddenly serious, leaning in close to me as Cathon did, but instead of increasing the distance between us, I tilt forward, drawn forward by his intensity.

"Then you waste much ink," he whispers dramatically.

A laugh barks out of me, and I swat at him. He bats away my arm with a simple gesture, and again I feel the heat radiating from where our skin met.

"No, honestly," Donil says, "if anyone can save us, you can, and I'm here to take my sister's place."

"Ah . . ." With my own problems so close at hand, I had not noticed Dara's absence. "I offended her past the point of returning?"

"I believe so. She's run off to the woods for a few days, something you get used to once you know her. I pity whatever she comes across, but her anger is better spent there than in castle walls. Dara's sworn to have my head off at least as many times as I've winked at pretty girls, and I think she's threatened to toss Vincent from the parapet once or twice. Temper comes easily to my sister, but the fire burns far hotter than it does long."

"If you're saying she'll forgive me eventually, that's not the best way," I tell him. "I prefer the fire not to burn at all."

There's a glib reply on his lips and a light in his eye that tells me exactly where the comment was headed, but he bites down on it and clears his throat. "In any event, my memories are at your disposal, if you're still so inclined."

I am inclined, but not for the sake of his Indiri memories. I don't want to rifle through dry pages and ask Donil to find the whisper of an overgrown path or a certain pattern of rocks. I realize I want his eyes open, and on me.

"Tell me more about your sister," I say instead. "Why are the two of you so different?"

Donil shrugs. "Why is the sea wet and the land dry? We are each of us what we need to be. Sometimes I think that, though there be only two Indiri left, fate handed us each a half of what was necessary for there to be a whole remaining."

I remember what Vincent told me. "You are life," I say.

"Yes, and Dara quite the opposite." There's a smile when he says it, but I've studied faces long enough to spot the shadow there.

"You would rather it were switched?"

Donil's mouth opens and shuts again, the quick answers I'm accustomed to from him not coming so easily. He remains still long enough that dust motes have settled in his hair before he speaks.

"Sometimes," he says, voice low and heavy with words I know he's never spoken before. "I know battle, and I can fight. But when the Feneen attacked, Ank waited until Dara had left King Gammal's side to kill him. He faced me and Vincent, shoulder to shoulder, but Dara he would not challenge."

"You think this makes you less of a man?" I ask, my hand searching for his and closing around it to give comfort.

"Does it make me more of a man to tumble girls?" he asks, then squeezes my hand. "Sorry, I should not have said that."

"It's all right, Donil," I say. "I know about . . . what you can do."

His brow furrows, and his hand clenches a little more than comfortable. "How?"

"Vincent told me."

The laugh that comes from him is dark and jagged, not fitting in his throat well. "I'm sure he gave you a truthful accounting of it," he says, shaking his head. "Khosa . . . it's not . . . I could never take a girl against her will, or even turn a head that wasn't already inclined my way."

I pull my hand out of his, but gently. "I didn't think you would . . . force a girl. It's not your nature."

"It's not," he agrees. "But it's also not in my power. There are girls who enjoy my company, surely. But there are many more that find my spotted skin repulsive, and no amount of flirtation could change that."

I falter, biting down on my lip. "So you can't . . ."

"Khosa," he says. "No one has ever thrown themselves at my feet, begging to be ravished, then woken regretting the act."

"I believe you," I say. The warmth this time comes from my own voice, and I know that it's true.

"Good, because they don't regret it," he teases. "Far from it."

"You are terrible," I tell him, and we laugh together, the sound deepening Merryl's frown.

"My lady," Merryl speaks up, and I feel a tinge of annoyance at the interruption, "I believe it is time you dress for dinner."

I've spent long hours in the library with food trays brought by servants cooling at my feet, formal dinners with the royals long abandoned once my stone face set their stomachs awry. But I can hardly contradict Merryl when I see the concern for me buried beneath his irritation at Donil.

"I'll go," Donil says, taking my hand as he rises. "Perhaps tomorrow we will save the world together?"

"Yes," I say, savoring the tips of fingers brushing as he leaves. "Tomorrow."

He turns in the doorway, a hesitation on his lips that doesn't fit with the boy I'm learning to know. When our eyes meet, his gaze drops to the ground, and the words that come seem to gag him as he forces them out.

"I know that you will save us all, Khosa. I know the sacrifice you make." His gaze meets mine again, a twist of his lips trying to resurrect the easy smile. "Until tomorrow."

His shadow has disappeared along the corridor before I realize there won't be a tomorrow, and the regret that comes with it is eclipsed only by the fact that the warmth of his touch has suffused me entirely, driving the twinges from my limbs. I ignore Merryl's glance and rest my head on the table, ignoring the history marred by the tears slipping down my nose.

CHAPTER 56

———⚬⚬◯⚬◦———

Witt

WITT STANDS ON THE BANK OF THE RIVER, THE HEAVY air dampening his shirt so that it sticks to his chest in patches. Beside him, Pravin coughs discreetly into his hand, the wet sound drawing a sideways glance from Hadduk.

"I put my mind around it more than once in the night, my Lithos," Hadduk says. "If the Feneen have a way to get across this river, it's beyond anything I know."

"How far does one have to search for that?" Pravin asks.

"You know a little about many things," Hadduk says. "But I know much about a few. And this entanglement with the Feneen makes the hairs on my neck stand up just as much as Nilana makes something else sta—"

"Regardless of how it's done, I believe it can be." Witt cuts him off. "You rode against the Indiri. Surely you remember the campaign to do the same to the Feneen?"

"I do. The Lithos before you said they posed no threat, but offered no benefit, either. We sent out scouts to report back, thinking it would be the work of a few days to dig a pit for them to match the Indiri's."

"And?"

"And we never found them. Party after party went out, looking for a whole tribe of people who should have been easy fodder for blades. Never saw the single turn of a sharp-edged leaf to say where they'd been."

"Because they were there." Witt nods to the opposite shore. "Happily safe from blades, arrows, and eyes. They'll get us across, Hadduk."

"I see you've brought a battalion." Ank's voice cuts through the clearing as his horse appears from the Hadundun trees. "Pity you didn't trust us with more. We could have the entire Pietran army safely on the other side by dusk."

"I'd prefer not to gather my entire army at a scheduled time and place, nonetheless." Witt closes his hand around the horse's bridle.

"Even to meet an ally?" Ank clicks his tongue. "Your trust is not easily given."

"It must be earned," Hadduk says, unable to hide his clear disappointment when he sees Nilana did not accompany Ank.

"And it shall be," Ank says, as Feneen come from the forest, seeming almost to sprout from the ground itself. The battalion of Pietra stand steaming and still in the heat, but Witt can see their eyes scouring the landscape as the number of Feneen grows, and their hands tightening on spears.

"Earn our trust, then," he says stiffly to Ank. "Show us, Feneen."

Ank motions to some of his men who lumber from the trees, their appearance drawing gasps from the assembled Pietra. Metal protrudes from their shoulders, a loop on each side of their head. They ignore the reaction, drawing small knives from their sides, making a few of the Pietra stiffen. But instead of approaching the battalion, they wade into the river, chopping through coarse reeds. Witt shifts his own shoulders subconsciously at the sight of the mutilated Feneen, and Ank smiles.

"We call them the Silt Walkers," he says. "It's a great honor among our people to join their ranks, but the choice must be made early. As a living tree will grow round a spike in the ground given time, so do humans knit with metal, if the spikes are driven while the bone is still soft with youth."

"Why would you do such a thing?" Witt asks.

"Watch and see."

Pravin glances at Witt, a question in his eyes, as Feneen march into the river and more reeds are cut. Witt shakes his head, their purpose a mystery to him. Ank raises his hand and the Feneen with reeds go deeper into the water, handing off knives to their replacements, who cut reeds themselves.

"My Lithos," Hadduk says, "if they start to pipe us a tune that reminds me of a dirge, I'll run them through, allies or not."

"Hold, Commander," Witt growls under his breath.

The Silt Walkers who went into the river first are far out now, the water to their necks, reeds held above the flow. With another wave from Ank they step still farther, and Witt finds himself holding his breath in empathy, a tightening in his chest that wants to erupt in a scream to tell them to stop.

They slip farther still, bringing the hollow reeds to their mouths in the last moment, their hair dancing at the surface until even that is gone, and the reeds grow shorter as they walk on the riverbed. Each reed is followed by another Feneen. Each plants his feet on the shoulders of the man beneath him, held in place against the current by their monstrous hooks.

"Fathoms," Hadduk says, as the water rises to the chests of the second men.

"Something to see, for sure," Witt says to Ank. "But even if I could convince our men to breathe through reeds and walk underwater, their armor will drag them down."

"Wait," Ank says as still more Feneen pour into the river, cutting reeds and climbing onto one another's shoulders. "You have forgotten. I promised that they would not even wet their feet. You need not convince your men of doing anything other than what they wish to do already: trample my people into the ground."

With that he whistles shrilly and a wave of flesh slices through the river as all the Feneen palms above the surface turn upward, forming a path of skin that snakes to the other side. Ank steps out onto them lightly, turning back to smile at Witt when he is halfway across.

"Don't go, my Lithos." Pravin's hand shoots out to stop Witt as he steps forward. "Who is to say they will not cave beneath you for the joy of watching you drown?"

"And who would command his soldiers to do something he has not?"

The trampled grass gives way to silt and the destroyed bed of reeds. Witt can't hide his grimace as the river water touches his boots, but he wades forward to the first upturned palm, nodding at the Feneen beneath it. He plants his boot, and then the next, the feel of soft flesh under his heel causing him to gag. Nonetheless, he holds his face impassive as he joins Ank at river's middle, ignoring the sway of the human bridge beneath him. Ank turns to the opposite bank at his approach and Witt follows, relieved when he lands on solid ground.

"Well done, Lithos," Ank says. "Welcome to the far shore."

Witt extends his hand. "Welcome to my army."

CHAPTER 57

<hr>

Vincent

CATHON KEEPS HIS FACE CAREFULLY BLANK AS HE ENTERS my measurements into the ledger, but it is this controlled neutrality that gives him away.

"Not all that impressive, am I?" I ask, stepping down from the scale. The stone on the other side drops, hitting the floor with a crash that has him scrambling for the inkpot before it splatters across generations of Stillean nobility, all of them taller than me. Even the column that holds Purcell's measurements is more impressive than mine, though the column itself is short-lived.

"It's not the height that makes the man," Cathon says, turning the book for me to see the carefully lined columns. "Runnar was about your height when he died, and he's remembered for a long and glorious rule."

"Runnar was my height when he died because he outlived his own children and walked nearly doubled over," I say. "How tall was he at my age?"

Cathon turns a few pages, scans Runnar's measurements, and deftly flips the book closed. "I wouldn't let it concern you overly."

I walk to the door of the chamber and glance out. We are utterly alone. The mundane task of measuring the royals has drawn no curiosity from anyone, exactly as we expected. I draw a folded paper from my shirt and hand it to Cathon.

"I'm no mapmaker, but it's the best I could do," I say, lowering my voice. "The tunnels are straightforward if you know where the entrances are."

Cathon unfolds the map I've drawn of the underground passages beneath the castle. "Made with a panicking royal family in mind, certainly," he says. "Not much fear of getting lost." He examines it more closely, a frown developing. "It leads to the beach?"

"Yes, there's a small cave there. We'll have to time it with the tide, of course, but I know the rhythms well. I had it in my mind more than once to run away. I would get as far as the mouth before going back."

"What changed your mind?" Cathon asks as he folds the map.

I shrug. "The sunrise. It's easier to imagine yourself doing the impossible in the dark. Light has a way of bringing you to your senses."

"Speaking of doing the impossible in the dark, I've heard a rumor about you." My father's voice brings me to my feet, positive that guilt must be painted on my face as clearly as the ink in Cathon's ledger.

"My lord." Cathon stands, takes a ducking bow, and flicks my map beneath his papers. "I was just taking the prince's measurements. He's becoming quite the man."

"Yes," my father says, a smile I don't like quirking his lips. "I've heard that as well."

Cathon glances between us. "I believe I have all I need."

"You're excused," my father says, and Cathon gathers his books, quills, and inkwell without glancing in my direction. Like any of the more informed servants, he knows my father well enough to close the door behind him as he leaves.

"What is it, Father?" I ask.

"We had rather harsh words last time we spoke," he says, crossing to the scale. He sits on the empty side I recently vacated, the rock on the opposite rising much farther than it did for me.

"We did, and I don't know they're the kind that can be taken back," I say.

He laughs a little to himself, the kind of chuckle that would've have sent Purcell and me running for our rooms when we were smaller. "You don't truly think I'm here to apologize, do you?"

"I don't believe I will, either," I say. "So why are you here?"

"Because I've heard whispers that you spend your nights with the Given."

My jaw clenches; an uneasiness spreads in my gut. I spent much of my childhood avoiding my father, and the better part of recent years either answering him with halfhearted mutters or full-fledged insolence. But I've never lied to him.

"Yes," I say. "It's true."

He eyes me carefully, as if this new development is something he could spot on my skin or in my stature.

"And?" he asks.

"And?" I repeat, shaken by the question.

"How do you find her bed?"

"I . . ." Of all the things I expected him to ask, this was not one of them. "It's very nice," I finally say.

He sighs and examines his fingernails. "I know you've never liked me, Vincent. Your mother got her claws in you too early. I didn't think much of it at the time, since Purcell was always at my side, but—"

"But he died and left you with me," I say.

"Yes," he says, rising from the scale. The rock hits the ground again, twice as loud as when I was on it. He crosses to me, and I have to will myself not to step backward as his hands land heavily on my shoulders. He is silent, staring into my eyes as if expecting to see Purcell resurrected there in this one moment when I have not failed him.

"It's an odd thing," he says quietly, almost to himself. "The Tangata care for their kits, wolves for their pups. I've seen great men handle their babes with extreme gentleness, and women raise infants not their own. How can this bond exist in abundance, yet have failed utterly between you and me?"

"I do not know, Father," I say, swallowing past the lump in my throat. "But it has."

"Quite," he agrees, stepping away from me. "Get the girl with child. You can make more on some other woman to fill the throne. Then perhaps we'll have something to talk about between us."

I watch him leave, hoping it is the last time I will ever have to hear his voice.

CHAPTER 58

MY DEPARTURE COULD BE THE DEATH KNELL OF AN ENTIRE kingdom, but the feelings of a single boy slow my steps. A permanent groove mars my fingers where a quill has pressed against my flesh as I piece out the fate of our world, but the one I hold now feels awkward in my hand. I am adept at stringing together facts and tallying numbers in cold columns, but I have no idea how to make ink tell the story of my feelings.

In the end, I know it's best that I don't.

Donil's parting words from the library echoed in my head last night as I walked with Merryl back to my chambers, their meaning lost to me. The whole country knows what sacrifice I would make if I were to remain here. Why should it weigh so heavily on Donil only now? The thought had itched, like the snag of a barbar weed on bare skin, a rash spreading through my mind. A maid slipped past us, dropping a curtsy, something that hadn't happened since the newness of my arrival wore off.

The turn of the corner brought another, and a deep nod, followed by the touch of a forehead from a sconcelighter, along with a breathy "good evening to you, Given." My face remained impassive to the last, until I saw Vincent waiting at my door and a gulf of heat opened in my stomach for my heart to descend into. Our ruse has been successful, and the entire castle believes that Vincent beds me to breed the next Given.

And if maids and sconcelighters know, then surely Donil does as well.

"Tides," I say to myself now, stabbing the quill through parchment in the privacy of my own room.

Leaving a letter could compromise everything, make a mockery of what Vincent, Cathon, and Merryl risk for my sake. But the combined weight of their fates feels fragile when set against the vision I see when I close my eyes—an Indiri boy's face crumpling with grief as he imagines me fleeing with his best friend, my supposed lover. I mutter an Indiri curse learned from Dara, its sharp edges tart on my tongue.

"Khosa," Merryl enters, bolting the door silently behind him. "It is time."

It is, and yet it is not. I crumple the page beneath my fingers, wet ink smearing my hands. No message is left behind, only a feeble attempt to open myself taking form in a splotch of black that I crush beneath my heel.

"I am ready," I say.

The draught that Merryl brings has been carefully measured to sink him into the deepest sleep. Those searching for me will find him on the floor of my room, a spilled water glass from Vincent's chambers close by, my lover come to save me from my fate, my guard easily dispatched with trust in his eyes as he accepts a drink from the royal visitor. Merryl sniffs from the vial, his eyes watering.

"I have a bit more sympathy for my wee babe, at least," he says, waving his hand in front of his nose. "The wife puts a drop of this in her mouth when she's colicky, and her face twists something terrible at the taste."

I rest my hand on his arm, our first and only touch. "You all take much upon yourselves for my sake," I say.

"I take nothing but a long nap," Merryl says. "Cathon has a life of boredom in front of him, and a touch more heat in his blood than is good for a Scribe. He'll treat it as an adventure."

"Vincent leaves a throne—"

"That he never wanted," Merryl cuts me off. "He was never good at hiding that fact."

I think of the first time I met Vincent, at the celebration of my arrival, his face tense and unhappy, palms curled in his lap as he surveyed the milling nobility.

"No, he wasn't good at hiding it."

"You're the one with the trial in front of you," Merryl says. "The coast will echo with screams for your blood, from the royals down to the maids. They'll hunt you, and them not the only ones. The cats in the forest will feast on anyone, Given or not. And always your feet will want to turn toward the sea, your own body betraying you."

I stare at him, my eyes brimming with tears at the truth in his words. "Always I have lived knowing I do so in order to die," I say. "Only now do I know the fear of losing my life."

I don't tell him the reason has light eyes, freckles, and an easy smile, or that the hesitation in my step has nothing to do with the fear that every day I draw breath I will be hunted. Instead I hold on to each passing second, because the warmth Donil leaves behind when he touches me could erupt into a bonfire if we allowed it the time. But that time would be measured by the growth in my belly, and end with a rush of blood, leaving him with a child and my footprints in the sand, not returning.

And yet, I falter. Because part of me believes that time might be worth trading for a life full of anything else.

Merryl's eyes are on me, intense. "I know why you linger," he says. "If I were told to walk away from my wife or die, I would lie down then and there. There may be something between you and the Indiri, but it is a seed without roots. Tear it out, carry it, keep it near your heart if you would. It will grow elsewhere. Go, Khosa. Lead a life, and let none tell you it was done in vain."

He puts the vial to his mouth before I can stop him, the muscles in his throat rippling as he drinks. I cry out, grabbing for him as he falls. We slump together against the foot of my bed, his head on my shoulder as the vial rolls from his hand. I splash water from Vincent's glass onto the floor around Merryl, then wrap his still fingers around the stem.

The steps of our plan have been so deeply seared into my mind that I'm enacting them before I realize the choice has been made not by me, but by Merryl. I brush his hair from his eyes as he sleeps, pressing my lips against his forehead for the briefest of moments, ignoring the shudder it brings.

"Clever man," I whisper. "Clever and good. May we meet again."

Cathon's knock is so quiet I barely hear it as I tie off a few things in the corner of my sleepshirt. I came into Stille with bloody feet and a dress in shreds; I'll leave better prepared. I take a quill and inkpot, a small scroll, and hunks of bread and cheese from my dinner. The sleeves of the sleepshirt knot together nicely and I duck underneath the loop I've made, the bulk of all of my possessions resting on my hip.

Cathon leans over Merryl, placing his palm on the guard's chest to make sure it still rises and falls.

"He may sleep longer than we thought," Cathon says, rising. "But the later he's able to say anything to anyone, the better. Are you ready?"

I nod, pulling a dark cloak over my dress, the hood over my face. Cathon peers into the hall, motioning for me to follow. We slip into the corridor soundlessly, keeping to the walls. The candle sconces are newly lit, tears of wax beginning to drop down their sides. The lighter is somewhere ahead of us, unknowingly illuminating the way for our escape.

Another hall and another, Cathon's breath coming faster and mine catching in my throat as time spent on stools in dusty rooms takes a toll. Neither one of us could run across the training field without stopping for a rest, and I feel a bubble of laughter rise at the thought of the two of us ruining the escape because we need to sit down.

Cathon pulls up short at the next corner, laying a finger on his lips. I nod, grateful for the break. A bead of sweat trickles down the side of his face and drops to the stone at our feet before we move again, ducking past the lit hall where I see the sconcelighter standing on tiptoe, stretching to replace a candle. The darkness folds around us as we slip into places she has not touched yet, but the stone under my fingers is warm and the smell of bread is in my nose.

"The kitchens?" I whisper.

"We're in the servants' hall, just behind the hearth," Cathon answers, his voice a thin thread in the dark. "In a moment we'll be in the dairy. There's an entrance there to the tunnels that will take us to Vincent, and the horses. Which"—he heaves a deep breath—"I think I'll rather welcome."

"We're scholars, not adventurers, you and I," I say, my own words barely audible as I gasp for air.

"A few steps down now," he warns, and I slide my feet forward in the dark, feeling for the drop-off.

There are more than a few steps, and I feel the air cooling around me as we descend. The sweat on my skin now feels chilly, and I shiver, pulling the cloak tighter at my throat.

"Almost there," Cathon says, and the floor beneath my feet evens out.

The air is heavy with the smell of fresh milk and the tang of aging cheeses. It presses against me and it takes real effort to breathe, as if the darkness itself is a weight on my chest.

"Where is the passage?" I ask, ready to leave this place behind.

I hear Cathon searching for the trapdoor. The pitch-black of the dairy matches the inside of my eyelids, and I don't know whether they are open or closed. I cross my arms, hugging my own elbows for warmth.

"Khosa," Cathon breathes, his voice directly in my ear, "I am sorry."

My whole body stills, even the air in my chest suspended for a moment as his arms encircle me from behind, his mouth hot on my neck. I am coiled like a snake in the grass, only I am not the predator, but the prey.

"There is no entrance to the tunnels here," I say, my voice flat and lifeless.

"No," he says, hands rising up my torso as he presses his whole body against me. My skin pulls away from him, but can only go so far, and I feel the revulsion all the way to my bones as his hands slip inside my bodice. A shudder rips through me, and bile rises in my throat. I gag and fall to my knees to retch.

Cathon follows me down, all apologies forgotten as his desire grows, emboldening his hands. I reach out in the dark with the palest idea of stopping him, but he swats my arms aside easily, pinning them above my head. It seems the time has come for my body to serve its purpose, and it has collapsed under the knowledge of what will happen, leaving only my mind in the darkness.

"I'm such a fool," I say. "A secret cadre of Scribes who wish to see the Given released?" I almost laugh as Cathon pushes my skirts up.

"Oh, they exist, and I am one of them," he says, trapping my wrists in one hand and fumbling with the front of his robes with the other. "But the king gave me a better offer. Now be still," he whispers, and I feel the nearness of him above me, the tightness of anticipation in his voice.

I have no intention of doing otherwise; the coldness of the stone floor beneath has penetrated my skin, dulling even the lifelong shudder that accompanies human touch. I am a shell on the beach, empty and hollow. Cathon's hand tightens on my wrist, grinding the bones together as he tears away my undergarments, and that flare of pain travels down my arms, igniting something I didn't know I owned, something inherited from a mother who would stare down a reviled tribe and decide who she wanted.

I don't want this. I don't want this man. And I am not his.

I buck suddenly, and Cathon falls away from me, not expecting resistance. I swing the bag at my shoulder blindly through the darkness, and it connects, the inkwell inside shattering. I dash for the stairs, but my skirts are loose and heavy, and he grabs me easily, all pretense of regret gone as he throws me face-first against the wall. He presses against me from behind, grinding my head against stone so hard my teeth scrape against grit. I spit and scream, kick and twist, but he is stronger and has no compunction about hurting me to gain whatever prize has been offered him.

"Khosa," he growls into my ear, "don't make this harder than it has to be."

I stomp down onto his foot, my riding boots crushing his toes and gaining me a moment to slip from his grasp. I wheel away, but he finds my flailing arms in the darkness, and I'm thrown off balance. I go down, reaching out for anything I can find to break the fall, my fingers glancing against glass bottles of milk. I grab one and turn, throwing it into the dark and hearing it crash against the opposite wall.

Cathon is still, and I reach behind me for another bottle, drops of water on the outside slicking my palms. My breath rises and falls loudly, and I shut my mouth to quiet it, listening for any movement. The stillness is so complete that my heart fills my ears and I barely notice the scrape of Cathon's foot to my right. I yell and throw the bottle, but it hits rock, and he's on me again.

I grab for another, my nails raking down wooden shelves as his arms circle my waist, pulling me away. I don't let go, and the entire shelf comes crashing down. Bottles shatter and cool milk splashes my heels, then soaks my knees as Cathon wrestles me down.

I have no strength left as he turns me over and tears my clothes away, wrenching my legs apart as milk flows into my ears. His face is looming over mine, and I am snapping at him, teeth clicking together on thin air when I realize that I can see him, lit by the fire of a torch.

"Stand up, so I can run you through."

I cry out at the sound of Donil's voice, and Cathon scrambles off me, adjusting his clothes as he rises to his feet. Donil stands on the stairs, a torch in one hand and his sword in the other. He descends the last few steps, eyes never leaving the Scribe, whose hands go out in front of him, as if they could ward off the bite of an Indiri blade.

"I was only doing what—"

Donil's sword leaps forward and slides through his mouth before he can finish. I flinch as Cathon's teeth close around the blade, his hands wrapping around it, producing rivers of blood that pour down his wrists.

"I know what you were doing," Donil says calmly, freeing his sword with a flick of his wrist, and sending Cathon's body tumbling to the ground, spilling blood into milk.

I try to get to my feet, but my knees shake and betray me, dropping me back into the mess on the floor. Donil's arm is around me, his sword forgotten as he pulls what remains of my dress into decency.

"Come to the stairs, out of the mess," he says gently. He leads me there, and I lean into him, the warmth I've always felt radiating from him seeping past the wetness of my cloak and into my skin.

We reach the bottom step, and he puts the torch in a wall sconce, both arms now free to hold me. I curl against him as the sobs start, my hands holding what's left of my clothes tight around me as I shake, my own breath tearing apart my body.

"It's all right," Donil says, over and over. "It's all right now."

His warmth embraces me, and I let it, aware that in this exact moment, maybe it is.

But a moment only lasts so long.

CHAPTER 59

—◦⊙◦—

Vincent

SOMETHING IS WRONG.

I know this cave, have known it since my fingers were strong enough to pull open the hidden panel in the library, my feet swift enough to carry me away from whatever new anger surged between my parents. Purcell shared the tunnels with me as soon as I could understand the importance of them, along with the need to keep them secret. We traveled them together often, but the last trip I made alone, tears streaming down my face at the death of my brother. Now I sit staring at a crack in the rock that Khosa should have come through some time ago, the tide lapping at my feet.

Outside, the horses snort to each other, unhappy with the water breaking around their hooves. I go to the tunnel entrance once more, leaning forward so that I can hear any murmur, any voice, above the rush of the surf. I throw caution to the wind and call her name, only to have it echoed back at me from wet walls.

I go out to the horses once the water has reached my middle. Whatever has happened, whether catastrophic or merely a delay, there will be no escape tonight. The cave will be entirely flooded soon, the end of the tunnel underwater.

I swing up onto my mount, gathering the reins of the other two in my fist. Our packs will keep for another day, and I hide them in the stables upon my return, giving an extra ration of grain to the mystified horses, who eat greedily at their unexpected meal.

The castle is quiet and my tongue feels like a weight in my mouth as I go to Khosa's room. I stand outside her door for a moment, not knowing what I will see when I push through. I prepare myself for the worst—Khosa and Cathon bound and at my father's mercy—and open the door.

What I find is almost worse—Khosa nestled against Donil by the fire.

"Vincent," she says, coming to her feet. Donil follows her, eyes on me. I don't know my hand is on my sword pommel until I see his movement echoing mine.

"Have a seat, brother," Donil says, motioning to the other chair.

"Khosa, what—" I begin, but am interrupted by a terrific snore and turn to see Merryl sprawled on Khosa's bed, mouth wide open as he dreams.

"Come Vincent, please," Khosa says, steering me to a chair. I go, dumbfounded by the light touch of her fingertips on my elbow. Only once I am seated do I realize her hands are shaking, and that her eyes are swollen, her cheeks streaked with spent tears.

"We were betrayed," she whispers to me, drawing her hand away. "Cathon. He led me to the dairy, and tried to—"

It's like a rock dropping into my gut, and a fire chasing it back up. "Where is he?"

"Still in the dairy," Donil says, his look telling me all I need to know.

"You're all right?" My hands go to Khosa without thinking, and she jolts but lets them remain on her arms.

"Yes," she says, patting my fingers lightly but then drawing away to sit in her own chair. "No harm was done."

"I wouldn't say that," Donil says. "You tore up the dairy, and a good thing too." He turns to me. "I was going to the kitchens to see what I could scrounge, and thought for certain someone had put a bull in the dairy for a laugh, all the glass that was breaking. What I found was something quite different."

I glance at Khosa, noting the beginning of a bruise on her cheek, and a line of scratches along her arm. While I was far away, she was misled and mishandled. Harm was done, but vengeance has already been exacted, and not by my hand.

"I'm so sorry," I say to her. "I had no idea he would—"

She holds up her palm to quiet me. "I didn't see it either, Vincent. The fault does not lie with you. It seems a reward for impregnating the Given was not offered only to the guards."

The fault may not lie with me, but the guilt certainly does. I trusted a man who laid hands on her, and with my father's blessing.

"We need to get the body, Vin," Donil says. "Cathon may have betrayed you, but your plan he kept to himself, twisting it for his own use. No one knows what you attempted tonight, and we must keep it that way."

Merryl mutters again in the bed, rolling onto his side.

"We can't leave Khosa alone," I say.

"Merryl gave me the names of men I can trust," Khosa says, counting them off on her fingers. "Cecil, Justus, Ornon, and Rook."

"Rook has the last watch on the east tower," Donil says. "I sometimes meet him for a game of ridking."

"Go," I say. "Tell him we need him to take Merryl's place at Khosa's door, that his friend is in his cups. We'll take Merryl to the guardhouse and then manage the other."

Donil nods and disappears into the corridor, leaving me with Khosa.

The silence stretches long after his footsteps are gone. I know she will not take comfort from me as she did with Donil, and that sends another streak of anger through my body, following paths that are beginning to burrow deep. For her part, Khosa remains staring at the fire, face set implacably against all that surrounds her, including me.

When Donil returns with Rook, she pretends to be asleep in her chair, bruising cheek and swollen eyes hidden by the fall of her hair. Rook unquestioningly takes Merryl's spot in the hall, but I see his brow furrow as Donil and I balance the burly guard between us on the way to the bunkhouse. I'm sure it goes against Merryl's character to drink himself to stupidity while on watch, but we have no better excuse.

Donil and I don't speak until we're in the dairy, the light of the torch he left behind playing over a sickening mix of blood and milk.

"Tides," I say, my nose wrinkling against the smell of curdle already at work. Cathon's eyes are open, his mouth splayed horrifically wide by Donil's blade. Teeth litter the floor around him, which Donil wordlessly begins to gather.

I prop the body in a corner and retrieve a bucket of wash water from the kitchen, splashing it around to thin the blood. It takes our combined strength to push the rack back against the wall, a testament to how hard Khosa struggled to defend herself.

"Him first," Donil says, breaking the silence. "Then we'll see what's to be done about the mess."

Glass crunches under our feet as we prop Cathon between us, his lifeless body heavier than Merryl's was. Two wet trails follow us up the stairs, milk dripping down his legs from his soaked robes. We rest at the top of the stairs and share a glance.

"To the library," I say. "There are tunnels there that lead to a safe haven for the royals; I was going—"

Donil holds up a hand to stop me. "Khosa explained, brother."

His use of the word adds guilt on top of an already heavy weight in my gut. "I couldn't share it with you," I say. "Even if I'd wanted to—"

"But you didn't want. And I know the reason. Truly, Vincent, you're the only brother a boy with my blood could have, and I won't let a woman come between us, even if she is worth it."

The torch in his hand sputters, and I drop my eyes, the guilt taking on a new facet—shame. "I have not treated you well, brother."

Donil nods, the apology accepted, then shifts Cathon back onto his shoulder. "We'll put him in the tunnels then?"

"He should have gone there in the first place," I say, taking my share of the weight as we struggle down the hall.

"If he'd done so, I never would have found them," Donil says.

"Going to the kitchens to see what you could scrounge?" I ask, repeating his reason for being near the dairy at so late an hour. "Certainly not going to see if Daisy was still awake?"

"A man can eat bread and talk to a woman at the same time," Donil says, but I hear his smile in the dark.

"What of Khosa, then?" I ask him, willing my voice to remain neutral, though the spike of anger still pricks at my gut.

Donil sighs. "She is the Given. I cannot deny that I have feelings for her, but neither will I seal her fate by getting her with child. I ask the same—what of Khosa? I know you have been spending nights with her."

The hurt in his voice overwhelms any false victory I might have felt otherwise. "There is nothing between us," I confess. "Merely a ruse to keep her safe from my father. One that failed as certainly as we did tonight."

I push aside the library tapestry that hides a loose rock, pressing in the right place for it to roll away.

"We'll have to take him far enough so that he won't be smelled," Donil says.

"I'll do it," I say. "Get back to the dairy and do what you can before Daisy awakes. What passed tonight must be as if it never were."

Donil nods once and is gone, leaving me the torch. I drag Cathon with one hand, lighting my way with the other. Despite Donil's advice, I don't take the body far, trusting the stone that shuts behind me as I leave to keep our secret for the time being.

I head for my father's room.

CHAPTER 60

Vincent

THE GUARDS AT FATHER'S DOOR STEP ASIDE AT MY GLANCE, and I find him abed, eyes bleary from sleep.

"Vincent?" he asks, for once no trace of guile on his face. "What has happened?"

"How can you not guess, Father, with so many in these walls vying for the right to Khosa's maidenhood?"

He actually brightens, and my fists clench. "Is it done, then?"

"It is not," I spit. "And a man lies dead because of you."

He doesn't ask who, merely gets to his feet to stir what remains of the coals in the fireplace, his robe billowing around him as he moves. "Because of me or you?"

"It was Donil who struck the blow while protecting her."

He tosses fresh wood into the fire and smiles as the first of the flames licks to life, a thread of heat reaching toward me from across the room. "You mistake my meaning, Vincent. I know you killed no man, as I knew you never bedded the Given."

"You know no such thing," I say, willing my voice to remain calm.

"But I do," he sighs as if disappointed, and rests the poker against the stones, its curled tip leaving a black line of soot in its wake. "You said yourself men compete for Khosa's *maidenhood*. I'd call the competition off if there were no prize, wouldn't I?"

My blood heats more quickly than the fire, and I feel my lip curl. Yet he only laughs.

"More than your words gives you away, son," he continues. "A boy with a willing girl of her qualities finds himself interested in nothing else. Yet I've seen you walking the halls, even leaning over old books with your supposed lover in the library, when if you were lovers, in truth, all your spare time would be spent between sheets."

"We are not animals," I say through gritted teeth.

His composure slips, and the first flare of the fabled temper I've inherited breaks through. "You *are*, boy. We all are. Every one of us exists to eat and breed, and that is all. Some of us do it in finery, some of us wallow in the mud, but we all follow the desires of our stomachs and our loins, and you, even with your mother's lofty ideals, are not above taking your fill."

I think of Khosa, how her teeth nibble at her own lips as she writes, the little gasps that escape her upon some new discovery. There is some truth to his words, as I have more than once thought of those lips beneath mine, her gasps brought on by my hands and more. Those visions have power, one that pulls at me even now, but the image of her by the fire, a bruise blooming on a cheek tracked with tears, is stronger.

"Yet somehow I have not taken anything, despite desires willing me to do so," I say.

"Then you are a fool," my father says. "You could have any girl you want, with or without her blessing, and never know retribution. This one that you've attached yourself to will find a lover in the sea, one that will tumble the flesh right off her bones before it's done with her."

He has always seen more of Mother than himself in me, so when I lunge for him, he's unprepared. Bone strikes bone as my knuckles crack against his nose and he goes over, hands dragging for purchase across the mantel to break his fall. He hangs there for a second, bright blood dripping from his nose. Our eyes meet, and he laughs.

"Now you find some nerve, boy? *Now?*"

The door that connects his room to my mother's flies open, and she rushes in, fumbling her dressing gown closed. Her hair hangs around her shoulders, the silver threaded through the dark strands more obvious now that it's loose. She glances between us, me cradling a bruised hand to my chest, Father's blood spraying into the fire as he shakes his head to clear it.

"Vincent, what have you done?" she says.

"Fulfilled my desires," I say, eyes still on my father, who laughs again.

"It seems he's not entirely your son," he says to Mother, fingers gingerly tracing the bulbous swelling of his nose. "Although even when he strikes in anger, it's in protection of another."

Mother turns to me, a question in her eyes.

"He set a man upon the Given," I tell her. "A man who died trying to gain what was promised to him in return. What was it, Father?"

"There were plenty who would do the deed for the pleasure of it alone," Father says.

I think of Cathon's face, the calculation in his eyes and the quickness of his mind. "Not this man," I say. "Cathon would have wanted more than flesh as reward."

"Ah, the Scribe." Father sits in the fireside chair and crosses his legs as if we are having a leisurely chat about the crop yield. "He had some demands, the position of Curator among them."

"But the Curator can be replaced only upon the death of the current . . ."

Father watches my face as my words trail off, the depth of how far he's willing to go apparent. Mother's hands have gone to her face, palms covering her mouth.

"How many men would you kill to see it done?" I ask.

"As many as necessary," he replies. "Even if the bodies rise as high as the outside walls, it is nothing in comparison to those that would float in the sea if she does not do her duty."

"You don't know that!" I shriek, the willful ignorance of his belief drawing out my anger. "Old stories are not fact, and tradition nothing more than a playact if you are wrong, one littered with the bodies of women damned because you blindly do as those before you have always done."

"Vincent," Mother says quietly, "mind your words. Tradition holds strong." She crosses to Father, her shaking hands going to his injuries, his blood slicking her hands. He pulls away from her touch, irritation flickering across his face.

"Tradition?" I ask. "Or habit? Just as you simper over a man who has never loved you, not questioning if there is another way."

"There is no other way, Vincent," he says. "Tradition. Habit. Name it what you will, but the Given is called for by not only the sea, but the people. If I deny them, they will rise, even if a wave does not. I may be king, but I am only one man."

"And Khosa only one girl," I say. "Yet I'll take the chance."

He shakes his head and comes to his feet, a bitter smile spreading. "If this Given were an ugly thing, she would pass to the water unnoticed by you. Are you so weak to be turned by a pretty face?"

It's my turn to laugh, and I don't need to speak my thoughts for him to follow.

"Yes, I've taken girls to my bed," he says, ignoring the choked sob from my mother. "Many and more, a long line of pretty faces. But I care for none, and endangered nothing by doing so."

"Must you be so callous?" Mother says, pulling herself into a chair. "Who is this man who speaks openly in front of his wife about other women?"

"Who am I?" Father turns on her. "I'm your husband. The one you chose above all others, knowing full well my nature."

"Yes, my *husband*," Mother spits. "A mockery of my womanhood, this marriage. A disgrace to my blood, that choice."

"Call your maids, woman," Father says, taking in her blotched, reddened face. "They'll have extra work to make you presentable today. Little wonder that I have a roving eye when you take so little care for yourself and willingly place nicely bodied tarts like the Indiri girl in my path."

"You bastard," Mother says, her rage a thing so long throttled that it shakes within her throat. "If you forced her—"

"Forced her?" My father laughs. "I've not had to. That girl desires only one thing, her children in a position of power, and I am the only one who can give it to her."

"She wouldn't," Mother says, but I feel a dark pit open in my stomach at the thought of Dara in my father's bed—and the possibility that it could be truth.

"No, she wouldn't," he agrees, turning his back to her to smile at me. "At least, not yet."

He doesn't see Mother change, the slide from heated emotion to cold calculation. He doesn't see her hand go to the poker or the slight trace of smoke it leaves behind as it arcs toward his head. His eyes are on mine, words of degradation on his lips.

And I hold them.

I keep my father's gaze locked on mine as my mother bashes his skull in.

The first swing garners a look of stunned surprise, an attack from behind unlooked for from a foe long considered vanquished. He goes down on one knee, and Mother's second swing shatters bone, the sound as incongruous as an egg breaking, the finality of the act belied by the quiet of the moment.

Mother's breath catches in her throat as the poker falls from her hand. "Vincent," she gasps. "I'm . . . I'm sorry."

"Don't be," I say, as blood pools around our feet.

CHAPTER 61

Dara

DARA KNOWS BETTER THAN MOST WHEN SHE IS BEING watched, can feel eyes on her much the way she imagines Khosa feels the sea—a constant weight. A lifetime of harsh scrutiny has taught her to filter the sensation while in the castle walls, but now, deep inside the Forest of Drennen, she is grateful for the warning that courses through her body, even if she can't name the source.

For two suns she's walked, forsaken the comfort of a feather bed for the cover of a leafy canopy. Her usual haunts—some caves near Hygoden, a secluded valley where she discovered the last of Hyllen's sheep, still scared and soot-covered—have not calmed her as they have in the past. Knowing Vincent's body as well as his heart is given to Khosa has undone Dara completely. Like a wounded animal, all she can think to do is put distance between herself and what is hurting her.

Her fire tonight is small, the hare she shot with her last arrow smaller. She leans back against a tree, her constant anger draining what energy she has left. Though she still feels eyes in the forest, her own grow weary. Dara's head hits her chest, but jerks upward when a stick snaps. The sound was purposeful, done the way Donil calls for her attention in the woods—without alerting others to their presence. She peers into the darkness, aware that the silence is a heavy, waiting one.

"Come in, then," she says, hand on her knife hilt. "I'll see your face whether you mean me peace or harm."

Shadows separate from the darkness, vague at first, their movement so slight even Dara's practiced eyes have to squint to follow as they emerge, finally, into the firelight. The Indiri's hand falls slowly away from her weapon, but her expression remains guarded. The two Feneen have five eyes between them and seven arms, though all their weapons remain at their belts and not in their hands.

She nods at them. "If you've come for my dinner, you can have it. My blood, and I'll put up a fight."

"We'd not tangle with you, Indiri," the taller Feneen says, slowly lowering himself to her fire. "Not after we saw you fight at the gates of Stille."

"If you were among that party, then you won't be leaving this fire with your throat closed."

The second Feneen opens all of his palms to her. "We mean you no harm."

"The harm is already done," Dara counters coolly. "The king was family to me, and there are few I call such. If a royal body falls by violence I'll see to it that more follow, of less consequence. Besides, you come upon me in a black mood."

"So I see," the taller Feneen says, his third eye blinking out of rhythm with the other two. "I am Filj, and this is Narr. Perhaps putting names to our faces may still your knives."

"Doubtful."

"In that case, a bit of your rabbit before you kill us?" Filj asks, his fingers going to the spit. Dara waves her permission, and he tears meat away from bone, handing some to Narr.

"You seem tired, Indiri," Filj continues. "Why are you so far from home and with red eyes?"

"My eyes are my worry, not yours," Dara says.

"All worries are the same in these days, I think," Filj says. "All minds go to the sea."

"Some in ways you don't expect," Dara agrees before she can remind her mouth to be still.

"Ah . . . ," Narr says, spitting a bit of gristle into the dark. "The girl is lovesick."

"Is this true?" Filj raises his eyes to hers, and Dara finds there the only pity she could ever accept, given from one who has also loved in vain.

"Tell me, Feneen," she says, without answering him. "Are there any male Indiri among you? Able-bodied or otherwise, mad as an oderbird trapped in a walled room, I do not care. Just tell me there is one among you, and my troubles matter not."

"Nay, girl," he says. "I could tell you there is, and say I'll take you to him should you spare me. But I will not lie to save my life, when I have no Indiri to lead you to."

Dara closes her eyes, rests her head back against the tree. "Then eat quickly, and go," she says. "Else I change my mind."

Narr watches her, expecting some trick. "I thought you would send us to the ground, to follow your king."

"It is not the dead bodies that trouble me, Feneen," Dara says. "But the living ones."

CHAPTER 62

———⚬◯⚬———

Witt

W ITT'S MEN WHO ARE ALREADY ON THE FAR SIDE OF the river aren't above taunting the stunned Pietra who arrive at morning light.

"Did you not know Pietra can walk on water?" one of them calls from the far shore to his friends.

"River water is solid as rock," another yells. "Never would have known, had we not taken the chance. Go on, then—step out."

The bulk of the Pietran army stand in formation, a lifetime of training unable to keep incredulity at bay. Hadduk frowns at the men across the river, and turns to his own soldiers.

"When you get to the other side, feel free to tell them a nomad troupe came through last night and I treated each of you to a woman."

A ripple of laughter goes through them, an ease of tension in its wake. Witt glances at Nilana, perched on Ank's back, but she is conversing with him in low tones and doesn't seem to have overheard.

"Pietra," Witt calls out, raising his voice, "there is nothing to fear, and no reason to disbelieve the sight of your brothers on the opposite bank . . . but I wouldn't take their advice."

More laughter, and sheepish grins from the soldiers across the water.

"You will cross," he goes on. "And safely. For this we owe the Feneen our thanks."

The chuckling stops, replaced by confusion and not a few frowns. From the other side of the river comes a cheer that sends a smile across Nilana's face.

"You doubt us?" she asks the assembled Pietra, her voice soaring over their ranks. "My people will see it done, and accept your gratitude after."

Ank calls the Feneen forward. Again, Witt feels his breath catching in his chest as the Silt Walkers stride into water past their heads, reeds their only link to life, their metal shoulder hooks disappearing last.

The Pietran army falls silent along with him, as if they too hold a collective breath as Feneen climb onto the shoulders of Feneen, and then again when necessary. Reeds float above the surface, some of them barely past the water, an innocent splash all it would take to end the life of the man below and send the bridge crumbling.

"How long to get them all across?" Pravin asks Witt, his voice lowered.

"Sunset, at least."

Ank brought more Feneen and Silt Walkers than the day before— enough to stand five across the width of the river—but the Pietran army is vast, and heavy.

Pravin glances at the sun's path, its light only now clearing the top of the woods. "How long can the knees of the Feneen below and the arms of the one above hold against the weight of men in armor?"

"I do not know," Witt says. "But their strength wanes as we wait."

As yesterday, he is the first across, to show the men that it is possible. Again, his throat closes against the soft give of flesh under his boots and the subtle swaying of each man beneath him as he walks across their upraised palms. But the Pietra who greet him on the opposite bank do so with slaps on the back and wide smiles.

"Who among you will have it said that you did not follow in the

Lithos's footsteps?" Witt goads his army, yelling across the water. "Will your children's children tell the tale of how their grandfather crossed the river to defeat Stille, or will they say that he waited at home for the victors to return?"

The response is a rattle of spears and a guttural roar, the sound over-powering even the rush of the river. Hadduk gives the order to the first detachment, and they step forward, knees buckling slightly at the odd-ness of the human bridge beneath them, knuckles white on their spears.

But they come, faces set against any rictus of fear, and when the first sets foot upon dry land, his breath leaves him in a rush, and he smiles at Witt.

"My Lithos," he says, "I am here."

They come on, spreading across the far bank like a moss, tents popping up and the smell of cook fires rising through the mist that gathers on the river as shadows lengthen. Hadduk crossed early, taking charge of the army so Witt could stay on the bank, encouraging the men as they strode across the Feneen, and eventually encouraging the Feneen as well, whose arms begin to shake as the day grows old. The Pietra on the far bank rest easy, bellies full or about to be, conversation raised in praise of the Feneen, though not all of their brothers in arms have reached safety yet.

Witt sees the first reed slip away on the current and locks eyes with Pravin, whose mouth remains in a grim line. The last of their men still huddle on the other side, Ank and Nilana with them. Another reed soon follows, and a gap opens in the bridge as a Feneen body floats away, fingers trailing in the water. The Pietra on the bridge halt, two of them unable to stop in time as their weight brings them forward.

Men roll forward like stones down a hill. Some fall to the side, instinct overcoming training as they reach for the man next to them, pulling him into the current as well. Feneen become entangled with Pietra as spears punch through hands, feet lace around arms, and panic overtakes all. Some Feneen gain the surface, but their strength is spent, their limbs as heavy as those of the armor-clad Pietra.

Witt runs alongside the bank, arms outstretched to those who are near. On the opposite shore, Ank does the same, wading into the water to his waist, Nilana wildly screaming directions to the Feneen who still stand. They regain their positions, the Pietra still on their palms and shoulders, clinging to each other for balance.

Witt hauls a man ashore, the only one he could save, collapsing against him in the mud as a Silt Walker sweeps past, eyes locking with Witt's before he is pulled under.

"My thanks, Lithos," the white-faced soldier says, coughing up river water.

Pravin pulls Witt to his feet. "Are you hurt?"

Witt shakes his head and looks to the damage. A few Pietra have turned their backs, unable to watch as their brothers sink to the bottom of the river that Witt promised them would not even wet their heels.

"I will cross for the rest," Witt says, ignoring Pravin's palm against his chest. "I cannot ask them to do so on my word alone that it will hold."

"My Lithos—" The Mason begins to argue, but Witt puts his hand up, silencing him.

The Pietra who are still on the river are gray-faced and grim, the sight of their Lithos alone not enough to encourage them to go on.

"Men," Witt says, swallowing his own fear as he feels the Feneen beneath him shift under his weight. "The shore behind you is for the weak, the one before for the strong. For the rest of you, there is a river to each side."

Ank himself swims out to the hole punched in the Feneen bridge, Nilana grim on his back. He pulls himself into position, filling the blank spot with their upturned palms.

"Pietra," Witt calls as he turns back to the shore where Pravin waits. "Forward."

He takes a step with all the conviction he can, not allowing the quivering deep inside to spread to his knees. He gains the shore, then turns to see if the men followed. They come, faces lined in fear and not a few with vomit streaking their chest plates. Witt stands to the side as the remainder of his army crosses and fans out among their comrades.

"How many lost to the river?" he asks Pravin under his breath.

"More than you think. Those who went in sank like stones. We'll not know the true count until morning call."

"Even then we won't know who drowned and who deserted." Witt assesses the last of the Pietra to cross. "There were more men on the far shore than I see here."

From the river comes Nilana's voice, raised in command. The weary Feneen climb over one another to reach land, many sliding off their comrades and into the water. Some find the strength to swim, others accept their fate with docility and disappear. Witt and Pravin go to the bank, grabbing Feneen hands and pulling them ashore. Pietran soldiers follow their lead without being commanded to do so, the fate of their brothers still heavy on their eyes, their inability to help them muted with every Feneen who sets foot on land.

Reeds float past once more, this time released by hands that had been long underwater. They break the surface, fingers deeply wrinkled pushing toward air, faces so pocked as to be unrecognizable finding the sun. Nilana and Ank move through them, helping where they can. The first of the submerged reaches Witt, and he pulls the man forward, both of them collapsing to the ground.

"Thank you, Lithos," the man says. His one working eye is buried deeply within grotesquely waterlogged flesh.

More Feneen emerge, some pulled from the water by Pietra, some gaining the shore on their own strength. The last of them clamber past Witt, rolling onto their backs, arms and legs spread wide beneath the dying rays of the sun.

Ank and Nilana come ashore last of all, and Witt meets them.

"There are still reeds in the water." He points to a handful that bob up and down in the current.

"They are mired," Nilana says, "and cannot free themselves."

"Can anything be done?" Pravin asks.

Ank shakes his head. "It would take the fresh strength of a man who could swim to release them now, and mine are spent. Yours do not swim."

"They have reeds," Nilana says. "If they still stand in the morning, we will send someone. To send a swimmer now would risk two deaths."

"We've spent more than that already." Witt's eyes are hard on Ank. "You promised me those who crossed would not wet their feet."

"I did. And I believe the men that made the far shore are dry. I never promised you would not leave some at the bottom of the river."

CHAPTER 63

Khosa

ERRYL AND ROOK TAKE NO CHANCES. I CANNOT TURN too quickly without my elbow catching one of them, or come to an unexpected halt without them crashing into my back. Their armor protects them, but leaves marks on me when we collide, bringing swift apologies and sheepish smiles.

"Merryl," I chide for the fifth time today, cupping my stinging elbow from where a nerve has been hit. "I understand tensions are high, but I'm in more danger from you than anyone else right now."

"The pr—" Merryl's teeth clamp on the title as so many often have in the days since the king took to bed, the Stoning that felled his oldest son catching him as well. With Gammal gone and Varrick as good as dead, calling Vincent "the prince" is more of a formality than anything, respect paid to a body waiting to die.

"Call him Vincent, as I do," I suggest.

"Vincent told me to stay beside you at all times," Merryl continues. "And I will."

Even though he means well, Merryl is so near that his shadow slips over mine, and I feel a rush of panic. Since Cathon attacked me, I've been edgier than usual, screams rushing into my throat at the creak of a door. I carry an alertness so constant that my body is always stiff, leaving me sore in the evenings when my door is double bolted and I can relax.

I reach to my neck and gingerly touch a cramped muscle there, wondering how Merryl and Rook can choose a life of such intensity, all their senses on guard at all times for another's sake. I make it worse by leaving my room, selfishly insisting on the comfort of the library, then berate Merryl for doing his duty too well.

"I'm sorry," I say. "It's only that—"

"No apologies," Merryl says in a tone that won't be argued with, and I return my attention to the book in my hands, fanning the pages as I take my seat at the table.

I hear Rook's voice in the hall in quiet conversation with another man. Merryl goes to the archway, glancing back at me. I nod, letting him know that the dagger he slipped to me this morning is tucked inside my boot, rubbing a sore spot on my ankle that brings its own source of comfort. Merryl's voice joins the others, a low hum that underscores my reading until a throat clears.

"Khosa." Merryl stands in the doorway, an elderly man in Scribes' robes beside him. The sight of the familiar clothing makes my hands clench into fists, fingernails digging into the softness of my palms. But his hip rope is braided finely, with a thread of gold spun through deep scarlet.

"Curator," I say, coming to my feet in respect.

"This man wants to speak with you," Merryl says, eyeing the Curator—who looks like a stiff wind would set him on his back—with suspicion.

"I'm sure it's fine. Please," I say, gesturing for the Curator to have a seat across from me at the table.

He settles onto the stool with a sigh, nesting the crooked neck of his walking stick in his inner elbow. "That a man of my age would find stone such a comfort," he says, shaking his head.

"I like it too," I tell him. "Any extravagance is wasted on me, if there is a book before my eyes."

"A kindred spirit, then." He smiles. "I had heard as much, and I would have saved that mind from the sea, but others had intentions for the flesh."

"I should not have trusted so easily," I say, dropping my eyes to the book before me, and the precision of the hand that lettered it.

"We both bear that fault, young lady," the Curator says. "Cathon's eagerness to be the Scribe to escort you away should have warned me, but I attributed it to his need to be in the books, not just around them."

"Not as my rescuer, but the father of my child," I say. "That would earn him a place on a page, certainly."

"Among other things," the Curator says. "Books talk to us through our eyes, but my ears are not deaf, and there are those who speak into them. When you fought for your dignity in the dark, you also saved my life, young Khosa. If Cathon had succeeded, his reward would have been my position, which can be filled only upon my death."

I think of Cathon on the day we met, how I had felt our like minds joining over dust and scrolls. My nose wrinkles now, the faintest reek in the air finding me. "I did not think him so cruel."

"Cruel? No, not Cathon," the Curator says. "Only ambitious, and in Stille that seed can rot before fruition. We live long and die easily in our beds. I am not surprised that some of the young have found violence to be the quickest route to ascendance."

The silence that falls after his words hangs heavily, and I raise my eyes to his. "Surely you aren't accusing Vincent of any wrongdoing?"

The Curator presses his lips together as if considering how much to say. "Vincent? No, I don't believe so. But Gammal died with his grandson beside him in battle, and the Stillness befell Varrick while his son stood in his chambers. Rumors are whirling, and with the training field more used for gossip than swordplay and the Pietra bonded with Feneen . . ."

He trails off, hoping for me to finish the thought on my own.

"All of Stille is in upheaval. If the Given were to disappear and the last royal along with her, where would the people place their hope?"

"Where indeed?"

"I won't be leaving," I say, the words having lost their sting since my skin has known Donil's touch. Known it and not pulled away.

"I am sorry, Khosa," the Curator says. "As much as I believe your sacrifice is a waste, I find my country with the threat of invasion from the outside. I cannot encourage instability on the inside as well."

"I understand."

"That being said, I believe Stille will have a new ruler shortly. And whatever the means were to his rise, I imagine you will find life in the castle much less threatening."

"A cage nonetheless," I say, motioning to the books around me. "And I spend my time in the one that damns me the loudest, surrounded by the writ of the past, which calls for my blood in the present."

The Curator rises to his feet, his body creaking with the effort. "The past is inked darkly," he says, "and cannot be changed. But the present can be smeared into illegibility, and the future is blank parchment."

I walk beside him, though I cannot bring myself to offer support. The scratch of his robe against my arm makes my skin prickle.

"Cathon knew the weight of futility," the Curator says when we reach the door. "He had a desire to make his mark, and a long wait before he'd even hold the quill. I cannot offer you my help, Khosa, or undo what has been done. But I know nothing better than ink and paper, and have five Scribes at work scouring Cathon from all mention. Stained out of existence, clipped from the pages, even his sign at the bottom of translations will be rubbed away."

The knowledge that the man who laid hands on me will have such an indignity visited upon him creates a heat that sweeps over my body. "Thank you."

"I cannot change what happened in the past, but I can alter what version the readers of the future will get," he says with a wink.

I laugh, a noise that makes both Merryl and Rook jump on the other side of the archway. "You sound like an Indiri now," I say to the Curator. "Dara insists that the feral Indiri child raised alongside white Tangata was born during the reign of Philo, because that fits her version better."

The Curator brightens at my laughter, but his eyebrows pinch together in confusion. "She was."

My smile fades. "No, it was during Konnal's time. I remember reading it."

The Curator crosses over to a bookshelf, his footsteps faster now that he is called to duty. His fingers trip over spines while he speaks, not needing to read the frontispieces to know what he touches. "You *read* it, or you *heard* it?"

"I . . ." My words falter as I remember sitting at my worktable, books stacked around me while Cathon told me—

I close my eyes, the familiarity of failure slipping through my skin. "I *heard* it. From Cathon, actually."

"Ah, well, we can lay much at that man's feet, but a slip of the tongue on a Scribe's behalf is no oddity. Our lives are lists of names and dates in columns. I wouldn't know offhand the ruler at the time of the white Tangata, except for this." The Curator pulls a book from the shelf, opening it before me.

"I compiled it myself," he says proudly. "A listing of the major events in the kingdom under each Stillean ruler. It's much easier to sift through for reference than reading the daily journals."

His finger runs across the page, tapping when he finds what he wants. "There you are, the white kits and the feral Indiri child. Both in Philo's time."

My head drops to the stone table, my hands buried in my hair. I feel the Curator's hand on my shoulder and straighten.

"Why should it trouble you so, the events long past?"

"Because I deeply offended Dara, and wrongly, as it turns out."

"The Indiri girl?" the Curator asks, and I nod. "Well, then," he sighs. "Perhaps you're more threatened in these walls than I thought."

CHAPTER 64

———◦◦⟨◉⟩◦◦———

Vincent

Y FATHER'S BRAIN BULGES FROM THE BACK OF HIS HEAD, artfully hidden from those who visit. Mother is the image of the perfect wife, staying by his bedside, hovering over his last days and dictating his care once the physicians have declared it hopeless. They never saw the hole in his skull, or suspected Mother's bridal pillow beneath him was for anything other than comfort.

Mother tore embroidery from the pillow while her hands were still streaked with soot from the poker, remnants of thread stitched years ago uncurling beneath her fingers as history came undone to aid us in the present. Half the sawdust stuffing went into the fire; the other half I pushed to the sides while she held his head in her lap, stitching the torn flaps of the pillow to his ruined scalp. His swollen brain rests inside, a linen beneath an opening in the back. We switch it for another when it is soaked through. No one questions that the queen and prince would want to be with the king constantly, or that we require privacy at times.

She looks at me now as we repeat our story to the Curator, and I reassess the woman in front of me. Gone is the haunted look of her eyes that I have always known. She looks like her father, as if

Gammal has returned to the castle. There is a grim determination in each movement, a plan behind each word. And all of them are for my benefit.

I will have gone from twice-removed heir to king once my father's life force leaks out under my mother's watchful eye. The Curator comes to record Varrick's fate, a lie that will go down in the histories.

Mother and I calmly tell the agreed upon story—Father had woken unable to feel his feet, the first grip of the Stoning having closed around them while he slept. He called for Mother, who sent for me, but in his panic, Father had not listened to our pleas for him to wait for the physicians. He'd rejected our assistance, struggling to his feet only to fall forward, breaking his nose against the floor and rendering him senseless. That he'd not recovered his speech or opened his eyes was attributed to the fast spread of the Stoning, an easy claim, impossible to disprove.

If the Curator has any qualms about the words he pens in the annals, he makes no indication, blowing our lies dry with a puff of his breath.

"Now, then," he says, "if I may speak with Vincent about plans for his coronation. I don't mean to be indelicate, but—"

"Of course," Mother nods, eyes fixed affectionately on my father's unmoving face. "But please, somewhere else. We do not know if he can hear us or not."

I follow the Curator to the hall, though a part of me hopes Father *can* hear us.

"Vincent," the Curator says, once he's assured we're unobserved, "I know of your plot, and Cathon's betrayal. Whether your father's imminent death is a part of that same plan I do not know, or care. It is Khosa whom I worry for, and the unrest of Stille."

I search his face for any sign of guile, any whisper of a lie in his eyes. I fervently wish for Khosa by my side; her lifelong study of faces would be priceless in this moment where a misspoken word could send us all reeling toward execution for treason. But I see before me only an aged man, worried for a young girl and the fate of his country.

"How will the people react to the news about my father?" I ask him.

He shakes his head. "Not well, I fear. We are a nation against change. The motion for allowing the sheep to graze on clover year round took twelve moons to pass through the Shepherds' Council. Now these same people have changed kings twice in a matter of short memory."

"So, not a good time to suggest we allow the Given to live?"

"Breaking with a tradition in a time of unrest would not be wise," he says.

"To the depths with tradition," I say, "and wisdom too, if it can even be called that when we send a girl to her death to keep at bay a danger that may not exist."

"The danger, my liege, now lies in the actions of the people, not the waves. You are a young king taking the throne during a war we are ill prepared for and under circumstances that are suspicious at best. The people must be willing to follow you, and that requires trust."

"And what do I require?" I ask, the image of Khosa on my mind. She does not want me, I know. To see her curled with Donil sliced my heart as deeply as any blade, and though the wound still gapes open, blood flows warmly beneath it. It will heal, I know, and the friend I've found in Khosa should be celebrated in the present, not only as a scar in the past.

"I wish there were another way," the Curator says. "But I do not see it."

A sconce reaches its end above his shoulder, the flame extinguishes, and the smoke wreathes his face, reminding me of another.

"Perhaps you lack the vision," I say.

❧❁❧

Madda hears my tread and enters from a side room, wry words already twisting her mouth. "Who is this boy who comes to me a king? Shortest one in lifetimes, I'm sure. Call the smithy to fashion a footrest for the throne; I doubt his feet will touch the fl—"

Her words die when she finally looks at me, and at Khosa hovering behind my shoulder.

"What is this?" she asks, all teasing dropped from her tone. "Why do you bring me the Given?"

I feel heat radiating from Khosa as she comes closer to me, and I draw strength from knowing that if she cannot touch me, at least she wants to be near.

"Read her," I say to Madda, who flips her hand at me as if I am an errant fly.

"For what purpose? Everyone knows her fate."

"Her name is Khosa," I say, approaching the table and pulling a chair out for Khosa to sit. "And I will have her read."

Madda's mouth is in a flat line, the wrinkles of laughter long spent slack to either side. I see her age around her eyes and in the crevices of her neck, and marvel that they have dug so deeply without me noticing until this moment. I see something new in her eyes too, something I never expected from her. I see fear.

"What is it?" I ask her. "You've held the blank palm of a town boy, told my mother in her misery there is only one marriage for her, two children's branches splitting away, and one quite short. How can you do those things yet not sit across from the Given?"

Madda takes the other chair without a word and holds out her hands for Khosa, who glances at me.

"It's all right," I tell her, and she slides her hands into Madda's. The sound of their skin brushing together is like sand through a sieve.

Candles flicker in the silence, incense clouds wrapping around them like a mantle made for two. I watch Khosa's face tighten, tiny muscles in her neck tensing at the feel of Madda's thumb rubbing across her naked palm. The Seer's mouth turns down, and she releases Khosa, who pulls her hands back into her lap as if they'd been burned.

"Madda?" I ask.

Instead of answering me, she gestures for my own hands, and I give them to her, succumbing to the hypnotic push of her worn flesh against mine. The sight of her heavy braid, plaited tightly against her scalp, is familiar, and I focus on it, willing my own lines to have changed.

Madda sighs, releasing me.

"You don't want to know," she says, rising from the chair. "Either of you."

I come to my feet violently, giving no heed to the jars of herbs and flickering candles that are knocked from the table. "Tell us. We are not children afraid of the dark and what it holds."

"Not children, no," Madda says, easing herself into a softer chair by the fire. "And the darkness is not what you fear. It is uncertainty that wakes you in the night, the anguish of not knowing that sends shivers down your spine. *Knowing* is one thing, is it not?"

She looks to Khosa, who nods. "When my fate was settled, I had only to wait," she says. "Now I see there could be a lifetime stretched in front of me, and I don't know if I'm more terrified at the thought of losing it or of having it."

"And you, Vincent," Madda says, "you'll sit on the throne, your greatest fear come to you long before anyone imagined."

Tears prick my eyes, and I look away. "All my life, every time you've touched my palms, I've hoped for some other fate, an escape."

"I know," Madda says, rocking in her chair. "There were times you would nap there in the corner, huddled into the rushes like a dog, and wake only to ask me to read you again, hoping that your fate had changed while you slept."

The tears overflow and drop from my face to the stone at my feet, stone more familiar to me than the paving in my own room. "I was happy here," I tell her. "I sometimes wished I were the child you never had."

"Please," Khosa interjects. "What did you see?"

"Nothing surprising for you," Madda says. "And no twist of fate on your part, Vincent."

Khosa looks to me, and I go to her, only a hand span between us as I breathe the words I know to be true. "We are both given to the sea, Khosa."

Her gasp fills the room, and she reaches for me against her own instinct, the rare meeting of our flesh a rash of fire on my own.

"He speaks truth," Madda says. "In part, at least. What makes you think I never had a child?"

CHAPTER 65

———— ❧❦❧ ————

Witt

"D EATH HAS AN ODD WAY OF UNITING PEOPLE."
Witt looks up as Pravin joins him on the ridge, the army's
campfires dotting the land below.

"I've seen it before," the Mason says. "My uncle was in one of the scouting parties sent to look for the Feneen after the desolation of the Indiri. There were rains that year, water falling from the sky so thickly he said it didn't come in drops but a wall. His party was trapped on a cliff as it washed away, the stone falling out from underneath their feet. Three of them went to their deaths before they found a cave— only a group of nomads had found it first."

Witt watches his men below. A shared fire is a sacred thing; the ring of people around it draw heat, food, and life from it together. Witt knows well that even one night at a fire can make friends for life. The people below him are shoulder to shoulder, but it isn't armor touching armor. Feneen, ragged and unkempt, are gathered around the fires as well, their presence easily spotted by blank spaces between armored bodies reflecting the flames.

"No one would have thought any less of your uncle and his men if they killed the nomads," Witt says. "Tossed them over the cliff, claimed their fires, ate their food."

"No one except themselves," Pravin says. "And I'm rather glad they didn't, as one of them became my favorite aunt."

Witt tears his eyes away from the men below. "He married outside of Pietran blood?"

"It happens. Bonds were made that night, and not just between the two of them. Food was shared, and stories about those both groups had lost to the rains. The nomads had little to nothing left, so the soldiers brought them back to Pietra, took them before the Lithos who served before you. He saw they were strong people, well built, fiercely proud. Adding their blood to ours would only strengthen us. And so they became Pietra, one night of a shared fire mixing their blood with ours forever."

"I never knew this."

"It was never spoken of, once the Lithos recognized them. He called them Pietra, and so they were, as if they always had been."

"I hear you, Mason," Witt says. "I know why you're telling me this. But those were nomads, strongly built, as you say. Not Feneen, some with eyes that point two different directions or hands with eight fingers."

"They can be Pietra and not wear a ring," Pravin argues, touching his own slim band of silver that gives him the right to breed. "There are Pietra who do not wear these; why not Feneen as well?"

A burst of laughter rolls up to their cliff-side seat, Nilana's high voice included.

"Whether you have accepted them or not, the men have," Pravin says. "They saw what the Feneen were willing to do to get our army to the other side of the river. Friendships will be built on this during the days of the march. There will not be many Feneen backs bristling with Pietra arrows littering the Stillean beaches, I think."

"Perhaps a few," Witt says.

"Perhaps, but not many, and if there are, you may hear grumblings among your men, even in the wake of victory. Unrest as brothers in arms discover there are those among them with less honor than they thought."

Witt picks up a stone and tosses it from hand to hand, thinking. "What would you have me do, Mason?"

"Send the Feneen to the front gate of Stille," Pravin says. "Don't waste them in a charge alongside us where they take the brunt of the resistance. They've attacked Stille before, and their return will draw men to the gates, making our march up the beach even more of a surprise."

The stone warms in Witt's hands, borrowing his heat. "They will break against those gates, lose many. Maybe more than they would fighting alongside us."

Pravin shakes his head. "Once we make our move from the beach, the Stilleans will be pulled in two directions. They are untrained, many unblooded, and a panic will send them reeling. They may open their own throats before our blades even find them. I'd wager we lost more men crossing the river than we will in the attack."

Witt's hands clench on the stone, its sharp edges digging into his fingers. "Ank is smooth with words, arguing that he held up his end of the bargain in that my men who crossed didn't wet their heels."

"Ank does what he must to keep a reviled people alive. Did you truly think we could take the army across the river—something no Pietra has done before—without losing a single man?"

"I had hoped."

"They lost as many as we did. More, even. And yet they stood firm as we trod on them, some knowing their feet rested on the shoulders of drowned men."

"Nilana says we do not have to cross like that again to attack," Witt says. "There's a shallow area near the beaches, a bar of sand below the water that will hold us if we step carefully, a few at a time."

"Good to hear." Pravin rises to go. "Give some thought to what I've said."

"I always do, Mason," Witt answers, eyes once again on the fires below and the rising voices of Feneen and Pietra so close in conversation he cannot tell one from the other.

CHAPTER 66

‹⦿›

Dara

THE QUEEN SLEEPS IN HER SEAT, FINGERS ENTANGLED IN the dying king's hair, while Dara keeps watch on his other side, face grim. Days have passed, days in which the linen beneath the king's head has been soaked through many times, yet he lingers, his penchant for torturing those around him tenacious, even in death.

Dara watches the rise and fall of his chest, the movement barely noticeable, like a breeze that stirs leaves but not branches. She found him thus upon her return, and Dissa related the truth of the matter over the body that still clung to life. As the queen shifts in her sleep, her hand falls away from the pillow, soft palm facing upward. Dara studies it, her eyes unable to find the future there like Madda does, but adept at recognizing the present.

Dissa's hands are delicate and soft, no calluses raised or scars marring their purity. Dara looks to her own hands, rough and gritty even now from days spent in the forest. Her fingernails are broken, dirt mired in the creases of her palms. She has never considered consulting Vincent's Seer, though as a child, he always invited her with him to visit Madda.

She has always known her fate: doomed to wander in search of a mate for her body with her heart left behind, trapped in a castle it never belonged in.

Filj's words fell heavy and wounded deeply. If there is no hope of an Indiri mate for Dara, she can follow her heart. Even if Stille will not see her on the throne, bastard children born of Stillean nobility will be looked after and cared for, her bloodline mixed with Vincent's to endure until the sea decides otherwise. For too long, death has been all Dara has known how to dole out. In a world where destruction awaits them all, why should she not be with the one she loves while she can?

The king draws a ragged breath and holds it, pulling Dara's eyes from her hands to watch as it slowly slips back out through his mouth, bringing a death rattle with it. Dara knows the sound, has heard it from animals and people alike, rising up from the battlefield like a dark miasma after blood has been spilled, or expelled in the woods with none but herself to hear.

"Dissa," she says, reaching across the body to rouse the queen.

Her eyes open and go immediately to her husband, fingers resting in front of his lips to feel no passage of breath.

"He's gone," Dara says, and the queen nods, a hitching breath of her own stuck in her throat. She bends over the bed, silent tears falling on her husband's face.

Dara slips through the door to the hall, and the guards on duty come to attention. "The king has passed," she says to them. "Send for the Curator and the Elders."

The taller guard shares a glance with his counterpart. "Perhaps we should see for ourselves before we rouse them."

"I know a dead body when I see one," Dara says, but the guard doesn't move.

"My duty is to guard the royal family." He looks down on her. "Not to take orders from Indiri."

Dara's lip curls, and she shoves him against the wall, his armor scraping her bare skin. "The royal family grows thin," she growls. "Perhaps you're not doing your duty so well."

He doesn't flinch, only smiles back at her coldly. "There's still more of them than there are Indiri."

Dara's hand drops to her dagger, and she hears the other guard's sword inch from its scabbard in warning. She backs away, and the guard she attacked adjusts his armor. "Gather the Elders yourself, girl," he says.

Anger burns brightly, tearing through her innards and wanting release through the flash of metal, blade on blade, but she wrestles it down. She cannot die in a battle of pride, her blood spilled in a dark hall by men who don't recognize its importance. Dara gathers her dignity and walks away, their guttural chuckling following her as she does.

She goes to the Curator, who sends a lower Scribe to fetch the other Elders. She hesitates before Vincent's door, unsure whether she will have better luck trying to find him behind Khosa's first. She raps her knuckles against the wood, heart slamming into her throat when she hears footsteps within. The door creaks open, and Vincent peers out.

"Dara?"

They have not spoken since she rejected him, only exchanged brief glances, their eyes bouncing off each other like sharp pieces of flint, sparks flying in their wake. He watches her now guardedly, and she feels keenly the hollow place inside her where their closeness used to be.

"Your father has passed," she says without preamble, voice low.

Vincent opens the door all the way. "My mother?"

"She is with him." Dara falls silent and they eye each other warily, unspoken words buried too deeply to mine at the moment. "I should return to her."

Vincent nods curtly. "I'll see you there," he says before shutting the door again.

Dara studies the wood for a moment; her hand rises to knock

again before reconsidering and turning back, the sconces casting her shadow long, head bowed in the only defeat she has ever known.

The outside air is a relief, coating Dara's skin with a freshness she can never find indoors. The bottle of wine sweats in her hand, slipping through fingers already growing numb with drink. She doesn't often seek solace in wine, but when she does, she takes no half measures. The bottle is much lightened, though the same could not be said of her spirits.

She leans against a tree in the gardens outside her own chambers, eyes on the full moon above. She returned to her room to retrieve her swords, meaning to gather with the family but remembering the challenge in the guard's eyes. If she'd been wearing her swords, he would not have been so quick to mock her. Her reflection in the mirror caught her eye as she strapped them across her back.

Her hair was tousled, one side of her speckled face flushing pink where she'd brushed against a vase of salium in the hall in her haste to retrieve the Curator. The other side was much darker. Her spots had deepened during the long days she'd spent in the woods—the very escape she sought had marked her as one who did not belong in the castle.

With her swords she looked fierce as a gathering storm, wild as a night wind, and strong as an ancient tree. Every bit of her screamed Indiri, and the usual pride she felt was tinged with bitterness at the thought. She did not return to the king's chambers to stand with the royal family, the blood flowing through their veins not her own. She did not want to see the quick private ceremony that would seal Vincent away from her forever.

She turns toward the tree, forehead pressed against the bark, the last of the wine burning down her throat. With Donil constantly shadowing the Given and Vincent doing the same, she has watched her life change—from trusted sibling to pestering nuisance, lifelong friend to stranger with whom awkward exchanges are made. Khosa has turned the two people she cares for most into ones she can only trade barbed or weighted words with.

It was unintentional, she knows. The Given no more meant or wanted to turn their heads than a boulder in the stream means to turn the flow of water. Still, though the boulder lacks intention, the damage is done, and floods unleashed. Dara presses her palm against the tree, letting rough bark dig deep against her skin until it draws pain and the wine bottle drops from her fingers, shattering on stone. She doesn't know what she is doing until the leaves touch her shoulders, the tree bowing as her anger draws its life.

"No!" she cries, slipping backward over shards of glass and landing hard. But the damage is done. The tree has wilted so badly that its branches scrape the ground with a gust of wind.

Dara crawls to it, wraps her arms around the trunk, and tries to push the life back inside, but she succeeds only in creating a springing moss that creeps up the dying bark. She drops her hands, leaving behind bloody prints from glass that sliced them open.

"I'm sorry," she says, words slurred. She rests her head against the trunk and finds that not all her tears are yet shed. They fall from her eyelashes, drip from her chin, and are blown away along with the leaves.

CHAPTER 67

Khosa

I CRACK OPEN MY DOOR TO FIND MERRYL AND ROOK SHOULDER to shoulder, blocking my way.

"I can't sleep. I was thinking of a walk," I say.

They exchange a glance, and Merryl sags, the duty of denying me falling to him. "It's best to stay in your room for now," he says. "The king has passed, and though the castle is quiet for the moment, word will spread."

I slide in between them, the flutter of my dressing robe snagging on Rook's spear. "Then I should stretch my legs while I can," I say over my shoulder.

I head toward Dara's room. She's swallowed my mind since I spoke with the Curator, the blaze of her eyes and indignant rise of her chin when I questioned the legitimacy of her Indiri memories keeping sleep from me. I know we will never be friends, but I can at least retract the words that made us enemies.

I pause at her door, and Merryl's spear bars the way before I raise my hand to knock. "What is this madness, Khosa?"

"You heard the Curator the other day; I was wrong about Dara's memories. She deserves an apology."

"I also heard your fight with her," Merryl counters. "You may trust her memories, but I don't trust her temper. You owe her an apology, yes. But will she accept it, or even welcome one in the middle of the night?"

I strike the door twice, my knuckles rapping sharply. "We'll find out."

I hear movement within, and Dara's voice calls out that the door is unlocked. When Merryl tries to follow me in, I stop him with a look.

"Some privacy, please," I say.

"If your privacy costs a hair on your head, I'll have hers off," he says, eyes dark. "I'm serious, Khosa. I don't trust the girl."

I think of Donil's face, so like his sister's, and the few times I've seen Dara's matching his, a blinding smile seen too little. "I do," I tell him, and close the door on his disapproving face, Rook hovering at his shoulder.

A breeze strikes me, dead leaves scattering across the floor of Dara's bedroom, their paths shooting in and out of long streaks of moonlight where one wall of her chambers is open to the outdoors, arches in full view of the sea.

"Dara?" I call, eyes adjusting to the darkness of her unlit room after the sconces of the hall.

"Over here," she says, one hand rippling out into a stream of moonlight from where she sits in a corner. "I wasn't expecting you at my door."

Her words are rough and broken, and I've seen enough of the royal gatherings to know why. I go to her regardless, alarmed by drops of blood that fell when she motioned for me.

"What have you done to yourself?" I go to her, finally able to see her outline in a chair. I take one across from her, eyeing the dark drops on the stone.

"Accident," she says, the single word drawn forth with effort.

"You should see a healer," I say, taking her hand in mine without thinking. She doesn't pull away, and instead of a cringe on my part I feel warmth, a draw not unlike the pulses that flow between Donil and me.

"No," she says, trapping a dead leaf on the floor with a stomp of her foot. She picks it up by the stem, which breaks in her hand. "*This* was an accident."

I don't understand her words and so dismiss them as drunkenness, taking a lamp from her bedside out to the hall where I reassure my guards that Dara is in no mood to hurt me, and no shape besides. I return with the lamp lit from a sconce, not questioning why my steps are quick, my need to be beside her strong.

"Let me see," I say, again drawing her hand into mine and thrilling at the touch. She lets me, but her eyes are hooded with mistrust.

I wash the slash on her hand with water from the basin, wrapping the drying linen around her palm. "I came to apologize," I explain. "You were right, about the white cats in Philo's time."

"I never thought I was wrong."

I tuck the edges of the linen in, raising my eyes to hers for the first time. They are bright, lit with an unnatural flame I've not seen before, but I feel something inside of me quicken at the sight. My hands rise to her face, like a child wanting to touch something pretty, and she jerks away.

"You've come to apologize, and now you've done it," she says, rising to her feet. I go with her as if a string attaches us, she the puppeteer and I at her bidding. She doesn't notice as she heads to the door, ready to see me out. I follow, fingers reaching out to touch her hair as it shifts in the wind.

She turns and smacks my hand away, dagger at the ready as if I'd meant harm. I laugh at the sight, a giddiness overwhelming me that I can't explain and don't care to. I spin around her, my dressing gown illuminated by moonlight, then lost in shadow as I do. Dara lowers her knife, brows drawn together as she backs away from me. I match her, step for step, taking her hands in mine.

"Dance with me," I say, and my feet drum out a rhythm only they know as the surf calls to me from the open arches.

Dara closes her eyes, dimming the light I see there, and my feet still, a quick rush of terror filling me in the moment before she opens them again. Then I'm lost, a conviction so bright inside of me that I squeeze her hands tightly in mine, fresh blood running from beneath her bandage.

"Dance with me," I whisper. She moves through an arch toward the sea as I follow, spinning.

"Oh, Khosa," she says, eyes still bright yet brimming with sadness. "Why must you make it so easy?"

CHAPTER 68

Vincent

THE WIND SUCKS THE DOOR TO THE ROOM SHUT BEHIND the last Elder to arrive at my father's deathbed, the wall sconces flickering in response. The Curator holds down the blank pages that he will fill with the details of my ascension, done quietly and with only a few witnesses.

Mother stands beside me, one hand on my shoulder. I do not know if I'm supporting her or she me. I followed Dara's summons despite my urge to run the other way, and though my father's bedchambers are large, the walls feel much too close, the air thick with the exhalations of old men seeing yet another Stillean take the throne.

The Curator clears his throat, dips his quill, and turns to the first page in the book that holds the words for the ceremony of coronation, said over countless Stilleans before me. He begins reading, and my eyes flick over the crowd, all of them silver haired and aging. Dara is not here. Donil has not come. I am surrounded by the weight of the accumulated years in the room, the very expectations of my Elders making their gazes heavy upon me.

Then, distantly, I hear a vein of life threaded under the intonations of the Curator, a youthful trill that trips through the air and brings a smile to my lips even in this dark hour. Khosa's laugh.

I'm so pleased at the sound I don't think to question it until movement outside the window catches my eye. I see her, a white shade on the beach, a spinning, glorious exultation of life dancing triumphantly toward her death, with Dara beside her.

I scream her name, throwing my mother's hand from my shoulder and breaking through the ranks of the elderly, knocking them aside in a lunge toward the window. I have no care for my own life as I jump, ignoring the drop and the alarmed cries of the room I leave behind me. All I know is Khosa.

Khosa with the tide already at her feet.

CHAPTER 69

Khosa

I AM DANCING.

I am dancing.

I am dancing.

This is how it should be, and I laugh for the joy of it, the exultation that thrills my very bones as I spin toward Dara, the life raging in her eyes and the welcoming, wet arms of the sea behind her. Why I have denied it so long I do not know. I only want to leave the sand of the shore behind me and feel the sea buoy me up as I go, ever onward.

"Onward," I yell, laughing at this, my newly discovered battle cry.

I spin and spin, my dressing gown now soaked with spray and sticking to my legs, my arms iridescent in the moonlight and the wind tearing my hair from my face. Dara is up to her waist in the sea, face twisted in disgust at the touch of the water but eyes still calling me forward.

And I go.

My name, splitting through the night, rending the incomprehensible song I've been singing. I shake it away and focus on Dara, on the wetness of the sea closing around my dancing feet.

I hear it again, in a different voice. A cry I can't ignore, and pain that can hardly be borne. It feels as if my heart is being ripped through my back as my mind moves blankly onward, my body motionless in between.

"Khosa!" Donil's voice comes again, and I turn to see him running, Vincent at his side. I fall to my knees, head in my hands and my screams echoing back off my fingers as I'm torn, half of me wanting Donil, the other half demanding the sea.

I scream and I scream until my mouth is filled with salt water.

CHAPTER 70

———◦◯◦———

Vincent

I HIT THE GROUND, AND SOMETHING RIPS INSIDE MY SHOULDER AS I roll, a white-hot pain that leaves my hand tingling. Still I run, sand kicking up behind me as I cross the distance between the dancing girl and me, yelling her name. It's echoed from the side, and I see Donil running from the castle, our paths meeting in a shared goal.

She stops for a moment, dropping to her knees at his voice, and I feel no jealousy, nothing but a pure relief that her dance knows a pause. Her laughter has stopped, as has her song. There is only screaming that is like terror unleashed, her throat surely tearing under the strain. We are strides from her when a wave knocks her to the side; her white dress is lost in the froth.

"Khosa!" I am in the water, feeling it break around me and tug at my feet, wanting to tear them from the bottom and drag me out to sea. Yet I feel no fear for myself, only a deep conviction that if I lose her now, I will let it take me as well.

Something glances on my legs, a soft wisp that could be seaweed or a fish. I plunge into the water, blindly groping, and come away with a fistful of her hair. I go under again and feel her arms, moving with the tug of the tide. I pull her up, and we break the surface, her body collapsed against mine.

Donil comes for us, his face twisted in a rage I've never seen painted there before. I almost drop Khosa to defend myself, but he passes us by, eyes pinned on Dara. I drag Khosa toward the castle and the people now pouring out of it, drawn by the cries of the Elders as they swarm on the beach.

We are on the shore, yet the castle seems far away as I drag Khosa, seawater foaming from her mouth. Hands meet us, ones withered with age and dark spots, and I welcome the help as I fall to all fours, crawling away from the depths that nearly claimed us both.

My mother is at my side, hauling me to dry sand when she screams, the sound splitting my head as I turn to see Donil wrap his hands around his sister's neck and force her under the waves.

CHAPTER 71

⟡

Dara

A S DONIL CUTS THROUGH THE WATER TOWARD HER, DARA sees he has no thoughts but death. The girl he attacks is not Indiri, not his sister, not the other half of his self. She is only an enemy, a threat to something more dear to him than their shared blood. Dara makes no move to defend herself, and not a word passes between them as he closes his hands around her throat.

Vengeance is something she understands.

CHAPTER 72

Vincent

MOTHER SCREAMS AGAIN, TEARING AT MY CLOTHES AS she points up the beach.

An army advances, shining silver beneath the moonlight. They're far away yet, their footfalls silenced by the wind and the spray, their spears in the air like a massive sea-spine come to end us. An Elder falls to his knees, hand on his chest, at the sight. Khosa is unconscious in the arms of one of her guards, the other hauling the Curator from the water, where he is screaming at Donil to spare Dara. My people are falling apart, my kingdom is about to perish, my friends are killing each other in the sea. The familiar anger rises in me, a rage so deep I welcome its power and the fearlessness it gives me.

I grab my mother's shoulder, turning her toward me. "Take Merryl and Khosa," I tell her. "Go to the tunnels in the library and close them behind you." She nods, terror replaced with action as her blood is called to duty.

I call for Rook, sending him to the guardhouse to sound the alarm, bringing any who can come to our aid. I know they will die, torn from their beds with a storm in their faces and an enemy they can't fathom marring their beach. My only hope as I plunge back into the water is that the Curator will live to write it all down. We will make an ending on the last page of Stillean histories that can be read with awe by those who conquer us.

I crash into Donil, tearing his feet out from under him as Dara comes up for air, fists swinging. I catch one of her punches, but the second lands its target, sending her brother beneath the tide. He comes back up with a dagger in hand, ready to swipe at me to get at her. I stand between them, a hand on each, a wall between two animals that want nothing more than to tear each other to pieces.

Donil spits salt back into the sea. "Stand aside, Vincent."

I shake my head. "No, Donil. We need her."

They see the army at the same time. I feel them both tense, each under a different palm, their anger turned away from each other to a shared target. Dara unleashes her blades, flinging seawater from them in two arcs. Our feet hit sand just as bells begin pealing from the castle. Cries erupt as men pour from the guards' barracks.

"The Feneen," one of them shouts when he spots me. "The Feneen are burning the gates!"

Pillars of smoke confirm his words, twin spires gray against the night sky, the flames beneath illuminating panicked men on the parapets. Too few.

I grab Donil by the shoulder. "The volunteers from the city will go to the front gates to fight. They need a good man to lead them. Get to the guardhouse; send as many as you can to the beach."

"We can't hold both for long," Donil says grimly.

"Then we'll hold them both for a short while," I say, shoving him toward the castle. "Go!"

He glances from me to Dara, who's still dripping water he would have drowned her in. "Go, brother," she says. "If I don't die on a Pietran blade, you'll have your chance."

He's gone, the wind tearing his response from my ears as the sound of the approaching army looms. Feet falling in time, a rippling mass of shining armor and stone shields that churns the sand so that I don't know what is land and what is water. Men are gathering behind me, guards in half their armor, some in less, armed with what they slept with. I see a few spears, a handful of swords; one man carries his bedside table for a shield and a shaving knife as a weapon. They are three deep behind Dara and me when the Pietra are close enough for us to see their faces.

"Dara . . . ," I say, but the words I mean to come after her name stop in my throat. Words of love and hate, mixed together in a fetid tangle that won't be spoken.

"I know you'd see me dead," she says, eyes on the Pietra. "Let me kill a few of them first."

And then she charges the entire Pietran army, alone.

CHAPTER 73

Witt

T HERE IS NO GLORY IN THE MARCH, NO PRIDE IN WITT'S heart as panic takes the castle. The Stilleans are like ants suddenly exposed when their rock overturns, their milling bodies a mass of chaos. A small group is forming on the beach, one that will be crushed easily by only a handful of Witt's men. He leads them on, Pravin by his side.

A figure breaks away from them, a wild shriek tearing through the night that sends a chill down Witt's back colder than river water. He misses a step at the sound, stumbling against Pravin.

"That's . . ."

"An Indiri," Pravin says. "Filthy fathoms, that's an Indiri."

Witt holds up a hand, and the entire army halts, their last step echoing off the walls of the castle, the Indiri's cry filling their ears. Blades slash wind as the first line draw their swords at Witt's command.

The cry comes again, and Witt can see that the Indiri is a girl, her speckled face twisted in fury, fiery eyes focused on him. Her hair is a black cloud in the wind, her blades shining bolts of light as she bears down on his army with no hint of fear.

Pravin pulls his bow from his shoulder. "Shall I?"

"Wait," Witt says, transfixed at the sight of her.

Then she is lost in shadow, the only thing that remains the lights in her eyes as a wave as high as the castle walls blocks the light of the moon.

CHAPTER 74

Vincent

THE PIETRA HALT AS DARA RUNS TOWARD THEM. I SCREAM her name, and am following her through the sand when I'm thrown facedown on the beach by one of my own men. I swing at him as I come up, my blade slicing open his tunic before he grabs me by the shoulders, forcibly turning me to look at the sea.

A wall of water rises, high as the moon. Its death roar fills my ears, and I'm screaming at Dara, screaming at my men, screaming the only thing I can think of.

"Run."

CHAPTER 75

Witt

WITT ORDERS HIS MEN TO RUN, KNOWING IT IS ALREADY too late. The armor meant to save them from an arrow or blade will drag them to their deaths in the water. Men trained to hold formation their entire lives break rank at the sight of the wave, some of them following Witt's order to run, some too awed to do anything but stand and be taken. Pravin drops his bow, grabbing Witt by the hand and steering him to a copse of trees at the beach's edge.

"Climb, my Lithos," Pravin shouts at him when they reach the base of the tallest one, offering a hand for Witt to step on. Witt jumps, grabbing the lowest branch and curling his legs around it. He reaches down for Pravin.

The wave hits the beach, knocking men down like reeds. Arms are torn from bodies by the force of the water, armor no longer covering chests blows though the air like leaves. Pravin's fingers brush Witt's for an instant and then all the Lithos feels is the cold grip of the ocean.

CHAPTER 76

—◦❦◦—

Vincent

I'M LOST TO THE SEA, JUST AS MADDA SAID.

It doesn't have me yet, but I'm lost all the same, unable to tear my eyes from the wet death that will claim me. It's magnificent, and in this moment, I can understand Khosa's dance and the smile that lights her face when she performs it.

Dara slams into me with a snarl, knocking me to the ground and then dragging me back up again. "Run, you witless filthy depth of a fool," she screams into my face.

I grab her hand, and we run together, stride for stride, a roar in our ears and the wet grabbing for our backs as our feet hit the paving stones in the garden outside her chambers. We're under an arch when she shoves me, and I crash through her door into the hall, my hands emptied as the water tears her away from me. It fills her room, flowing into the hall and sweeping me with it.

I'm pushed all the way to the great hall and slammed into the wrought iron of a table leg before the roaring wave is gone. And what comes next is worse.

Silence.

CHAPTER 77

◦◦◦◦◦

Vincent

THE WAVE RECEDES, TAKING WITH IT BLADES AND BOWS, furniture it wrapped watery fingers around from the lower levels of the castle. It took soldiers and scholars, the young and the old, tore Tangata cats from trees and replaced them with fish drowning in air. It left behind a young monarch, broken and entangled in metal, his childhood friend struggling to set him free.

"Vin, bend your arm back the other way," Donil says, face red as he pulls against the unmoving table leg.

"Can't," I say.

"Then I'll do it for you," he says, and I find strength left in me to scream as he jams my arms back through the metalwork. I lie heaving, taking a moment of rest in a pool of water on the flagstones.

Donil helps me to my feet, and we make our way down the beach as a second wave rolls in, much smaller than the first, the cries of people cresting along with it. Stilleans race to the surf, grabbing outstretched hands where they can, holding on when the wave pulls back. Donil drops me to the sand and strides forward to stand firm in water that breaks around his knees, pulling out a Pietran soldier, who nods to him, walks five paces inland, and collapses. Five are saved this way, Daisy among them, her blue eyes big and vacant as she clutches the guard who saved her. The moon lights up the sand, the shadows of unmoving armor and drowned men cast long.

"Khosa?" Donil asks, her name barely a whisper.

"Safe inside, with my mother," I assure him, before saying darker words. "I lost Dara. She pushed me into her room and . . . I don't know, Donil. I don't know."

"We'll find her," Donil says, but his face is grim.

We walk the beach, pulling Scribes to their feet while I hear reports from the guards. The Feneen fled at the roar of the wave, and the men in the castle celebrated their victory for a brief moment before turning to see their brothers on the beach swept away.

"Nothing like it," one man says to me, his legs shaking so violently he cannot stand. "They were there, and then they weren't."

"I know it," I say, wincing as a healer binds my broken arm to my chest. "And while we feel our losses keenly, the Pietra lost an entire army."

"They did, my king. That they did," the guard says, with no hint of celebration. "Wiped the beach clean. The Pietra army stood strong, men upon men. And then there was nothing."

"We're gathering the dead on the beach, wherever they hail from," Donil reassures him. "They'll know respect, in the end."

I am needed everywhere, and Donil is at my side. Decisions need to be made about the living Pietra the waves returned to the beach, and the surviving Stilleans need care. The moon sinks and the sun rises, and still the sand bristles with the dead and the choked cries of the living just discovering them.

Sweat is beading on Donil's brow as we move through the gathering crowds on the beach, shouldering past a group of Scribes who are bringing damp scrolls out to the sun. A few are perched like birds on a rock, their pages flattened as they furiously write the stories brought to them by all who were there, capturing it with ink as well as they can.

A hand claps on my shoulder. "You saw, my king, did you not?" the Scribe asks.

"I saw the wave, yes," I say, but the Scribe shakes his head.

"No, did you see the Given? She called that wave, she did. Brought it in from the rim of the sky and delivered us from the Pietra scourge."

"She . . ." My voice dies as the Curator approaches, shutting the Scribe's book and delicately sending him in another direction.

"What was that?" Donil asks us. "Khosa wasn't even on the beach when—"

"Shhh," the Curator whispers, one finger to his lips. "You know that, and we know that. Yet a story that hurts no one and redeems her entirely is being born here this morning. A quick mention, an implication, a buried word. I've planted them, and they grow on their own."

The Curator rests a hand on my arm, walking with us along the surf. "Already if you asked ten people eight of them would claim to have been on the sand when the wave hit, yet you know there were only three."

"Four," Donil says. "Dara was with us."

"Yes," the Curator notes the correction. "The Indiri girl has not been found."

Donil's throat constricts, and he looks to the waves as if he might see a flash of speckled flesh in the froth.

"My men are working," the Curator continues. "But already fact and fiction are braided together; some would argue the weave is stronger for it. I counsel you, my king, to take advantage of the situation. Yes, this wave was a horror, but nothing like the one in the histories. That wave dragged most of Stille out to sea, tore whole houses from the ground. This one barely brushed the castle, taking with it an entire army about to spill our blood. This wave didn't destroy us. It delivered us."

"And so Khosa will be seen as a hero rather than a sacrifice?"

The Curator smiles, hands in the air. "Who is to say that the Given was never cursed, but a blessing? One that needed the right mixture of elements to deliver its boon."

"That's your story, then? The Given called the wave that claimed the Pietra?" I keep my eyes on the sea as I think, the weight of a simple lie insignificant against the possibility of Khosa's death sentence being lifted. "What country would demand the death of a beautiful girl who saved them from annihilation?"

"Indeed." The Curator smiles. "I think instead they would make her their queen."

CHAPTER 78

—◦◦◦—

Vincent

I ANSWER QUESTIONS AND ASK THEM; I PULL ASIDE DEAD BODIES and shake living hands. I set fires in rotting flesh and wash wounds that will heal. I am everywhere and everything. I am the king.

Mother comes to me, face still pinched against the smell of Cathon's body in the tunnels where she locked herself and Khosa. She tells me that Merryl discreetly added the Scribe's corpse to a pile on the beach.

"Rotted flesh mixed with old milk. I'll not thank you for that memory," she says, shading her eyes against the sun as we gather the last of what remains on the beach. A broken chair. A shattered wash-basin. The guards keep their distance, allowing us some privacy.

"You'll explain about the body later," Mother says.

"I will," I assure her. "There was good reason."

"There usually is," she answers, and I imagine I see her hands clench a poker that isn't there. "Have you spoken with Khosa?"

"Not yet," I say. The Curator has moved between us all, spinning lines of conversation and murmured agreements that have made a web strong enough to hold Stille together and bind Khosa to me.

"She's not displeased at the arrangement, if that's what you're worried about," Mother says.

"I'd rather she were, in fact, pleased," I say, bending to pick up a pommel with no blade attached to it.

"She's pleased enough to be alive. More may grow in time."

Khosa will be my wife, the girl who would've been taken from me by the sea now delivered into my arms because of it. I pitch the pommel away from me, and it sinks to the depths, mired with more things than anyone knows down in the darkness.

A cry breaks down the beach, a child running toward me, who bursts through the arms of my guards and wordlessly grabs my hand, dragging me to the castle. We break into the garden and the girl points wordlessly, eyes shining.

Dara lies unconscious, the arms of a dying tree wrapped around her in a lifesaving embrace.

CHAPTER 79

Witt

FIRES LIGHT THE WILDERNESS, AND WITT COMES TO THEM one by one, gathering what remains of his army until they are enough to form ranks. Hadduk's men rally, their vicious war cries splitting the night when their commander walks in from the darkness, pulling seaweed from his hair. The Feneen follow the sound and find them, their people more numerous now than the Pietra.

Ank sleeps, his smooth face resting on lined hands, Nilana leaning against a tree beside him. Witt feeds their fire, rejecting her words when she says he needs to eat.

"What good is a Lithos dying of hunger?" she chides him.

"What good is a Lithos whose army is drowned, yet he lives?"

Nilana's eyes find his and hold them, even though he wants nothing more than to look back into the mesmerizing flames of the fire and not the demanding ones in her eyes.

"The wave can hardly be laid at your feet," she says.

"No, indeed, it only wetted my toes," Witt says bitterly.

He dropped from the tree the moment the water receded to find the beach swept clean of his men. Flashes of armor against moonlight in the distance proved that some had heard the order to run in time, and Witt had followed them, to find they were only a handful.

"I led them there to die," he says. "Pravin—" The Mason's name in his mouth is too heavy a word, his tongue folding under it.

"I am sorry," Nilana says. "He seemed a good man."

"He was," Witt says, angrily wiping tears from his cheeks before anyone can see them fall.

"And you seem one as well," Nilana says softly.

"I am the Lithos. We do not have the luxury of being good men or bad, only the Lithos."

"Ah." Her voice is a whisper for the two of them alone. "But I see before me a Lithos who doesn't have the heart to be a Lithos."

"A Lithos doesn't have a heart at all."

"Then perhaps that is what I meant."

A wind gusts around them, flaring the fire and sending Nilana's hair into her face, catching in her long eyelashes. She blows on the strands, but they stay. Witt leans forward, tucking the errant curl behind her ear.

"You'll need a new Mason," she says.

"Hadduk," Witt says. "He can shave these softer edges from me, in a time when they must go."

"Perhaps," Nilana says, her voice pitched low. "Or perhaps a softer hand is exactly what you need."

"Nilana," Witt sighs. "I know what you propose. That fire burned out long ago."

The Feneen woman smiles, her beauty brilliant in the firelight. "An ember is all I need."

CHAPTER 80

Dara

"NOT GOING TO SAY GOOD-BYE?"

Dara rests her head against her horse, a heavy sigh escaping against its coat. "I thought the wedding preparations would have everyone too busy to notice the quiet exit of an unwanted Indiri girl."

"Not her twin," Donil says, joining her in the horse's stall. "And why do you call yourself unwanted?"

"Because I *am*, brother," Dara says. "I damned myself when I drew the Given out to the sea before she bore a child, and now she will be queen . . ."

"Khosa will see no harm done to you," Donil insists. "A cooler head rests on her shoulders than on yours, sister. Revenge is not her way."

"It is not revenge that prickles my skin, merely the fact that she is queen."

"And Vincent her king," Donil finishes.

"You can bear things I cannot," Dara says, eyes on the ground. "Drive a spike through my leg, and I'll laugh at the pain; shoot an arrow in my eye, and I'll use the good eye to track you down and pull out your own. But break my heart, and I am of no use to anyone."

"You are of great use, Dara," Donil argues. "There is no fighter such as you, and the ferocity of your will knows no bounds."

"Yes," she agrees, and swings into the saddle. "And I go to vent it elsewhere. You saw him, too."

Donil nods, the memory of the Lithos of the Pietra standing on a Stillean beach, his face the last sight their Indiri mother saw. "I understand," he says. "But the very thing that sends you away anchors me here."

"I know, brother. And you must stay where your heart is. Mine knows only death, and I go to visit it upon another."

Donil rests his head on his sister's knee for a moment and mutters an Indiri blessing for safe travels against the rough fabric of her cape before she spurs her horse and is gone.

CHAPTER 81

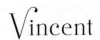

Vincent

TODAY I MARRY.

Khosa is resplendent in white, the bodice of her gown crafted like the sea, waves reaching toward her face but falling short. She is no longer the Given, a sacrifice to ensure long life for our kingdom. They are calling her the Redeemed, a savior to guide us in our rebirth.

The ceremony is performed quickly, Donil gray and guarded alongside my mother and the Curator. The crown is heavy on my head, the scepter a deadweight in one hand, Khosa's touch on my other even less lifelike. Words are spoken by the Curator, repeated by me and then Khosa. The crown that made me realize my heart had turned to her moves from Mother's head to hers, and we are married.

The Elders take us to the balcony, drawing back the heavy curtains so that all of Stille can see us. We are ushered to the edge, announced as the king and queen, a joyful noise that deafens me greeting the statement. I stand, useless as ever, between my mother, who made me king, and the queen who saved my kingdom.

I slip my fingers in between Khosa's, giving her hand a squeeze.

My wife turns her head to vomit discreetly into a cup.

CHATPER 82

Khosa

I AM DOOMED TO LIVE.

I am the Redeemed. The girl who called the ocean down on the heads of an invading army. Yet I remain the Given, a girl whose feet still dance toward the sea, a yawning ache deep inside me matched only by a desperate want for one who is not my husband.

I am the queen of Stille; a queen who cannot touch her spouse to create an heir. A queen who despises the blood flowing in her subjects because it so recently demanded her own.

I am drawn to the water, yet I now know that is not what calls me. It is inside Donil, and I go to it. It was in Dara for a moment, after she drained life from the earth, and I felt it. I do not dance into the sea mindlessly, for it is not what I yearn for, but something beyond.

I have become the queen of a dying land.

It is not the water that I am given to, but life.

ACKNOWLEDGMENTS

I've had a fantasy story in me for the past twenty years, and though it had percolated long, it was definitely the most difficult one to put onto paper. A huge thanks to my editor, Ari Lewin, for helping mold the beast and gamely rolling with any and all inappropriate things I managed to say over the phone.

As always, thanks is due to my agent, Adriann Ranta, who nodded and said, "Why not?" when I suggested my fourth genre jump in as many years. Critique partners are a necessary part of my process, and I need to thank my regulars, R. C. Lewis, MarcyKate Connolly, Demitria Lunetta, and Kate Karyus Quinn, for all being perfectly amenable to weighty attachments on emails. The same is true for amazing fantasy author Cinda Williams Chima, to whom I owe a huge debt of gratitude!

Inspiration can strike at any time and ideas rear their heads in odd situations. Thanks to fellow Ohio author Emery Lord for listening patiently at a book festival when I turned to her and said, "Hey, listen to this thought I just had . . ." and then ate all her cookies.

Lastly, thank you to my family and friends, who know my facial expressions well enough to know when I'm working, even if I only seem to be staring into space.